WHITE DEATH

Daniel Blake is the pseudonym of award-winning novelist and screenwriter Boris Starling. *White Death* is his seventh book, and he also created the BBC1 franchise *Messiah*, which ran for five series. He lives in Dorset with his wife and children.

Praise for Daniel Blake:

'*City of Sins* starts with a tsunami and ends with a hurricane, and nothing in between slows it down. A smart, scary, and relentless storm overtaking a city held hostage by greed and disaster.'
— ANDREW GROSS, *Sunday Times* bestselling author of *The Blue Zone* and *15 Seconds*

'Stunning. A *Chinatown* for the 21st century'
— CHARLES CUMMING, *New York Times* bestselling author of *The Trinity Six*

'Hugely entertaining'
— SEAN BLACK, author of the Ryan Lock series

'Daniel Blake makes New Orleans the setting for a story that's as hot, steamy and shot through with voodoo madness as the city itself. As the victims of a ritualistic serial killer mount up, *City of Sins* is not just a first-rate crime thriller, but also an impassioned, powerfully evocative attack on social injustice, racial prejudice and the unfettered power of the rich. Highly recommended!'
— TOM CAIN, author of *The Accident Man* and *Dictator*.

By the same author

AS DANIEL BLAKE
Soul Murder
City of Sins

AS BORIS STARLING
Messiah
Storm
Visibility
Vodka

DANIEL BLAKE

White Death

HARPER

Harper
An imprint of HarperCollins*Publishers*
77–85 Fulham Palace Road,
Hammersmith, London W6 8JB

www.harpercollins.co.uk

A paperback original 2012
1

Copyright © Daniel Blake 2012

Daniel Blake asserts the moral right to
be identified as the author of this work

A catalogue record for this book
is available from the British Library

ISBN: 978-0-00-738448-8

Typeset in Meridien by Palimpsest Book Production Limited,
Falkirk, Stirlingshire

Printed and bound in Great Britain by
Clays Ltd, St Ives plc

MIX
Paper from
responsible sources
FSC
www.fsc.org   FSC™ C007454

FSC™ is a non-profit international organisation established to promote
the responsible management of the world's forests. Products carrying the
FSC label are independently certified to assure consumers that they come
from forests that are managed to meet the social, economic and
ecological needs of present and future generations,
and other controlled sources.

Find out more about HarperCollins and the environment at
www.harpercollins.co.uk/green

For Caradoc

ACKNOWLEDGEMENTS

Thanks to: Sarah, Julia, Emad, Kate and Anne at HarperCollins; Caradoc, Yasmin, Linda, Louise and Elinor at A.P. Watt; Charlotte, Judy and David Starling; John Saunders and the gentlemen and players of the José Raúl Capablanca Memorial Chess Society.

PART ONE

Opening

'Play the opening like a book.'
Rudolf Spielmann, Austrian chess player
(1883–1942)

1

It's not hard to shrink a human head.

First, you make a slit up the back. (Well, first you sever the head from the body, but I guess you figured that out already.) Then, you peel the skin and hair away from the skull. Slow and careful does it: you gotta keep it all in one piece, else you'll spend hours tryin' to make it right again, and even then it won't look quite the same. And it's not like human heads grow on trees, and you can just go out and find another one. So take your time and get it right. Sorry to sound all bossy, but it's gotta be said.

You don't need the skull no more, least not for this process, so do what you want with it. Chuck it away (someone else's dumpster's better than your own, in case the cops come knockin'), or, I don't know, put a candle in it, save it for Hallowe'en, give it to the next guy you know playin' Hamlet, whatever.

But you still need somethin' to keep the head's shape, so put a wooden ball in where the skull used to be. Sew the eyelids shut; the finer the thread the better. You need delicate fingers; think piano players rather than piano movers. Close the lips and skewer 'em with little palm pins, the kind you get on dog brushes.

Then take the head over to the stove, put it in a cookin' pot, and simmer for a couple of hours – no more, you hear, not unless *you want all the hair to fall out and the skin to end up as dry and cracked as a summer riverbed. A couple of hours, and the skin'll look and feel like dark rubber. That's what you're aimin' at. Take it out the cookpot, remove the wooden ball, flip the skin inside out and scrape out all the gunk and fat on the inside. Flip it back again and sew shut the slit you made at the back to kick this whole thing off.*

You don't need the wooden ball no more today, but of course keep it close to hand if you're plannin' on shrinkin' more heads any time soon.

Now you need a heap of hot stones, to shrink the head even more and sear its inside clean. Drop the stones through the neck openin', one at a time. Make sure you keep movin' 'em around, else you'll leave scorch marks. When you got too many stones in there to keep rollin' 'em around nice and easy, take 'em all back out, one by one.

The stones all gone, tip hot sand into the head. The sand gets in the places the stones can't reach, the little crevices of the nose and ears. Attention to detail, folks. But you ain't finished with the stones yet, no sir. You press 'em to the outside of the face: shape and seal, shape and seal. Gotta keep those features lookin' good. Think of it like moldin' a clay face, like you're Patrick Swayze and Demi Moore in Ghost. *Love that movie.*

Singe off any excess hair and cover the face in charcoal ash. This is supposed to let you harness the dead person's spirit to your own ends; you don't put on the ash, the soul'll seep out and avenge the death. That's what the old-timers say, at any rate. Not sure I believe 'em, but what the hell. Can't do any harm, can it?

The head should be about the size of an orange by now. Hang it over a fire to harden properly, and you're done. You can do what you want with it now.

Like I said, not hard. Not hard at all.

2

There are several types of hangover. There's Hangover Lite, a mild but insistent ache in the temples; there's Hangover Medium, where you ride greasy swells of nausea which rear and ebb without warning; and there's Hangover Max, when a team of roadworkers are jackhammering behind your eyes, your heart is doing a one-man Indy 500, and the thought that you might die is eclipsed only by the fear that you won't.

And then there's the kind of hangover Franco Patrese had at the precise moment his cellphone jolted him from sleep with a brutality that was borderline sociopathic.

But Patrese was a pro. In the time it took for the phone to ring once, neither the shock of the rude awakening nor the monumental combination of toxins gleefully racing round his body could prevent him from assembling a few salient points.

First, it was still dark outside.

Second, he was in a hotel room, which he remembered as being on the outskirts of Foxborough, Massachusetts.

5

Third, there was another bed in the room, and in that bed was a man named Jeff whose snoring had the rhythm and persistence of waves breaking on a shore. Jeff was one of Patrese's college buddies. A whole bunch of them had hooked up to come see their beloved Pittsburgh Steelers play the New England Patriots in Foxborough this coming afternoon, and, as Patrese hadn't seen much of his old friends since moving down to New Orleans, they'd decided to make a weekend of it, all boys together. For someone like Patrese, a single guy who lived in party central, this was just another weekend of good times. For those of his buddies who were married with kids, and whose usual weekends were therefore kids' soccer practice, home-improvement jobs and putting up with the in-laws, this was pretty much their only free time all year, and by hell they'd made the most of it.

Fourth, Patrese had been first a cop and then an FBI agent for more than a decade, so he knew that no one rang that early on a Sunday morning unless there was a good reason for it. And nine times out of ten, a good reason means something bad has happened.

He answered on the second ring. 'Patrese.'

Well, 'Patrese' was what he'd wanted to say. 'Ngfrujghr' was how it had actually come out.

'Hello?' It was a woman's voice. 'I'm looking for Franco Patrese?'

Bile rose fast and hard in Patrese's throat. He took a deep breath and forced it back down. This time when he opened his mouth to speak, his tongue felt like a desiccated slug.

'Hello?' said the woman again. 'Hello?'

There was a glass of water by the bed. Patrese reached for it. Felt sick again. Hangover motion sickness, he thought: you move, you feel sick. No matter. He grabbed the glass and drank it down in one.

'This is Patrese.' His voice still sounded like Darth Vader

6

with flu, but at least he was now speaking recognizable English.

'Agent Patrese, my name is Lauren Kieseritsky. I'm with the police department in New Haven, Connecticut.'

No apology for waking him so early. Patrese didn't expect one. Law enforcement personnel don't apologize to each other for doing their jobs. In any case, Patrese was already trying to think. New Haven, Connecticut? He'd never been there in his life. Never been, didn't know anyone there, probably couldn't even point to it on a map.

'I got your number through ViCAP,' Kieseritsky continued.

Patrese sat straight up, nausea be damned. ViCAP is the Violent Criminal Apprehension Program, a Bureau database which collates information on violent crime, especially murder. ViCAP is linked to police and sheriff departments across the country. Local officers can enter details of crimes committed on their patch and see if these details match anything already in the system. ViCAP is particularly useful in catching serial killers, who often murder in different jurisdictions and over many years: crimes which beforehand had simply been written off as unrelated and insoluble.

ViCAP definitely meant something bad had happened.

'What you got?' Patrese asked.

'Two bodies found an hour ago on the Green.'

'The Green?'

'Sorry. New Haven Green. Grass square, center of the city.'

'OK.'

'White man, black woman. No IDs on either yet, though we've taken fingerprints and are running them through the system. Both been decapitated. No sign of the heads. Both missing an arm. Both with skin taken from their chests and backs.'

'The arms – that's why you called me? Limb removal?' Patrese's first case as an agent in New Orleans had been a serial killer who, amongst other things, had amputated his victims' left legs.

'Yes, sir. Well, not just that.'

'Then what?'

'The dead man. We found him on the steps of a church, and he's wearing a signet ring with a cross emblem on it. We think it's the Benedictine medal. We think he's a monk, a priest, something like that.'

Before Patrese had been a Bureau agent, he'd been a Pittsburgh cop. He'd taken down a killer nicknamed the Human Torch, whose victims had included a bishop – a bishop who, as a young priest, had befriended Patrese's family and done the kind of things to a teenage Franco that no human being should ever inflict on another.

Patrese ran to the bathroom and threw up.

3

New Haven, CT

Early on Sunday morning, no traffic on the road and a crime scene to get to, it took Patrese dead on two hours to make it from Foxborough to New Haven. He drove fast but not ridiculously so: he was still way over the alcohol limit, so the last thing he wanted was to get stopped. It was a dollar to a dime that any highway patrolman who did pull him over would let him go on his way once Patrese had explained the situation, but it wasn't inconceivable that Patrese would run across a trooper who disliked the Bureau (most people did), didn't see what the hurry was (the folks were dead, right? They weren't going nowhere), and would take great pleasure in busting his ass for DUI ('The law's the law, sir'). Either way, better not to risk it.

Kieseritsky had said she'd hold the crime scene for him once he'd made it clear he was just down the road rather than in New Orleans. Patrese had texted his buddies back in Foxborough to explain his absence, and chuckled to himself at the thought of the ragging he'd endure *in absentia* once they eventually hauled their sorry asses out of bed.

He'd have given an awful lot to be at the stadium this afternoon rather than poking round the entrails of yet more lives snuffed out, but when the dead said jump, anyone who dealt with homicide could only ask one question: 'How high?' That was the way it was and always would be. You don't like it? Get another job.

The crime scene came with the sound-and-light show that all major incidents did: rotating blues and reds on top of patrol cars, men and women in sterile suits and shoe covers talking urgently to each other or into handsets, striped tape flapping in the breeze, and a crowd of onlookers both thrilled and appalled to be part of all this. A uniformed officer was subtly videoing the crowd: some killers like to hang around the crime scene.

Patrese parked up on a side street, opened his door, checked to see no one was looking, shoved a couple of fingers down his throat, and parked what was left of the contents of his stomach into the gutter. He hadn't vomited at a crime scene for many years, but the way he was feeling right now, he couldn't guarantee continuing that streak. It would do his image and authority no good if, the moment he saw the corpses, he started yakking his guts up like a teenager who'd had too much Coors. Hence the precautions: get it all out now.

When he was sure his stomach was well and truly empty, he popped some gum in his mouth, got out of the car and strode towards the Green. The Green was the kind of space which would have made the Founding Fathers purr: a large expanse of grass criss-crossed with paths and surrounded – protected – on all sides by buildings which reeked of civic pride. A neoclassical courthouse with columns out front; red-brick office blocks designed in Georgian Revival; and what looked like an enormous Gothic castle gatehouse.

A uniform checked Patrese's badge and lifted the tape for him to duck under.

'Detective Kieseritsky's over there, sir.' The uniform pointed to a small lady in a charcoal trouser suit. Patrese nodded his thanks and walked towards her.

'You must be Agent Patrese,' said Kieseritsky when he was still ten yards from her.

She was mid-thirties, all lines and angles: hair parted at the side and cut short at the back, cheekbones tilting above a pointed chin, arms forming triangles as she splayed her hands on her hips. If there was any warmth in her voice or bearing, Patrese couldn't detect it: then again, he wouldn't have been full of the milk of human kindness either if he'd spent the first part of his Sunday at a double homicide.

'Looked you up while you were on your way,' she added. 'You ready?'

'Sure.'

'Any preference?'

'Preference?'

'Which one you want to see first.'

'Whichever's nearer.'

'John, then.'

'John?'

'John Doe. That's what they still are. John Doe and Jane Doe.'

There were three churches on the east side of the Green, arranged in a neat line: one at the north end, one at the south, and the third smack in between. Kieseritsky headed toward the middle one. Patrese fell into step alongside her.

He gestured all round them. 'Big place,' he said, and instantly cursed himself for being so facile.

Kieseritsky shot him a look which suggested she was thinking exactly the same thing, but her tone was polite.

11

'Sure is. Designed by the Puritans to hold all those who'd be spared in the Second Coming.'

Patrese tried to remember the Book of Revelation. 'A hundred forty-four thousand?'

'You a religious man, Agent Patrese?'

'Used to be. Not anymore.'

'Then we're gonna get along just fine.'

She led the way through a line of trees, and now Patrese could see the headless corpse on the church steps. The man was lying naked on his back, though curiously the pose didn't look especially undignified, at least to Patrese's eyes. Perhaps, he thought, it was because the cadaver hardly looked human anymore, not without its head.

'Snappers have all been and gone,' Kieseritsky said.

Patrese nodded. She was telling him that the crime scene had already been photographed from every conceivable angle and distance, so he could – within reason – poke around to his heart's content.

Crisp fall morning or not, dead bodies stink. Patrese gagged slightly when the stench first reached him, but not so obviously that anyone would notice. Just as well he'd gone for the gutter option a few minutes before, he thought.

He crouched down beside the corpse.

No head, no right arm, and the skin gone in a large circle from sternum to waist. Hard to tell too much from any of that about whoever this poor soul had once been, but from the crinkly sagging of fat around the man's waist, the faint wrinkles on his remaining hand and the gray hairs on the arm above it, Patrese guessed his age as mid-fifties.

No blood, either: no blood anywhere around the body, even though it had suffered two major amputations. John Doe had clearly been killed elsewhere and brought here.

Patrese peered closer at the points where the killer had performed those amputations. Clean cuts, both of them, even though taking off a head and arm involved slicing through tough layers of tissue, muscle, cartilage and bone. Must have used something very sharp, Patrese thought. Must have been skilled at using it, too. A surgeon? A butcher?

The man's neck looked like an anatomy exhibit: hard white islands of trachea and esophagus surrounded by dark-red seas of jugulars and carotids. The stump of his shoulder was a sandwich in cross-relief: skin round the outside like bread, livid muscle and nerves the filling within. And where the skin on his chest had been was now a matrix of areolar tissue, thousands of tiny patches like spiders' webs which Patrese could see individually up close but which blended into formless white from even a few feet away.

Patrese looked at the signet ring on the man's pinkie. Kieseritsky had been right when she'd called it as the Benedictine medal: Patrese had grown up a good Catholic boy, and symbols such as these were now hardwired into his memory. There on the ring was Saint Benedict himself, cross in his right hand and rulebook in his left, and around the picture ran the words *Eius in obitu nostro praesentia muniamur.*

'May we be strengthened by his presence in the hour of our death,' said Kieseritsky.

Patrese nodded, wondering whether John Doe had indeed felt the presence.

'This isn't a Benedictine church, though?' he asked.

Kieseritsky shook her head. 'United Church of Christ.'

'And the other two?'

She shook her head again. 'That one' – pointing to the church at the north end of the green – 'is also United Church. The other's Episcopal.'

Patrese looked over the rest of the corpse. Indentations on the skin of both ankles: restraints, Patrese knew. That apart, nothing: no watch, no jewelry, no tattoos.

There *was* something next to John Doe's hand. A playing card, by the look of it.

Kieseritsky handed Patrese a pair of tweezers. He picked the card up.

Not a playing card; well, not one of the standard fifty-two-card deck, at any rate.

The card pictured a man in red priestly robes sitting on a throne. On his head was a triple crown in gold, and in his left hand he carried a long staff topped with a triple cross. His right hand was making the sign of the blessing, with the index and middle fingers pointing up and the other two pointing down. At his feet were two crossed keys, and the back of two monks' heads could be seen as they knelt before him.

Beneath the picture, in capital letters, **THE HIEROPHANT**.

Patrese knew exactly what it was. A tarot card.

4

There was a tarot card by the cadaver of Jane Doe, too. Hers was **THE EMPRESS**. The figure on this card was also sitting on a throne, though this one was in the middle of a wheat field with a waterfall nearby. She wore a robe patterned with what looked like pomegranates, and a crown of stars on her head. In her right hand she carried a scepter, and beneath her throne was a heart-shaped bolster marked with the symbol of Venus.

Like John Doe, Jane was also naked, and also missing her head, an arm (the left one, this time), and large patches of skin front and back.

The more Patrese looked, though, the more he saw that there were at least as many differences between the two corpses as there were similarities.

For a start, Jane was lying on the grass under a tree, a couple of hundred yards from the church where John had been left.

More pertinently, perhaps, she'd been killed where she lay.

Patrese saw the splatter marks of blood high and thick on the tree trunk: the carotid artery, he thought, spraying hard and fast as her neck was cut. The ground around and beneath her body squelched with all the blood which had run from the cut sites.

And whereas John had been killed with what looked like clinical precision – clean lines of severance at neck and thigh, neat removal of the chest and back skin – Jane had been attacked with a far greater, unfocused fury. The wound at her neck gaped open and jagged, as though the killer had sawn or twisted or yanked her head: possibly all three. Flaps of skin and muscle hung messily from the stump of her arm. The perimeters where the patches of skin had been taken were uneven and torn. No restraint marks on her remaining wrist or her ankles: the attacker must have set about her instantly.

Heads, arms, skin, all gone. Had the killer taken them with him, as proof of his skill and tools to help him relive the fantasy he'd just acted out?

'Any thoughts?' Kieseritsky asked.

'Lots. Some of them might even be right.' Patrese pushed himself to his feet. 'John was killed elsewhere and brought here. Jane was killed here. Pretty risky, to decapitate someone in a public place. Lot of people round here at night?'

'Up to midnight, sure. Most of 'em the kind of people who keep you and me in business, of course. Same for urban parks the country over. But we ain't talkin' murderers usually, let alone something like this. We're talking pick-pockets, drug dealers, muggers, those kind of guys. The guys who know the process system as well as I do, they come in and out of the station house so often.'

'New Haven's got a high murder rate, right?'

'Where d'you hear that?'

'Bureau report. I remember it 'cos after Katrina, when all the criminals had been shipped out of state during

16

reconstruction, New Orleans dropped out of the top three for the first time in years. Big rejoicing in the Big Easy.'

'Yeah, well. I seen that report too. We're fourth highest in the US proportionate to population, it says. Only ones in front of us are Detroit, St Louis and some other hellhole, can't remember where. But it's bullshit, Agent Patrese.'

'Yes?'

'First off, our crime figures are *down* year-on-year, and that's what matters to me, not how we rank against some-place else. Second, it all depends on where you draw the municipal boundaries. May I speak freely? New Haven ain't no different to any other damn place in the States. The vast majority of crime is committed *by* poor black people, *on* poor black people, *in* areas full of poor black people. Don't make it right, of course, but that's the way it is. You must know that.'

Patrese nodded. He'd worked in Pittsburgh and New Orleans, and it was the same in both those places. Kieseritsky continued:

'But round here, downtown, this kind of thing just doesn't happen.' She gestured toward the Gothic gatehouse on the edge of the Green. 'That's the main entrance to Yale, you know. That's the kind of place this is. Ivy League, old school, full of the kids who in twenty years' time will be running the country.'

'And screwing it up, same as generations before them have done.'

She raised a sardonic eyebrow. 'President Bush went to Yale.'

'I rest my case.'

She laughed. 'Anyway. Like I said, most law-abiding folks wouldn't hang around on the Green late night, but those that do are only going to lose their wallets and cellphones. Not their lives.'

17

'And the lowlife? They here all night?'

She shook her head. 'Most of them have cleared out by two or three in the morning, even on weekends.'

'And no one saw Jane Doe being killed, or John Doe being dumped?'

'Not that we've found so far.'

A uniform hurried across the grass toward them, eyes bright with the importance of the news bearer.

'We've got a match on Jane's fingerprints, ma'am,' he said.

'Previous offense?'

'Arrested in New York on the Iraq war demonstration, February 2003.'

Patrese remembered that day well: there'd been protests all over the world. He'd intended going, but he'd spent what had started as the night before and ended up as the whole weekend with a waitress he'd met on the Strip in Pittsburgh.

'Regina King,' the uniform continued.

He must have seen both Patrese's and Kieseritsky's eyes widen in surprise, because he nodded. 'Yes, ma'am. Sir. *That* Regina King. Kwasi King's mom.'

5

Kwasi King was twenty-four years old, and he had been famous for exactly half his life. A month after his twelfth birthday, he became the youngest chess grandmaster in history. Before he reached fourteen, he won the US championship. Chess was pretty much a minority sport as far as the mainstream media were concerned, but one story was always guaranteed to get their attention – a child prodigy who might, just might, be the next Bobby Fischer.

Especially when that prodigy was a black kid raised by a single mom in America's largest public housing project.

Regina King had been seventeen when she'd given birth to Kwasi. The name meant 'born on a Sunday', because he had been. If she knew who Kwasi's father was, she never said so. She had no qualifications to speak of, but what she *did* have was a work ethic that was positively Stakhanovite and a tidal desire to give her son a better start than she'd had.

She took two jobs at once, sometimes three, just to keep them afloat; but the jobs were minimum wage and childcare cost money, so the only place she could afford was a small apartment high up in a Queensbridge tower block. Six thousand people lived in the Queensbridge complex, peering with hopeless longing across the water to Manhattan's glass-and-steel canyons.

Drug dealers worked shifts along the development's main commercial stretch, punching clocks as diligently as stevedores. You wanted to go get something from the store, even a loaf of bread or a bar of candy, you had to walk past them. *This is the life*, their very presence seemed to hiss, *this is the life, this is the only life you'll ever know*. In the daytime, they shouted and snarled at each other: when night fell, they started shooting.

Some of them tried their luck with Regina: she was a good-looking girl, and still only twenty. She turned them down, politely but firmly. A couple of her wannabe suitors weren't used to women turning them down, and liked to use their fists on such occasions: but there was something about Regina which made them meekly accept it and walk away.

One day, shortly before Kwasi's fourth birthday, Regina took him into Manhattan for the day. They walked through Washington Square Park, past the corner of the world which is forever chess: an array of checkered tables in poured concrete, and round them an endless flow of players and spectators. All human life is here: alcoholic hustlers who'll bet you a handful of dollars a game, Eastern European grandmasters down on their luck, bankers and lawyers in their lunch hours, students, bums, sages, fools. And the play is strictly speed chess. No two-hour games in reverential library-style silence: five minutes each player, tops, with trash-talking not so much encouraged as mandatory.

Kwasi stood to watch one of the games, his little face barely at table level, so he was peering through the pieces rather than over them as adult players do. The game had ended in a flurry of moves and insults, both players' laughter deflecting any malice. Come on, Regina said, game's over, let's go.

One more, Mom. Can I watch one more?

She'd been at work all week, farming Kwasi out to friends. She owed him a little indulgence, no? Sure, honey, one more. Just one more.

One more became one more after that, and another one, and another one. Nine games later, when a hotshot lawyer had been checkmated seven ways to Sunday by one of the regular park hustlers and grudgingly handed over the five bucks stake, Kwasi turned to him and said, quietly but precisely: 'You missed checkmate in three moves.'

Regina, swaying from foot to foot in her impatience to get going, stopped dead.

She knew two things for sure. First, Kwasi had never so much as seen a chess set in his life, let alone played with one. Second, he wasn't the kind of kid to come out with something like this unless he meant it. She'd always known he was bright: talking at six months, reading at a year, glued to *The Price Is Right* at eighteen months – but this, if this was what she thought it was . . . well, this was something else entirely.

Lawyer and hustler both laughed: the hustler with some good humor, the lawyer with none. The hustler, breath sweet from his paper-bag rum, leaned toward Kwasi. 'Mate in three, huh?'

Kwasi said nothing: simply put the pieces back to where they'd been halfway through the game, and played through the three-move sequence. When he finished, the lawyer took the pieces from him and played it through himself, muttering 'I'll be damned, I'll be damned' with every slap of piece on board.

21

'I done seen *all* that at the time,' the hustler said. Kwasi merely looked at him, his face completely still like a little black Buddha, until the hustler's mouth cracked into a goofy raggedy-tooth smile and he threw up his hands in mock surrender. 'OK, kid, OK, you got me. I never saw that neither, none of that. How old are you?'

'Three years, eleven months and twenty-six days.'

'A'iiiight. It's good to be precise. And when you learn to play chess?'

'Thirty-eight minutes ago.'

The hustler laughed again, until he saw that Kwasi was serious.

When it came to chess, Serious was Kwasi's middle name. This is my boy, Regina would proclaim, and he's not taking no crap off of nobody. Not in the years he spent playing all comers in the park, and certainly not when some of them tried to cheat by making illegal moves or subtly nudging a piece off its square; not when people tried to trash-talk him, because the regulars understood that Kwasi didn't trash-talk and that, get this, it didn't matter, 'cos he was so damn good; not in the proper tournaments he played, the ones that had TV crews and arbiters and trophies; not at school when the other kids swung between admiring his talent and calling him a freak; not when the cops came round after yet another gang murder to ask whether he'd seen anything from his apartment window six stories up; not when as a teenager he threw away his polo shirts and acrylic sweaters, started wearing long black leather coats and motor-bike boots, and ran his hair into dreadlocks; not even when he went on *Letterman* or *Conan* or *Leno* or any of those shows. He didn't give a shit about what folks did or said to unsettle him, he didn't take any shit off of them. He wasn't in the shit business.

And all the time around him, the endless whispering

22

undercurrent of hope and fear: *the next Fischer, the next Fischer, the next Fischer,* for Fischer had been both genius and lunatic, the two sides of him waxing and waning against each other until the lunatic had taken over, ringing radio stations after 9/11 to exult in the destruction of the Twin Towers and tell the world that America had had it coming for years.

Wherever Kwasi was, so too would Regina be. To give him more time to play chess, now his tournament winnings were enough to let her go part-time at work, she pulled him out of school and began to home-tutor him herself. The deal was simple: he played chess, she did everything else. She dealt with anything that might stress or distract him even before he knew it existed.

Kwasi had a growth spurt around thirteen or fourteen, and after that people who didn't know them sometimes thought that he and Regina were brother and sister, or even boyfriend and girlfriend, as she still looked so young. When he went to college – none of the Ivy Leagues would take him, but the University of Maryland, Baltimore County, offered him a chess scholarship and a major in computer science, and he led the varsity chess team to three consecutive Pan-American Championships – she came with him, setting the two of them up in an apartment near campus.

In America of all places, there's fame and there's *fame*; and there was no doubt as to the moment when Kwasi made the jump from one to the other. Three years ago, at the age of twenty-one, he played for the world championship in Kazan, the ancient Tatar capital which was now part of modern-day Russia, a night's train ride east of Moscow. His opponent was Rainer Tartu, a thirty-something Estonian (long after the fall of communism, the old Soviet republics still dominated the chess world) with

23

wire-rimmed spectacles, a bouffant of sandy hair, an expression of benevolent openness, the fluent English of the international cosmopolitan, and the long slim fingers of a concert pianist, which was what he was when he wasn't playing chess.

The match was twelve games, with a tie-break procedure if the scores were still level at the end. A dozen US reporters and analysts went out to Kazan to cover the match: the networks carried highlights, and there was full, real-time, coverage over the Internet.

To start with, it all seemed for nothing. Kwasi, this great natural talent, this badass who'd steamrollered all the other candidates to get here, who wore a suit at the board because those were the rules but who wouldn't cut his hair – indeed, he'd woven red, white and blue ends into his dreads – Kwasi was off the pace.

Tartu won the first game at a canter, played out draws for the second and third, won the fourth and had the better of draws in the fifth and sixth. A succession of draws can appear boring, but these were anything but. They were see-saw games where the initiative swung first one way and then the other, where pressure led to mistakes and mistakes led to pressure. Each player had to dig deep within themselves to hold the line, slugging each other to a battered and exhausted standstill, knowing that it was just as important not to let your opponent draw blood as it was to try to hurt him: because sometimes when the blood starts to flow, it's hard to staunch.

With one point for a win, half for a draw and none for a loss, Tartu was 4–2 up at halfway. Kwasi looked shell-shocked, and all Regina's soothing could do nothing to stop the rot. Kwasi was letting it slide through his fingers, little by little. The reporters wanted to go home.

Game seven was another draw, though for the first time

in the match Kwasi was the better player. But draws weren't going to be enough: he had to win two games of the remaining five even to force a tie-break.

In game eight, he finally, triumphantly, magnificently got it right, playing a game of such breathtaking brilliance that when Tartu resigned, he – Tartu – led the audience in a standing ovation. Kwasi peered through his dreads in shy appreciation.

Now it was Tartu's turn to look shell-shocked. He lost game nine inside twenty moves, almost unheard of at this level. Four and a half points each, but the momentum was all with Kwasi. The reporters were getting their front pages again. Game ten, Kwasi missed a difficult winning chance and had to settle for a draw.

Then came game eleven. In a routine opening, Kwasi made a knight move that brought gasps from the spectators in the hall. Even a casual player could see it was a blunder. Tartu, blinking in astonishment, looked at the position, then at Kwasi, then at the arbiter, then back at Kwasi, then back at the position. There was no trap, no swindle. A genuine, twenty-four-carat mistake, or so it seemed. Five moves later, Kwasi resigned.

In the press conference afterwards, Kwasi explained what had happened. He'd reached out to move the knight, and as he'd done so, he'd realized it would be a mistake: but before he'd been able to withdraw his hand, he'd felt the tips of his fingers brush the head of the knight. Chess rules state that if you touch a piece, you have to move it. He'd touched the knight, so he'd had to move it.

Sitting next to Kwasi, in front of the world's press, Tartu shook his head in astonishment. I didn't see you touch it, he said. The arbiter concurred: Me neither. Kwasi could have chosen a different move, a better move, and no one would have been any the wiser. How did he feel about that?

25

He shrugged. At the chessboard, he said, rules are rules. Nobody's fault but mine.

And now he needed to win the last game just to take the match into a tie-break. Tartu could try to close things down, go for the easy draw. Kwasi would have to shake things up: go for the victory even at the risk of losing.

Mikhail Tal, a former world champion and the most dashing player the modern game has seen, once said: 'You must take your opponent into a deep dark forest where two plus two equals five, and where the path leading out is only wide enough for one.'

In game twelve, that's exactly what Kwasi did. He piled complication on complication, trying to scramble Tartu's powers of concentration and calculation. Feint left and go right: feint right and go left. Knights jumping around at close quarters, rooks battering down open lines. In between moves, Kwasi got up and walked around, pawing at the ground like a bull.

A well-aimed, well-timed counterpunch from Tartu would probably have taken the game back to Kwasi, but Tartu was – as Kwasi had hoped – too conservative, too wedded to the idea that he could ride out the storm if he battened down the hatches. Kwasi sacrificed two pieces and then a third to rip open Tartu's defenses; and when Tartu finally extended a hand in resignation, he looked almost relieved that the agony was over.

Tie-break: first ever in a world championship.

The twelve games so far had been played with classical time controls: each player given two hours to make forty moves. Now there would be four games at 25/10: twenty-five minutes for all moves, with ten seconds added to each player's clock every time he made a move. Kwasi won the first game and Tartu the second. The third and fourth were both draws. Still level.

The ratchet got even tighter, and up went the excitement. Two games at 5/3: five minutes for all moves, three seconds added per move. If the scores were still level after these two games, another set of two would be played, and another, up to five: ten possible games in all. NBC cleared its schedule and started beaming the matches live. Viewing figures later released would show that, on average, quarter of a million more people started watching every minute as news of the showdown spread across America.

Kwasi won the first game. He was five minutes from the world title, all he needed was a draw – and he blew it, letting Tartu's pieces strangle the life out of his position. Third and fourth games, both draws. Fifth game, Tartu won, and now he had the advantage. That meant shit or bust for Kwasi: win or go home.

He crouched low on his seat like a panther, wild and beautiful. When he reached across the board, it seemed that he was not so much shuffling wooden figures from one square to another as unleashing some long-hidden primal force. The cameras zoomed in on his face. He winced in agony, gasped in delight. He put his head in his hands. When he bared his teeth, a couple of the spectators in the front row recoiled instinctively.

This wasn't just chess anymore, the commentators panted breathlessly: this was heavyweight boxing, this was a five-set Wimbledon final, this was Ali and Frazier, Borg and McEnroe, where the momentum swings first one way and then the other, and both men can practically smell the prize they want so much.

Frantic scramble with seconds left for both men in game six, but it was the flag on Tartu's clock that dropped first. He'd lost on time. They were even again. The crowd stamped and cheered, not because they were against Tartu but because they recognized that what they were seeing was a once-in-a-lifetime drama.

Seventh game to Kwasi. Eighth to Tartu, at last beginning to sweat under the tension. Punch-drunk, perhaps trying to save themselves for what they knew really would be the final decider, they played out the final two games as draws.

Now came sudden death, Armageddon chess: and for once the sobriquet didn't seem inappropriate. The colors had so far alternated game on game, but since this was a one-off, they tossed again. Kwasi won, and chose Black. In Armageddon chess, White has five minutes to make all his moves and Black only four: but White has to win, because a draw is counted as a Black victory.

By now, thirty-two million people were watching in the United States alone, and three or four times that worldwide.

Tartu and Kwasi shook hands, gave brittle smiles for the cameras. The arbiter checked their clocks, and off they went.

Most all the chess teachers Kwasi had ever had – and every one of them had been obliged to provide their services for free, as Regina had never been able to afford lessons – had tried to stop him playing speed chess in Washington Square Park. It's not real chess, they'd tell him; it's cheap stuff, trickery, simple two- or three-move patterns. Real chess takes time and contemplation, real chess requires vision and strategy. Real chess is the Four Seasons: speed chess is Mickey D's.

But they'd all been wrong, because it was exactly those thousands of two- and three-minute games in the park that won Kwasi the world title now. All the things that were gradually leaching Tartu's energy from him – the ever-tightening vice of quicker time controls, the barely controlled pandemonium in the hall, the insane pressure of playing a blitz game for the greatest prize in his sport – these were the very things that energized Kwasi, that arced through him like electricity. Four minutes on his clock, spectators who couldn't keep still or shut up, all eyes on him. This wasn't a hall in Kazan, this was the park, rain and shine and summer and winter, this was where he felt at home.

Now, with no time in which to think and even less in which to move, Kwasi played with deathless precision, mind and eyes and fingers everywhere on the board at once. He made moves like a tennis player plays shots, all instinct and muscle memory, pieces finding their way to the perfect square time after time as though by homing instinct. Some called it the zone, some called it a trance. It was both, and neither. Kwasi was no longer playing chess. He *was* chess.

And when he came back to the States as world champion, the youngest in history and America's first since Fischer, he remained chess in a different but equally all-consuming way. Suddenly, the game was no longer a refuge for weirdos and sad sacks, for guys with pocket protectors and BO, sweating out fast-food toxins in gloomy rooms.

Kwasi, single-handedly, had made chess cool.

He played against celebrities. He guested on hip-hop albums, rapping about the ways in which chess mirrored life. He said he was going to hire himself the best architect available and build himself a house shaped like a rook, replete with spiral staircases and parapets. Sponsors fell over themselves to sign him up, this perfect synthesis of every marketing man's dream: hip enough to appeal to kids, smart enough to appeal to adults, wholesome enough – never much talk of girls, let alone drugs – to be held up as a model for the black community. Kwasi had Tiger's reach, Jordan's smarts, 50 Cent's cred, Denzel's looks. Will Smith wanted to play him in a movie.

The one thing he didn't do was the one thing that had made him famous. He didn't play competitive chess. As world champion, he was guaranteed the right to defend his title, so he didn't have to go through the official qualification process again, but there were still plenty of other tournaments in which he could have played, names that tripped off the tongue of chess fans the world over: Linares, Wijk aan Zee, Dortmund.

The less he played, the more his mystique grew, this Gatsby of modern-day chess. Was he working on some new fiendish openings? Could anyone else call themselves a winner without playing him?

It wasn't as though Kwasi needed the tournament income. The championship prize money had made Kwasi a millionaire literally overnight. In the year or two that followed, endorsements multiplied that at least tenfold, probably more. The only two people who knew the exact figures were Kwasi and Regina, and they weren't telling. And yes, she was still there, always at his side. No one got to say so much as a single word to him without going through her first. No sponsor got to pitch him a proposal until she'd read it and sat in their boardroom for three hours going over it point by point.

When he bought a condo in the Village, she moved in with him. When he played in exhibition matches, she was right there in the auditorium, front and center. When they stayed in hotels, they had a suite, two bedrooms, one for him and one for her. At home or on the road, she made sure his cooking and laundry were done. She was mother, manager, promoter, gatekeeper.

Time ran a profile on her. YOU KNOW THE KING, ran the headline, NOW MEET THE QUEEN. She cut it out and put it on the noticeboard in their kitchen, alongside one that showed her on the street outside their old tower block, a farewell to their old life. THE QUEEN OF QUEENS, that one said.

And now Kwasi was due to begin the defense of his title
– against Tartu once more – at Madison Square Garden in
less than two weeks' time, and Regina was dead.

6

'I don't understand,' Kwasi said. 'She's never late.'

Marat Nursultan tapped his Breitling. 'We get on with it? We suppose to start a half-hour ago.'

'Of course,' said Rainer Tartu.

It was only the three of them in the room: the three most powerful men in world chess. Not that it was an equal triumvirate, of course. Kwasi was the box office: his presence, and his presence alone, determined the dollars. Tartu just happened to be the one on the other side of the board. If Kwasi could have somehow played against himself, the sponsors wouldn't have given Tartu a look-in; and if he, Tartu, didn't like it, there were plenty of other grandmasters who'd take his place in a heartbeat.

As for Nursultan . . . well, he was the kind of guy that everyone had an opinion about. He liked people to call him Mr President, as he held two such offices: the presidency of Tatarstan, the semi-autonomous region of Russia whose capital Kazan had hosted the first match between Kwasi and Tartu; and the presidency of FIDE, the Fédération

Internationale des Échecs, the governing body of world chess.

Rumors of bribery and corruption had swirled around both elections, and Nursultan had done little to dampen them: how else, his sly smile and calculated bonhomie seemed to ask, how else was one supposed to win elections? Nursultan was pretty much the prototype for *homo post-sovieticus*: after completing a doctorate in applied mathematics from Kazan State Technical University, he'd seen which way the winds of perestroika were blowing in the late 1980s and had positioned himself accordingly.

In the chaos that had followed the collapse of the Soviet Union in 1991, he'd made a small fortune in car dealerships, a medium one in oil and banking, and an enormous one in technology. The Kazan Group, of which he was chairman and CEO, was now at the forefront of mobile communications and software development. On a good day he was worth $12 billion, on a bad day $10 billion. He was comfortably one of the richest hundred people in the world. He had mistresses whom he paraded in public and a wife whom he didn't. He claimed to have been abducted by aliens and given a tour of their galaxy.

And he loved chess with a passion. His Rolls-Royces were only ever black or white, the floors of all the houses he owned around the world were checkerboard marble, and he'd made the game a compulsory subject at every school in Tatarstan. He spent as much time out of Tatarstan as he did in it, leaving the day-to-day running of the place to the prime minister, who happened to be his brother. As far as Nursultan was concerned, both Tatarstan and FIDE were his own private fiefdoms. He liked to answer to one person only: himself.

Now he sat in his suite – the presidential suite, naturally – at the Waldorf-Astoria, graying hair slicked back above his brown, watchful, flat Asiatic face. 'Kwasi, we not wait any longer. Your mother not here, that too bad.' He put out his hand. 'You have demands, no? You give them to me.'

Kwasi handed a sheaf of papers to Nursultan and another one to Tartu. 'They're both the same,' he said.

Nursultan flicked to the last page. 'Sixteen pages.' He looked up, eyes glittering with the prospect of challenge. 'One hundred and eighty demands!'

'We've divided them into sections. Prize money, playing environment, and so on.'

'This is a laundry list,' Tartu said.

'And they're not demands,' Kwasi added. 'They're conditions. I'm entitled to have match conditions which suit me.'

'And me?' Tartu added. 'Am I entitled to conditions which suit *me*?'

Kwasi shrugged.

'If we not accept these, er, points,' Nursultan said carefully, 'then what?'

'Then I don't play.'

'They *are* demands, then.'

Kwasi shrugged again.

'The match starts in two weeks' time.'

A third shrug. 'I know.'

Nursultan looked at Tartu and raised his eyebrows.

They started to read Kwasi's list. Nursultan jotted notes in margins, pursing his lips and giving little dismissive laughs from time to time. Tartu read the whole thing very fast, and then went back to the start and did it again, more slowly. Kwasi walked over to the window and looked down at Park Avenue, as though he could will his mother into arriving simply by the power of his gaze.

'Well,' Nursultan said at last, 'Rainer and me, we should talk about this, no?'

'OK,' Kwasi said.

He didn't move. Nursultan laughed. 'We want to, how you say? Talk about you behind your back.'

'Oh. OK. Sure.'

'You go into room next door,' Nursultan said. 'I call you when we finish.'

Kwasi left. Nursultan batted the back of his hand against Kwasi's list. 'This: outrageous. You know how much money on this all? He want to hold us ransom.'

'He's not trying to hold you to ransom.'

Nursultan snorted: hard-headed businessman telling airy-fairy chess player the ways of the world. 'Two weeks before biggest chess match since Reykjavik? What else he do? Rainer, they not coming to see you. Sorry, but true. They come to see him.'

'You don't get him, do you?'

'Get him?'

'Understand him.'

'Sure I do.'

'No, you don't. Why does he make all these demands?'

'To get more money. To, how you say, unsettle you.'

'No. He makes them because they're what he wants. He has no agenda beyond that. He's a child. He doesn't want to play in Linares, so he doesn't. He doesn't want to play in Dortmund, so he doesn't. He sees the world like a child. Black and white.'

'He not behave this way last time.'

'He wasn't world champion last time. He wanted that prize so much, he didn't care about anything else. But now he wants everything to be the way he wants it.'

Nursultan flicked through the pages. 'Some of these, reasonable. Some, no. I see ten, twelve, simply no good. Cannot accept.'

'Then we won't play.'

'You will play.'

'*I'll* play. But he won't.'

'Then I negotiate with him.'

Tartu's smile meant the same thing as the snort Nursultan had given a minute or so before: I know the truth of this situation better than you. 'He won't negotiate.'

'Everyone negotiates.'

'Not him. These aren't one hundred and eighty demands: they're one demand. Take it or leave it.'

'We'll see.' Nursultan called out. 'Kwasi!'

Two doors opened at once: the one that led into the room where Kwasi was waiting, and the main door of the suite, which was guarded round the clock by Nursultan's security men. Two of them stood in the doorway. As Kwasi came back in, one of the security men walked over to Nursultan and spoke quickly in Tatar. Nursultan nodded. The man by the door stepped aside, and Patrese walked in. Nursultan remained seated. People like him didn't get up for government agents.

'I'm looking for Kwasi King,' Patrese said.

'That's me,' Kwasi said.

'Franco Patrese, Federal Bureau of Investigation.'

'Have I done something wrong?'

Patrese looked around the suite. 'Could I talk to you in private, sir?'

7

Patrese led Kwasi back into the room from where he, Kwasi, had just come, and shut the door behind them. Deep red sofas, antique escritoires, carpets thicker than some of the surfaces he'd played football on, and a wicker chair that JFK had used for his bad back: Patrese figured that, on a Bureau salary, he too could afford to stay in this place. For about five minutes.

He'd volunteered to tell Kwasi. In terms of gathering evidence and following leads, the first twenty-four hours after a homicide was critical, and so it made sense for Kieseritsky to stay in New Haven and supervise the investigation there: it was her turf, and she knew it backwards. The easiest thing to do would have been to phone the nearest precinct to Kwasi's apartment and get them to send a couple of uniforms over, and perhaps that's what they would have done had Jane Doe turned out to be an ordinary Jane, but this: this was something else.

The news was going to get out sooner rather than later, and the moment it did the press would be all over them like the cheapest suit on the rack. In that situation, you didn't need some guy barely out of police academy, so Patrese had hauled ass from New Haven down to New York, a couple of hours' drive to add to what he'd already done. En route, he'd checked in with his boss at the Bureau's New Orleans field office, Don Donner – yes, that really was his name and yes, he had eventually forgiven his parents. Donner was one of the least territorial Bureau guys around, which made him a rare and precious beast. Sure, he'd said, do whatever you have to, help them for as long as they need you. We're all the Bureau: we're all the good guys.

And Patrese's hangover had disappeared somewhere around Stamford.

Death notification is the redheaded stepchild of law enforcement work, the dirty job that no one really wants to do; but one of Patrese's partners, an old-time Pittsburgh detective named Mark Beradino, had always believed it to be one of the most important tasks a police officer could have. It wasn't merely that you owed the living your best efforts to find whoever had killed their loved one; it was also that the skilled detective could ascertain a whole heap from what the bereaved said or did. Shock and grief, like lust and rage, flay the truth from people.

Patrese knew the rules of death notification. Talk directly. Don't be afraid of the d-words – dead, died, death. Don't use euphemisms. Driver's licenses expired, parcels were passed on, keys were lost. Not people. People died.

Patrese gestured for Kwasi to take a seat, and sat down opposite him.

'Mr King, your mother is dead.'

Kwasi stared at him. Patrese held his gaze, rock-solid neutral. He didn't try to take Kwasi's arm or touch him in any way. Everyone reacts to news like this differently. Some people clap their hands to their chest and catch their breath;

some fall sobbing to the floor; some even attack the messenger.

Kwasi did none of these things. He stared at Patrese for fully half a minute, totally blank, as though his brain – this vast, amazing brain that could see fifteen moves ahead through a forest of pieces on a chessboard – was struggling to comprehend the very short, very simple, very brutal sentence he'd just heard.

'You sure?' he said at last.

'Yes, sir.'

'How?' He blinked twice. 'How? Where? When?'

'Her body was found this morning on New Haven Green.'

'Where?'

'New Haven, sir. Connecticut.'

'What the hell she doing there?'

'I was hoping you could tell me that, sir.'

Kwasi looked around, as though seeing the room for the first time. 'Can you take me home, officer?'

'Sure.'

Manhattan slid past the windows of Patrese's car. A church on Lexington spat worshippers out on to the sidewalk. In a Union Square café, a man jabbed his fork in the air to make a point amidst pealing laughter from his friends.

The journey passed in silence. Kwasi said nothing, and Patrese didn't try to make him talk. Some people gush an endless torrent of questions, wanting to know everything about how their loved one has died: others are silent, perhaps in the hope that if they don't ask, don't know, don't listen, then it won't have happened.

Kwasi didn't move the entire journey. He sat bolt upright and stared straight ahead. Only once, when they turned past Washington Square Park, did he so much as glance out of the window.

Kwasi's apartment was on Bleecker Street. Patrese pulled up outside. A little further on, at the junction with Sixth Avenue, police barriers were being erected on the sidewalk.

'Do you have anyone you can call?'

Kwasi shook his head.

'No one at all?'

'No.' Kwasi made no move to get out of the car.

'Would you like me to come up with you?'

'Yes. Thank you.' Kwasi looked at Patrese for the first time since leaving the Waldorf-Astoria. 'That would be' – he searched for the right word – 'helpful.'

There was a doorman in the lobby; a young guy with tight curly hair and teeth white enough to be visible from space. He got to his feet as they came in.

'Hey, Mr King. Looking forward to the parade tonight?'

Kwasi didn't hear; or if he did, he didn't acknowledge it. Patrese nodded at the man. 'Parade?' he asked.

'Hallowe'en parade. Expecting a million folks, they say.'

The apartment was typical Bleecker: gentrification writ large over smatterings of old-school authenticity. Exposed brickwork and windows framed with industrial steel: wooden floorboards and subtle uplighting. Poliform kitchen with corian countertops and Miele appliances: pre-wired Bose sound system and fifty-inch plasma TV.

And on pretty much every surface was a chess set. There must have been hundreds, jostling on shelves and squatting on tables. Standard sets were very much the minority. Think of a theme, and it was there somewhere. Cowboys faced off against Indians, Crusaders against Saracens, Red Sox against Yankees, Spartans against Athenians, angels against demons. There were Egyptian gods, Norse gods, Greek gods. Terracotta warriors peered sideways towards *Harry Potter* characters. *Star Wars* figurines backed on to samurai. One set was made of automobile parts; another had skeleton keys as pieces, fitting into a hole in each square; a third had squares of all different heights. Blue pieces eyeballed green ones, pink played yellow, red played orange. A hexagonal board was designed for three players; a multi-dimensional set stacked four boards atop each other.

Kwasi looked at Patrese, saw his interest.

'Can never have too many sets,' he said.

This was Kwasi's refuge, Patrese sensed. When the world got too big and complex and nasty – and it must have been all those things right now for him, and more – here's where he came, back to the chessboard, where everything had order and rules and where he was the master.

'Which one's your favorite?'

'Don't have one. If I did, the others would get upset.'

'The others? The other sets? The pieces?'

'That's right. Tell you one I haven't got, though. It's this one from Wales; you know, part of England. The chessboard of Gwenddoleu. The board's made of gold, the men are made of silver, and when the pieces are set up, they play by themselves.'

'That's a nice story.'

'It's not a story. It's true. It really exists.'

Patrese decided to change tack. 'Mr King, I'm sorry to do this, but I have to ask you some questions about your mother. Help us find the person who killed her.'

'She was killed?'

'I told you that.'

'You told me her body was found on New Haven Green.'

'Well, I'm sorry, but yes. She was killed.'

'How?'

Patrese had thought about this one already. 'A knife was used.' Not a lie. Not the whole truth either, of course, but

41

not a lie. 'Now, you said you don't know why she might have been there. In New Haven.'

'I didn't say that.'

'You did, sir.'

'I said, "What the hell she doing there?"'

'I took that as you not knowing why she was there.'

'I don't.'

Patrese wondered briefly whether Kwasi was being deliberately obstructive. No, he thought, I've just told the man that his mother's dead. Cut him some slack.

'When did you last see her?'

'Yesterday.'

'You remember what time?'

'A quarter of ten exactly.'

'That's very precise.'

'I know the time of everything that happens.'

'What was she doing?'

'Leaving for Baltimore.'

'What was she planning to do when she got there?'

'She was attending a symposium run by the National Council of Black Women.'

'You know where this symposium was?'

'The Hyatt Regency in Baltimore's Inner Harbor: 300 Light Street, Baltimore, Maryland 21202. Phone number 410-528-1234.'

Hell, Patrese thought, was this what you needed to be world chess champion? *Rain Man* with dreads?

'How did she get there?'

'By train. Amtrak. Depart Penn Station, New York, yesterday at 10 a.m., arrive Penn Station, Baltimore 12.13 p.m. Return journey, depart Baltimore 9.34 a.m., arrive New York 11.52 a.m.'

Patrese did a quick calculation. 'You last saw her at quarter of ten when she had to get a train at ten?'

'I drove her to Penn Station.'

'And dropped her outside?'

'There was nowhere to park.'

'And then you came back here?'

'Yes.'

'So you didn't see her get on the train?'

'No. I saw her go into the station.'

'And what did you do after that?'

'I came back here.'

'You were here all weekend?'

'Yes.'

'What were you doing?'

'Playing chess.'

'With who?'

'Myself.'

'You play against yourself?'

'Sure. Against computer programs, and against myself. I have a world title match in two weeks. I'm preparing. Practicing. Training.'

'What does that involve?'

'Some general stuff. Get a position, turn it round, see how best to play against it. Also preparing specific openings, a lot of the time. Opening lines are constantly getting developed and refined. You try 'em out, see what works for you. You find a variation you don't like, you move on to another one.'

Checking through different lines, trying to look at positions from your opponent's point of view: chess sounded a lot like detective work to Patrese.

'Did you go to Penn to pick her up today?'

'Yes?'

'Were you concerned when she didn't turn up?'

'Yes.'

'What did you do?'

43

'I rang her cellphone. She didn't answer.'

'You think of doing anything else?'

'Like what?'

'Like ring the hotel in Baltimore?'

'I had to meet with Nursultan and Tartu. She knew where I was going. I figured she'd gotten the wrong train and had no cellphone reception. I guessed she'd come right along to the Waldorf when she arrived.'

'So your car's still at the Waldorf?'

'Yes.'

'And you have no idea why your mother would have been in New Haven?'

'No.'

'No friends, family there?'

'No.'

'She lived here, that's correct?'

'Yes.'

'May I see her room?'

'Sure.'

It was clear from even a first glance that Regina had been a neat freak. Her bed was made to a standard that wouldn't have disgraced the Waldorf-Astoria, the bottles and tubs on her dressing table were arranged with millimetric precision, and the clothes in her closet were color-coded. In the en-suite bathroom, the same level of order.

'How many bedrooms are there here?'

'Two.'

Patrese looked round the room again: high ceilings, south-facing, plenty of light. 'If this is anything to go by, the master bedroom must be quite something.'

'This is the master bedroom.'

Patrese looked surprised. 'Where do you sleep?'

'Next door.'

Kwasi's room was smaller. His bed, a single, was jammed hard up against the far corner, the better to make room for as many bookshelves as possible. Chess books, Patrese saw, with titles that might as well have been double Dutch as far as he was concerned. *An Anti-Sicilian Repertoire for White. Caro-Kann: Bronstein-Larsen. The Strategic Nimzo-Indian: A Complete Guide to the Rubinstein Variation.*

'Your mom had the master bedroom?'

'Sure.'

'Why, may I ask?'

'Why not?'

Patrese was getting used to the rhythm of Kwasi's speech and thought patterns now. Kwasi might be a genius on the chessboard, but quotidian details that seemed obvious to Patrese clearly passed Kwasi by.

'Mr King, *your* success, *your* skill, *your* money bought this place. Most all homeowners I know, it's the same thing: whoever buys the house gets the nicest room.'

Kwasi shrugged. 'Don't bother me. Bedroom's just a place to sleep.'

Most twenty-four-year-old men thought bedrooms were a place to do pretty much anything and everything other than sleep, Patrese thought: but then again, most twenty-four-year-old men didn't buy a Bleecker penthouse and then ask their mom to move in with them.

Patrese excused himself and went out on to the apartment's private roof terrace. He had to talk to Kieseritsky, and thought it best to discuss gory details of beheading and amputation in private.

The terrace had wrought-iron railings set six inches too low for comfort. A few blocks to the south, floats and giant puppets were already beginning to gather in preparation for the parade. Patrese looked out over the river toward Hoboken.

As he dialed, Patrese could hear a low noise from inside the apartment. He wasn't sure, but it sounded as though Kwasi was crying.

8

In the first few hours of any major homicide investigation, no news is most certainly not good news. Forensic evidence is fresh, eyewitnesses can remember what they've seen, people are willing to offer information. If detectives don't get decent leads right from the get-go, their chances of solving the crime are seriously jeopardized.

Lauren Kieseritsky had two pieces of news for Franco Patrese.

First, they'd found a fingerprint on John Doe's chest, and it belonged neither to him nor to Regina. They were running it through the system, so far without matches.

Second, they'd found a knife in the undergrowth on the Green: a hunting knife covered with Regina King's blood. No fingerprints on it, and no evidence that it had been used on John Doe too. The knife was manufactured by a German company named Liberzon. Officers were trying to get hold of the company to check their US retail outlets.

Talking of John Doe – the Reverend John Doe – well, he was still unidentified. They knew that he wasn't from

New Haven itself or the immediate environs, as they'd checked every Catholic church within that area. They were now spreading that search outwards, looking for any missing priests within an hour's radius of the city. If that brought no joy, they'd extend it to two hours' radius, and so on.

No one had come forward to say they'd seen anything suspicious on the Green. Shortly before one in the morning, a couple had walked past the church and treeline in question and had seen nothing. Whoever had killed Regina King and dumped John Doe's body must have therefore done so after that time.

This concurred with the medical examiner's preliminary findings. Taking into account the bodies' exposure to several hours of a crisp fall night and the subsequent effect on the temperatures of the cadavers, the medical examiner had put Regina King's time of death as between 1.30 and 2.30 a.m., and John Doe's as between 3.00 and 4.00 a.m. In other words, John Doe had been killed after Regina, in a different location, and then brought to the Green.

There were no bullet holes in the bodies, and no stab wounds to the vital organs. A full toxicological analysis was still pending, but the most basic tests had showed up no evidence of poisons, sedatives or intoxicants. Blood splatter and flow patterns – particularly the difference between pre-mortem and post-mortem bleeding – suggested that the victims' arms and skin patches had all been removed post-mortem. It was therefore most likely that the act of decapitation itself had killed both Regina King and John Doe.

Wouldn't they have screamed? Not if the killer had put a rag in their mouths. Certainly not once he'd severed their larynxes.

No sexual interference in either case. That was

interesting. Dismemberment is usually sexual and often connected with picquerism, where the killer is aroused by stabbing, pricking or slicing the body; all obvious substitutes for penile penetration, of course. The slicing was here – both in terms of the missing arms and heads, and the patches of skin removed – but there was no sexual interference and no stabbing.

Criminology theory holds that there are five forms of dismemberment: the practical, the narcotic, the sadistic, the lustful and the psychotic.

Practical usually involves cutting up bodies to make them easier to transport or store, which didn't seem to be the case here. Regina had been alive when she'd come to the Green; it was hard to see how removing John Doe's head and arm would have made him materially easier to move.

Narcotic, as in the perpetrator being off his head on drugs; well, that was a possibility in Regina's case, given the frenzy with which she had been attacked, but not for John Doe, whose killing had been a work of clinical precision.

Sadistic; unlikely, even given the gruesome method of death. Those things which would inflict unimaginable pain on a person, such as amputating their arm and removing their skin, had been done post-mortem.

Lustful: no, for the absence of sexual interference.

Which left psychotic. The killer was doing all this for his own reasons, and those reasons would be buried somewhere unfathomably deep within his psyche. It might turn out that they would find the reasons only by finding the killer, through traditional police work and evidence-gathering. Taking wild guesses at what was driving him might simply distract them from genuine leads.

But as for such evidence-gathering: well, so far there was no forensic evidence worth the name, as was often the case when bodies had been left outside. The police lab was doing its best, though no one was holding their breath for a break-through: not because the lab wasn't good – it was as good as could be expected of any short-staffed, underfunded public body – but because this was real life, and in real life cases don't get solved in fifty-eight minutes minus commercial breaks.

The tarot cards were part of a standard Rider-Waite deck, the most common tarot deck in the United States and Europe. They were trying to trace the manufacturer, but that was easier said than done, especially on a Sunday. Manufacturers tend to put their details on the packaging box, but not on individual cards themselves.

As for the symbolism of the cards, they'd managed to find some basic information on the Internet: the mighty Google, helping cops and porn fiends since 1998. 'Hierophant' was more or less a fancy ancient word for a priest: 'Regina' was Latin for 'queen', which would tie in with 'empress'.

The curator at Yale's Beinecke Rare Book and Manuscript Library was one of the country's foremost experts on the history and symbolism of tarot – the Beinecke had one of the oldest decks in the world, dating back to 1466 – but she was returning from vacation and wouldn't be at her desk until tomorrow morning.

Kieseritsky had scheduled a press conference for an hour's time. Patrese said he'd look after Kwasi, keep the press away from the world champion, and at the same time do some digging to try to find out what had happened to Regina King.

He hung up and dialed the Hyatt Regency in Baltimore, number helpfully supplied by Kwasi's incredible memory. No, the receptionist said, we didn't have a Regina King staying last night. Yes, sir, she was absolutely sure. Not in the general register, and not under the National Council's discount rate block booking.

Could she have registered under a false name? Patrese asked.

Yes, the receptionist said, but only if she had a fake ID too: each guest had been obliged to present some form of photocard. The receptionist had a copy of the National Council's own attendee list, and there was no Regina King on that either.

Patrese thanked her and hung up.

Regina had told Kwasi she was going to Baltimore. He'd dropped her off at Penn Station. She hadn't gone to Baltimore. She'd gone to New Haven. Trains from Penn Station ran to New Haven too.

Time to go to Penn Station.

Patrese stepped back inside the apartment. Kwasi was sitting at a computer. Patrese noted without surprise that there was a chessboard on the screen.

He explained what he'd found out from the Hyatt receptionist, and said he was going to Penn Station to try to find out where Regina had gone from there. 'I'll give you my cell number. You got a pen?'

'Tell me. I'll remember it.'

Patrese did, and he had no doubt that Kwasi would.

'Will you come back when you've finished?' Kwasi said. He sounded so like a little boy lost that Patrese instinctively put a hand on his shoulder.

'Sure, Kwasi. Sure I will.'

Penn Station was no one's idea of a grand railway terminus, the kind of place movie crews would dress up in period detail and have steam trains come hissing to a halt beside men in thick tweed suits. It was a catacomb, mostly underground and as bland as it was dark. Armed police stood with their feet wide apart and tried to look as though they weren't dying of boredom. The government had warned of terrorist attacks on transport hubs a few weeks back, so everyone was going through the motions of pretending to do something about it.

A bomb in this place might actually improve it, Patrese thought.

He found his way to the control center after a couple of wrong turns and a station worker who'd been less impressed by a Bureau badge than Patrese would have liked. The control center was half movie theater, half trading floor: rows of workstations, many of them empty, and an enormous wall covered in intricate maps of the railway system. Trains inbound and outbound were marked by little symbols in various colors. It looked pretty busy even now, midway through a Sunday afternoon. God alone knew what it must be like during a Monday-morning rush hour.

The train to Baltimore that Regina had said she'd catch had left at ten o'clock. The train to New Haven had left at exactly the same time: ten o'clock, on the dot. Patrese asked for CCTV footage of both platforms from the moment the gates had been opened until the moment the trains had departed. The angles weren't great and the picture resolution left much to be desired, but after going over the footage in fine detail, often asking to rewind a frame two or three times, Patrese had to accept a simple fact. Regina had been on neither of those trains.

He looked at other services that had departed at round about the same time: the Adirondack line up to Montreal, the Empire service to Buffalo and Niagara, the Vermonter to, well, Vermont, and a plethora of smaller commuter trains. No joy on any of those either, nor on the next two trains to New Haven and Baltimore respectively, nor anywhere on the station concourse between 9.45 and 10.00.

Kwasi had dropped his mother off at Penn Station at 9.45 yesterday morning. She'd gone inside, vanished into thin air, and rematerialized without her head in New Haven almost eighteen hours later.

9

There was a crowd of perhaps twenty people outside the main door of Kwasi's apartment block by the time Patrese returned there, and they weren't part of the Hallowe'en parade. As Patrese got out of his car and walked toward the building, large lenses swiveled to follow him for a moment before being lowered. The photographers clearly deemed him of little interest. Fine with him.

The toothpaste-ad doorman was standing just inside the door, eyeballing the posse of reporters with a sailor's determination to repel boarders. Patrese didn't want to have to flash his badge in case the reporters saw and clocked who he was, but Toothpaste Man recognized him from earlier and unlocked. Patrese slipped inside, checking out the nameplate on the man's lapel: BEN SHERWOOD.

'Thanks, Ben,' he said. 'I'm Franco Patrese, FBI. You know why they're here?'

'Saw it on the news. Damn shame.' Sherwood gestured toward the reporters. 'Freakin' vultures.'

'They're only doing their job.'

'Flockin' round when someone's dead, waiting to get fed. Like I said. Vultures.'

'Any of them tried to get in?'

'Not yet. They can try all they want. I know all the residents by sight, and if I don't know you, you ain't comin' in.'

'Good man. I'm going back up. You have any problems, give me a shout.' Sherwood had a pad on his desk; Patrese jotted down his cell number.

'Will do. I'll ring up to Mr King, let him know you're on your way.'

Kwasi was waiting at the door of his apartment. Behind him, a phone was ringing.

'Been like that the last twenty minutes,' he said.

'You answered any of them?'

'First couple of times. People jabbering about my mom. I hung up.'

'Good. Let me deal with this.' Patrese walked over to the phone, crouched down and pulled the jack from the wall. The phone stopped ringing.

On Kwasi's fifty-inch plasma TV, Fox News' Chris Wallace was interviewing a young woman with limpid eyes and a cascade of black hair. A caption appeared as she spoke: INESSA BAIKAL, US WOMEN'S CHESS CHAMPION.

'What it means for his title defense, no one can yet know,' she said. 'For a world championship match, you need to be at your absolute peak, total concentration. Even for someone like Kwasi, who's so good at shutting things out, you have to ask: Will he be in the right frame of mind? Could anyone be in the right frame of mind after something like this? He's so strong, mentally, but this is so . . . so awful.'

'You know him better than most,' Wallace said. 'You used to date him, is that right?'

'That's not right,' Kwasi said from beside Patrese.

'You want to switch over?'

55

Kwasi shook his head. 'Everyone got an opinion about me. I'm used to it.'

On the TV, Inessa said: 'Date him? A couple of times, sure, but nothing too serious.'

'How will he be dealing with this?'

'Badly, I think. They were so close, Kwasi and his mom. They were inseparable. I— I can't imagine what he must be going through right now.'

Kwasi had had enough. He picked up the remote and muted the sound. Inessa talked silently on.

'No, bitch, you can't imagine,' Kwasi said to her image. 'You know shit about me, you know shit about chess. So shut the fuck up.'

Patrese pointed at the caption. 'Says she's the national women's chess champion.'

'So?'

'So she must know something about chess.'

'She knows nothing about chess. She's a woman.' There was real anger in Kwasi's voice now. 'National women's champion means fuck all. You know her ranking? She's the 812th best player in the world. She knows nothing about what it takes to be world champion. And she knows nothing about me.'

'You don't think women are good at chess?'

'I *know* they're not good at chess.'

'Why?'

'Too emotional. Chess is rough and hard. You have to be a man to win. Control your feelings, be a machine. You let feelings and emotions in, you're fucked. The only women who can ever play well are those who change their character, suppress their natural instincts, take on a man's qualities. And *she*' – he flicked his hand dismissively toward the screen – 'she's too busy lying round on the beach in her underwear,

56

doing photoshoots for fashion magazines and pretending she's a model.'

Wow, Patrese thought: it was like listening to some bitter old misogynist of a bachelor uncle rather than a black kid with dreadlocks. He wondered how many of Kwasi's sponsors would drop him in a heartbeat if they heard him talk this way. And he wondered, too, what exactly had happened between Kwasi and Inessa.

Probably not the best moment to ask.

Kwasi and Regina had been inseparable, and now she was dead. In the circumstances, a little spleen was no bad thing.

Kwasi stared at Inessa, who was giving a coquettish smile as Wallace ended the interview.

'Bitch,' he spat.

Thinking that it might prove a welcome distraction, Patrese took Kwasi up on to the roof to watch the parade. Hallowe'en on Sixth Avenue wasn't a bunch of schoolkids dressed up as zombies and trick-or-treating: it was a three-hour extravaganza like nothing else on earth, apart perhaps from Mardi Gras in New Orleans.

In fact, Patrese remembered, the 2005 parade had been a gathering point for those New Orleans residents living in airport hotels near JFK after Hurricane Katrina, having been displaced from their homes two months before by that iconic catastrophe through which Patrese had hunted another serial killer. The parade organizers that year had put on a mock-up jazz funeral with a second-line band and dancers, and all those folks whose houses had been washed away and who weren't used to fall temperatures south of the eighties, all those folks knew that George W. Bush might not have cared about them, but New York sure did.

Now the crowds on Sixth Avenue were ten deep, and they cheered the parade as though every passing costume was the winning play in the Super Bowl. The dancing skeletons came first, as they always did, a reminder that tonight death danced only to celebrate life. After them came giant illuminated caterpillars; a Statue of Liberty stabbed in the chest; a group of bulldogs on leashes all dressed as Batman. Giant Scrabble tiles rearranged themselves time and again to spell different words. Decks of playing cards – not tarot ones, Patrese saw – shuffled up the avenue.

'Look!' Kwasi shouted suddenly. 'Look!'

Two armies of chess pieces were coming past, one black and one white: adults as pieces, children as pawns. They threw candy to the crowd and posed happily for photos. Kwasi was rapt.

Patrese thought back to his childhood, when he and his buddies had daubed their faces with chalk, put on some of their moms' lipstick and rung a few doorbells.

'You ever go trick-or-treating as a kid, Kwasi?'

Kwasi watched the chess pieces disappear into the distance before answering.

'No.'

'Never?'

'Never.'

'Why not?'

Kwasi shrugged. 'Just seemed silly.'

'What about your friends? They must have asked you to go with them.'

'You have a happy childhood, officer?'

'Franco. Please, call me Franco.'

'You have a happy childhood, Franco?'

Patrese thought for a second. 'Most of the time.'

'Good for you. Me? Never had one.'

'Never had a happy one?'

'Never had one, period. I'm the youngest world champion in history. I had to fight every day for it. I became a soldier too early. That's the price. I had no childhood.'

10

For the second morning in succession, Patrese was woken in a hotel room by a phone call. This time, however, he didn't have a hangover, and he knew who was calling: KIESERITSKY flashed up on his cellphone's display screen.

It was half past six. She wouldn't be calling to ask how he'd slept. He picked up.

'Hey, Lauren. You found John Doe?'

'Damn straight. Darrell Showalter. A monk who teaches school in Cambridge.'

'As in Cambridge, Massachusetts?'

'As in Cambridge, England.'

'Really?'

'No, not really. Yes, Cambridge, Massachusetts.'

'You sure it's him?'

'Pathologist found a small birthmark on the ankle: could have been livor mortis until you knew better.' After death, with no heart to pump it round the body, blood settles toward the parts of the corpse nearer the ground, causing a purplish-red discoloration of the skin. 'One of the other teachers came up in the middle of the night to give us an ID. You want to go and talk to the school, they're waiting for you.'

Monday-morning traffic on the eastern seaboard meant it took Patrese four hours to get to Cambridge, and he knew it could have been worse than that.

He'd finally taken his leave of Kwasi at around ten the previous evening, and had found a hotel off Washington Square that had charged him – which was to say, had charged the Bureau – a couple of hundred bucks for a bed less comfortable than a landmine, a shower smaller than Gary Coleman, and Art Deco furniture less tasteful than Trump Tower. By that stage, however, Patrese had been beyond caring.

He'd spoken to Donner again en route to Cambridge and told him what was going on. Well, Donner had sighed, it's not like we haven't got enough to do here. True, Patrese had replied, but we *are* a federal organization, and these folks want me to help them out. OK, Donner had said at last. There was a Bureau field office in New Haven itself: he'd get them to give Patrese any help he needed.

Darrell Showalter, the corpse formerly known as John Doe, had taught at the Cambridge Abbey School, a few blocks up from Harvard Square. Patrese instantly clocked the school as the kind of place that turned out muscular Christians: young men who half a century ago would have traveled the world bringing gospel and gridiron to the natives. Organ music swelled from inside a chapel; students hurried through cloisters.

The principal introduced himself as Michael Furman and offered Patrese a seat, some coffee, a photograph of Showalter, and thanks for coming.

'The school's in shock, as you can imagine,' Furman said. 'Terrible business.'

'What was it that Darrell did here?'

'The school's attached to the abbey, which is an institution in its own regard, of course. Most of our staff, like myself, are lay teachers, but some of the monks also teach: religious studies and spiritual guidance, mainly. It's a tradition we value greatly. Darrell was one of those.'

'So no family? No wife, no children?'

'Absolutely not.'

'Was he popular?'

'Extremely. Both with the staff and with the boys. One doesn't necessarily mean the other, as I'm sure you know.' Furman looked around as though about to divulge an indiscretion, though only he and Patrese were in the room. 'And the monks aren't always that popular with the boys, either. Men who give their lives to God . . . sometimes they don't understand children too well.'

Or sometimes, Patrese thought bitterly, they understand children all too well.

'No enemies?' Patrese asked. 'No disputes? No one who wanted to do him harm?'

Furman shook his head. 'Absolutely not. He wouldn't have hurt a fly.'

'Could I see his room?'

'Sure.'

Furman led Patrese down corridors that smelled faintly of disinfectant.

'Do you know when he was last seen?' Patrese asked as they walked.

'In the refectory on Saturday evening, around seven o'clock. He was on roster then, one of the staff due to eat with the boys. After that, no one knows. I guess he'd have gone back to his room if he had no other engagements, and no one would have thought anything strange about not seeing him again that night.'

'Next morning? Sunday, in a religious establishment; someone must have noticed him missing?'

'Of course. His absence was noted at first morning prayers, seven a.m., but people just thought he was ill; there's a virus going round the school, plenty of pupils and staff have got it. His room was checked to see if he was OK, but there was no sign of him.'

'That didn't cause alarm?'

'At that stage, no. This is a big school; he could have been anywhere, doing anything. It didn't seem sinister. But when he didn't appear for the main chapel service at ten thirty or for lunch afterwards – that's when we started to search for him in earnest.'

'And when you couldn't find him?'

'We called the police.'

And Patrese knew what the police would have said: he's an adult, adults go missing, we'll take a note of his details and let you know if we find anything. Meanwhile, the search for John Doe would have been working its way slowly outwards from New Haven, and Cambridge was far enough away not to have shown up in the first sweep.

Not that it would have made any difference. Showalter had been dead several hours before anyone had even thought to look for him.

'How easy is it to get into this place?' Patrese asked.

Furman shrugged. 'We have security guards, of course, and gates, but we're a school of young men. They go on sports and cultural trips, we encourage them to help out in the local community, the abbey itself is open to the public at certain times. We don't want to shut ourselves away from the world. We wouldn't be much of a school if we did.'

'But anyone acting suspiciously would be challenged?'

'I'd like to think so.'

The problem, as Patrese knew, was that anyone who could

63

kill a woman on New Haven Green and leave another body there was almost certainly pretty good at *not* acting suspiciously. If killers walked round rubbing their hands and cackling like pantomime villains, they'd be much easier to catch.

'You have CCTV here?'

'At the main entrance.'

'Nowhere else?'

'No.'

'How many entrances are there?'

'Four or five, depending on how you count.'

'So why not have CCTV on them too?'

'I wouldn't have had it at all if it hadn't been required by the insurance company. I want to bring these young men up properly, and you can't do that if they think they're being watched the whole time. I know most of them are good kids; but they're also kids, and kids sometimes do what kids do. I come down like a ton of bricks on them when they screw up, but I want to let them make their own mistakes too. Within reason, of course.'

Heck, Patrese thought. If he'd had a principal like Furman when he'd been at school, maybe he wouldn't have ended up hating religion so much.

'And you have no idea how Darrell could have ended up in New Haven?'

'None whatsoever. As far as I know, he had no family there, no friends. I've been here eight years, and I never heard him mention the place once.'

Patrese looked out of the window, toward the spire of the chapel and a concrete sports hall beyond. Something about the solidity of both buildings made him think of the Gothic gatehouse on one side of New Haven Green.

'You're not far from Harvard here, are you?' he asked.

'Not at all.'

'You ever do anything with them? Meetings, programs, any of that?'

Furman shook his head. 'Not really. We take the boys in twelfth grade to look round the place – not just Harvard but MIT too, of course – in case any of them are thinking of applying there, but that's about it.'

'Did Darrell ever go on these trips?'

'Not that I recall. Why?'

'You're near Harvard. His body was found near Yale. I was wondering whether there could be a connection.'

'Not one that I'm aware of. Darrell certainly didn't attend either Harvard or Yale as a student. Thought they were a little too elitist, if I remember rightly.'

'And yet he taught in a private boys' school.'

'A third of our boys are on some sort of financial assistance. And religious instruction is a major part of the curriculum here. I think his conscience was satisfied that he was doing the right thing. Here—' Furman pushed open a door and stood aside to let Patrese through. 'This is – was – Darrell's room.'

It reminded Patrese a little of Kwasi's room in Bleecker Street: a single bed, hundreds of books. None about chess, though, or at least none that Patrese could see at first glance. Shelves of religious texts, unsurprisingly. The obvious giants of the postwar American novel: Mailer, Updike, Roth, squashed close together like rush-hour rail commuters. Tolstoy and Dostoevsky in translation, and not only the famous ones about war, peace, crime and punishment either: Patrese saw *The Cossacks*, *The House of the Dead*, *Hadji Murat*, *The Idiot*, *Resurrection*, *Demons*, all with broken spines and fraying corners.

'Loved Russia,' Furman said, following Patrese's gaze. 'One of the classes he liked to teach was about religious survival in times of persecution. In particular, how the Russian

65

Orthodox Church kept going under the godless Soviet regime. Lessons for us all in how to keep the faith.'

There was a laptop on a desk by the window. Patrese turned it on, waited for it to boot up, and tapped on the Outlook Express icon. Forensics could crawl over the machine later, but if Showalter had made any arrangements for Saturday night by e-mail, they'd probably still be on here.

The program opened. No password demand: most people don't bother when they have sole access to a machine. Patrese scanned through the inbox. All school-related business, by the look of it: circulars about staff meetings, refurbishment work, and so on. He glanced toward Furman. 'Do you know whether he used a personal account too? Hotmail; that kind of thing?'

'I very much doubt it.'

'Why so?'

Furman stepped forward and clicked on the 'sent items' folder. It came up empty.

'Darrell didn't use *any* e-mail unless he had to. He'd read the incoming stuff, because he knew that's how people communicate nowadays, but if he wanted to reply, he'd ring you up.'

'Why?'

Furman shrugged. 'Just the way he was. Not everyone likes to filter their lives through electronics.'

When he'd finished with Furman, Patrese went over to the school security office by the main gate and asked to see the CCTV footage from Saturday evening. No sign of Darrell leaving at any time; though, as Furman had said, there were other ways in and out. Plenty of people entering and leaving, though it was hard to make out any more than the most rudimentary of features: this had all been filmed after dark, and the picture quality was as bad as it had been in Penn Station.

It was like this in many investigations: questions way, way outnumbered answers. There was one thing Patrese knew for sure, however. Regina King had left New York alive and been killed in Connecticut; Darrell Showalter had left Massachusetts alive and been found dead in Connecticut. That meant interstate transportation, which in turn made it federal jurisdiction. The Bureau would take over from the New Haven PD.

It was Patrese's case now.

11

Since Patrese needed some cash, he pulled up at the nearest bank. The ATM in the wall was out of order, so he went inside, where there were three more machines: all working fine, but all with queues. That wasn't surprising: it was the start of the lunch hour. Patrese scanned the queues, trying to work out from the kind of customers there which queue would move fastest. Businessmen in suits would be in a hurry; little old ladies would take their time.

A bark of laughter came from the tellers' counter. Patrese looked over. One of the tellers, a young guy with the kind of hair-and-moustache combo that hadn't been in fashion since East Germany had ceased to exist, was holding up a piece of paper. A black man in a hooded sweatshirt stood in front of his position.

'You demand money?' the teller scoffed. 'This is a practical joke, right?'

No, Patrese thought. No, never say that. What the fuck was the teller playing at? The police tell every bank, and every bank tells its employees, not to stand up to bank robbers. Just give them the money and get them out of there. Hell, most banks use some kind of dye pack that makes the notes unusable, or they hand over bait money, whose serial numbers are recorded and the police alerted when the notes are back in circulation. But even if they don't do either of those, it's still only money. Better that someone gets away with a couple of grand than that someone gets shot because of some fool teller who thinks he's Dirty Harry.

All this went through Patrese's head in a split second. In that same split second, Hoodie Man had pulled a gun from his waistband with his right hand and grabbed the nearest customer, a young Asian woman with red eyeglasses and a crimson Harvard top, with his left. He pressed the gun to the woman's head. Her eyes and mouth made perfect circles of shock and fear.

'Look like a practical joke to you now, motherfucker?' yelled Hoodie Man.

Shrieks and screams all around Patrese, people falling to the floor or backing away as far as they could. He had his own gun out now, though he wasn't aware of having drawn it: that was Bureau training, where in times of danger you armed yourself without conscious thought.

He drew a bead on Hoodie Man. 'Let her go!'

'*You* drop it, man! Drop it, or I smoke the bitch!'

The man's face was half hidden beneath his hood. He looked to have smooth skin and regular features, but beyond that Patrese couldn't see enough to tell for sure whether he was serious about this threat or not, let alone whether he was juiced on crack or meth or whatever else junkies out there liked to hit on nowadays.

Could take the shot anyway, Patrese thought, but Hoodie Man was moving around, pulling his hostage with him. Hs gun was pressed hard against her temple: the pressure was turning her skin white around the end of the barrel. Even if Patrese got off a clean shot, head or vital organs down the centerline of the trunk, Hoodie Man might still fire his own gun, as a reflex shot if nothing else.

Patrese remembered Samantha Slinger, a crack addict whom he'd shot dead in some scuzzy Pittsburgh rowhouse because he'd thought she'd been going for a gun. She hadn't. And her death had helped set in motion a series of murders that had reached five before he'd managed to finish it. That kind of thing stayed with you. It hadn't stopped him taking shots in difficult situations since then – he'd put a bullet through the head of a wannabe suicide bomber during a Steelers match at Heinz Field, for a start – but it *had* made him more cautious about weighing up risk and reward.

And right now there was no contest between the two. Hoodie Man wants to steal some cash rather than work for it? Sure. Let him. Guys who hold up banks in broad daylight aren't criminal masterminds. They get caught sooner rather than later. Give him the money, get him to let the girl go. That's what Patrese thought. That's what the teller should have thought too, before he started to get wiseass.

'OK,' Patrese said. 'OK.' He crouched down and put his gun on the floor.

Hoodie Man swiveled his eyes toward the teller. 'Money, now. In a bag, twenty seconds, or I smoke her.'

Patrese could hear only two sounds: a quiet, breathless sobbing from somewhere behind him, and the panicky rustle of the teller frantically shoving shrink-wrapped packs of notes into a carrier bag.

Hoodie Man glanced across at the teller again. 'Enough!' he said. 'Give!'

The teller reached out, bag juddering from the tremors in his arm. Hoodie Man tightened his left arm around Harvard Top's neck and took the bag with the outstretched fingers of the same hand. The gun in his right hand never left her temple.

'Fool,' he spat at the teller.

Patrese rather thought he had a point.

Hoodie Man began to walk toward the door, still holding his hostage. She looked round in silent supplication. Do the right thing, Patrese thought. Get out of the door and let her go. You've got what you came for. You keep a hold of her, and within minutes it'll be a situation with armed cops and all that, and those things tend to end the hard way.

And that's exactly what Hoodie Man did. He got out of the door, pushed Harvard Top away, and took off down the sidewalk like a scalded cat.

Patrese grabbed his gun from the floor and went after him. No good. By the time he was out of the building, Hoodie Man was halfway down the block and moving fast toward the lunchtime crowds. Chasing him would only risk flaring the whole thing up again. He might take another hostage; even worse, he might start shooting. Letting him go wasn't the macho thing to do, but it was the right thing to do.

It didn't stop Patrese stamping the ground in frustration, though.

12

When the Cambridge police arrived at the bank a few minutes later, Patrese pulled rank and got himself interviewed first. It wasn't just that he wanted to get to New Haven and didn't have time to spare hanging around here: it was also that law enforcement officers are trained in observation and recall, which made his testimony more accurate and useful than that of a random member of the public. Most of the people in that bank, he knew, would hardly have remembered their own names when confronted by a man with a gun.

Witness statement given, Patrese headed for the interstate. In the last day and a half, he realized, he'd driven from Foxborough to New Haven, New Haven to New York, New York to Cambridge, and now Cambridge back to New Haven. Heck; he should have been a trucker, not a Bureau agent. Probably get paid better, too.

He drove straight to the New Haven police headquarters. They'd set up an incident room, done all the right things: two dozen officers manning the phone lines, one wall covered in photos of the cadavers and the crime scene, a buzz of industry and determination that told good things for the department's standards.

Kieseritsky showed Patrese into her office and told him what they'd got so far. It didn't take long. She'd had little news for him yesterday, and she didn't have a whole lot more for him today.

No joy with the fingerprint they'd found on Showalter's chest. There were millions of fingerprints on the Bureau's database, most of them belonging to various shades of scumbag, but none of them matched this one.

The Liberzon knife company had sent over a list of their US retailers. These were being checked to see if anyone connected with the victims had purchased the hunting knife in question: though if that person had used cash rather than a card, they'd be none the wiser.

Still waiting on any other possible clues from forensics.

Still no one who'd seen anything strange on the Green at that time of night.

Still no idea how Regina had gotten to New Haven in the first place. They'd checked every hotel within a ten-mile radius of the Green, and she hadn't stayed at any of them.

Still no joy on the provenance of the tarot cards. They'd managed to establish that the cards were made by US Games Inc., who had copyright over the Rider-Waite design in the United States; but US Games Inc. sold hundreds of thousands of sets a year, all pretty much identical. The set the killer was using could have been bought in any state in the union, not to mention online. Where would they start?

And, as far as could be ascertained, still absolutely no overlap whatsoever between the lives of Regina King and Darrell Showalter. A single mom from the projects and a monk teaching at a private school in one of Massachusetts' most upscale areas: it wasn't as though they'd have had much in common to start with.

Showalter seemed to have lived a pretty blameless life; not even a speeding ticket or a parking fine. Regina, on the other hand, had been a bit of a firebrand. Remember how they'd got her fingerprints from the arrest docket at the Iraq War protest in 2003? Well, that hadn't been the end of it.

She'd sued the NYPD for bodily harm, alleging that the officer who'd arrested her, Howard Lewis, had used excessive force, which had damaged ligaments in her shoulder and neck. The case had dragged on a couple of years before being settled for an undisclosed sum; which was to say that the NYPD had worked out the minimum they'd have to pay her to make the problem go away, and had done precisely that.

Settlement had been reached about six months before Kwasi had won his world title, which had made his fame and earnings go stratospheric. Patrese wondered whether Regina would still have accepted the NYPD's offer had she known the financial windfall around the corner. Principles were good; eating was better.

When Kieseritsky finished, Patrese told her kindly but firmly that this was now the Bureau's case, and that the incident room must be transferred lock, stock and barrel to the Bureau field office a half-mile up State Street.

Kieseritsky was disappointed but not surprised. She knew the rules of federal engagement as well as Patrese did; but any detective worth their salt doesn't like giving up a case that has been theirs from the outset.

'You know this is no reflection on you personally,' Patrese said.

Kieseritsky shrugged. 'You sure? It's not like we're about to catch the murderer any minute now, is it?'

'Some cases just don't fall that way. As far as I can see, you've done everything exactly as you should have done. I appreciate it.'

'Don't be kind.'

'Oh?'

'It makes it harder for me to hate the Bureau.'

13

If there was a prize for the most striking building in New Haven, Patrese thought, he was standing outside the runaway winner right now.

It was a rectangular box without windows. In their place were panels of white, lightly veined marble framed with pale gray granite. It stood in the middle of a quadrangle on the edges of which glowered edifices in Gothic and Classical styles, as though this box was an alien spaceship that had dared to disturb the old-world tranquility around it. It was Yale's Beinecke Rare Book and Manuscript Library, and a sign by the main door informed Patrese that this was the largest building in the world reserved exclusively for the preservation of rare books and manuscripts.

Anna Levin, the curator, was waiting for him inside. Patrese was expecting some tweedy old dame with reading spectacles dangling from her neck, and so he almost walked straight past her. Only when she put her hand on his arm did he realize who she was. She had the bright eyes and deep tan of someone who spent as much time as possible outdoors – no mean feat if you worked in this place, Patrese thought – and, like an athlete or a dancer, she walked on

76

the balls of her feet. He'd never have put her as a librarian in a million years. She was this side of dotage, for a start.

When they'd introduced themselves, Anna gestured around her, at the inside of the library. 'Whadd'ya think? Quite something, huh?'

Quite something indeed, Patrese thought. The marble panels, which from out in the quad had appeared solid, were now revealed to be translucent, almost like blank television screens. They let in a small amount of filtered light: presumably to allow rare books to be displayed without risk of damage.

And in the middle of this enormous space, rising six stories like a monolith from Atlantis, was a glass tower full of books: a shrine to volumes bound in leather of olive green, Mikado yellow, burnt umber, carmine and a hundred other colors besides.

'I think they're the most beautiful things in the world,' Anna said. 'Books.'

Her office was two stories below ground. She couldn't offer him coffee or tea, she was afraid – no food or drink allowed, because they couldn't risk damage to the books. That was fine, Patrese said. Too much caffeine gave him a weird St Vitus dance.

'I've got a whole heap of things to do,' he said, 'so I can't spend too long here. Nothing personal. You know why I'm here?'

'Something about tarot cards being found at those dreadful murders yesterday.'

'That's right.'

'Well, listen . . .'

'I need hardly tell you that anything I say to you is confidential. We keep a tight lid on information from crime scenes: helps weed out the tons of crank callers you always get.'

'Sure. Do you know which cards were found?'

'There were two victims. Regina King, who's been all over the news . . .'

'I know. My sister . . .'

'. . . and a monk from Cambridge, Massachusetts named Darrell Showalter. The Empress was found by her body, the Hierophant by his. Both in the Rider-Waite design.'

Anna nodded. 'And you want to know what they might mean?'

'Exactly.'

She steepled her fingers. 'OK. A bit of background first, if that's OK. Help you get a sense of context for all this.'

'If it's quick.'

'The reason I got interested in Tarot was from working here. The first known sets of tarot cards in the world were made around 1442 for the Visconti family of Milan. There were three sets, of which we have the very first, the proto-type, right here in this building. There were no printing presses at the time, of course, so all the cards had to be hand-painted. That's why they're so rare, and so valuable.

'Tarot cards nowadays are used for two main purposes. One, games, as with conventional playing cards, though this is confined mainly to Europe, particularly France and Italy. Tarot games are almost unknown in English-speaking countries. Two – and this may be more relevant to your investigation – divination, predictions, mapping mental and spiritual pathways, those kind of things. A tarot reader will predict your future according to which cards she draws for you and in which order.'

'And this *does* occur in the States? Tarot divination?'

'Absolutely.' Anna pulled a Rider-Waite pack out of her drawer. 'There are seventy-eight tarot cards in all, divided in two main categories. The first is called the major arcana, which means greater secrets. The major arcana consists of twenty-two cards, all without suit.' She took a handful of cards from the top of the deck and spread them on the desk in front of her. 'The first twenty-one are numbered. In order – and you'll recognize the ones you found yesterday – they're the Magician, the High Priestess, the Empress, the Emperor, the Hierophant, the Lovers, the Chariot, Strength, the Hermit, Wheel of Fortune, Justice, the Hanged Man, Death, Temperance, the Devil, the Tower, the Star, the Moon, the Sun, Judgement, and the World. Unnumbered, or assigned zero, sometimes twenty-two, is the Fool.'

She arranged the remainder of the deck alongside. 'Second category: minor arcana, the lesser secrets. These are much more like conventional playing cards. They're divided into four suits: wands, pentacles, cups, swords. Wands correspond to clubs, pentacles to diamonds, cups to hearts, swords to spades. But each tarot suit has fourteen cards rather than thirteen: there's a Knight which goes between the Queen and the Jack.'

'But both the cards we've found belong to the major arcana?'

'That's right.'

'Then let's focus on that for now. What do the Empress and the Hierophant signify?'

'OK.' Anna handed the Empress card from her deck to Patrese. 'The Empress is the third card in the major arcana. A mother figure, she's fertile, sexual, sensual, natural. She's the Great Goddess, she's the Queen of Heaven. The scepter represents her power over life. The twelve stars of her crown represent her dominance over the year. See her throne in a field of grain? That's her dominion over things that grow: food, plants.'

Anna tapped on the Empress' gown. 'Pomegranates. In Greek mythology, Hades, lord of the underworld, kidnapped and raped Persephone. Persephone's mother Demeter, the harvest goddess, stopped every plant from growing for a year

79

until she and Hades came to a deal about Persephone's fate. But while she was in the underworld, Persephone ate some pomegranate seeds. Anyone who consumed food and drink in the underworld had to stay there – so, even after the deal her mom had struck with Hades, Persephone had to spend part of each year in the underworld.'

Patrese thought of how close Regina and Kwasi had been. 'Tell me more about the Empress as a mother. What kind of symbolism is there on that?'

'Oh, a whole heap. The Empress often represents mothers, good and bad. She's the blood flowing through all living things, which starts in the womb. She's also the object of desire, the love children feel for their moms.' Anna flicked her fingers. 'Tell me something. When you found the card, which way up was it?'

'Which way up? Er . . . face up.'

'No, no: which way was it *pointing*? In line with the body, or inverted? Was the Empress' head towards the victim's head?'

Patrese thought for a moment, trying to recall exactly what he'd seen on the Green. There'd be crime-scene photos against which he could check if necessary, but he wanted to do this himself. Think. *Think.*

He'd seen the Hierophant first, by Showalter's corpse, and then gone over to Regina's body, looking to see whether she had a card too . . .

'Inverted,' he said suddenly. 'The Empress' head was facing towards Regina's feet.'

'You're sure?'

'Absolutely. The Hierophant was the right way up, but the Empress was inverted.'

'An inverted card can mean the opposite of whatever the usual symbolism is. With the Empress, it would be something like she was a bad mother, an unhealthy over-attachment somewhere, that kind of thing. Take the qualities and reverse them. In her usual, positive aspect, the Empress gives, nurtures, celebrates life. In her negative aspect, she takes it, either literally or figuratively.'

Patrese didn't know what kind of mother Regina had been, but 'over-attachment' when it had come to her and Kwasi was pretty much spot on. As to whether that had been unhealthy, who knew? Only she and Kwasi for sure, perhaps. Or not even them. As Patrese knew full well, people in dysfunctional relationships find so many ways of justifying these dysfunctions that they end up not being able to see them at all.

'OK,' Patrese said. 'What about the Hierophant?'

Anna handed him the Hierophant card. 'This is the fifth card. The word "Hierophant" means "the one who teaches the holy things". See here. His right hand is performing a blessing: two fingers pointing up, two pointing down. This forms a bridge between heaven and earth. The pillars either side of his throne represent law and liberty: the crossed keys at his feet are the keys to Heaven. The Hierophant represents assistance, friendship, good advice, alliances, marriages, and religious interests. When he's inverted, that means bad advice, lies, and persecution. If he appears in a spread, it's a warning to the querent to re-examine their understanding of the meaning of things, of the structure of the world, of the powers-that-be.'

'A spread? A querent? What are those?'

'When you do a reading. The querent is the subject, the one who wants to know their future. The spread is how the cards are arranged. There are several different ways, depending on the reader's skill or preference. Would you like me to show you?'

'What? Give me a reading? I'm the querent?'

'Sure.'

'Thank you, no. I haven't got time, and in any case I don't believe in all that stuff.'

'It would purely be for interest.'

'No.' He stood. 'Thank you. You've been helpful.'

'Might give you an idea as to why the cards are being left there. Might even give you an insight into how best you'll solve the case. In a reading, some people believe the cards chosen are guided by a spiritual force. Others, like Jung, think the cards help us tap into a collective unconscious.'

Patrese was torn. He really didn't believe in this stuff, and he really didn't have time to waste: but if someone was going round killing people and leaving tarot cards by their bodies, shouldn't he be exploring all possible avenues to help catch that person?

He sat back down again. 'All right. But only a quick one.'

Anna smiled. 'Sure. I'll keep it to the major arcana, twenty-two cards rather than seventy-eight, and give you a simple horseshoe spread rather than some of the more complex ones.'

She took the Empress and Hierophant back from Patrese, cleared away the minor arcana cards, and shuffled the major arcana with a speed and dexterity that wouldn't have disgraced a Vegas croupier. Then she laid out seven cards, all face down, in a horseshoe.

'This is just for interest,' Patrese said.

'Each card in this pattern means something different,' Anna replied. He wondered if she'd heard him. 'The first one' – she tapped the one to her extreme left – 'is the past: any events that have already happened which affect your current situation. The second is the immediate present. Self-explanatory. Then the immediate future; also self-explanatory.' She rested her finger on the fourth card, the middle one. 'This is what's occupying your mind: what you're thinking of, whether you know it or not. The next, the fifth, is the attitudes of others around you. Then there's the obstacle you must overcome. And finally the outcome, the ending: how the situation will finish. Ready?'

If I don't believe in all this, Patrese thought, then why do I suddenly feel so nervous?

He swallowed hard. 'Sure.'

She smiled. 'OK. This first card is the past.'

She turned it over. Card number VII, the Chariot. A prince in armor sitting in a chariot pulled by two sphinxes, one black and one white.

'The chariot symbolizes conquest: a battle that can be won if you have the willpower. The battle is usually external, with a clear goal and plan of action. The charioteer fights alone. He succeeds by attacking from the side rather than straight on. To win the battle, you need self-reliance, hard work, and the conviction that you're right and that you'll achieve victory no matter the odds. But, but . . . this can easily tip over into a ruthless desire to win at any cost.'

Patrese thought of the cases he'd pursued in the past. Some of them had gone on for months, and in each one he had at times felt frustrated, depressed, ready to jack it all in; but in the end he'd always kept going, and he'd always gotten a result. He was here now because he'd solved those crimes; he'd solved those crimes because he was good at what he did; and he was good at what he did because he kept plugging away and because he'd try anything to get a breakthrough.

Yes, Patrese thought: he could see how the Chariot card applied to him.

'Next card,' Anna said. 'The immediate present.'

A young man standing blithely on the edge of a cliff. He carried a rose in his left hand and had a hobo's bindle over his right shoulder. The sun shone; a small white dog played next to him.

83

Card zero. The Fool.

Patrese clenched the muscles in his jaw. Anna leaned forward and put her hand on his. 'No, don't be insulted. The Fool doesn't mean "idiot". In Tarot, the Fool is the spirit seeking experience. He represents the mystical intuition within each of us, the childlike ability to tune into the inner workings of the world. Each card in the major arcana can be seen as a point on the Fool's journey through life. It's that journey you're on now. Where it'll take you – well, who knows, but almost certainly not the place you think.'

Idiot or not, Patrese didn't like being the Fool. He gestured to the next card.

'The immediate future,' Anna said, as she picked up.

Card XVIII. The Moon. The moon itself with a frowning face at the top of the card; great drops of dew falling from the moon to land; two tombstones; a dog and a wolf howling at the moon; a crayfish crawling from the water on to the land; and a path that disappeared into the distant unknown. Despite himself, Patrese shuddered.

'The moon is tension, doubt, deception, confusion and fear,' Anna said. 'It's sleepless nights and unsettling dreams. The dog and the wolf are our deepest fears: the crayfish hauling itself up from the deep is the base animal nature we try so hard to hide. You must make like the moon itself, Franco. Look at the frown on the face of the moon. Look at the drops of moisture. Look how hard it strives to keep those instincts down.'

Patrese wanted to get up and leave, but he couldn't: how would it look, a Bureau agent walking out of a tarot reading? If it ever came out, he'd never live it down.

He reminded himself that it was all mumbo jumbo: cards chosen at random, images so old that no one knew any more why they'd been chosen in the first place. It might mean something to Anna, or to the wacko who'd killed Regina and Darrell, but to Patrese – determined, rational, secular Franco Patrese – it meant nothing. Nothing. Didn't it?

Anna's hand moved on to the fourth card, the middle one. 'This is what's occupying your mind right now,' she said.

An old man standing in a wasteland. He wore a long hooded robe and a white beard. A lantern in his right hand, a staff in his left. Card IX. The Hermit.

Kwasi, Patrese thought instantly; a man always a step out of sync with the rest of us.

'This card is introspection, solitude, the search for understanding,' Anna said. 'The hermit must withdraw from society to become comfortable with himself; but he must also return from isolation to share his knowledge with others. The hermit can give the insight we need to open a sealed door or conquer the forest beasts. Some say the hermit is the time we learn our true names, when we see who we really are.'

'Fifth card,' she said. 'The attitudes of others.'

A young man in a red robe with a wand held high in his right hand. Above his head was the sign of infinity, a sideways figure of eight looping back endlessly on to itself. On the table in front of him was another wand, a sword, a cup and a pentacle: the four suits of the minor arcana. Flowers bloomed on the ground.

Card I: the Magician. Reversed, inverted. Anna blew through her teeth.

'An inverted magician . . . that means there's a manipulator around. He may appear helpful, but he doesn't necessarily have your best interests at heart. He may not even be a real person: he may just be your ego, or the intoxication of power.'

Patrese looked at his watch. 'Can we hurry this up? I have things to do.'

'Don't shy from this, Franco. It could be very important for you.'

'So's getting back to the incident room. Come on. Sixth card.'

Anna looked at him for a long moment. 'The obstacle,' she said eventually, reaching for the penultimate card in line. 'Something you must overcome to resolve the situation.'

Card IV; the Emperor. An armored king on his throne, with a scepter in his right hand and a ram's head at the end of each armrest.

'Absolute power,' Anna said. 'Control, discipline, command, order, structure, tradition; also inflexibility. The Emperor symbolizes your desire to rule over your surroundings. You need to accept that some things aren't controllable, and others may not benefit from being controlled. The emperor's strength is stability, which brings comfort and self-worth. But his weakness is the risk of stagnation, and the sense of personal entitlement beyond your rights. You must separate one from the other.'

She looked up at Patrese. 'Tell me. Are you impatient, or are you uncomfortable?'

He started to push his chair back. 'I have to go.'

'Sit.' A sudden flash of steel in her voice. 'Last one. The final outcome. Surely you want to know how this is going to end?'

He stayed seated. He had a feeling she'd known he would.

'Last card.' She rested her fingers on top of it. 'This is how the situation will end.'

Card XVI. The Tower. Lightning striking a tower and knocking an outsize crown from off its top. Fire at the windows and two men in the foreground, falling head first towards the ground.

If Patrese had thought the Moon card was disturbing, this

86

was another level entirely. There was nothing comforting about the image, nothing whatsoever: just violence and anguish. Even Anna looked a little taken aback.

'What's wrong?' Patrese said.

'This is . . . this is the card I fear the most.'

'Now you tell me.'

'In order, it comes right after the Devil card. It's a bad omen. When they play tarot games in Europe, they often leave this one out. The deck we've got here, the original one from the fifteenth century, that doesn't have it either. The Tower is bad, Franco. *Bad*. Chaos. Impact. Downfall. Failure. Ruin. Catastrophe. You want to know how bad it is? It's the only card that's better inverted. That way, you land on your feet.'

Anna took Patrese's hand again, and this time the fear was in her eyes rather than his.

'Be careful out there, Franco.'

14

Building 32 of the Massachusetts Institute of Technology, better known as the Stata Center, is a whimsical cartoon village, a riot of angles and perspective. Walls swerve and collide, columns lean like Pisan towers, surfaces change color and texture at the drop of a hat, from dark brick to brushed aluminum, saffron paint to mirrored steel. Crumpled and concertinaed, the building looked as though it had suffered an earthquake.

In an office with walls that sloped so violently no bookshelves would stand flush against them, Marat Nursultan sipped at his coffee.

'You're *sure* you haven't heard from him?' he said.

Thomas Unzicker shook his head. He wore square-rimmed glasses and a WHO THE FUCK ARE HARVARD? sweatshirt. He was twenty-four, and still got ID-checked in pretty much every bar from here to Cape Cod.

Nursultan clattered his spoon into the saucer. 'We *have* to get hold of him.'

Unzicker stared at Nursultan a good ten seconds before replying. Nursultan didn't break the gaze. Unzicker rarely spoke unless the subject was computers, when you couldn't shut him up; but otherwise, almost nothing. Nursultan didn't know whether Unzicker was just shy or whether it was something deeper, more pathological. He didn't care, either way. He wanted Unzicker for his peculiar form of genius, not for his company.

'His mom's dead.' Unzicker's voice was little more than a whisper. Nursultan had to lean forward to hear it. It was always like this. If a door slammed or someone was talking outside, you had to ask Unzicker to repeat himself; that's how quietly he spoke.

'I want to talk with him. Much important on this, you know. He being difficult before his mother dead. He try to play me both way, yes? Be difficult with title match, get advantage on this project. Or maybe other way round. But I not have it. I not do business that way. So tell me: you need him for this?'

'Yes.'

'*Really* need him?'

'Yes.'

'You can't do it on your own? Or get someone else in for him?'

'No.'

'Why not?'

'This thing's only going to work with the kind of chess Kwasi plays.'

'There are other super-grandmasters.'

Unzicker shook his head again. 'Too much to explain to someone new.'

'If someone beats us to it . . .' Unzicker shrugged; Nursultan kept talking. 'You *sure* no one else know about this?' Headshake. 'What that mean? Yes, no one know, or no, you not sure?'

'I haven't told anyone.'

'The police? They been round?' Headshake. 'They check up on things. They want to find out about his mother, they examine every bit of his life, then they find us.'

'We're not doing anything illegal.'

'No. But what we do, it is secret.' He rubbed his fingers together. 'Valuable.'

Unzicker said nothing. In the corridor outside, a quartet of students in gym shorts padded past. A squeal of laughter from the day-care center echoed off the walls.

Nursultan looked out of the window, across a roofscape dotted with Technicolor huts. MIT, he thought, was supposed to be about reason, logic, engineering excellence. But this building was like one of those car-crash sculptures, like someone had just thrown it up. It didn't even look finished. And that was the point. What Unzicker was doing here, what everyone was doing here, it was all nothing more than work in progress. Science was an open question. Every discovery made was merely a stepping stone to the next one.

Frank Gehry, who'd designed this place, had said the same about his buildings: they always looked more interesting under construction than when they were finished. That's what he'd wanted here: that restless sense of something still happening. The floorplans looked like fractals. That was deliberate, to make sure the people inside didn't think linearly. They were doing research that could change the world, they had to think in weird dimensions. If the building looked like it was leaping off the planet, so were the people inside. That was the theory, anyway.

Nursultan smiled and stood. 'Moment you hear something,

you tell me. Remember who pay you. Remember how much more I pay when we make this work.'

He patted Unzicker on the shoulder. It felt to Unzicker like the grasp of a bear's claw.

15

Thursday, November 4th

Patrese had settled in to New Haven for the long haul, whether he liked it or not. The Bureau had booked him a room – special rates for government employees, naturally – in the downtown New Haven Hotel, conservatively named and conservatively decorated in various tones of corporate taupe.

He'd had the New Orleans field office FedEx him up a bunch of his suits, dress shirts and black leather Oxfords so he'd actually look like a Bureau agent. All he'd had packed when Kieseritsky had first called on Sunday morning was casual clothes for a weekend at the football.

He'd spent the past couple of days following up leads that had started without promise and had become even more hopeless. In the process, he'd gotten himself acquainted with the city's geography and neighborhoods. Westville, East Rock and the East Shore were the 'best' – for which, read 'richest' – places to live. Fair Haven, the Hill and Dwight-Kensington were at the other end of the scale. As was so often the case, Patrese thought, the prettier the name, the bigger the shithole.

The first forty-eight hours after the murders had come and gone, and with them the hope that this thing might get solved quick and clean. The task force had followed up any known cases of criminal pairings, be they siblings, couples, friends, colleagues or any other imaginable permutation. Nothing doing.

And meantime, pressure was mounting from several directions at once. The press were clamoring for more information, which meant an arrest or another victim. Kwasi King wanted his mother's body back so he could give her a proper burial, but the medical examiner wanted to keep hold of it a while longer, perhaps even till the crime was solved. Patrese had rung Kwasi to tell him. Kwasi had delivered himself of an unflattering opinion of medical examiners in general and the New Haven one in particular. Kwasi was well into the anger phase of grief, Patrese had thought.

Anna's tarot reading had freaked Patrese more than he wanted to admit. The Fool had annoyed him; the Moon had unsettled him; and as for the Tower, men diving to earth while the building burned behind them . . . it reminded him of the pictures from New York on the day seared into America's collective memory, when some of those trapped above the firelines in the Twin Towers had been pushed or jumped to their lonely, brutal deaths. An uncanny harbinger of that tragedy, no? If the Tarot was right about that, what else might it be right about?

Now Patrese was in the hotel bar, about to order dinner before turning in for the night. He couldn't be bothered to go out, but equally he thought it defeatist to order room service. Hence the bar.

The waitress informed him that tonight's special was apizza, a white clam pie pizza with a thin crust and no mozzarella. Apizza was New Haven's main contribution to world cuisine, and boy did you know it when you were

93

here. If one more person in this town asked Patrese whether he'd tried it, he might start committing murders himself rather than trying to solve them.

His cellphone rang. He held a finger up to the waitress: let me get this.

The display showed a 212 number. Manhattan code. Kwasi?

'Patrese.'

'Agent Patrese?' A man's voice, deep and rough: not Kwasi's. 'My name is Bobby Dufresne. I'm a detective with the NYPD, Twenty-Sixth Precinct.'

He didn't need to tell Patrese why he was calling.

16

It's seventy-five miles, give or take, between downtown New Haven and the campus of Columbia University in Upper Manhattan's Morningside Heights district. Lights flashing and sirens blaring, Patrese managed the journey inside forty-five minutes.

He found his way to the murder site easily enough: it was lit up by the blues and reds lazily rotating on the roofs of the half-dozen police cruisers in attendance. At the main entrance to an austere-looking stone building, two uniforms stood guard behind crime-scene tape. A hundred or so students milled around, weeping on each other's shoulders or talking dazedly into cellphones. A shrine seemed to be growing organically on a patch of grass nearby: candles, photographs, T-shirts, scarves.

HARTLEY, proclaimed letters on the building's front wall. Patrese turned sideways, edged through a gap between two students, and flipped his badge at the uniforms. One of them stepped forward and lifted up the tape for him to duck under.

'Down the corridor, sir. It's right at the end, in the corner.'

'Thanks.'

Crime-scene officers flitted through bright pools of arc

lights. Halfway along the corridor, Patrese stopped one of them and asked where he could find Detective Dufresne.

'Right over there.' A finger swathed tight in blooded latex pointed at a black man by the far wall. Dufresne had a sports jacket and a goatee beard trimmed to what looked like an accuracy of micrometers. He came across, hand extended.

'Agent Patrese?' A glance at his watch. 'Where's Mario?'

Patrese stiffened. An Italian insult right off the bat?

'Mario?' He kept his voice neutral.

'Andretti. No other way you could have got here this fast.'

Patrese laughed. 'Mario's got the night off. Dale said he'd drive instead.'

Dufresne clapped him on the shoulder. 'Glad you made it. Pleasure to meet you. Heard a lot about you, all that stuff down in New Orleans round about Katrina. Took an interest in the voodoo side, for obvious reasons.'

Patrese made a quick calculation: black skin, French name, voodoo, New York's diaspora. 'You're Haitian?'

'Came here when I was nine. Never going back. Anyhows, I can give you my life story sometime else.' He gestured toward the corner room. 'You wanna go on in?'

'Sure.' Patrese started to walk toward the room. 'What happened?'

'Deceased's name is Dennis Barbero. President of Columbia's BSO, the Black Students Organization. Not as minority as you might think, this being Ivy League and all. Columbia's got more black students than most, and the, er, head guy, the president of the university, he's a big fan of affirmative action.'

'You got an ID so fast?'

'Excuse me? Oh, you mean 'cos he's got no head and shit? Yeah, yeah, definitely him. Definitely Dennis Barbero. Public Enemy T-shirt he always wore, that's on the, er, body, and also, he's one of the few who had a key to open this room up.'

They reached the door. Dufresne gestured: After you.

'G-body meeting of the BSO, every . . .'

'G-body?'

'General body. General meeting. Every Thursday, nine till eleven, right in here, but it's locked when not in use. Dennis had to open it up.'

There was a sign on the door. MALCOLM X LOUNGE, 106 HARTLEY HALL.

Patrese stepped inside.

Blood everywhere, all over the walls and floor, as though a herd of pigs had been slaughtered in here rather than one man. Dennis' body was sprawled between a table and two chairs. Unlike Regina King and Darrell Showalter, he was clothed. Like them, he was missing a head and one of his arms.

The Public Enemy T-shirt had the band's famous logo: the silhouette of a black man's head with a beret, as seen through rifle sights. The shirt had ridden up to reveal the missing patch of skin. The left arm of his shirt had been severed, along with the arm itself. There was a tarot card near the body, but it was too far away for Patrese to make out exactly what it was.

He looked round the room. On the near wall, a painting – Sherman Edwards' *My Child, My Child*, according to a card alongside – from which a staggeringly beautiful black woman, dressed in a purple shawl and clutching a naked baby tight to her chest, stared at Patrese in silent, reproachful challenge. Directly opposite was a poster-sized photo of Malcolm X himself, lips pursed, right index finger raised, old-fashioned radio microphone in front of him, and beneath it a quotation:

'*We declare our right on this Earth to be a human being, to be*

97

respected as a human being, to be given the rights of a human being.'

And to be killed like an animal, Patrese thought bitterly.

He went closer, careful not to step in any of the outlying islands of blood. He peered at the tarot card. A young man in armor astride a charging horse, sword held high in his right hand. The Knight of Swords.

Since Anna had told his fortune, Patrese had pondered and studied the major arcana with a fervor some might have thought obsessional. He knew this card wasn't among them. The knight of swords was minor arcana, the lesser secrets. He'd have to go back to Anna tomorrow and pick her brains all over again.

No tarot reading, though; not after last time. That was for damn sure.

He turned to Dufresne. 'Give me the timescale. What do we know?'

'I'll walk you through it; it's easier. Let's get out of here.'

17

The Columbia campus stretches over six city blocks, but in the last few hours of his life, Dennis had moved within only one of them. Hartley Hall was located at the eastern side of this block, on 114th and Amsterdam: Dufresne took Patrese over to Alfred Lerner Hall on the western side, 114th and Broadway. Patrese glanced at the 114th Street sign.

'Across 110th Street, huh?' he said.

Dufresne laughed. 'Oh, you're not in Harlem yet. 110th Street's the marker only over to the Upper East. Round this side of the park, us niggers don't start in earnest till north of 125th. Matter of fact, this precinct's one of the safest in the city. Till tonight.'

There was another uniform at the entrance to Lerner Hall. He snapped to attention as Dufresne approached.

'Easy, son,' Dufresne said. 'This ain't *Crimson Tide*.'

Dufresne and Patrese rode the elevator to the sixth floor, where Dufresne led the way through two sets of fire doors to a sign: WKCR, 89.9 FM. Columbia University Student Radio Station.

'Dennis was here, seven thirty till eight thirty. Did it every week: Dennis Barbero's Black Music Hour. Played whatever he wanted to play, long as it was black. Could be Martha Reeves or Kool Herc, could be Gladys Knight or Grandmaster Flash. One of the most popular shows they have.' He made a face. 'Had.'

Patrese smiled: it was the most natural mistake in the world.

'Anyhows,' Dufresne continued, 'show finishes eight thirty. Dennis hands over to the guy doing the news headlines – on the half-hour, short ones only – says adios to the producer, and leaves.' He took Patrese back through the fire doors, down again in the elevator, and through the main foyer. 'A couple of people see him here, leaving the building.'

'What time is this?'

'About eight thirty-five.'

They left the hall and headed across the quadrangle.

To their right, on the south side, was an enormous neoclassical library fronted by an arcade of Ionic columns. Above the columns ran a frieze of famous writers' names, starting with Homer and Herodotus and ending with Voltaire and Goethe. To their left, a sculpture of the goddess Athena sitting on a throne, with a laurel crown on her head and the book of knowledge balanced on her lap. Her arms were raised as though welcoming the knowledge all around her.

Whatever accusations you could level at Ivy League colleges, Patrese thought, understatement wasn't one of them.

'From Lerner to Hartley, probably seven minutes, walking at normal pace,' Dufresne said. 'Well-lit, people around, usually a couple of campus police patrols too.'

'You think he was followed?'

'Maybe. Wouldn't have dared jump him out here, though. No chance of getting away unseen. But maybe he wasn't followed. Every Thursday, Dennis had the same routine: his radio show, walk across the quad, open up the Malcolm X

Lounge, make sure everything was ready for the G-body meeting at nine. Didn't need to follow him. You could set your watch by him. Hell, you could set the atomic clock by him.'

'So Dennis unlocks the lounge, the killer slips in there with him—'

'Or has gotten access to the room beforehand, and is lying in wait.'

'—or that, and then he kills Dennis and hauls ass. Must have had a holdall or something, to carry the head and arm in. Anyone see anyone like that?'

'Not that we know.'

Patrese shrugged. If the killer was smart – and they knew he was that, if nothing else – he'd have made sure that he attracted as little attention as possible. On a student campus, that meant dressing like a student, whether you were one or not. Sneakers, jeans, college sweatshirt; someone dressed in those would pass unnoticed, even with a holdall. Going to the gym, helping set up a party . . . plenty of reasons to carry a soft bag.

'Security measures in Lerner and Hartley?' Patrese said.

'The time of night we're talking, not much. Lerner's a public building, so people come in and out the whole time. Hartley's primarily residential, but it has a few communal rooms like the Malcolm X Lounge, which means the main door's kept open till those meetings are over.'

'CCTV?'

'No. Students. Human rights.'

'So we're looking at, oh, several thousand possible suspects.'

Dufresne rubbed his chin. 'In that neighborhood.'

Patrese thought for a moment. 'Unless . . .'

'Yes?'

'Ivy League colleges: they stick together much?'

'What do you mean?'

'They have a lot of meet-ups just for Ivy League places? Parties, conferences, tournaments, I don't know. That kind of thing.'

'No idea. Why?'

'Two people killed within sight of Yale's front entrance. Now one on Columbia's campus itself. Columbia and Yale are both Ivy League colleges. It must be worth seeing whether anyone from Columbia was at Yale last weekend, or . . .'

Dufresne finished Patrese's sentence for him. 'Or whether anyone from Yale's here at Columbia right now.'

18

Dufresne's men and the campus police had been on the case
most of the night. The campus block where Dennis had been
killed had been locked down: no one allowed to leave till
they'd spoken to police, no one allowed in without proof
they lived there. Hartley apart, there were four other accommodation blocks: Wallach, Furnald, Carman and John Jay.
Every resident had been interviewed, some at two or three
in the morning. A lot of them had grumbled about this.
Patrese couldn't have given a damn.

He and Dufresne had kept themselves awake by mainlining
black coffee the consistency and taste of peat sediment. When
even that hadn't been enough, Patrese had grabbed a couple
of hours' restless sleep on a cot bed in the precinct station
house.

Now Dufresne took him to breakfast in a diner across the
street, where they filled up on waffles and hash browns.
Law enforcement officers, like soldiers, march on their stom-
achs: it might be many hours before they got to eat again.

They reviewed what they had so far.

103

No connections they could find between the first two victims and the third. Dennis Barbero had known neither Regina King nor Darrell Showalter. Patrese hadn't set much store by any links between the two male victims – a radical black student and a white Benedictine monk were hardly natural bedfellows – but he *had* wondered whether Dennis and Regina had come across each other. Dennis had been president of Columbia's Black Students' Organization: Regina had been a member of the National Council of Black Women. Two black activists? It was hardly unheard of. But no, nothing doing. They'd never even attended the same conferences.

One small breakthrough: a connection between Columbia and Yale. The Columbia Lions football team had played Yale Bulldogs in New Haven the previous Saturday. Even that, however, seemed to lead nowhere. The Columbia team had stayed in New Haven the night before the game, on Friday, but had returned home after the game on Saturday. None of the team or its support staff had been in New Haven at the time of the murders.

Travelling supporters? Very few. The Lions' home attendance was by far the worst of all Ivy League colleges; not surprising when you considered how hopeless the team were. The Lions found it hard to muster 1,500 people for an average home game, and less than 100 had made the trip to Yale last week. All but one of those had returned to Columbia the same night, and the exception had stayed up to spend the weekend with his girlfriend, a Yale sophomore.

Yes, they'd been together all weekend. The girl's neighbors were adamant, their testimony shot through with equal parts annoyance and admiration at the prolonged sexual symphonies resonating through the walls. After all that, it was a wonder the guy had had enough energy to eat breakfast, let alone go out and murder someone.

But there'd been no events at Columbia last night involving anyone from Yale. So maybe the timings of the murders were sheer coincidence.

'Coincidence' isn't a word that homicide investigators like to hear.

They'd also found out a little more about Dennis Barbero. Columbia was hoping to extend its campus into the largely Hispanic Manhattanville neighborhood to its north. Dennis hadn't just joined the local Manhattanville protest campaign: he'd ended up running the damn thing. He'd addressed rallies, chained himself to railings, demanded audiences with congressmen and senators.

The expansion plans were incompatible with the need for affordable housing in Manhattanville, he'd said: they represented nothing but more forcible gentrification, more unthinking white property appropriation. Publicly, the university authorities had said they welcomed dialogue and debate, and valued Mr Barbero's freedom of speech even – especially – when his opinions were opposed to their own.

What they'd thought privately might have been another matter entirely.

Breakfast done, Patrese and Dufresne went back to campus around nine. The campus was no longer locked down – only Hartley House itself – and the morning shifts of both precinct and campus officers had taken over, putting up notices and buttonholing students as they passed. Did you see anything? Do you know anything? All information confidential. Phone this number or talk to an officer.

There was a crowd around the entrance to Hartley House, as there had been last night, but Patrese could see instantly that the mood was very different. Where people had been shocked and tearful, now they were angry. Their bodies made angular lines of self-righteous defiance; their voices came in shouts, barks, growls. A couple of TV crews were filming them. Patrese spat out a curse. TV crews always made these things worse.

Dufresne walked over to the nearest uniform, exchanged a few words with him, and came back to Patrese.

'What's going on?' Patrese asked.

'People getting real pissed now. Say the police been hassling them.'

'There's been a murder. The fuck do they expect?'

Dufresne shrugged. 'They're students. Always think they know everything. Student who knows they don't know everything is like a woman who don't nag: a strictly mythical creature. You know how it is. We can't do anything right. We ask questions, we're hassling them. We don't ask questions, we don't care 'bout some dead black guy.' He gestured to one corner of the protest. 'Some fools over there, they're stirring things up even more. Saying Dennis was killed 'cos he took it to the man.'

'The Manhattanville protests?'

'I guess. You ask me, they just want to make him a victim.'

Patrese thought for a moment: then he started towards the posse Dufresne had indicated. One of the TV cameramen came closer, lens tracking Patrese as he walked. A reporter shouted a question. Patrese ignored them both. He was tempted to tell them to butt out altogether, switch the camera off, but he knew that would cause more problems than it solved.

The students Dufresne had called stirrers were a mixed bunch: a handful of black guys dressed in the kind of low-slung pants that always made Patrese want to pull them up and tell the wearers to look smarter, but also some white and Asian kids with backpacks and earnest faces.

'I'm Franco Patrese. I'm with the FBI. Is there anything I can help you with?'

You could try not sounding like a damn shop assistant, he thought to himself.

One of the guys with Rikers pants stepped forward. 'You goin' round aksin' all the students if they killed Dennis, but why ain't you investigatin' the administration?'

'We're following several lines of enquiry.'

'That's what the police always say. The administration hated Dennis, man. Hated him. He was a pain in all their asses. You gotta talk to the president, the provost, the vice-presidents, all the trustees. I'm at law school here, and you know what they teach us? *Cui bono*? Who benefits?'

'I know what *cui bono* means.'

'Then go look, man. You keep on hasslin' the students here, this thing's gonna blow up. We ain't afraid of protests at Columbia. We got a long tradition of that shit.'

The cameraman took a step toward them. Patrese kept his voice calm.

'Sounds to me a little like a threat.'

'Everyone got the right to protest, man.'

'You know your rights, huh? What about your responsibilities? What about your responsibility to let us do our job? I didn't just tumble out of high school and find myself in the Bureau. I worked hard, I got trained. I know what I'm doing. All the officers who stop and ask questions, they know what they're doing too.' Patrese clapped his hands, raised his voice. 'Listen up. All of you.'

The crowd noise rose, subsided. Patrese spoke into its ebb.

'I know you're all upset about what happened last night. But please: let us do our job. You got any thoughts or information, ring the number on the noticeboards all around campus, where a trained officer will take your call. I ask you: disperse in an orderly fashion, and this whole thing will get solved quicker.'

For a moment, Patrese thought it had worked: and then the shouts went up, police trying to cover things up, just another nigger dead, and all that. This was the Ivy League

107

in the twenty-first century, Patrese thought, not sixties-era Kent State: but this wasn't all about race, he realized, this was students kicking against the system, and that was as old as education itself. He wanted to tell the protestors that in a decade's time they'd be rich bankers or lawyers, and they'd sure as heck want the police to come quick enough when their condo got burgled: but he didn't think that would do any good right this moment.

The crowd jostled and surged. It seemed to have grown bigger. A couple of campus police officers came hurrying over from outside the library, radioing for back-up as they did. If he wasn't careful, Patrese thought, he'd have a full-scale riot on his hands.

Someone was leaning over the barriers, trying to attract his attention. A black guy with dreadlocks. Looked like Kwasi.

Not just looked like Kwasi, Patrese realized with a start. It *was* Kwasi.

'Hey, Franco,' Kwasi said, as though they were meeting in a coffee shop rather than on the fringes of incipient public disorder.

Patrese went over. 'What are you doing here?'

'Saw it on the news. Same guy who killed my mom?'

'Think so. I was going to call and tell you.'

'OK.'

'That doesn't answer my question.'

'What question?'

'What are you doing here? You wanted to talk to me, you could have rung me.'

'Thought I could help.'

'*Help?*'

'Sure. Calm things down a little.'

Patrese almost laughed. Only Kwasi, with his weirdly direct logic – some form of mild autism, perhaps, maybe Asperger's – only Kwasi could see a student protest and think he could help. Patrese opened his mouth to say, 'Thanks, but no,' and in that exact moment thought: Well, why not? It could hardly make things worse, could it?

He opened the barrier for Kwasi to squeeze through. Dufresne's eyebrows practically attained escape velocity. 'What the . . .?' he mouthed.

'Trust me,' Patrese mouthed back, though in truth he wasn't sure he trusted himself.

Kwasi walked to the building's entrance, where the whole crowd could see him.

The transformation was amazing. Aggression drained from the chants as though a plug had been pulled. In its place came the happy shock of unexpectedly seeing a properly famous person up close.

The crowd whooped and hollered. 'Hey! Kwasi! *Kwasi!* Over here, man!'

Dufresne came over to Patrese. 'Never seen nothing like this.'

Kwasi held up his hands. The crowd quietened. Give him a beard and a robe, Patrese thought, and he could have been Jesus.

'My mom was killed last weekend.' Kwasi spoke slowly and carefully, picking each word with care: not a natural orator, but perhaps the more effective for that. The protestors saw he was speaking from the heart. 'Whoever killed her also killed Dennis, and another guy too. Agent Patrese, the Bureau guy who's here behind me, he's leading this case. He's a good guy.' Patrese felt the start of a blush. 'He personally came to tell me about my mom, and he stayed with me that day, looked after me, when he had a ton of other things he needed to do.'

Kwasi paused, swallowed, continued. 'You guys here, Ivy League college kids: it's a hell of privilege, what you've got here. I got turned down. Went to UMBC instead. Kick-ass chess team, but the rest of it, nothing like this place. All of you, show you're as smart as everyone thinks you are. Do me a favor. Let the police get on with it, let them find the killer, we can all get some closure. Do what Agent Patrese said, and disperse.'

And that's exactly what they did.

19

An hour later, Patrese felt he'd done all he could here. Kwasi had given interviews to the TV stations on site and gone back home. Forensics was in the hands of the NYPD, who'd promised to let him know the moment they had anything. Since the central incident room was in New Haven, Dufresne said he was happy to come up there any time to help work on things. And New Haven was where Patrese needed to be, running things.

His car was at the precinct house, twelve blocks north. A squad car would have given him a lift, but Patrese wanted to walk: stretch his legs, clear his head. Too much coffee and too little sleep were making his face feel like it was about to slide off. He wondered vaguely whether he was safe to drive. If he wasn't, there were stops on the interstate. He could always pull in and doze off if need be.

He'd walked no more than a half-block when a car pulled up alongside him. Not just any old car, either. A white Rolls-Royce. The nearside rear window opened soundlessly.

'Agent Patrese.'

'Mr Nursultan.'

'You have moment?'

'If it's going to help me solve a triple homicide, then sure. If you're telling me I've won the state lottery, also sure. Otherwise, no.'

'Maybe both.' The door swung open. 'Please. It's important. If it save you time, I can take you to where you go. We can talk on the way.'

So much for clearing heads and stretching legs. 'OK.' Patrese ducked his head, stepped inside the Rolls, and settled himself into the black leather. He felt as though he were Billy Ray Valentine in *Trading Places*, being made his offer by the Duke brothers. The door swung shut again.

'Where to?' Nursultan asked.

'West 126th.'

Up front, the chauffeur nodded. Traffic parted as the car slid away from the curb. You saw a Rolls, you let it in, even in New York. Especially in New York.

'I get you something?' Nursultan was the model of solicitousness. 'Whiskey? Cigar?' Again with the Duke brothers shtick.

It was barely mid-morning. 'Thank you, no.'

'You have a good, how you say? Thinking, make things up.'

'Imagination?'

'Yes. Imagination. You have a good imagination?'

'Listen, no disrespect, but I've had two hours' sleep, I've got police departments in two separate states to deal with, and I'm not in the mood for riddles or obscure questions. You got something to say, say it. I was enjoying my walk. I'm happy to enjoy it again.'

'OK. In Theater at Madison Square Garden in six day, at eleven seconds past eleven minutes past eleven o'clock on the eleventh day of the eleventh month' – the detail clearly pleased him – 'I press a chess clock, I start biggest match since Fischer and Spassky. Twelve games in three weeks. Five thousand seats for each game, all sold out. Every single

112

seat. I could have sold each seat four, five times. I have announcers and cheerleaders, like in boxing, no? I have big screens to show players' faces close up, so spectators can feel the emotion, see the agony. I have live TV coverage, every move. I have grandmasters analyze for audience, best graphics in world.'

'And?'

'And right now, I have none of this. I have none of this, because Kwasi King give me sixteen pages of demands and won't discuss a single one with me. You want to know these demands? I tell you some. For Tartu, only one flavor of yoghurt per game, in case his seconds try send him, er, message through the flavor, through which flavor they choose. Electronic sweep of theater for devices, you know, bugs, before every game. Board to be this size, pieces this weight, table this high. And on, and on, and on.'

Patrese gave Nursultan a long, appraising look. If he let Nursultan intimidate him, he'd never get him off his back. He's the money, Patrese thought, but I'm the law. Remember that. Always remember that.

'I guess you stand to lose a lot of cash if this doesn't go ahead.'

'Of course. Not only me. Sponsors, venue, insurers . . .'

'Don't ask me to feel sorry for insurers.'

Nursultan laughed. 'Even insurers not feel sorry for insurers. Yes, people lose money. But you know, money just money. For me, what I lose, I make back, two minutes on stock market. For me, much more important here is chance to blow chess up, make it explode, make it huge. Fischer could have done it, but he too mad. Kwasi, everyone love him: but if he play now, he seal it forever. The game, not only him. This most important to me. This greatest game in world. I want every child to play it. Kwasi, he only one who can inspire. I see him on news today, with the protestors.

113

You there with him, you see it too. He has it. The gift, the touch. Now imagine: this kid, this chess, er, *messiah*, very cool, very weird, his mother just killed, he play anyway . . .' Nursultan clicked his fingers. 'Hollywood, no? It's Hollywood.'

Patrese made a conscious effort not to let his jaw drop. 'You want to make capital out of this? You want to play on his tragedy? You're sick.'

'No. Not sick. Real.'

'Real?'

'Real, how you say? Realistic. Kwasi do same, too. Every time something bad happen, he make advantage of it, he turn it round so best for him. That one of reasons why he so good.'

'So why isn't he doing it now?'

'He try to get as much from me as he can.'

'Christ!' Patrese slammed his fist on the seat. 'His mother's been murdered. If he doesn't want to play chess, then . . . I wouldn't want to play either, in that situation.'

'Chess not your whole life. For Kwasi, his whole life. Match right now is good for him. Take his mind from his mother.'

'You care about his health now? Spare me.'

'I not care what you think of me. But I need help. From you.'

'From *me*? What do you expect me to do about it?'

'You find man who did these kills, you give Kwasi, how you say, peace of mind.'

'One less reason to keep holding out on you, you mean.'

'Maybe.'

'I don't think it'll make any difference to him. His mom's dead. Catching whoever did it isn't going to bring her back. He'll play or he won't. That's between you and him. And anyway' – Patrese mimicked Nursultan's voice – '"You find man who did these kills"? What the *fuck* do you think I'm trying to do? I've thought about nothing else for the past six days. You've got any bright ideas as to who it might be, do let me know.'

'You can make arrest, no?'

'I can make hundreds of arrests. Not much good if they're all the wrong guys.'

'No?'

'No what?'

'They wrong guys. So what?'

And there it was. Patrese had felt that Nursultan was leading up to this, but he wanted to be sure, he wanted to hear it loud and clear.

'Why don't you tell me what you want?' Patrese said.

'You bright guy. You know what I want.'

'I'm sure I do. But tell me anyway. Just to be sure.' He saw the hesitation in Nursultan's face, and knew what it was: a doubt about how freely they could talk without comeback. Patrese went on. 'Oh – if you're worried about recording devices, don't be. I came straight from my hotel last night. I'm not wired, I don't have a digital recorder, nothing. So say what you want.'

'And if it not what you want to hear?'

'Then it'll be your word against mine. And I'm sure you have very good lawyers.'

Nursultan considered. 'OK. I want you to make arrest and press charge, so you can say that you catch man who killed Regina King.'

'Who would you like me to arrest?'

'Homeless. Junkie. Criminal. Any like that.'

'That's obstruction of justice.'

'Sure. Is serious offense. So I compensate you. Big.'

'And that's attempted bribery of a federal official.'

'Listen. If this match in Kazan, and I want arrest, I have a thousand policemen who do anything for this kind of money.'

Patrese leaned forward and tapped on the partition. 'Stop the car, please.' He turned back towards Nursultan. 'I don't wanna sound like an asshole, but . . . no, actually, I don't give a fuck what I sound like. This match isn't taking place in Kazan. It's taking place in New York City, and I don't take to being bribed by you or anyone else. I'm not perfect, but I *am* honest. That means something to me.'

The car pulled up. Patrese opened the door, got out, and then leaned back in. 'I like Kwasi, and I want him to do what's best for him. I understand the power you have in the chess world, and I don't want you to make things any more difficult for him than they are already. So I'll forget what you've just said. This time. But never again.'

20

Back in New Haven, Patrese stopped at his hotel long enough to shower, shave and change clothes before heading to the Beinecke Library. It was a few minutes' walk, no more. Central New Haven was three square blocks by three, with the middle one of the nine – the Green – left open, as is the tradition with many New England towns. Patrese walked down streets whose names told the tale of the city's corner-stones: College, Chapel, Court, Temple.

Anna said that this time it was she who couldn't stay too long: she was heading to Manhattan this evening in preparation for running the New York marathon on Sunday.

'OK, I'll get straight to the point: Knight of Swords,' Patrese said. 'Regular aspect, not reversed.'

'Minor arcana,' she said instantly.

'Exactly. Why the change?'

'The main difference between major and minor arcana is the meanings the cards have when it comes to divination. Major arcana are supposed to represent seismic events; minor arcana are life's more mundane aspects. There are four knights in the minor arcana, of course, one of each suit – wands, pentacles, swords and cups. Whatever the suit, a knight usually symbolizes a young man, perhaps a teenage boy.

'When it comes to the Knight of Swords in particular – well, he's confident, articulate, visionary. He's an idealist, a crusader. See the birds flying above the knight on the card? They symbolize these higher ideals. And the horse here, that shows his energy and vitality. He's got a passion for truth and a brilliant mind. He can cut to the heart of a matter, he can stand up to people in power.

'But he can also be impetuous, unrealistic and foolish. He can rush in without thinking. Since he lives in his head rather than his heart, he's not good at developing attachments to people. And his level of commitment can be questionable. He's a champion of the truth, sure, but sometimes he prefers the fight to the outcome.'

A lot of that applied to Dennis, Patrese thought. Some of it applied to him too.

Three victims. Three tarot cards, all providing fairly accurate descriptions of the victim in question. Was this it? Was the killer hoping to go through an entire deck? Seventy-eight cards meant seventy-eight victims. That was an absurd amount. No killer could expect to remain undetected over the course of that many murders, not when he chose such visible victims.

Seventy-eight would be a national record. America's most prolific serial killer, Gary Ridgway – the Green River Killer – had confessed to seventy-one murders and been convicted of forty-eight. His killing period had lasted eighteen years, and his victims had been mainly Seattle prostitutes. No police force in the world put maximum effort into investigating dead hookers, whatever they might say publicly.

That was the only way for a killer to get away with murdering again and again, into double figures and beyond: to choose victims who wouldn't be missed. Alexander

118

Pichushkin had preyed primarily on elderly homeless men in a Moscow park. Like Ridgway, he'd also been convicted of forty-eight murders, though he claimed sixty-three and was furious to have been caught one short of his target: a victim for every square on a chessboard.

Besides, the presence of the tarot cards didn't explain why the killer was taking the heads and arms, or why he was cutting away the patches of skin. No: it couldn't simply be down to the Tarot. The Tarot was part of the killer's psychosis, but it wasn't all of it.

In the incident room at the New Haven FBI field office, Fox News was on: the afternoon program, *Studio B*. Patrese saw footage of Kwasi getting the Columbia protestors to disperse; then back to the studio and a raven-haired young woman whom Patrese took a second or two to place. He got there a moment before the caption went up: INESSA BAIKAL. The national women's chess champion.

'I think he's scared,' she said, leaning forward slightly over the studio desk in what Patrese thought a fairly blatant attempt to show some cleavage. 'It's not all to do with the tragedy of his mom. He hasn't played competitively for three years. He has this great mystique around him now, but that mystique goes the moment he steps back into . . . I was going to say "into the ring", 'cos that's what it feels like.'

She'd had Kwasi hurling insults at the screen last weekend. It didn't look like he was going to be much happier this time round, Patrese thought.

'I'm no chess expert,' the interviewer was saying, 'but doesn't Kwasi King play totally *without* fear? Isn't that part of what makes him so good? How does that square with this idea of him being scared?'

'The problem's not when he's at the board. The board's where he's most at home: it's ordered, it has rules, it has patterns, and he understands them better than anybody. At the board, he's scrupulously correct, as we saw in the famous game last time out when he called his own touch-move and lost, even though no one else had seen it. No: the problem's getting him *to* the board.'

'Hence all these, what is it, one hundred and eighty demands we keep hearing about?'

'Yes.'

'And you think they're a smokescreen? A way of avoiding playing Tartu?'

'That's what a lot of people think. But I'm not so sure.'

'Oh?'

'Kwasi doesn't think like other people. You ask me, he's making these demands because he feels they're necessary. Sure, to everyone else in the world they appear extravagant, absurd, but maybe not to him. He sees everything as a zero-sum game: one person wins, one person loses. He never compromises. Ever. I know that first-hand.'

'From when you dated him?'

'Right. In a lot of ways, he's still a child. He doesn't get the way the world works. Maybe that's even part of his charm, part of his appeal. He's this, like, man-child. Look at today, that clip you were showing. He went to help. Most people wouldn't have done that. But he did. He didn't think of all the reasons why not; he just thought of something and did it, like a child. And the conditions he's demanded for the title match: I haven't seen them all, but the ones I *have* seen are mainly about playing conditions. That tells you he might not like playing chess too much any more.'

'He doesn't *like* playing chess? But he *lives* for chess, no?'

'That's not the same thing.'

The interviewer laughed. 'Whoa. Now you're losing me.'

'This might sound bizarre, but saying Kwasi doesn't like playing chess isn't the same as saying he doesn't like chess.

120

Quite the opposite. As you say, he loves chess. But I think that what he loves is the, er, I don't know quite how to put this . . . is the . . . holy perfection of chess itself, as a game, as an intellectual exercise. Tournament chess is a very different thing. Your opponent's a couple of feet away, the clock's ticking down, people are shuffling and coughing . . .'

'And more, in those time-scramble tie-breaks. They're practically shouting then.'

'Exactly. Everywhere he's been since becoming world champion, Kwasi's been photographed, filmed, followed, interviewed. He's got a level of fame which I think he's totally unsuited to, temperamentally. I wouldn't be surprised if his true happiness – perhaps his only true happiness – is on his own, late at night, playing endless variations against . . . well, against himself. Against chess itself. Against God, maybe.'

'Against God?'

'There are more possible positions in chess than there are atoms in the universe.'

'You're kidding me?'

'Not at all. That makes the game pretty much insoluble. It's not checkers: there's no perfect line. So man can struggle all he likes to penetrate chess' inner secrets, but he'll never get all the way there. Kwasi, though – he wants to get further than anyone.'

'If you were a betting person, Miss Baikal, would you put money on Kwasi being at that table next week, when the match starts?'

'No. No, I would not.'

21

Universities across the United States make demi-gods out of those who represent them at sports. Nowhere is this more true than in the Ivy League; nowhere in the Ivy League is this more true than at Harvard; and nowhere at Harvard is this more true than on the river.

Year on year, the Harvard men's eight is one of the fastest crews in the country. The competition within the squad just to make the boat is so intense that sometimes the racing itself comes as a relief: it's easier to beat another college than rise to the top of your own. The guys who *do* make it, therefore, are the kind of alpha males who end up earning millions on Wall Street or in the law: tall, muscular men with the confidence of those who believe that the sun in the sky has no purpose other than to shine directly on to them. They race each other up and down every step in the Harvard stadium. They drive themselves to collapse and beyond on the rowing machines. They argue and fight and never, ever admit that someone else might be better than them.

They're not the kind of guys, therefore, who take kindly to their cox not showing up for an outing.

No cox means the boat can't go out: eights are too big, heavy and fast to be left unsteered. No outing on the water means another session in the gym, which the rowers hate. Another session in the gym means the cox – half the size of everyone else in the boat to start with – runs the serious risk of having seven shades of shit kicked out of him when his oarsmen finally run him to ground.

Chase Evans was cox of the Harvard men's eight, the one that had beaten Yale – again – in their annual match a few months ago, and he hadn't showed up for training on the first Sunday in November. They'd called his cellphone: no answer. His voicemail had asked them to leave a message, and they'd done so. Several messages, in fact, each more abusive than the previous one. None of the messages had exhibited the slightest trace of concern, even though this no-show was totally out of character for Chase.

Chase was old-school Harvard. His father had been there, and his grandfather too, and probably a couple more generations of the dynasty fading back into the mists of sepia-photographed time. Chase loved the traditions and the ethos. If you'd pricked him, he'd probably have bled Harvard crimson rather than the plain red everyone else does. He was reliable, organized, solid. His crew trusted him absolutely. On the water, they just rowed: he did everything else, juggling steering, tactics, coaching and motivation with a deft calmness. Crews love coxes like that.

But still, there was no concern in their messages. The Harvard men's eight don't show concern. Concern is weakness. Weakness is for losers.

No one saw Chase all Sunday, either. Those oarsmen who gave it any thought in between half a dozen hectic stops on an average Harvard day might have figured that Chase was

123

so embarrassed about missing the outing that he'd chosen to hide away rather than face them. He'd be there tomorrow morning, they were sure, and he'd stand on the concrete hard in front of the Newell boathouse, the most famous boathouse on all the Charles, and apologize with the same kind of concise elegance that he used to gee his crews up for one more push when it was fifty strokes to the line and they were dying.

Chase Evans was indeed at the boathouse on Monday morning. In fact, he was on the concrete hard itself. But he wasn't going to be saying anything. Not without his head.

22

Patrese had spent more of his weekend than he would have liked dealing with the president of Columbia University, who had told him repeatedly that (a) Columbia would do anything they could to help find Dennis Barbero's killer, (b) Columbia couldn't allow this tragedy to affect their ongoing search for academic excellence – 'academic excellence', Patrese had thought, in this case being used under its lesser-known meaning of 'snow-white public image and high levels of endowments'.

If that was Columbia's attitude, Patrese thought, he could hardly wait to see what Harvard would say about this one. They'd probably demand a cover-up somewhere between the levels of Watergate and Roswell.

The detective on scene at the Newell boathouse was tall enough to carry his weight well, and his eyes were as gray and cold as the river. 'Max Anderssen,' he said. Patrese resisted the temptation to wince as they shook hands: the man had a grip like a mangle. Patrese glanced down at Chase's body, looking for the tarot card he knew would be there. Another knight: the Knight of Pentacles, this time.

'The crew found him when they arrived here at six,'

Anderssen said. The bane of rowers' lives, Patrese thought: dawn starts to fit training around lectures and make use of the river before it got too busy. Anderssen nodded toward sprayed piles of vomit. 'Bit of a shock for some of them, as you can see. The guys who barfed, they're now the ones yelling loudest about how they want to find the guy who did this and rip *his* head off.' He gave a little smile, acknowledgement of testosterone's predictable pathways.

'Media?'

'Not yet, but that's only because this ain't a homicide town, so they're not clued up to the police department the way they are in big cities.'

'But when they *do* find out, it'll be huge.' Homicide in a safe town was always news: many times more so when it was part of a series, and many times more so again when it took place at perhaps the most famous university in the world.

'It sure will. This is our first in a couple of years.'

Patrese was surprised. 'You haven't had a single homicide in two years?'

'That's what I said.'

'I should move here.'

'You'd be out of a job.'

'I know. Sometimes I feel that wouldn't be a bad thing.'

'Longest clean run in fifty years. But even in normal times, we only ever get one or two a year. I've been here more than a decade: most I've ever had was five.' That was impressive, Patrese thought. Cambridge had 100,000 residents, give or take: cities of that size averaged about ten murders per annum. 'The usual stuff,' Anderssen continued. 'Husbands and wives, vagrants intoxicated on God knows what, young street punks too quick to pull a knife or a gun.' He looked around him: at the yellow tape cordoning off the scene, at the river police boat blocking this section of the Charles. 'Not this.'

'Not this kind of killing, or not Harvard?'

'Not this kind of killing. I've had Harvard before: my very first case, actually.'

Patrese thought for a second. 'The roommates?'

'You got a good memory.'

'Remember reading about it. Big news at the time.'

'Just that.' Anderssen gave Patrese a précis of the case. It had involved two female students, both from overseas. Sinedu Tadesse had come to Harvard from Ethiopia, Trang Ho from Vietnam. They'd roomed together and gotten close: fellow students in their hall of residence had said they were inseparable, always going places in tandem. Co-dependent, some had even sniped. But it hadn't been co-dependent, not really. It hadn't been a relationship of equals.

Tadesse, struggling academically and with mental problems – she'd written to strangers picked from the phone book, describing her unhappiness and pleading with them to be her friend – had clung obsessively to Ho. Ho, more popular and balanced, had found the friendship increasingly suffocating.

At the end of their third year, Ho had told Tadesse she didn't want to room with her anymore: she was going to room with someone different for their senior year. Tadesse had brooded, planned, made oblique hints to fellow students about her intentions, and finally stabbed Ho forty-five times with a hunting knife before hanging herself.

The fallout had been long and complex. Ho's family had filed suit for wrongful death, emotional distress and negligence against Harvard, alleging that the university had had plenty of evidence of Tadesse's mental state and fixation on violent vengeance, and could have prevented Ho's death had they acted sooner. Harvard had set up a scholarship in Ho's name, but not before a long debate over whether it should be in both girls' names, as though this had been some lovers' mutual suicide pact. And several other students had come forward to say how inadequate they had found Harvard's mental health policies.

That might be the heart of it, Patrese thought. What it took to succeed here didn't necessarily help build a healthy psyche. Attending Harvard wasn't simply a matter of going to college: it was a sign that you'd been chosen, it was a talisman to put on your résumé. It was a guarantee that you could do pretty much what you wanted to in life, be it something interesting, something lucrative, or both.

Four victims now. One at Harvard, one at Columbia, the other two found near Yale. Patrese thought of Sinedu Tadesse, and wondered how many students there were at Ivy League colleges who harbored mental problems: how many with violent fantasies that might play out in the way he was looking at right now.

Oh, the universities themselves wouldn't want to give out that kind of information, that was for sure. They'd cite patient confidentiality, which in this case meant the same as the Columbia president's 'academic excellence'. There were eight universities in the Ivy League – Harvard, Yale, Columbia, Princeton, Penn, Brown, Cornell and Dartmouth. They'd spent many years building up their collective reputation. They weren't about to roll over and let their names be trashed.

Patrese didn't care.

23

The press conference was held in the Bureau's Boston field office. The field office was used to holding them, and the local reporters were used to going there.

A lot of law enforcement officers don't like the media, and make no secret of that. They dislike being second-guessed by reporters they consider uninformed at best and irresponsible at worst, and they hate the media's tacit demands that the police work to news deadlines rather than at an investigation's natural pace. Some detectives prefer simply to read out a statement, usually written in excruciatingly pedantic officialese, and flatly refuse to take any questions.

Patrese took a more pragmatic approach. He figured the media were part and parcel of every major homicide investigation, so he might as well accept it. Better to have them inside the tent pissing out than vice versa. The more he could run them, the less they could run him. And there were also ways of using the media to put pressure on a killer, to bluff or double-bluff him, but you had to be pretty sure of your ground to do that, and Patrese wasn't yet there on this one.

He practiced his demeanor in the mirror before going on.

He had to look confident but not cocky, serious but not depressed. Yes, these were tragedies, but he was in charge of solving the crimes, not leading the mourners. Others could weep and wail. What the public wanted to see was a flint-eyed, square-jawed G-Man who would run down the bad guy with implacable remorselessness. Think Jack Bauer meets Dirty Harry.

Flashbulbs like a meteor shower as he walked in, and a copse of microphones on the table in front of him. He took his seat and shot his cuffs. What he was about to perform was a balancing act: give enough information to keep the media happy, but not enough to jeopardize the investigation.

'Good morning. My name is Franco Patrese, and I'm the agent in charge of this case. A few hours ago, the body of a young man named Chase Evans was found outside Harvard University's Newell boathouse. Mr Evans was a third-year student at Harvard, and he was the coxswain of the university's rowing eight. I need hardly tell you that his murder has sent shockwaves through the university, just as the killing of Columbia student Dennis Barbero did at that university last week. We believe the same man is responsible for both killings, as well as the murders of Regina King and Darrell Showalter, whose bodies were found on New Haven Green in Connecticut eight days ago. In each case, the victims had been decapitated and had an arm removed.'

No mention of the skin patches or the tarot cards. That information was being kept secret – well, as secret as something involving three separate police forces plus the Bureau itself could ever be – in order to weed out the crank callers, of which there were inevitably hundreds.

'We are pursuing several lines of enquiry,' Patrese continued, 'which for operational reasons must remain confidential. But we're confident that, with the public's help, we'll catch this man before too long. If anyone's got any questions, I'll do my best to answer them.' He indicated a blonde reporter in the front row. 'Yes?'

'Sandra Olsen, WBZ-TV. Is there an Ivy League connection to the murders?'

'I don't know for sure, but of course it's an avenue we're exploring pretty closely. Two of the victims were Ivy League students; the other two were found more or less by Yale's front door. I've already requested all eight Ivy League colleges, not just the three involved so far, to provide a list of students who've shown aggressive tendencies, been involved in violent incidents, or expressed any kind of murderous fantasies in classwork, therapist sessions, anything like that.' Nod to a woman with frizzy hair. 'Yes?'

'Bethany Bryan, *Boston Globe*. That sounds a lot like invasion of privacy. Aren't therapy sessions confidential?'

'Under normal circumstances, sure. Psychotherapy is a private process which often involves discussion of very sensitive issues, and I respect that. I've got no intention of rootling through the files of innocent folk who've got nothing to do with this. But in cases where the patient's believed to pose a danger to himself or someone else, then confidentiality can be broken; that's established case law. The protective privilege ends where the public peril begins.'

This was all true, but it was also a tactical move on Patrese's part. He guessed that at least some of the eight colleges, the Ancient Eight, would try to drag their heels: acceding to police demands for sensitive information didn't sit well with lofty liberal academic ideals. By making his request a matter of such public record, Patrese hoped to shanghai any recalcitrant authorities into co-operating.

'Doug Turner, WBZ news radio 1030. The victims have been both black and white, and male and female. Isn't that a little unusual?'

'You mean, serial killers don't usually cross race or gender lines? Yes, it is. But it's also unusual – and I'm not meaning to be flippant here – it's also unusual to decapitate your victims and remove their arms. That it's unusual doesn't mean it's impossible. We're clearly dealing here with someone who's got a very rare and serious pathology. He's not going to think and act like normal people. Unusual is the very least that he is.'

'Barrie Golding, *Christian Science Monitor*. You're coordinating investigations in three separate jurisdictions. Does that cause problems?'

'That's what the Bureau was set up for. Detectives Anderssen, Dufresne and Kieseritsky – they're the ones in Cambridge, Manhattan and New Haven – they all understand that. They've been extremely helpful so far, and I'm sure they'll continue to be. We all want the same thing: to catch the guy who's doing this. I don't care if it's me that runs him to ground personally after a tri-state manhunt or if an old lady trips him up with her walking stick. I just want him caught. When that happens, then everyone can start arguing about who gets the credit.'

Everyone in the room surely knew the phrase as well as Patrese did. Success has a thousand fathers; defeat is an orphan.

There was still a forest of hands showing. At this rate, Patrese thought, he could be here all day. He'd made his statement, he'd shown willing. Keen though he was to keep the media onside, he had a task force to run; and besides, it did no harm to have them always wanting a little bit more. He held up a hand.

'I'd love to stay, but as you can appreciate, I have a thousand and one things to do. Before I go, though, let me say something.' He looked down the lens of the nearest camera: a trick he'd learnt back in Pittsburgh, that a direct appeal could work wonders. 'I'm asking you, the public, to help us on this one. We, the Bureau and the police, we can't be everywhere. You can; you *are*. Be our eyes and ears. Please, if you've seen anything, heard anything, noticed anything unusual; please, ring in and tell us. Don't worry if it seems too small or insignificant or irrelevant. Let us be the judge of that. You never know; your piece of information could be the one that makes the difference.'

That kind of logic – *it could be you* – got people buying lottery tickets, so Patrese figured it was worth a try here. And the more publicity a case received, he felt, the greater the chance of it being solved. He didn't know whether that was statistically the case, but logically it seemed that the more people who knew, the more likely they were to offer help. Too much information could, and often did, swamp homicide task forces, but better too much than too little. Sooner or later, the snippet they needed would bubble up through all the dead ends and red herrings. Given enough time, manpower and luck, you could always find the needle in the haystack.

But if the needle wasn't there to start with, you had no chance.

24

Patrese headed back to New Haven after lunch. Anderssen's men were questioning people on the Harvard campus in the same way that Dufresne's officers had done down in Columbia: sealing off the accommodation block where Evans had lived and working outwards from there. And, Patrese thought, Anderssen would face exactly the same problems Dufresne had: not in terms of protests – Harvard students didn't protest unless their port was of insufficient vintage – but in the impossibility of keeping strangers off an open campus.

Patrese rang Anna from the car. She too was on the road, en route back from Manhattan. She'd done the marathon in 3:47. She'd been hoping for 3:30, but was happy to have got round inside 4:00. Pretty good, Patrese said. If he ever ran it, he'd be lucky to finish before the maintenance crews arrived to take down the crowd barriers.

He told her about Chase Evans at the boathouse.

'The Knight of Pentacles?' she said. 'That's a funny one. Funny peculiar, not funny ha-ha. There are four knights in the deck, but Pentacles is the only one who's reliable and steadfast. The others are daring but flighty. Pentacles is very thorough, very methodical. He's pushy, bossy, a control freak. Loves being in charge, loves responsibility.'

In other words, Patrese thought, a typical cox.

But all this was getting him nowhere. That wasn't Anna's fault: she couldn't have been more helpful. The problem was that, so far, the tarot cards showed Patrese only what *had* happened. Dennis Barbero had fitted the characteristics of the Knight of Swords, Chase Evans those of the Knight of Pentacles. But they were already dead: the cards had merely confirmed their personalities. Patrese needed to know in advance, and right now he could see no way of achieving that.

Sure, he could try to extrapolate likely targets from the remaining seventy-four cards in a tarot deck, but the search fields were way too wide to be of any use. Even if Patrese got it spot on in working out what kind of victim corresponded to what card, that would still be no good – not unless he knew the very next intended victim. Not the one two or three down the line, but the next one, the one who was going to die in a matter of hours, days, weeks unless Patrese got to him before the killer did. Knowing your next victim might fit one of seventy-four different parameters gave you roughly the same odds of saving him – or her – as not knowing anything at all.

In my next life, Patrese thought, I'm going to do a different job. Something simpler. Something easier. Something less frustrating. Astrophysics, perhaps. Or brain surgery.

The figures that Patrese had requested from around the Ivy League, if not the specific cases behind those figures, were starting to come in by the time he got back to New Haven. There were 125,000 students between the eight universities, and almost one in six of them, 18,000, were on record as attending therapy. The one-in-six ratio was similar when staff were counted too: 8,000 therapy patients out of just under 50,000.

Even by the standards of modern America, Patrese thought those staggering figures.

But perhaps it wasn't so surprising, not when he considered it some more. Parents, professors, peers all put these kids under insane pressure to succeed, to make the most of their opportunities. Perhaps the kind of person who got an Ivy League place was inherently more susceptible to mental trouble in the first place. Just as finely tuned athletes often get sick or injured, so too a brain overstressed by studying too hard or worrying about measuring up to high standards all around might start to malfunction.

Then again, maybe he was making it all too sinister. Bipolar medication had allowed bright but mentally ill students to get to college in the first place, where beforehand they'd never have made it through high school. And therapy was no longer the stigma it used to be, especially amongst the educated classes. More people seeing therapists might not indicate more people needing therapy, simply more people prepared to seek it out.

There was a similar phenomenon when it came to serial killers, Patrese knew. There had always been serial killers throughout history, but they hadn't been recognized as such until crime detection methods had reached a point where crimes hitherto thought unrelated could be cross-referenced and correlated. Jack the Ripper wasn't the first serial killer; just the first serial killer to be known as such.

The majority of the therapists' cases would be sexual identity issues, substance abuse, eating disorders, anxiety, apprehension about the future, and so on. Patrese wasn't interested in those, not unless they came with violent undertones attached. If the killer was among the student body, and had been seeking therapy, it was almost inconceivable that he wouldn't have shown some aggressive tendencies. The killings were too savage.

Patrese stayed in the incident room for a couple of hours, finding out what they had (a ton of leads to follow up after his press conference earlier) and didn't have (anything else). Still waiting on forensics, not just on this one but on Columbia too: it could take weeks sometimes, high-profile case or not. Nothing useful from eyewitness reports.

The hell with Ivy League kids, Patrese thought. Much more of this, and *he'd* be needing a damn therapist.

When he'd been at college, his first choice of therapy had always been exercise. Getting some air into his lungs, feeling the cleansing burn of lactic acid through his legs – that had been better for him than a dozen sessions on a shrink's couch. If Anna could manage twenty-six miles, he could surely manage a few himself?

'Where's good to go running round here?' he asked the room.

Lighthouse Point Park, came the answer: a nice park on the city's east shore. It was five miles dead from New Haven Green to the titular lighthouse, hence the name of the point it stood on: Five Mile Point.

Patrese hadn't been running for so long that five miles dead might leave him just that. And then it would be five miles back too. Well, that was what taxis were for, wasn't it?

The city center gave way to smaller residential streets, which gave way in turn to the industrial area round the city's harbor. The park was the other side of the water from the city center, and two bridges spanned the bay: the Pearl Harbor Memorial Bridge, which didn't permit pedestrians, and the Tomlinson Lift Bridge, which did. The slap of Patrese's sneakers echoed off the girders as he crossed. His breathing came fast and ragged, the hard first few minutes of a run while his body adjusted itself to the effort.

Feet wandering, mind wandering. The charioteer approaches things from the side, Anna had said. You can stare a solution straight in the face and not see it; but when you turn your head away and squint through the corner of your eye, it might become clear.

In the press conference earlier, the guy from WBZ news radio had asked whether it was unusual for a killer to cross gender and race lines. Patrese's reply – that 'unusual' was the very least this killer was – had sounded to him more flip than he'd meant it to be. Thing was, news radio man had a point. Lines of race and gender *are* heavily marked in the human psyche, and serial killers rarely cross them. Wayne Williams killed young black men and boys. Ted Bundy killed pretty white girls who looked like his ex-fiancée. Peter Sutcliffe, the English Yorkshire Ripper, killed prostitutes. Killers go for the same kind of victim over and again because the victim represents something specific to them.

Patrese ran down off the bridge and past the seaport. Gas tanks huddled together in dirty white clusters. A rusting red crane lowered its boom towards the deck of a moored freighter like a bird pecking for food.

MO, *modus operandi*, and signature. In the most basic terms, how and why a killer kills. MO comprises a crime's functional components: the time of day, the means of access, the weapons used, and so on. Signature reflects the killer's emotional and psychological drivers: specific patterns of mutilation, ways in which the body is posed, those kind of things. MOs can change over time as killers become more experienced or refine their techniques. Signatures never do.

In all four killings so far, the signatures were identical: amputation of the head and one arm, removal of the skin patches, and the tarot cards. But the MOs were very different.

Darrell Showalter and Chase Evans had been killed with clinical precision elsewhere and brought to the places their bodies had been found. Regina King and Dennis Barbero had suffered frenzied attacks at the spots where they'd died.

WELCOME TO LIGHTHOUSE POINT PARK, said the sign. TAKE NOTHING BUT PICTURES, LEAVE NOTHING BUT FOOTPRINTS. Soccer pitches, Little League diamonds, jogging paths. Patrese swiped a sleeve across his forehead to wipe away the sweat. He was breathing better now, slower and deeper.

The Bureau likes to divide serial killers into two categories: organized and disorganized. The organized killer is intelligent and plans his crimes methodically. He's socially adept and proficient at luring victims away from safe places, which means he can leave three crime scenes: where he meets his victim, where he kills them, and where he dumps the body. He has friends and lovers, sometimes even a wife and family. He follows his crimes in the media and takes pride in what he's done. He might like to go back to the crime scene or play games with the police. He tends to have a nice car and travels a lot, often with his work. He's the guy who helps his neighbors and runs the kids' Little Leagues; when he's caught, everyone's shocked and says he's the last person they suspected. But sometimes he's not caught. Since he's forever trying to improve his techniques, the longer he kills, the more difficult it is to find him.

Darrell Showalter and Chase Evans appeared to be the victims of an organized killer.

The disorganized serial killer is just the opposite. He's of below average intelligence and doesn't plan his crimes too much. He strikes on a whim, whenever the bloodlust takes him – hence the frenzy of his attacks and the carelessness to leave the murder weapon at the scene. He's often unemployed, a loner with few friends and no spouse or family. He has poor hygiene, drug or alcohol problems, a history of mental illness. He doesn't take much interest in the media coverage of his crimes. If he plays games, it's with the victims' families rather than the police; if he drives, it's a battered old sedan or pick-up. He doesn't go far from home. His inconsistency can make him hard to catch – How do you predict the movements of someone who doesn't know himself when he's next going to kill? – but when he *is* caught, people queue up to say they always knew he was a wrong 'un, and why the hell hadn't the police gotten to him quicker?

Regina King and Dennis Barbero appeared to be the victims of a disorganized killer.

Up ahead, Patrese could see the lighthouse that marked five miles. It was octagonal and made from whitened sandstone. No light at the top, even though the sun was setting. Must have been decommissioned. Most of them were nowadays.

Organized killer for Showalter and Evans. Disorganized killer for Regina and Barbero. Showalter and Evans had been white, and had come from the Cambridge area in Greater Boston. Regina and Barbero had been black New Yorkers. It could almost have been two separate investigations: Anderssen in Boston, Dufresne in New York.

Anderssen was white, like 'his' victim. Dufresne black, like his.

If Regina and Showalter had been killed in their home-towns, Patrese would never have had to come here, to New Haven.

New Haven was pretty much halfway between New York and Boston. Halfway. A midpoint. A meeting point. A rendezvous.

You need two people for a rendezvous. You also – solitaire aside – need two people to play cards.

Patrese sprinted the last few yards to the lighthouse and

sagged against it, spent. A runner going past the other way smiled sympathetically.

No, Patrese thought as he sucked in air and felt the endorphin flush on his face. I've got it all wrong. I'm not dealing with a serial killer. *A* serial killer. One.

I'm dealing with two.

25

Patrese didn't need the taxi to get back to town: he ran all the way without stopping, adrenalin outstripping the fatigue. When he got back to the hotel, he called Anderssen and Dufresne and asked them – told them – to get here within the next two hours. Then he called Kieseritsky and told her the same. Eight o'clock meet in the incident room, and all the apizza they could eat. Finally, he called Anna and asked her a few questions.

When Patrese arrived in the incident room at five to eight, the three detectives were already there. They'd introduced themselves and were swapping stories in the way detectives do the world over. Common theme – the stupidity of criminals. Cops liked nothing more than, say, robbers who left their wallets at the scene of the crime: the double whammy of an easy arrest and a good story in the bar after work.

This might be a good story, Patrese thought, but it sure as hell wasn't an easy catch.

He told them his theory. Two killers: a white one in the Boston area, a black one in New York. The white one was organized, the black one disorganized. They'd met in New Haven last weekend for the first kill. Maybe they'd never met before that, though they must have been in touch with each other to start with. How they'd gotten to know each other, let alone how they'd decided to start killing, Patrese had no idea.

If they were of different races, it was unlikely they were related. But they could have been friends, colleagues, lovers; something pretty close, in any event. In the rare cases Patrese knew of where killers were operating in tandem, their signatures tended to vary more than their MOs: signatures being behavior innate to the perpetrator's psyche, MOs being learned and malleable. But in this case, it seemed the other way round. It was as though the killers shared a psychosis, but not a way of executing it. And you don't divulge your deepest neuroses to another person without knowing and trusting them.

Whatever the killers' relationship, they seemed to be murdering in turn. The presence of the tarot cards no longer suggested merely symbolism or divination: it looked very much like a game of some sort too. Anna had told Patrese that most tarot games use the full 78-card pack, with the Fool card acting like a Joker. Although games are usually for four players, there is a version of French tarot that is for two players only. Whether or not the killers were following established game rules was another thing entirely, of course.

Either way, they surely had some means of communicating with each other. Back in the day, criminals had used the classified sections of newspapers to plant coded messages. Such a method nowadays seemed as remote and antiquated as the telegraph. There were plenty of ways two people could communicate without ever needing to leave a trace of their real names: e-mail accounts, Internet forums, pay-as-you-go mobiles. Losing yourself in the endless chatterings of the electronic ether was as hard as falling off a log.

Yes, the authorities have ways to punch through that

chatter. The FBI can mount surveillance operations and intercept communications, but only if they know who to watch. The NSA – the National Security Agency, for a long time so secretive that it had been nicknamed 'No Such Agency' – has supercomputers that can analyze improbably large amounts of data in improbably short fractions of time. Set some trigger words – 'tarot', perhaps, or 'behead' – and its banks of processors can race through billions of phone calls, e-mails and texts, plucking out any containing those words.

But there are two problems with this. First, the NSA isn't allowed to spy on US citizens while they're on US soil. This isn't in itself insurmountable. The US, along with the UK, Canada, Australia and New Zealand, is part of a network called Echelon, which eavesdrops on those same billions of phone calls, e-mails and texts across the world. When the NSA wants to spy on people it's not allowed to, it simply asks one of the other four signatories to Echelon to do it and pass the information over.

And that's where the second problem comes in. These are government operations, and as such are always overstretched. They'll pull out all the stops if you're a terrorist plotting on taking down an airliner out of JFK. But if you're a common-or-garden serial killer, forget it. Only four victims? You'd get that many in a road smash on the turnpike. Not a reasonable use of our time or resources. Sorry.

Here's what I suggest, Patrese said to Anderssen and Dufresne. You each treat your own investigation as an entity unto itself. Anderssen was looking for a serial killer who'd killed two people; Dufresne was also looking for a serial killer who'd killed two people. They just happened to be different serial killers. Every piece of information either detective got was to be duplicated to Patrese in New Haven. Patrese would pull it all together, look at the big picture, try to connect the dots, and any other management-speak bullshit bingo you could think of.

They all thought that was a good plan.

We need names, Anderssen said. Names? Nicknames for the killers, till we find them. Cops are like soldiers: they need to personalize the enemy. The Viet Cong had been 'Charlie', the First World War Germans 'Jerry'. This was no different.

Dufresne started humming a track and miming a piano. They all laughed, getting the reference instantly, and the nicknames were decided there and then.

Ebony and Ivory.

26

Tuesday, November 9th
New York, NY

'Only you do I let in here,' Kwasi said. 'Only you.'

Unzicker looked around in what appeared to be distaste. A Bleecker loft apartment, the kind of place that featured in trendy urban magazines, and right now it looked like a crack den: Babel towers of washing-up teetering in the sink, archipelagos of half-empty pizza boxes sprawling across the floor. Whatever state the apartment was in, however, was mild compared to that of its owner. Kwasi's hair was matted, his eyes looked like a shattered ketchup bottle, and his BO would have taken down a buffalo at ten paces.

Kwasi's defense of his title was due to start in two days' time, and there was still no guarantee that he'd play. The press attention would have been intense even in normal circumstances: but with the will-he-won't-he? saga going on, and with the clock ticking down, it was through the roof. There were similar media encampments outside the Waldorf-Astoria, where Nursultan was staying, and Madison Square Garden, where the match was due to take place.

Kwasi had been to see Nursultan on Saturday. His original list had detailed 180 demands. Nursultan had agreed to 179 of them. The only standout was what percentage of gate receipts Kwasi should get. But as Tartu had said, there weren't 180 demands: there was one demand in 180 parts. Take it or leave it. And if Nursultan wouldn't take it, Kwasi would leave. He wouldn't play, and he didn't care if he was portrayed as the bad guy: the one who walked away from the match of the century for nothing more than a bit of cash. Don't agree, won't play. Like a child: shan't, won't, hate you.

'Clean up,' Unzicker said softly. He picked up a couple of pizza boxes and, looking to clear some space to put them on, began to slide Kwasi's Red Sox and Yankees chess set along a table.

'Don't touch my set!' Kwasi barked.

Unzicker jumped back as though he feared Kwasi would bite him.

'I want this place cleaned, man, I'll do it myself,' Kwasi said. 'Now: if Nursultan didn't send you here, why did you come?'

Unzicker unzipped his computer bag, brought out a laptop and turned it on.

'You hear about the Harvard kid?' Kwasi said.

'No direct programming since last time,' Unzicker replied. 'Just played around with the hardware.' He clicked on one of the screen icons. A stylized graphic of a chess king with eyeglasses appeared. Below it was the word MISHA.

'White or black?' Unzicker asked.

'Don't care.'

Unzicker got Misha to select colors. It chose to play black.

Kwasi looked out of the window at the photographers below and called out his first move. Unzicker played it on screen. When Misha responded, he called that move back to Kwasi. They continued like this: Unzicker inputting and relaying, Kwasi playing without looking at the screen.

The first time Unzicker had seen Kwasi do this, he'd been speechless with admiration, as though Kwasi was some kind of sorcerer. Now, he didn't even notice. When you played chess like Kwasi did, the board itself was strictly for ornamental purposes. Kwasi carried thousands of games in his head; this was just one of many.

On move twenty, Kwasi turned round. 'You can stop it there,' he said.

'Why?' Unzicker looked at the position on the screen. 'Looks pretty even to me.'

'Misha and I played these exact moves on twenty-first February this year. I won that game. This is the point where I won it, when Misha played his bishop to c5 rather than b4. Now it's played the same move again, c5. Twenty moves' time, I'll have this game won.'

'You sure?'

Kwasi didn't even bother to answer.

'OK,' Unzicker said. 'Try something else. You play black this time . . .'

'No. I'm tired. Tommy, you gotta go now.'

'But . . .'

'But nothing.'

Unzicker slapped the back of his hand against the screen, a flash of annoyance that seemed at once out of place and deeply characteristic. 'We are *so* close. We get this right, we're going to be like Watson and Crick, Page and Brin, you know? We're going to be immortal. We're going to make history.'

'Tommy.' There was no smile in Kwasi's eyes. 'I already am. I already have.'

27

Wednesday, November 10th
Cambridge, MA

Twice a year, in November and January, the Massachusetts Institute of Technology experiences a striking phenomenon. When the path of the setting sun crosses the axis of MIT's Infinite Corridor, which runs more than quarter of a kilometer from the institute's main entrance and links five different buildings, the sun fills the windows and blazes light down the corridor's entire length. Inevitably, and with a nod to one of the world's most famous solar shrines, this phenomenon is known as MIThenge.

MIThenge only lasts a few minutes, and Unzicker was in position a quarter-hour beforehand. He'd become a minor fixture of the occasion himself, dressing up in solar-themed costumes. His first year, he'd come as the Egyptian sun god Ra, with a falcon mask and a golden disk on his head. Last year, he'd turned up as the Hindu deity Surya, hair and arms painted gold and sitting yogi-like in a cardboard chariot pulled by a cardboard seven-headed horse.

At MIT, such exhibitionism was practically encouraged:

149

the wackier the students, the more likely it was thought that they'd produce works of genius. The tight asses at Harvard, where Unzicker had been an undergraduate, would have sneered.

This time round, Unzicker came as tarot card XIX: The Sun.

The crowd began to gather, pressing themselves to the sides of the corridor to allow others the best view possible. Someone enterprising was selling special eyeglasses – smoked glass, usually used to observe eclipses – for five bucks a pair, cajoling the reluctant with the sales pitch 'Cheaper than being blind for the rest of your life'.

As the sun approached, the outer rays started to filter through the window, dappling on the corridor's reflective floor. Unzicker tapped the design on his costume and began to speak. 'An infant rides a white horse under the sun. The child of life holds a red flag, representing the blood of renewal.' A couple of people tried to shush him, but they in turn were shushed by others, veterans of the occasion: if Unzicker wanted to behave like a freak, let him. 'All the while a smiling sun shines down on the child. The sun represents accomplishment. See too the sunflowers behind.'

There was a gasp as a corner of the sun proper appeared in the window. Light snaked down the corridor, bathing walls and ceiling in hues of flaming orange.

'"Who are you?" you ask the child. The child smiles at you and seems to shine. And then he grows brighter and brighter until he turns into pure sunlight. "I'm you," he says. "I'm you." As his words fill you with warmth and energy, you realize that you've just met your own inner light. Your mind's illuminated, your soul light and bright as a sunbeam.'

The sun filled the window now, nothing but the sun, no

sky visible around it. Every part of the corridor, all the way along and all the way around, was ablaze with light, and the light thickened and darkened until it was the red of blood.

28

New York, NY

It was long gone eleven when Howard Lewis clocked off from his shift in the Twenty-Sixth Precinct. He felt as though he'd spent pretty much an entire week at Columbia University, first asking every student he could find whether they had any information about Dennis Barbero's murder, and then interviewing those kids whose therapists had reported them for violent propensities.

Listening to some of the therapy kids talk, Lewis had thought it surprising not that there were so many high school and college shootings, but that there were so few. These kids might be brainy as all hell, but boy were they screwed up. Perhaps that was the price of being so intelligent. Lewis was no idiot, but he knew he wasn't Einstein either. He'd made sergeant, and knew that was probably the top of the ladder for him. He had a wife and two kids, and he thought himself a good father and husband. He'd never cheated on his wife, never raised his fists to her or the kids. He'd raised his fists to criminals, sure – that was the only way to knock sense into some of the punks who came through Central Booking – but never to good people.

He'd never been to a therapist, never taken anti-depressants or any of that shit. Howard Lewis had yet to come across a problem that couldn't be solved by chewing it over with his buddies over a beer. People complicated life unnecessarily, he thought. It was very simple. Get up, work hard, don't be a dick. Repeat.

He changed back into civvies, walked to the subway and caught the last C-train going north. The C had a dire reputation for reliability – the line's stock was the oldest on the entire system – but this particular train got Lewis to his stop at 155th Street, and that was all he cared about.

Located in the Sugar Hill district, 155th Street is part of Harlem. A lot of people – more precisely, a lot of white people – think of Harlem as one big slum, but that's not the case. In the thirties and forties, Sugar Hill had got its name because it offered the sweet life: big old houses up on the bluff, famous residents like Ralph Ellison and Paul Robeson. By the seventies and eighties, it had become Crack Central. Now it was halfway between the two: you could still find pushers on street corners, but some of those big old houses were going for north of two million bucks.

Howard Lewis didn't live in one of those houses, of course: not on a cop's salary. He had a three-bedroom, split-level maisonette on 152nd, and that did him just fine. He was a black man raising a black family in Harlem, and he wouldn't have changed it for the world. His maisonette was less than a block from the Thirtieth Precinct's station. Maybe one day he'd get round to putting in a transfer request, and have the shortest commute of any cop in the NYPD.

To get home, he used as a shortcut an alley that ran from 153rd through to 152nd. Perhaps it wasn't that sensible to walk down a secluded alley late at night – not in any big city, let alone Harlem – but heck, he was a police officer. He

153

was trained, he had a gun. Any punk tried to rob him, they'd soon be wishing they hadn't.

He reckoned the shortcut saved him a couple of minutes each time.

Tonight, it cost him his life.

29

A garbage collector found Lewis' body at dawn. There was no problem identifying it: the wallet with Lewis' police badge and ID card was still clipped to his belt. Dufresne was on site a half-hour later, and Patrese an hour after that. Dufresne was still shaking when Patrese got there, and it wasn't the cold or the gruesome sight of a man without his head.

It was anger.

Ebony had just graduated from serial killer to cop killer, and police departments the world over reserve a special level of hell for anyone who kills one of their own. Patrese put his hand on Dufresne's shoulder. Dufresne nodded, the muscles in his jaw bunching under the skin like walnuts. Patrese didn't say anything. He didn't have to.

Dufresne handed him a transparent evidence bag. A tarot card with a prince in armor sitting in a chariot pulled by two sphinxes, one black and one white. The Chariot.

The Chariot was one of the seven cards that Anna had picked out for him, Patrese remembered. It symbolized a battle that could be won with the requisite willpower:

155

alternatively, it marked the ruthless desire to win at any cost. The charioteer succeeded by attacking from the side: it was that kind of lateral thinking, letting his brain go blank while he ran down to the lighthouse in New Haven, that had given Patrese the twin killer theory to start with.

He'd seen in the library at Yale how the Chariot card applied to him: and now it was the marker of a dead cop. Coincidence? A symbol that worked for law enforcement in general? Something against Patrese personally? Or another reason entirely? Some weird Ivy League intellectual game-playing shit? Lewis had been part of the team investigating Dennis Barbero's murder at Columbia, and the task force was still interviewing those Ivy League students flagged as potentially violent. No joy on that front yet.

'He was a good man,' Dufresne said. 'I know folks always say that about people when they're dead, but he was. Not a saint. None of us are. But a good man.'

The leather wallet with Lewis' police badge and ID card was in another evidence bag. Patrese looked at it through the plastic. The badge was a gold shield with an eagle and Lewis' number. The ID card had a serious-looking photo of him above his name: HOWARD LEWIS, SERGEANT, 26TH PRECINCT.

Howard Lewis. The name rang a bell. Where had Patrese heard it before? It floated on the edge of his memory like Tantalus' grapes, right there yet out of reach. He relaxed, imagined himself crouching down and then leaping for the answer . . .

Got it. 'He was the one who arrested Regina King at the Iraq demo, wasn't he?'

Dufresne looked at Patrese in surprise, realization dawning. 'Yeah. Yeah, he was.'

'And she brought a case against him . . .'

'. . . which was all bullshit, and which we settled in the end just to be done with it.'

'Really?'

'Really what?'

'Was it really bullshit?'

'Yes.'

'Did she have a case?'

'Depends whether you ask a lawyer or whether you ask someone with horse sense.'

'Five victims. First, Kwasi's mom. Now, the guy she sued.'

'Looks like we got ourselves a prime suspect.'

'Who? Kwasi?'

'Who else?'

'No.'

'Why not?'

'He didn't kill his mom.'

'Why not?'

'He was in New York that weekend.'

'Says who?'

'Says he.'

'Anyone else?'

'No, but . . . he and his mom were, you know.' Patrese wrapped his middle and index fingers round each other. 'Like that.'

'Franco, have you lost your mind? Those are exactly the kind of relationships where one party *does* kill the other!'

'Sometimes. But . . . I told him his mom was dead. I stayed with him that evening. Kid's halfway autistic. No way could he be that good an actor, to have played me like that. No way. So he can't have done it. And, and, it was because I stayed with him, because he liked me, that he came to help us out when things were getting hairy at Columbia that day.'

'Help us out? Or insert himself into the investigation, the way some killers do?'

'He's got no connection with Dennis Barbero.'

Dufresne shrugged. 'Maybe not. But he's got a hell of a connection to the other two.'

Patrese looked at his watch. 'His world title match is due to start in a couple of hours. If you think he's been preparing by going round killing people . . . no. Far more likely that someone's trying to get to him.'

'Why? Why would they want to do that?'

'Who knows? To stop him playing. Lot of competing interests in something like this.'

'Stop him playing? Everybody *wants* him to play, surely?'

'Maybe that's what we're supposed to think.'

'Far as I can make out, the only person who's gonna stop him playing is Kwasi himself. He's the one making all these conditions, no?'

'I'll go and see him.'

'I'll come with you.'

'No.'

'No?'

'No.'

'Why not?'

'Because he trusts me, that's why not. Listen, Bobby, I know this is going to sound weird, but he's not like others. He doesn't see the world the way we do.'

'All the more reason to bring him down the station and question his ass.'

'Two hours before he goes on stage at Madison?'

'I couldn't give a damn if it's two minutes before.'

'We'll bring down the shitstorm to end all shitstorms if we do. Imagine the press. Imagine the lawsuits. Kwasi doesn't show up, that's his lookout. We stop him from going there, we're the ones who get blamed.'

'If we have a case, we have a case. Fuck everything else.'

'No. Listen. He doesn't need arresting. If anything, he needs protecting.'

'Protecting?'

'Sure. His mom's dead, so's the dude she sued. Why shouldn't Kwasi be in line?'

'Why *should* he?'

'If we knew why these killings were taking place, I could give you an answer.'

'Franco, you're in charge, it's your case. You think you're better off going in there alone, because he trusts you and only you, and you and he have some big mystical connection, then sure. You're worried about screwing him up before a match – even assuming he wants to play the damn thing, which don't seem to me the case – I see that too. But you ask me, you're being an asshole.'

30

Patrese went to Bleecker Street alone. Dufresne went back to his precinct house.

The press pack outside Kwasi's condo block looked to be almost a hundred strong. As he'd done on previous visits, Patrese ignored them and their catcalls. The doorman, Sherwood, opened the main door, and Patrese went up to Kwasi's apartment.

'You gonna play?' Patrese asked.

'You come here to ask me that?'

'Not exactly. But what I'm about to tell you might alter your decision.'

'I'm going to play if he agrees to my terms.'

A matter of hours before the biggest chess match in almost half a century, and Kwasi and Nursultan were still playing brinkmanship? Patrese didn't know whether to be impressed or appalled. This wasn't chess, he thought: it was some gigantic game of poker, each side daring the other one to call his bluff first.

'And if he doesn't?'

'Then I won't play.'

'I read that if you don't turn up for the first game, you forfeit. Is that right?'

'Sure. He starts my clock, I'm not there after an hour, I forfeit that game.'

'But not the match?'

'Only the game.'

'You'll lose the first game without playing just to make a point?'

'He has my conditions. He has a car waiting outside for me. I even heard he's got the city to keep all the traffic lights from here to Madison Square Garden on green so we can get there fast. All he has to do is say the word.'

Well, Patrese thought, Kwasi was certainly more talkative than when they'd first met.

'What is it you've got to tell me?' Kwasi added.

'We found a body this morning. Howard Lewis.'

'The one who beat up my mom?'

'The one your mother sued, yes.'

'The one who beat up my mom. How did he die?'

'Same way as your mom.'

Kwasi ran a hand through his dreads. 'Jeez, Franco. What the fuck is happening?'

'That's what we're trying to find out.'

'I can't . . . I don't . . . You think they're connected, right?'

'They *are* connected. Kwasi, I've got to ask: where were you last night?'

'Here.'

'That's what you said last time, when your mom was killed.'

'I live alone. I don't have friends. I don't have convenient alibis every time you come round asking things. You believe me or you don't. I was here, asleep, 'cos if Nursultan stops being a jerkoff in the next hour or so, I have to go and play

161

a world championship match, and to do that I need all the rest I can get.'

'I want to take you into protective custody.'

'What?'

'Your mom was killed. That might have been to unsettle you.'

'What are you talking about?'

'I don't really know. But now Howard Lewis is dead too. It might be a coincidence, but cops don't believe in coincidences too much.'

'And Barbero? Showalter? Evans?'

'You know their names.'

'I know thousands of chess games, move by move. I knew the address and phone number of the place my mom was supposed to be staying the weekend she got killed. I remember things, Franco. So yes, I know their names. Wouldn't you, if they'd all been killed by the same person who murdered your mom?'

Patrese held up his hands: fair point. 'You have any connections to those guys?'

'None. I never heard of any of them till they turned up dead.'

Kwasi's cell rang. He picked up. Patrese could hear Nursultan's tinny, agitated voice at the other end. Kwasi listened impassively. 'You agree?' he said at last. 'No? Then I got nothing more to say.' He ended the call and turned back to Patrese. 'Man rings me every half-hour. Wants me to break first. Not gonna happen.'

Another ring tone. 'Rings you every half-minute, more like,' Patrese said.

'That's your cell, man. Not mine.'

Patrese reached in his pocket and brought out his phone. 'So it is.' He looked at the screen: DUFRESNE.

'What's up, Bobby?'

162

'Where are you?'

'With Kwasi.'

'Go somewhere he can't hear you.'

'What?'

'Go somewhere he can't hear you. Just do it.'

'Er . . . sure.' Patrese gestured at Kwasi that he was going on to the roof terrace. Kwasi made a mime: sure.

Patrese stepped outside. 'OK,' he said. 'I'm on the terrace. What's up?'

'You gotta get out of there.'

'What?'

'You gotta get out of there. I just got a call from forensics. They found some DNA on Dennis Barbero's body: strand of hair or something. Partial match with Regina King.'

'So? We already know the same guy killed them both. Hairs and fibers get transferred from person to person the whole time.'

'That's what I told them. And they said that wasn't what partial match meant, not in this context. It means they found DNA which partially matches Regina, but which partially doesn't.'

'As in a relative?'

'As in a son.'

A dark shadow moving fast and furious in the corner of Patrese's vision. With instinct faster than thought, he threw up his free arm, his left, to protect himself; which was why the marble chessboard Kwasi was wielding like a baseball bat only broke Patrese's wrist rather than fracturing his skull.

Deep pain, such as that caused by a broken bone, often takes a few seconds to kick in. Patrese knew this, and he used it. He dropped his phone and went for his gun. Chessboard clattering on the floor, Kwasi darted back inside the apartment. Patrese followed.

Glimpse of a leg disappearing round a corner, and then a

gust of wind. Open window. Fire escape. The first shockwave of pain rippled up Patrese's arm, sharp enough to make him catch his breath. One second. Two. No more. Grit your teeth. Keep moving.

He ran to the window and looked down. Kwasi was a story below and moving fast, dreadlocks bouncing as he ran across the landing and on to the next level. Patrese climbed out of the window and began to follow. Wrought-iron staircase, beautifully crafted: a goddamn work of art for something so functional. Typical New York. Patrese couldn't grip the banister with his left hand, needed his right free for the gun. Felt like he was about to fall the whole time. Couldn't slow down without losing sight of Kwasi.

The fire escape ended up in a courtyard round the back of the condo block. Kwasi jumped the last six feet and headed towards an iron gate. Patrese was a flight above him. Lost his footing halfway down. Part jumped, part fell the same last six feet. Landed heavily, rolled hard to avoid smacking his broken wrist.

Pushed himself upright again, weight through that very wrist for a split second before he realized. A welter of agony. Kwasi through the gate and gone. Follow. Move. Should have listened to Dufresne first time round. Stupid Franco, thinking he knew best. He'd be more sensible next time.

The gate was still swinging where Kwasi had passed through. Patrese followed, looking left and right. A passageway that forked left and right. Big commercial dumpsters one side; the back of a restaurant. A bodyshop the other side, cars with their hoods up. A couple of mechanics looked at Patrese with surprise.

He thought fast. They wouldn't have been surprised to see him if they'd just seen Kwasi run past, would they? So Kwasi must have gone the other way, past the dumpsters. Patrese headed that way. He felt lopsided, no real way of keeping balance with one arm hanging useless by his side and the other trying to keep a gun aimed halfway straight.

The passageway widened beyond the dumpsters: fifty yards straight, no doors Patrese could see on either side, and no sign of Kwasi, which meant either that a man who spent most of his life sitting down could run like a cheetah when he had to, or that . . .

. . . and the thought – *he's behind the dumpsters* – hit Patrese at the same time as Kwasi did. A roundhouse in the solar plexus followed by a jab to the face. Patrese sank to his knees as though someone had cut his strings. A kick jarred his fingers, making him drop the gun; and before he could even start reaching for it, Kwasi had picked it up and was aiming it straight between Patrese's eyes.

No one around. Dumbass mechanics must have gone back to their repairs. This was New York. People come running past looking wild-eyed the whole time. Nothing doing. Nothing to see. Move along now.

Patrese was aware that he was kneeling in front of Kwasi. He tried to stand up. Kwasi put a foot on his chest and pushed him back down on to his backside. Better for Patrese's pride at least, if not for his immediate prospects of survival. The barrel never wavered. Shot by his own gun. Not exactly a heroic end. Not one for the Bureau's wall of honor.

He wouldn't beg. It wouldn't do him any good anyway. He'd been wrong about everything. He'd fallen for Kwasi's little-boy-lost act. He'd seen exactly what he'd wanted to see. He'd never thought, not for a minute, that someone who destroyed his opponents on a little board of sixty-four wooden squares would be every bit as merciless in real life. Killer instinct, that's what they said about Kwasi: he had the killer instinct, the unerring ability to go for his opponent's jugular given half a chance. Killer instinct.

165

At another time and in another place, Patrese might have laughed.

'Who's white?' he said.

Kwasi looked at him with eyes of serene emptiness.

'Who's white?' Patrese said again. 'Who's Ivory? Who's in Boston? Who are you playing against?'

The pistol whip came so fast that Patrese hardly even saw it. Unlike his wrist, this one *did* hurt instantly. He toppled over. The ground was cold against his cheek. He pressed his good hand to the wound.

Kwasi squatted down beside him. Two cards in his hand, their backs facing Patrese.

'This is what I am,' Kwasi said, turning the first one round. 'I'm the Magician. Watch me vanish.'

Another pistol whip, this time a backhand, the other way across Patrese's face. As Patrese rolled on the concrete, trying to shake the pain out of himself, he heard the fading sound of running feet. By the time he was sitting up again, Kwasi had gone.

Kwasi had left the other tarot card face down on the ground. Patrese knew what it would be even before he turned it over.

Card zero. The Fool.

PART TWO

Middlegame

'Play the middlegame like a magician.'

Rudolf Spielmann

31

It's not hard to carve a human bone.

In this case, the humerus, the bone of the upper arm. The rest of the arm you can get rid of, though you've gotta be careful where you do this. Body parts got a nasty habit of turnin' up and gettin' in the hands of the cops if you don't make damn sure of your disposal methods.

You cut away the skin, muscle and tissue till you got yourself just the bone. There's still goin' to be lots of blood and goo on it, of course, so you put it in a large cookin' pot – same one you use to shrink the heads, if you like – and cover it in hot water. Very hot, very hot indeed, but not, repeat not, boilin'. Anyone say you gotta boil the bone, they're a fool, 'cos that's horseshit. Boilin' bones makes 'em hard and brittle, and when they're hard and brittle, that's when they break. Never boil.

The hot water'll help you get the blood and goo off. You also gotta scrape out all the marrow that's inside the bone. Then you tip away the water and fill it back up again, this time with detergent and Nappy-San: three times the amount of each you'd use normally. Leave the bone in there for a coupla days, soakin'. Take it out after that, it'll be clean as a whistle.

Now the cuttin'. Most of the humerus is pretty much a cylinder, straight up and down, but there are bits at the top and bottom, all with fancy medical names: greater tuberosity, lesser tuberosity, lateral epicondyle, medial epicondyle, trochlea, capitulum. Don't matter what they're called, you gotta get rid of them. All you want is the straight bit.

So you take a fretsaw, blade probably 18 tpi – that's teeth per inch, you get to know these things after a while – and you saw right through the damn thing. You might want to wear a mask and goggles while doin' this: it kicks up some bone dust, and that shit ain't so good to breathe. When you've cut off both ends of the humerus, all the fancy-named knobbly bits, you should be left with something around a foot long.

You put the bone in a vice. You gotta be careful here, as the last thing you want is to damage it. So you put leather pads on the jaws of the vice, and you pack a leather bag filled with rice around the bone. Only now can you tighten the vice.

You take your files and your gravers. Only use the ones made by Vallorbe. They're a Swiss company, and they're expensive, but in this game you get what you pay for. You use cheap tools, your work will look cheap.

You file away all the rough edges and protuberances on the bone, and there are plenty of those. With the gravers – they're like little chisels – you can make all the patterns you want in the bone. Nice and slowly does it. You don't want to rush. You don't need to rush. Like I told you before, no one's going nowhere.

When you've finished your carvin', you're nearly done. Now you just gotta sandpaper it all down to get it as smooth as possible. Sandpaper comes in several grades, and you want to use four or five of them in turn, getting finer each time. Start with 240 grit, very fine, and then work your way through finer and finer ones: extra fine 400, super fine 600, and finally ultra fine 800. By the time you've gone through that lot, the bone will feel smooth as glass.

Like I said, not hard. Not hard at all.

32

If you're going to run from the law, New York City must be one of the best places in which to do it. Hiding out in a heavily populated urban environment is far easier than doing so in an isolated rural area. People in cities don't know their neighbors, don't notice the unusual, don't like to get involved in anyone's business but their own. There are endless cheap hotels that take cash and ask no questions: homeless people have an underworld and subculture all their own, and don't talk to the authorities in a month of Sundays. If you do want to leave the city, that's the easiest thing in the world. Airports are easily monitored, and all flights require ID checks and passenger lists: but an endless traffic of cars and trains flows like blood through arterial bridges and venous tunnels.

All this was to Kwasi's advantage, Patrese thought. Kwasi alone knew where he was going and how he intended to get there. Unlike most criminals, who can hardly find their own assholes without a mirror, Kwasi was super-smart, not just to have killed three people the way he had, but to have had Patrese in his apartment more than once and to have come

171

to 'help out' at Columbia. He'd murdered his mother, the person to whom he'd been closest in the whole world, and had acted all shocked and surprised when Patrese had arrived to tell him of her death a few hours later. The man could pick daisies in a minefield and never miss a beat.

The cops who found Patrese wanted to take him to hospital straight away. No, he said, he had too much to do. Dufresne arrived, having hauled ass all the way from Morningside Heights, and told Patrese the same thing: go to hospital. You didn't listen to me last time, Dufresne added, and look what happened.

The manhunt for Kwasi was already in motion: Dufresne had seen to that. An APB of Kwasi's name and description had gone to every one of the NYPD's seventy-six precincts, plus the local offices of the Bureau, the ATF, the DEA, the US Marshals, and so on. Bridges, tunnels, airports and railway stations were all being watched.

So there was no reason for Patrese to keep being ornery. A couple of hours in ER, some industrial-strength painkillers, and he would be back on the case. It was either that or him keeling over in half an hour's time when the shock kicked in. Dufresne would see him back at Kwasi's apartment. No ifs, no buts, no arguing.

Kwasi had spent a long time preparing for this moment. Life, like chess, was a matter of planning. He didn't simply show up at the board and play whichever move came into his head; he had strategies, schemes. So too here. He wasn't making this up as he went along. It had all been in place way beforehand.

First things first: nothing could be traceable to him. He had a spare truck and a second home, both registered to a company based in Gibraltar. His mom had done night school in accountancy, and the moment he'd started earning serious money, she'd set up an offshore company. He'd won the Gibraltar chess tournament three years in a row, he'd liked the place, and it was a less obvious location for going offshore than the Caribbean.

He kept the truck in the parking lot at Pier 40, right on the Hudson. It was self-park, so he didn't have to get valets involved; he paid monthly rent in advance, so he didn't have to worry about being chased for payment; and the lot had a capacity of 3500 vehicles, which greatly reduced the chances of his truck being noticed.

It was seven blocks from the dumpsters where he'd left Patrese to the Pier 40 parking lot. Kwasi walked purposefully but unhurriedly, hood pulled up to hide his dreads. He'd have to get rid of them now: they were too obvious, too much of a trademark. But that worked both ways. Because people so associated him with them, he'd be harder to recognize without them. Cut his hair, grow a beard, put on eyeglasses and puff out his cheeks with cotton wool pads: to the casual observer, he'd seem a totally different person. Of course, he had extra levels of disguise too, but he didn't want to use those except when necessary. A disguise was only a disguise when no one knew it was a disguise.

No one noticed Kwasi on his way to Pier 40, let alone stopped him or tried to talk to him. A couple of police cruisers with sirens raced past, but they could have been going anywhere. This was New York: emergency calls were as unremarkable as traffic lights.

He got to the parking lot, found his truck, put his ticket into the exit barrier, and turned on to West Street, heading north. The river rolled lazily away to his left. He felt no panic, no fear: just the cold thrill of assessing a position with gimlet eyes, and there was no one in the world better at that.

Catch me if you can, he thought.

* * *

173

The cops put on the sirens and took Patrese to Bellevue, where he flashed his badge, jumped the queue, and got seen to instantly. An X-ray told him what he already knew, that his wrist was broken. The doctor gave him a local anesthetic, manipulated the bones back into place, and put a cast on his arm. A nurse iodine-swabbed the cuts on his face where Kwasi had pistol-whipped him and put plasters across them.

Dufresne had said a couple of hours: the whole thing had taken forty-five minutes. You want good medical service, Patrese thought, you need one of two things: money, or a badge. On the way out, one of the scores of people sitting in the waiting room started mouthing off at Patrese for jumping the queue. Patrese gave him the finger with his good hand, and glanced at the TV set high on the wall, out of range of drunks or junkies. BREAKING NEWS: POLICE SAY WORLD CHESS CHAMPION KWASI KING IS MURDER SUSPECT, FUGITIVE FROM LAW.

Chess' Tiger Woods was now its O.J. Simpson.

The mini-forest of reporters outside Kwasi's apartment was growing minute by minute, blocking roads, crowding sidewalks, broadcasting breathlessly to a nation agog. Nothing else was running on the news channels. This was no longer simply a story: this was an *event*. Uniforms cleared a path for Patrese when he got there.

In the apartment itself, Dufresne was arguing with one of the uniforms. The uniform was pointing out that this was the Sixth Precinct and that Dufresne was about a hundred blocks out of his jurisdiction. Patrese stepped in. Sixth Precinct or Twenty-Sixth, he said, it didn't matter. This was a Bureau case, end of story. He, Franco Patrese, was in charge, and he wanted Detective Dufresne to head up the New York end of a federal investigation. If the man from the Sixth Precinct wanted to help, he could go get some coffee and donuts.

The man from the Sixth Precinct turned on his heel and left. Patrese doubted whether either coffee or donuts were high on his immediate agenda.

Patrese turned to Dufresne. 'Sorry.'

'Huh? Sorry? *I* should be thanking *you*, sorting out that jobsworth asshole. What are you sorry for?'

'For not listening to you before. About Kwasi.'

'Hey, we all make mistakes. Ask my wife. You know Kerouac wrote *On the Road* on one long sheet of paper? My wife's got a sheet twice as long, filled with all my failings.'

Patrese laughed, winced at a jag of pain that had snuck past the pills, and gestured round the apartment. 'What have you found?'

'No heads or arms or skin, if that's what you mean. But these; these are interesting.' He tapped a pile of books on a table. 'Got these from one of the bedrooms.' Patrese remembered the rows of bookshelves in Kwasi's room. 'Had a team of five guys skim through every book there, see if they could find anything. Look.'

Colored Post-it notes peeked from various pages. Patrese picked up the first book. *Game and Playe of the Chesse*, by William Caxton. It was a modern printing – Medieval Institute Publications, Kalamazoo, MI, and beautifully bound in dark red leather – but the copyright page informed him that the book itself had been written in 1474, and illustrated with woodcuts from that time.

The first woodcut was of an execution.

A king had just been beheaded. His head, crown on top and eyes closed, lay on the ground next to a chopping block. The executioner was cutting one of the king's legs with an axe, and four vultures flew around the scene, each with some part of the king's dismembered body in their beaks.

Decapitation. Dismemberment. Patrese raised his eyebrows. Dufresne nodded.

The text itself was in medieval English, which was hard to read. Fortunately for Patrese, some learned professor or other had written an introduction that explained what the book was about. *Game and Playe of the Chesse* was a *speculum regis*, a mirror for a prince: a political instruction manual with chess as an allegory for a community where each citizen contributed to the common good according to their station.

In life as in chess, the king and queen stood for themselves. The king was the most important piece, and had to be protected at all costs. The queen was the most powerful piece, both representing and protecting the king. Next, flanking king and queen, came the bishops, representatives of organized religion. Then the knights, wealthy and educated, with the freedom to jump around denied any other piece. On the outside were the rooks, the walls of the medieval castle, representing those who protected the community – soldiers, usually. Finally came the pawns, divided by Caxton into eight walks of life: laborers and workmen; smiths; scriveners, drapers and clothmakers; merchants, changers; physicians, spicers and apothecaries; taverners, hostellers and victuallers; toll gatherers and town keepers; dice players, ribaulders, messengers and couriers.

Patrese ran through the victims in his head.

Regina King. Tarot card: Empress. Empress was another word for queen. Regina was Latin for queen. She'd been the most important woman in Kwasi's life.

Darrell Showalter. Hierophant. Bishop. He'd been a monk teacher.

Dennis Barbero and Chase Evans. Knights. Educated, wealthy in future life if they wanted to be: that was Ivy League for you.

Howard Lewis. Chariot. Chariot?

As though reading his mind, Dufresne opened another

book and handed it to Patrese. It was a glossary of chess, and under the entry 'rook', it said: 'Often (though incorrectly) known as a castle, the word 'rook' comes from the Persian *rukh*, chariot.'

Howard Lewis. Chariot. Policeman. Protector. Enforcer.

'He's playing a chess game,' Patrese said. 'We said "Ebony" and "Ivory", didn't we? Kwasi's playing black. He's Ebony. He's Black.'

'Looks that way,' Dufresne said. 'But some weird-ass chess game. Are they following normal rules? They playing out some sort of game already famous? There must be classic chess games, no? The same way there are classic football and baseball games?'

'I guess. But what about the body parts he takes?' Patrese pointed to the Caxton woodcut of the executed king. 'Because of this? But that's only the king, not the others.'

Dufresne shrugged. 'We don't know. But we did find a couple of variations on the same tale about the history of chess. Genius in ancient India or wherever invents the game. The emperor's so enthralled with it, he says to the inventor, I'll give you anything you want. Sure, the inventor says. I'd like a grain of rice on the first square of the chessboard, two grains on the second, four on the third, eight on the fourth, so on and so on, doubling each time. That all? says the emperor. That's all, says the inventor. So the kingdom's treasurer starts counting out the rice, and soon realizes that, by the time they get to 64 squares with it doubling each time, they'll need more rice than there is in the whole world. Furious at being tricked like this, the emperor cuts off the inventor's head.'

'Moral of the story: no one likes a smart ass.'

Dufresne laughed. 'Ain't that the truth.'

'Even if that's something to do with it . . .'

'. . . it still doesn't explain the arms and the skin. I know, I know.'

'And it still doesn't tell us who he's playing against. Who's White?'

Patrese went into the living room. All Kwasi's chess sets were gone: packed up and taken away for evidence, no doubt. Patrese remembered that one of them had featured the Red Sox and the Yankees: Boston against New York, perhaps the fiercest rivalry in all American sport. If you were going to choose two cities as opposing sides in a game, it would probably be those two, a competitiveness that went back centuries.

In the nineteenth century, Boston had been a powerhouse in every way: cultural and artistic as it was nearer Europe, educational through its elite schools, economic because of its manufacturing hubs. New York had then been the upstart: dirty, dangerous, crowded, edgy. You'd have gone for a beer with New York, but you'd have wanted Boston dating your daughter. Since then, of course, New York had taken over as the epicenter of national and international capitalism; but the rivalry remained. Was this the latest, weirdest arena in which it was being played out?

A crime-scene officer was tapping away with latex gloved fingers at one of Kwasi's computers.

'Found anything?' Patrese asked.

'Just got it now. Took a while to break the password.' The CSO swiveled the screen round so Patrese could see: a list of e-mails, most recent at the top. Patrese scanned down quickly, looking to see which names appeared the most often.

He counted four or five messages from **Unzicker, Thomas**.

'Open that one,' Patrese said, pointing to Unzicker's latest message. It had been sent on Wednesday, 10th November at 23:12. Last night.

Hey KK. Good to see you yesterday. I know you're busy and everything, but we really need to talk. Think I might have found a way to make Misha work. Ring me when you can. T. PS Awesome MIThenge. You should come see it sometime. Next one's in Jan.

There was an automatic signature below the message. Thomas Unzicker, MIT CSAIL (Computer Science & Artificial Intelligence Laboratory), The Stata Center, Building 32, 32 Vassar Street, Cambridge, MA 02139, USA.

Cambridge, Patrese thought.

Darrell Showalter and Chase Evans had both been killed in Cambridge.

He dialed Anderssen. 'Max? Franco Patrese. Got someone I think we should visit.'

There were cops at the toll booths on the George Washington Bridge; looking for him, Kwasi thought, if the radio reports were anything to go by. He hadn't intended to go across to New Jersey anyway, but seeing the cops made his mind up for sure.

He swung right, heading for the Alexander Hamilton Bridge and the Cross Bronx Expressway. There were no tolls in that direction, least none that he could think of, which meant he was just another driver going about his daily business. Sure, the cops could pick his truck out at random and stop him, but as long as he stuck to the speed limit and didn't do anything dumb, the chances of that were minimal. They wouldn't be looking for this truck, they wouldn't have time to see him clearly as he went past, and they didn't have the manpower to stop every black man on every road out of the city.

Patrese and his men would be all over the Bleecker Street condo. Too bad. All Kwasi's stuff was there, but none of what they were looking for. They'd take all his lovely chess sets, all his books, everything he'd spent years accumulating, but that didn't matter. He carried the memories of them all crystal clear in his head. The cops couldn't touch anything inside there, nor anything inside the place he was going to.

That place was where he was heading now: his second home, his fortress, turned by necessity into full-time residence. It wouldn't take him too long to get there, but he thought it best to arrive under the cover of darkness. A fortress wouldn't be a fortress very long if anyone saw him entering or leaving.

So he'd have to park up a few hours until the light had gone. Not at a service station; he couldn't risk being seen. He'd pull off the interstate once he was well out of town and head down towards the sea. This time of year, way out of season, there'd be no one around. He could stop somewhere secluded, grab a few hours' sleep, and then complete his journey after dark.

He imagined the FBI, NYPD and all those other goons as a pack of hounds, barking furiously as they chased their own tails. He was the fox running before them, the quarry. And the fox was cunning. Too cunning for them. Way too cunning.

33

There were two men in Unzicker's office when Patrese and Anderssen walked in; Unzicker, whom they'd expected to be there, and Nursultan, whom they definitely hadn't.

'What are you doing here?' Patrese asked Nursultan.

'Maybe I ask you same.'

'I'll bet your answer's more interesting than mine.'

'Maybe.'

'All right. I'm here because Kwasi King, who half killed me this morning' – he held up the arm with the cast on it – 'is now on the run, suspected of three murders. We found e-mails from Mr Unzicker on his computer. I'll come to that in a second. But what really interests me is this. You, Mr Nursultan, were at Madison Square Garden a few hours ago. The biggest star in your firmament is now making like O.J. Your championship match has gone down the can. Half the reporters in New York City must want to talk to you. I bet your sponsors sure do. You could spend your next forty-eight hours locked away in crisis meetings. And what do you do? You come up to MIT,

181

which takes time, even if you *do* have a private jet, and you see a postgraduate student. Of all the things in the world you could be doing, this must be the most important to you. And if it's the most important to you, I reckon it's going to be pretty important to me.'

Nursultan regarded him levelly for a moment. 'We work together. Unzicker and me.'

'Work on what?'

'Project.'

Patrese thought back to Unzicker's e-mail, and took an educated guess. 'Misha?'

He could almost hear Nursultan's calculations: to lie, or not to lie? 'Yes. Misha.'

'And Misha is what?'

'Misha nothing to do with you.'

'Misha is something to do with Kwasi King, yes?'

'Yes.'

'Then it's something to do with me. What is it?'

'Can't say.'

'Can't, or won't?'

'Very sensitive. Commercial. Very commercial sensitive.'

'If I was any good at using things that were commercially sensitive, I wouldn't be a Bureau agent. I'm not going to steal your idea or tell your competitors. But this is a direct murder investigation of Kwasi King, and if you don't co-operate, I will have you seven ways to Sunday on obstruction of justice. That clear?'

Unzicker looked terrified. Nursultan weighed the odds. He'd tried to bribe Patrese before, asking him to manufacture a suspect in order to get Kwasi playing. Now Kwasi was a suspect himself, and he wasn't playing. Nursultan had no leverage any more.

'Misha not finished yet,' he said.

'And when it is?'

'When it is . . . it first real artificial intelligence program in history.'

Unzicker explained the science to them.

When it comes to chess, he said, there are three main lines of computer application. The first was among the goals of the inaugural AI conference, held at Dartmouth – Ivy League again, Patrese thought – in 1956: to create a computer program which could defeat the world chess champion. At the time, that seemed a pipe dream, the very peak of human intellectual endeavor.

Forty years later, the first match between man and machine took place: Garry Kasparov, the world champion, against IBM's Deep Blue. Kasparov won. A year later, Kasparov and Deep Blue played again. This time, Deep Blue won. The primacy of the machine was irrefutably established; so much so that nowadays there are several programs – all readily available in the shops for around $50 – that will get the better of any human on earth. Yes, even of Kwasi King. Not every time, not every game, but under anything approaching match conditions, a series alternating black and white, the machines will win. So far, so *Terminator*. No mileage in that for Unzicker.

The second line of application is the solution of chess itself; that is, with perfect play, is chess a win for White, a draw, or even a win for Black? Checkers was solved not so long ago; computers found a perfect line of play against which there is no defense. Effectively, checkers is over as a competitive sport. It's like doing a crossword that someone's already filled in.

But chess is a different matter altogether. Checkers pieces all move more or less the same. Not so in chess. The differing moves of the pieces leads to a bewildering array of possible positions: 10^{120} give or take a few. A thousand trillion trillion trillion trillion trillion trillion trillion trillion trillion trillion trillion possible positions. To put that into perspective, there've only been 10^{26} nanoseconds – not seconds, *nanoseconds* – since the universe was formed, and there are only around 10^{75} atoms in the entire universe. To all intents and purposes, chess is a road with no beginning and no end on which you could travel through eternity.

Yes, some positions have been solved: endgame positions with no more than six pieces (including both kings, who can never be taken) on the board. Supercomputers are now working on solving seven-piece endgames, and after that they'll move on to eight, and so on. But each extra piece adds an exponential layer of complications and possibilities, not to mention the requirement for storage space. There are thirty-two pieces on a chessboard at the start of a match. At current rates of progress, it'll be at least a couple of centuries before chess is solved, if indeed it ever is. No mileage for Unzicker here either.

It's the third line of application, Unzicker said, that most interests him and Nursultan: the idea that chess is the perfect vehicle with which to create an intelligent computer program. A proper self-teaching, self-learning, self-changing program. One that would pass the Turing Test, the famous litmus test posed by Alan Turing, the father of modern computer science: that a device can be deemed intelligent if its answers to a set of human-posed questions are indistinguishable from those of a human.

As things stand, what makes computers so good at chess is precisely the fact that they *aren't* human. They never get tired, flustered, hungry. They never worry about marriage problems or paying the bills. They never get upset by sudden noise or stale air. Their decisions are reliable, consistent and disciplined. They're completely unemotional: a win, a draw, and a loss are simply three states, none of which affects their ability to play the next game. They have full knowledge of everything programmed into them: openings, endgame positions, middlegame strategies. They rely solely on logical inferences, and make no catastrophic errors: a computer never overlooks mate in one, either in its favor or against it. They evaluate 200 million positions per second, using complex algorithms to work out several different functions – placement, attack, blockade, exchange, skirmish, negation, and so on – crunching numbers with a brute force way beyond the furthest imagination of the keenest brain.

But they don't have two things.

They don't have intuition, gut feeling: that sixth sense that leads them to the right move through some process both inexplicable and primal.

And they can't learn from their own mistakes. Whatever knowledge they have comes from new human input. When a computer makes a mistake, it will make that same mistake in the same conditions again and again until a programmer corrects it.

Why? Because the human brain and the computer chip are structured differently. The brain has what the chip does not: functional plasticity. In the human brain, memories are stored at a cellular level in the framework of the synapses. This framework can be altered, reconstructed, reconfigured, adapted to different functions. The brain's plasticity is so great that it can even generate new specialized centers: for example, epileptics who lose the functions of one cerebral hemisphere can reorganize the other to take on the job of both. In contrast, a computer chip is literally hardwired, constrained by the rigidity of its own architecture.

What I'm doing, Unzicker said, is trying to combine the two. I'm growing neurons within a computer's silicon circuits. And chess is the ideal proving ground for this. When it comes to exploring the cognitive processes, and developing problem-solving methods, chess has it all. There are six different types of pieces, all of which move in a different way. A pawn's line of motion is different to his attack, a knight moves in three dimensions rather than two, a king and rook can perform a double move, the values of the pieces are constantly shifting, depending on their positions, and the king's value is infinite. Strategy and tactics must combine in an endless dance. All these are priceless tools for reasoning. Goethe called chess the touchstone of the intellect.

And this, Unzicker said, is where Kwasi comes in. They've been constantly refining the project, experimenting, trying new things, failing, trying something else. At each turn, they'd needed Kwasi to play against the program and test its parameters. You want a program to think like a human, play chess like a human, with creativity and intuition? You have to test it against the best human around. Testing it against other chess programs would simply make it play like them.

Ever-increasing processing power and number-crunching wasn't what the Dartmouth conference had had in mind all those years ago. Deep Blue and all its successors were intelligent only in the way a programmable alarm clock is intelligent. But that's the way things are going now. Brute-force programs play the best chess. The market demands the best programs. So there's no point bothering with anything other than brute-force programs. The competitive and commercial aspects of making computers play chess have taken precedence over using chess as a scientific proving ground.

But this one, Misha, will be different. I don't care about computation, Unzicker said: I care about *understanding*. And with Nursultan providing backing, I don't have to worry about running out of financial resources. As long as I keep working towards the goal, Nursultan will keep funding me.

Why Misha? In homage to the great Soviet player Mikhail Botvinnik. Botvinnik was world chess champion three times after the Second World War: he was also an electrical engineer and computer scientist of great repute, trying to develop artificial intelligence not only in chess but also in economic management. His ideas were way ahead of the technology available at the time. This is their way – Unzicker's, Kwasi's and Nursultan's way – of honoring him.

Patrese saw two things more or less at once.

First: this project would, if successful, revolutionize science. Proper, provable artificial intelligence was the Holy Grail: perhaps the final triumph of science over religion, the assertion of man's primacy through the generation of life itself from inert matter. Whoever accomplished it would end up revered through the ages: a Newton, a Darwin, a Watson and Crick. That promise of immortality alone would explain Unzicker's obsession with the project, and perhaps Nursultan's too: whatever else you thought about him, the man wasn't short of an ego.

But it was the second thing that really got Patrese thinking. He remembered reading somewhere that IBM's share price had spiked 15 per cent in the immediate aftermath of Deep Blue beating Kasparov: a result which had, in essence, proved little other than that computers were very good at being computers. If Project Misha, potentially several magnitudes of achievement greater, were to come off, the effect on the Kazan Group – its share price, its market capitalization, its pretty much everything – would be astronomical.

'What's in it for you and Kwasi?' Patrese asked Unzicker.

'You mean money?'

'I mean money.'

'More than you can imagine,' Nursultan said.

187

34

The manhunt for Kwasi had been going twenty-four hours, and had now spread across the entire north-east of the country. Police and sheriff departments in twelve separate states, plus federal law enforcement personnel, were all on the lookout for Kwasi, so far without joy. Not that there was a lack of information: quite the opposite. There seemed to be as many sightings of Kwasi as there were of Elvis, and they were all just as unreliable. The task force was receiving hundreds of calls an hour, and even with every available person dragooned into service – not only Bureau agents and cops, but administrative support staff, press officers, guys who worked in HR and IT, pretty much anyone who could answer a phone and take down basic details – they were still over-whelmed. Someone rang to tell them that they'd never find Kwasi because he'd been abducted by aliens; another said the murders were connected with the Kennedy assassination. Crazy Kwasi, the papers were calling him; but he was no more crazier than some of the folks out there, Patrese thought.

Patrese was always wary of letting facts fit theory rather than vice versa, but at every turn he was becoming more convinced that Kwasi was indeed playing some murderous chess game. For example, he'd realized while out running in New Haven early this morning how closely the layout of the central streets mirrored that of a chessboard. The Green, where the first two bodies had been found, was the middle of nine squares, each one delineated by street boundaries.

In chess, a king can move one square in any direction. If a king – Kwasi King? – was standing on the Green, he could move to any one of those eight adjacent squares, those eight city blocks. And if this was a chess game, who better to ask advice from than the second-best player in the world? Well, the best player in the world, perhaps, but he was currently indisposed. Which was why Patrese had come to see Rainer Tartu in New York.

Like Nursultan, Tartu was staying at the Waldorf-Astoria. Unlike Nursultan, he didn't have a suite all to himself, though his room was still hardly tenement standard. He was packing when Patrese arrived.

'You leaving already?' Patrese asked.

'I have no reason to stay here. The match is indefinitely postponed.'

'Going back to Europe?'

Tartu shook his head. 'To New Haven.'

'New Haven, Connecticut?'

'That's right.'

'That's where I am. That's where we're based during this . . .'

'Then maybe I'll see you around. It's not such a big place, I hear.'

'What are you doing there?'

'I have three passions, Mr Patrese. Chess is the first, of course. I'll be playing a few simultaneous exhibitions up around there.'

'Simultaneous exhibitions?'

'When you play multiple people at once. Don't want to let all my preparations go to waste now, do I? Music is the second. I'm a trained concert pianist, and as luck – perhaps not luck: perhaps fate, or kismet – would have it, the New Haven Symphony have got a temporary vacancy. They're due to perform Rachmaninoff's Second and Third Concertos next weekend, and their pianist has taken ill. No time to find a replacement through the usual channels. So I volunteered myself. I know Rachmaninoff like the back of my hand. And I know my presence there, because of all the – well, you know what I mean – all the *events* of the past few days, it'll help sell tickets. That's the way it is.'

'And the third?'

'Yes: the third concerto, and the second too.'

'No. Your third passion.'

'Oh! Excuse me. Rare books. The library at Yale has some of the most exquisite examples to be found anywhere.'

'The Beinecke?'

'That's right. How did you know?'

Patrese thought fast. There was no reason to tell Tartu about the help Anna had been giving him. 'It's pretty famous. And I walk past it most every day now.'

'I've never been. I can't wait. I have quite a collection of rare books back home.'

'I'm sure. Listen – I'd like your help.'

'I don't know what help I could give.'

'We think the murders have a chess theme. Kwasi's playing Black, if that makes sense. We don't know who's playing White. We need to find that person, and we need to find Kwasi. If we can get a sense of their tactics, their strategy, then maybe we can do that. But we need someone who plays chess at Kwasi's level.'

'And that's me?'

190

'That's you.'

Tartu pressed his hands to his face, covering his nose. He studied Patrese over the top of his fingers, as though Patrese himself were a chessboard. It was some time before Tartu took his hands away and spoke.

'In a world championship match, you go very deep into yourself, you know? You're like a diver, exploring hidden worlds no one else has ever seen. No one else apart from the man sitting opposite you, that is. You go deeper and deeper, and then when it's all over, you have to come up very fast. That does strange things to you. After Kwasi and I played last time, in Kazan, I was depressed for a year, and only a little of that was because I'd lost. I wanted Kwasi's company, I missed him.'

'He's a murderer.'

'I wanted to warn him. I wanted to say, Kwasi, you'll feel like a god, people will love you, history will obey you, you'll think your problems are over; but in those high places it's very cold, very lonely. I wanted to warn him that soon would come depression, the fall. I was afraid for him. I like him.'

'He's a murderer,' Patrese repeated.

'So you say. But has he told you that? Has he confessed? There are many reasons a man might run from the police, especially someone like Kwasi. The only place he feels comfortable, the only place in the whole world, is the chessboard. But even there it's not safe. Until you play at that level, you don't understand the stress involved. Your heart rate can easily double during a game, especially when you're having to play quickly in time trouble. Normally when your heart rate's doubling you're moving around, being active, but in chess there's no outlet for this. So you develop problems with your mind.'

'Mr Tartu, I asked you a simple question.'

'And I'm giving you a simple answer.'

'Are you?'

'Yes. You're just not listening.'

'Will you help me try and find Kwasi?'

'No.'

'No?'

'No. Kwasi's my friend. I understand him, perhaps better than anyone else in the world, certainly now his mother's dead . . .'

'Dead? Murdered. By him.'

'. . . again, so you say. If you find him, and then you want me to talk to him, try and help him, then yes. But while you're hunting him like dogs, no.'

'You're duty bound to help . . .'

'I'm duty bound to do nothing. You can't arrest me. I'm not in any way obstructing your process. I've spent the past year preparing for a match that isn't going to take place. I'm tired, and I don't want any more to do with this. Is that so hard to understand?'

He picked a pair of shoes off the floor and put them in his suitcase.

'No,' Patrese said. 'No. I guess it's not.'

35

There were days when Officer Sinclair Larsen, Boston Police Department, felt he was actually doing some good, actually contributing to the nation's well-being. A day, for example, when a shopkeeper would stop him and say how much safer they felt now that foot patrols were being reintroduced to some of Boston's higher-crime areas; or a day when he had to give evidence in court, knowing that his testimony would be part of the proof that put a gang of organized criminals behind bars.

And then there were days like today: an endlessly depressing litany of all the shit that the city's detritus could scoop up and fling in his direction. Stolen cars, convenience-store robberies, and now the inevitable domestic violence call-out. What really got Larsen was the paucity of ambition in these crimes. These weren't daring or exotic master criminals taking on the police in a battle of wits; they were nasty, brutish, squalid.

Squalid was the word of the day, he decided. The city's Egleston Square district, sandwiched between Roxbury and

Jamaica Plain, was squalid. The apartment complex outside which he was pulling up was damn sure squalid. It might have been OK when new, but now it looked like a trailer park without wheels. The perimeter fence sagged where it had fallen away from its supports, and the cars parked up against it all had dents in their hoods: sure signs that people climbed the fence and used the cars to break their fall, Larsen thought. Beer cans lay toppled on the ground like felled trees. Dogs barked, couples shouted at each other. Just another day in paradise.

Other units were en route, Larsen knew. The sensible thing would be to wait for them. All cops in the Greater Boston area had been briefed about Howard Lewis' murder, and warned that they might be targeted in a similar fashion. The advice sheet circulated had contained the usual mix of health'n'safety overcaution and the bleeding obvious: be vigilant, vary your routes home, try to avoid being alone when out on the streets. Sinclair Larsen, along with at least 99.9 per cent of his fellow officers, reckoned that a cop who couldn't be trusted to look after himself didn't really have the right to call himself a cop at all.

Alone on the streets? He was a first responder, that was his job. If he got there before everyone else, so be it. The 911 call had described a screaming match and furniture crashing in apartment 24. The kind of low-lives who lived here weren't above using fists on their women, and where fists came, knives and guns often followed. Larsen didn't know whether he had time to spare. He didn't want to find out too late that he hadn't.

He came out of the car fast, gun drawn. No one in the communal gardens. The apartments were built on two levels. A quick check of the numbering showed him that 1–20 was first floor, 20–40 was second. There was a stairwell away to his left. He ran for it.

194

It stank of piss. Of course it did. There wasn't a public staircase anywhere in the world that didn't. He took the stairs two at a time, turned back on himself at the landing, and felt a blow to his face so sharp and savage that for a second he thought he must have run full tilt into the wall without realizing.

Sinking to his knees, hands coming to his face, gun clattering to the ground. A man above him, punching him for a second time, this time hard in the solar plexus, and the breath whistling out of him like a freight train. As he pitched forward, reflexively trying to get some air – any air – back into his lungs – Larsen caught a quick glimpse of his assailant. Hoodie. Smooth features. White skin. Gloves.

No sirens. Other units weren't yet here. Have to get to apartment 24, Larsen thought, have to get to the domestic violence . . . and through the fog of pain, he realized dimly that there *was* no domestic violence in number 24. This was the call-out, right here; an ambush, an attack, first unwary copper gets it.

A couple of kicks to his ribs. He'd have screamed if he hadn't been so busy sucking in breaths. Not that it would have made a difference. Places like this, no one came to investigate a fight, not unless they wanted to be next.

Hands turning him over, under his armpits, grabbing and dragging him up the stairs. The concrete slammed into Larsen's back. He winced and twisted, grabbing upwards at the man's chest. Couldn't reach all the way to the man's face, but Larsen's fingers brushed against something. A chain, a medallion, something like that. He reached again, shirt and jacket riding up on his chest as he fastened his hand round the chain . . .

. . . and suddenly, just like that, the man with the hoodie dropped him and took off. By the time Larsen had struggled to his feet and half run, half tumbled back down the stairs to retrieve his gun, his attacker had run across the complex' front yard, through the gates and was gone, weaving down the lines of dented cars till he disappeared from sight.

Patrese had asked that any attacks on Boston police officers be reported to him. A Columbia student had been murdered shortly before a Harvard student; by the same logic, the murder of a New York cop should presage something similar in the Boston area.

That Sinclair Larsen was white was unsurprising; apart from him fitting the tarot/chess pattern, four in every five Boston police officers were white. That he'd survived *was* surprising. That his attacker had voluntarily let him go seemed inexplicable.

Patrese didn't like inexplicable. He got Larsen to tell him what had happened, blow by blow, no detail too small, no recounting too exhaustive.

Larsen went through the whole thing. When he finished, Patrese was still mystified. The $64,000 question: Why had Larsen's attacker suddenly dropped him? No other cops had arrived, no curious resident had poked their head out of another apartment. Yes, Larsen had gotten hold of the chain round the man's neck, but it had only come away in his hand once the man had dropped him; it hadn't been the action of Larsen yanking the chain that had caused the man to drop him.

It didn't make sense.

So Patrese made Larsen tell him again, even slower and more painstakingly than before. This time, Patrese played the part of the attacker: mimicking the ambush, pretending to drag Larsen along the ground, seeing how Larsen reached for the chain, shirt and jacket riding up . . .

There.

Larsen had a tattoo on his stomach. A Red Sox logo, perhaps nine inches in diameter.

Right on the place where the patches of skin had been removed on the other victims.

The killer had seen the tattoo, and that had spared Larsen's life. Whatever he and Kwasi wanted with the patches of skin, a big tattoo didn't seem part of it. If the skin wasn't clean, they weren't interested. None of the other victims had had tattoos.

'You want to see the chain?' Larsen said.

Patrese was still thinking about the tattoos. 'The chain?'

'The one I grabbed from his neck.'

'Oh. Yeah. Sure.'

Larsen passed over a transparent evidence bag. 'We've got people checking it out. Mainly sold at the gift shop, I think.'

Patrese took the chain from the bag. It was silver, and had a circular charm bearing a seal. There were two men pictured: one with a hammer and anvil, the other engrossed in a book. They were leaning against a plinth marked '1861', and below them was the legend *Mens Et Manus*. Mind and hands.

Words ran round the perimeter of the seal, but Patrese didn't need to read them. He knew what they'd say, as he'd already seen this seal; two days ago, in fact.

Massachusetts Institute of Technology.

36

Patrese called a sitrep meeting first thing Monday morning. Anderssen and Dufresne had come up the night before, and they'd been drinking with Patrese in his hotel bar till the small hours. Patrese had put it all on his room tab. God alone knew how he was going to get that one past the Bureau bean-counters. Perhaps he could call it a 'liaison meeting with multi-jurisdictional law enforcement personnel'. Or maybe food was chargeable as a legitimate expense. Trouble was, every item on the tab was strictly liquid. Ah well.

Now he stood in front of the task force and outlined where they stood. Officer Larsen had been attacked by someone with an MIT pendant. Forensics were seeing what, if anything, they could get off that pendant by way of evidence. So far, all they'd managed to ascertain was that the pendant had been purchased from the MIT shop, where they sold hundreds each year, and that the only fingerprints were those of Sinclair Larsen where he'd grabbed at it during the attack.

Kwasi King was working with Thomas Unzicker of MIT on Project Misha. There was no way of knowing for sure whether Unzicker had been the guy who'd attacked Officer Larsen, or if Unzicker had called in the fake 911 call himself. Analysis of the tape revealed that the caller had used some sort of electronic voice modifier. But at the very least, they'd needed to investigate Unzicker further, which was exactly what they'd done. The task force had spent most of the weekend digging up whatever they could find on him, and boy was there a lot of it.

First, the Ivy League connection.

Not only was MIT just down the road from Harvard, with well-documented friction between the two, but Unzicker had been at Harvard beforehand: he'd done his undergraduate degree there. Patrese had asked for any Harvard therapy reports on Unzicker – the initial request to Ivy League colleges had been for current students only, so Unzicker hadn't been included in that – and Harvard had come back with plenty.

That led Patrese on to the second point: Unzicker's mental problems. In childhood, Unzicker had suffered from a condition called selective mutism, an anxiety disorder that manifests itself in the sufferer speaking very quietly and infrequently – and often not at all – in situations most people would find entirely normal and unthreatening. The mutism had, with sad predictability, been exacerbated by the reactions of other children. They'd teased him, offered their lunch money just to hear him talk, called him Trombone Boy for his habit of walking to school alone carrying his trombone, stuffed him in garbage cans and made him eat trash. When a teacher had threatened to fail him for not participating, he'd begun talking in a strange, deep voice which had sounded as though he'd been possessed by an alien or had something stuck in his mouth.

Unzicker had told his therapist all this. The mutism had

begun to fade in adolescence, perhaps because his skill with computers had given him the confidence to believe he wasn't a total loss at everything. Not that he could be described as entirely normal even now. During his time at Harvard, Unzicker had used his cellphone to take photos of female students' legs under their desks, and had written poetry which was in various measures obscene, deranged, pathetic, violent, and almost totally lacking in literary merit.

He'd railed against rich kids and hedonists with their 'Mercedes, golden necklaces, trust funds, vodka, cognac and debaucheries'. He'd written an ode to his girlfriend Jelly, who he said lived in outer space, traveled everywhere by spaceship, and called him Spanky. He'd signed these poems with a simple question mark, and had started referring to himself as Mr Question Mark or Mr Eroteme, another word for the punctuation mark.

The therapist had been sufficiently alarmed by Unzicker's behavior to have arranged a duress code with her assistant: if she ever spoke the name of one of her former colleagues, now dead, the assistant was to call security at once. She'd never needed to use it, but in other fields Unzicker's behavior had been reported to three separate bodies: the student affairs office, the dean's office and the campus police. They'd each said the same thing: as long as Unzicker made no overt, direct threats against himself or other people, there was nothing they could do.

Why hadn't Harvard disclosed any of this to MIT when Unzicker had applied for his postgraduate course there? Because federal law expressly forbade it. Only if Unzicker gave his consent could Harvard hand over the files; and he hadn't done so. Patrese could get the information, but MIT couldn't. Even if they could have, perhaps it would have made no difference. Unzicker was by all accounts a computer scientist of egregiously rare talent: no university, let alone the top technological institute in the world, was going to pass up a candidate like him. He was odd, he was a genius. They went together. Deal with it.

And now to the third point: Unzicker's behavior at MIT itself. He was famous, or perhaps infamous, for his 'hacks' – MIT slang for practical jokes, usually with a technological element. During a keynote speech, he'd patched his own electronics into the audio hook-up and gradually made the speaker's voice sound higher and higher. He'd hacked into the MIT website and changed the home page to an announcement that Disney was buying MIT. He'd altered elevator announcements so they said dumb things.

People who pulled these kinds of stunts at MIT were often seen as folk heroes, but Unzicker wasn't going to be winning any popularity contests. People thought him arrogant, aloof, obnoxious. They rarely saw him with anyone who might constitute a friend. He ate every meal in the dining hall alone, and discouraged those who tried to be sociable and sit with him.

No one had officially complained about him at MIT, but that could be explained by two things: his immersion in Project Misha seemed to leave him little time for extra-curricular activities; and MIT liked to think of itself as less uptight and more freewheeling than Harvard. MIT girls might be more likely than Harvard princesses to laugh off a clumsy weirdo's approach.

Whether that was the case or not, however, paled into insignificance against one thing: that the previous Thursday, less than twenty-four hours before Kwasi had gone on the run, Thomas Unzicker had attended MIThenge – which he'd mentioned in his e-mail to Kwasi – and had gone as a giant tarot card. The presence of tarot cards at the murder scenes was still not public knowledge, so Unzicker's choice of costume was either incredibly coincidental, incredibly arrogant or incredibly stupid. And Patrese needed to remind no one what he thought about the prospects of coincidence.

Opinion in the room was split: not on whether Thomas Unzicker was a person of interest to the investigation, as he clearly was, but what their best course of action was. Anderssen wanted to bring Unzicker in, shake him down, smack him around if necessary. Dufresne wanted to bug Unzicker's office and room, and see what they could get that way. Patrese agreed with neither of them.

There were two things here, he said. They had to find White, the person playing with Kwasi, but they also had to find Black, Kwasi himself. Assume Unzicker's White. Bringing him in is only going to cause problems. We bring him in, arrest him, charge him, Kwasi breaks off contact. We bring him in and release him, that messes up his mental state still further, he freaks out, Kwasi realizes he's no longer reliable, Kwasi breaks off contact. As for bugging Unzicker: the guy's a tech whiz, he can probably spot a recording device or some software monitoring program at a hundred paces. He finds it, he freaks out, we're back to square one again.

No. What they were going to do was this. Mount surveillance on Unzicker; not electronic watching, but proper human surveillance. Everywhere he went, everyone he met. If he was White, and he was the one who attacked Officer Larsen in Egleston Square on Saturday, then he'd want to try again soon. His bloodlust would be up, and Ebony and Ivory were killing in turn, so presumably Kwasi couldn't kill again till Ivory had done so. Chess rules: one move each, strict rotation. They'd catch Ivory – Unzicker, perhaps – in the process of killing, and then try and use him as bait to lure Kwasi out.

But they had to catch Unzicker first. And, of course, there was always the possibility that it wasn't him at all. That he was the most likely suspect didn't mean he was the only suspect. If Kwasi was playing some form of warped chess with people's lives, his ego was such that he'd only consider an opponent whom he deemed worthy. And there were two other people Patrese could think of who fit that bill: Tartu and Nursultan.

Tartu was now right here in New Haven, where the first two bodies had been found. Kieseritsky had put discreet surveillance on to him – he was staying at the same hotel as Patrese, which was either convenient or awkward, depending on your point of view – and so far he'd done nothing other than that what he claimed to be there for. If he wasn't in the library, he was in the symphony hall. He'd been in New Haven all weekend, so he couldn't have been the one who'd attacked Larsen. But he was still, if not an outright suspect, certainly a person of interest, if only for his refusal to help them. Were his reasons purely innocent, or more nefarious? Only time would tell.

Nursultan was a trickier case, not least because he had diplomatic immunity. When in the US, he spent most of his time in New York, with odd trips up to Cambridge to visit Unzicker – including one this weekend, which put him in the frame as at least a possibility for the attack on Larsen. If Nursultan did turn out to be involved, they'd have to tread very carefully or risk an international incident. But they'd cross that bridge when they came to it, and in the meantime there was nothing to stop them keeping tabs on him.

Unzicker, Tartu, Nursultan. Cambridge, New Haven, New York. Anderssen, Kieseritsky, Dufresne. Each individual surveillance operation would be the responsibility of the respective detective in charge. They'd all answer to Patrese, who'd oversee the whole thing, the entire tri-state operation.

And though waiting for one of them to slip up was all well and good, Patrese wanted to be more proactive. He wanted to know how it felt to be playing such a game, wanted to know the pressures, the strategies, the tactics. Since Tartu had refused to help, what Patrese needed was someone who was an excellent chess player, who knew Kwasi well, and who had no reason to want to protect him.

And if she looked like Inessa Baikal did, so much the better.

37

New Haven, CT

Inessa was a postgraduate student at Harvard, which Patrese hadn't appreciated until he rang her. While they talked, he flicked quickly through the list of those students seeking therapy. Her name wasn't among them.

Yes, she said, of course she'd help: not just because of the Kwasi connection, but because of the Harvard one too. She'd been wondering whether or not to volunteer her services anyway, but she'd been sure that the Bureau had been deluged with offers of help. Yes, he could come and see her at Harvard any time, but if he wanted to see her right now she could make it even easier for him. Right now, she wasn't at Harvard at all.

She was in New Haven.

Business or pleasure? Patrese asked.

Both. She'd come to consult some texts for her doctorate, and she always got special treatment when she came to examine Yale's rare books. Her sister was the librarian.

Anna Levin's your *sister*? Patrese spluttered.

Sure, Inessa said. Different surname, because Anna had

gotten married – briefly – but as sisterly as sisters could be. They'd been born in St Petersburg – Russia, not Florida – but after their mother had been killed by a vagrant seeking vodka, their father had brought them to the US and Brookline, a town encircled by, but fiercely resistant to, Boston. When its neighbor, West Roxbury, had become part of Boston in the late nineteenth century, Brookline had refused to follow suit, a position it had maintained ever since. The town was more than a third Jewish, many of them like Inessa and Anna of Russian heritage, and the inhabitants liked to think of themselves as both reflecting and reinforcing the town's spirit of independence.

Anna came on the line herself. I tried to tell you, she said, the first time you came to ask me about the tarot cards. I tried to tell you twice, in fact, but you were in such a hurry that you'd talked over the top of me, and then I figured maybe you knew anyway, which is why you'd come to see me in the first place.

Patrese asked Anna if she'd come across Tartu. Of course, she said. He comes in every day. Very nice, very knowledgeable. The softening in her voice made Patrese wonder whether she had a soft spot for the Estonian.

It could all be harmless coincidence, of course: Inessa and Anna being sisters, Tartu coming to New Haven. In fact, Patrese couldn't see how it could be anything else. He'd sought out both Anna and Inessa independently of each other, not knowing their relationship. Neither of them had come to him. And Tartu would still have been in New York playing for the world title had Kwasi not hightailed. If there was anything suspicious in any of this, therefore, Patrese couldn't see it.

Inessa said she'd be round at the Bureau's office in a half-hour.

* * *

She was smaller than Patrese had expected – five two, five three at most – but perhaps that was because he'd only ever seen her on TV. In the flesh, her eyes seemed larger, her hair darker. She came half a step too close when she introduced herself, held on to his hand a beat too long. Patrese wondered whether these were signals, or whether that was just the way she was with everybody; a flirt, a space invader, someone who – if the gawps of several task force members were anything to go by – enjoyed the effect she clearly had on men.

'Ready to start?' he asked her.

'Listen, I've been stuck in front of a computer half the night – online poker tournaments, that's how I make most of my money these days – and then in the library these last couple of hours, so what I'd really like to do is get outside and stretch my legs. I've brought my running kit. I was going to ask whether you want to come with me, but . . .' She pointed to his plaster cast.

'I don't run on my hands.'

Her laughter tinkled round the room. 'OK. Then let's go.'

He drove her to his hotel. They changed in his room: her in the bedroom, he in the bathroom. The plaster cast made things slower and more difficult than usual, but he was getting better and quicker at it. When he was in his running gear, he knocked before going back in, to check he wouldn't be surprising her half dressed.

He opened the door, and tried very, very hard not to look her up and down.

And failed.

She was wearing black lycra leggings and a lime green long-sleeved top. Her hair was tied back, and she fizzed with suppressed energy. How she managed to sit still long enough to play chess – or poker, for that matter – he had no idea.

They set off quicker than Patrese would have liked. It

wasn't his arm that was the problem; the cast was light, and it didn't bother him too much. It was rather that he preferred to start slowly, ease himself into the exercise, let his body get used to the work. After a couple of minutes, he was breathing hard and half considered asking her to slow down, make some excuse about his broken wrist; but he knew that she'd only look at him and laugh, and shred his male pride to the four winds.

Be subtle, he thought. Give her an open-ended question, get her to do the talking. Maybe that would force her to slow down a bit.

'Tell me about Kwasi,' he said, timing it so he could talk between breaths.

'God, where to start? Everything you see or hear about him is true, and yet it's also untrue. Everything he does, he can do exactly the opposite. He's so secretive about lots of things, and then sometimes he'll say something so candid it takes your breath away. One minute he can be really generous, the next he wouldn't give you a dime to save your life. I've seen him be kind and consoling to someone who's just lost a game, and I've seen him take people apart not only at the board but in the postmortem afterwards.'

'Postmortem?' Three syllables was about Patrese's limit as he puffed.

'Oh!' She clapped her hand to her mouth. 'Not your kind of postmortem. A chess postmortem. After the game, the players, and sometimes the spectators too, discuss where the game was won and lost, what different moves you could have played, and so on. If you've won, you're supposed to be, you know, magnanimous. But I've seen Kwasi call his victims trash, fools, losers, all those things.'

'We all have that.'

'What?'

'Contradictions.' Puff, puff. 'Paradoxes.'

'Sure. But his are so extreme. He's like two different people. Sometimes he's the biggest jerk in the world; arrogant, rude, uncouth, spoilt, egocentric, greedy, vulgar. And sometimes he's all sweetness and light.'

'He's a killer.'

'I know.'

'Were you surprised? Him on the run?'

She made a face. 'Sort of. It's a shock, sure, but you see the way he plays chess . . . He's a killer on the board too. Two things about his play always stand out. One, it's so clear. He doesn't make mysterious or obscure moves, at least not when you analyze them properly. He's very direct. Very logical.'

'You make it sound easy.'

'Isn't that genius, though? To make the difficult, the almost impossible, look easy?'

And the other way round, Patrese thought: Kwasi could make the easy, the quotidian understandings of human relationships and social functions, look supremely difficult.

'What's the other?'

'What's the other what?'

'Thing about his play.'

'His will. It's granite. He never gives way to anyone else. If he loses a game – and everyone does sometimes, even the greatest players – he *never* loses the next one. Some people crumble when they lose. But Kwasi, it only makes him stronger. Never seen him lose two straight, ever. I remember one time, a Pan-American tournament. University chess champs. He was top board for UMBC, I was third for Penn State. I watched him play; not the moves on the board, but *him*. It was like looking at, I don't know, a bird of prey, a hunting animal. A predator. A raptor. Just ruthless. He plays every game as though it's his last.' She paused. 'To the death.'

'He ever violent to you when you dated?'

'Physically? Never.'

'Emotionally?'

Inessa didn't answer immediately. They ran in silence for a few moments, heading towards the bridge across the harbor. Patrese didn't press her; he thought her hesitation was more a question of finding the right words than a reluctance to answer.

'Yes,' she said at last. 'But not deliberately, if that makes sense. He never abused me, told me I was worthless, any of that. The violence, the psychic violence, he uses it against himself as much as against other people. He had to win everything. Not only chess but everything. We played tennis, he had to win. Poker – Jesus Christ. Couldn't stop till he was up, didn't matter if you'd been playing all night.'

'Sounds pretty wearing.'

'It is. But then again, you know you're with a genius; a proper, unalloyed, twenty-four-carat genius. Seriously. You know anything about chess, you see the clarity of his play and the brilliance of his ideas, and you think he's every bit a Mozart, a Rembrandt, a Shakespeare. All the girls, every female chess player, we all wanted to be with him. Like his status would reflect well on us, you know? The time I was with him, all the other girls despised me. I had what they wanted. But they admired me too, for getting him. Just like you can admire Kwasi's chess and despise his personality.'

'How long were you with him for?' Patrese's breathing was coming easier now.

'Not long. Month or so.'

'Hardly a great romance.'

'It's a month longer than he managed with anyone else.'

'You sure?'

'Absolutely.'

'How?'

'Because of why we finished.'

'Go on.'

'Two things. First, his chess was suffering. He lost more games in the month we were together than he had in the two years beforehand. You know what it's like: young love, you can't think straight, you can't eat properly, your mind keeps wandering. To a chess player, all that is death. You've got to be strong, focused, clear-headed. Maybe it would've settled down, I don't know: the first flush of the crush fades, you become a proper couple. But he never gave it a chance. I was affecting his chess, so I had to go. That was how he saw it.'

She wiped her sleeve across her brow.

'That was sure as hell how his mother saw it. She's the second reason we finished, of course. Relationship like they had, no other woman ever stood a chance. She hated me. Not me as such, I guess, but what I represented. *She* was the only woman in his life, that was how she saw it. She did everything for him – took him to tournaments, cooked, washed, managed, negotiated – and in return she expected total loyalty.'

'And of course her attachment wasn't just to him, but to his success too.'

'Exactly. I threatened that success. If I got too close, not only would she be pushed out, but he might not end up what they'd both planned for: world champion, best ever, all that. Her or me. Chess or me. I lost, on both counts.'

They headed into the park. Patrese pointed ahead with his good arm. 'I usually run to the lighthouse and back.'

'Oh?'

'You sound surprised.'

'Not a bit. I thought we'd be going further, that's all. Well, if that's as far as we're going to get, you want to race there?'

He laughed. 'And you told me *he* was competitive.'

211

'He is. But so am I. Come on. You're a Bureau agent, and you won't race a girl?'

'You want a head start?'

Her eyes flashed. 'You want to patronize me a bit more?'

'What's the bet?'

'Winner buys dinner.'

'Sure. When do we start racing?'

'We already have,' and she was off, arms pumping and feet splayed as she sprinted.

Patrese won, but he had to work hard for it, overhauling her only in the last hundred yards or so. They collapsed against the side of the lighthouse in heaving laughter.

'Double or quits on the way home,' she said.

'Sure.'

After a couple of minutes' rest, Patrese turned round and led the way back toward the city, heedless and ignorant of who might be watching them.

38

Kwasi had never liked to think of himself as a voyeur. It wasn't the furtiveness that bothered him but the dirtiness. His mother had told him all women were whores, apart from herself, and that no woman would ever love him as much as she did.

But it wasn't like he was being a voyeur now. Sure, he was watching them, but they weren't having sex. Just running.

Funny, he thought. Patrese was looking for him, and yet Kwasi could see Patrese rather than vice versa. Kwasi was the one on the run, but he was standing still while Patrese ran. There were a multitude of ways in which you could watch someone without them knowing – you didn't even have to be within sight of them; hell, you could be on the other side of the world as long as you had a camera and a web link – and yet he, Kwasi, was hiding from the world almost in plain sight. Going out only in darkness, staying in during daytime. The world was a topsy-turvy place. White was black, black was white.

He wondered how Inessa had portrayed herself to the cops, and whether it had been the same way she'd sold

213

herself to the news networks. *I used to date him, I know him better than anybody, I can help, let me help.* He wondered if they'd see through her, or whether they were so desperate for comment and insight that they'd take anything.

This was a game, wasn't it? That's what Patrese had asked him by the dumpsters in Bleecker – nice plaster cast, by the way, from where he'd fended off the chessboard. Another split second, and Kwasi would have stoved in Patrese's skull. *Who's white? Who's Ivory? Who's in Boston? Who are you playing against?*

It was a game. And if it was a game, then he should start playing properly.

The thing about chess is this: it's a game of perfect information, entirely without chance. Perfect information, because both players can see all the pieces on the board all the time; entirely without chance, because there's no outside force to provide the element of luck. In poker, you can't see your opponents' cards; in backgammon, you rely on the roll of the dice. Not so in chess. That's why poker and backgammon are poor relations to the game of kings. Chess is a contest of pure skill.

So too here. Patrese was trying to find Kwasi; Kwasi was trying to remain hidden. Patrese would find Kwasi only if Kwasi made a mistake. But the equilibrium in this game was different than in chess. In chess, you begin at stasis; an even position, the pieces symmetrical with the board undisturbed. Then you create chaos out of order. Here, the positions weren't equal. If the status quo was maintained, Kwasi would win; that was, Patrese wouldn't find him. Chess starts as a draw. This was starting as a win for Kwasi. Kwasi knew things Patrese didn't.

Everyone always said Kwasi was scrupulously fair at the board. And the fair thing to do when you're much better than your opponent is to offer him odds, to play handicap;

compensate him for the imbalance in skill, even things up. Odds make things even. In chess, there are many ways of doing this. You can play without a pawn or a piece, you can give your opponent more time or extra moves, you can play blindfold while your opponent has sight of the board, and so on.

In this game, though, where the rules weren't clearly defined, it was harder to think what was best.

Knowledge, Kwasi thought. That was what Patrese wanted with Inessa, of course; he, Patrese, wanted to know about him, Kwasi. Wanted to know what made Kwasi tick. Kwasi had looked Patrese up, of course, after the very first time they'd met, and read about his previous cases. The Human Torch in Pittsburgh, that business down in New Orleans with the axes and the mirrors.

Kwasi had read a lot, and he'd worked out something about Patrese. Patrese always wanted to know *why*. Most cops were happy with what, where, when, how. Patrese wanted the fifth, why, at once the most and least important of the list.

And if that would even things up a bit, that's what Kwasi would give him. Not all at once, of course: where was the fun in that? But little by little, and things that would be useful if Patrese was smart enough to work it all out.

If.

39

Americans don't have much time for smart kids. The media does, because it can make a story out of you – a freak story if it's the National Enquirer, a chatty but serious one if it's the New York Times – but ordinary people don't. They say they do, but they don't. Adults don't like having a little kid telling them they're wrong. Teenagers don't like being beaten at chess by someone half their age. College kids don't like sitting in class alongside someone who should still be in ninth grade.

That's the curse of being a prodigy. You're as bright as adults – brighter than most of them, in fact – but you don't have the life experiences they have, so you can't really talk to them about things. And everyone your own age feels like a dumbass, stupid and juvenile and just variations on the central theme of being a douchebag.

You're a 32-bit child in an 8-bit world. You're not going to fit in anywhere. Show me two stools, any two stools, and I fell between them. The only kids I could possibly hang out with were other chess players, but even then there was a problem. Most of them I could beat with one hand tied behind my back, so they were no contest. The very few who could give me a good game became threats, so I couldn't let them be my friends either.

The only person who knew what to make of me was my mom.

Some doctors wanted to diagnose me hyperactive or with attention deficit disorder, give me Ritalin, dope me up to be a good little zombie. Others thought I was autistic, retarded. She told them all to get fucked. She pulled me out of school to home tutor me. The principal told her she was going to mess up my life. She told him to get fucked too.

It was us against the world. She taught me everything, the whole curriculum, even when she was having to learn it herself. Most of the time, I was teaching her as much as she was teaching me, often more. She insisted that I do all the subjects and get into college, not just because I should have more than chess, but because it would make me better at chess. The first part I could see. The second I thought was bullshit.

I was ready to go to college when I was fourteen. I applied to four Ivy League colleges – Columbia, Princeton, Brown and Dartmouth – and they all turned me down. Didn't think I'd fit in. No doubts about my intellect or my grades, but concerned that I wasn't ready for the rest of the college experience. Home schooling did not a rounded young person make, or some shit like that. Patronizing fucks.

Then some guy from the Baltimore Sun came to do a piece on me, and mentioned in it that I was hoping to go to college. The day the article came out, the very same day, I got a call from a guy named Neal Marsh, professor of computer science at UMBC. UMBC was building up a chess team to take on the best, and they were offering scholarships. They'd pay my fees as long as I played chess and majored in computer science. Marsh said he'd always wanted to have a future world champion at UMBC.

He let me play as much chess as I wanted. The computer science part helped a lot in that, with search engines and stuff. Turns out I was wrong about getting into college not making me better at chess. Everything I did was to make me better at the game.

You heard of synaesthesia? It's when your senses get muddled up; you hear colors, you see smells, that kind of thing. Saturday to me is purple and smells of coffee. Red is Beethoven's Fifth. The taste of eggplant is those little indentations you get on a thimble.

And it's like that on a chessboard for me too. I don't see the pieces. I see the paths they make, I hear the squares they can go to. A bishop is a blinking light, a rook is a straight tunnel. Patterns swirl and collide. Every move makes something new, and I'm in control of it all, this board which is the whole world, quivering with tension.

Other people – and I didn't know this for the longest time, because you think everyone sees the world like you do until you know better – other people have to calculate. This piece goes there, so that piece goes there, and if the rook takes the knight then the pawn can take the rook and no, start again, what if the queen goes to that square . . . I don't have to do that. I just see it. I don't know how, I just do. It's like everyone else is hacking through the jungle with trees all around them, and I'm hovering above and can see which way's out and where all the dead ends are.

So you get better than everyone else, and suddenly you're a freak show. Everyone wants part of you; no one wants you for yourself, they only want you because they think you can make them money, or that being with you will somehow bring them glory or status or some bullshit like that. You know that movie The Truman Show? My favorite movie of all time, because the Jim Carrey figure, Truman – the true man – he's me. He's the only honest Joe in a world full of scheming, dissembling shysters.

I tell you this, Franco, and I don't say it to make you feel sorry for me, or for any reason apart from that it's the truth: I have never had a friend in my life. Not a true friend. Not a single person who's ever accepted me for what I am and wanted nothing from me. Not one friend, ever.

40

Inessa had won the race back to the hotel, so they were quits. The government would pick up the tab for dinner, Patrese said, as if it hadn't been going to all along. Inessa went back to her sister's place to change, and then met Patrese in the hotel restaurant.

They made a pact not to talk about the case, and instead spoke easily about themselves; the kind of mutual dance you get on a not-quite-date, when each side is trying to portray themselves in the best possible light while simultaneously trying to discern the other's intentions. Yes, the chess parallel did occur to Patrese, and he stamped down on it. Too much thinking about Kwasi would make Patrese as insane as Kwasi was.

She was doing a PhD in comparative literature, she said. More precisely, and to give her doctorate its full and specific title: Russian Formalism, the interaction of math and physics theories with twentieth-century literature from a thematic and stylistic perspective: kitsch and camp aesthetics in post-Soviet Russia: the insect metaphor in literature and media studies. She liked maps, austere buildings and primary colors.

Before Harvard, she'd gone to Penn State, so she was

inordinately impressed when Patrese told her he'd played in the Pitt–Penn State football match. College football was huge at both universities, and the guys who made the teams were revered across campus. Patrese told her what it felt like to run out at Beaver Stadium, Penn State's home turf: the largest stadium in North America, and boy, did you feel it. Banks of people rising high and vertiginous in a tidal wave of blue and white, banging out their chant like an earthquake, shock waves round and round the stadium, the physical force of the sound battering against your chest.

Inessa took up the famous Penn State chant, clapping her hands.

'We Are!'

'Penn State!'

'We Are!'

'Penn State!'

The other diners glared at them. Inessa and Patrese collapsed with laughter.

They'd got to coffee, Patrese debating not so much whether to make a move as when, when his BlackBerry bleeped. He clicked on the message folder, and caught his breath.

One message. Sender: Kwasi King.

'Problem?' Inessa said.

'Let you know in a moment.'

He read the e-mail twice: once fast, to get the gist, and then again more slowly. **Americans don't have much time for smart kids . . . It was us against the world . . . I have never had a friend in my life.**

He handed Inessa the BlackBerry. Probably against the rules, showing an outsider evidence like this, but since they'd brought her in specifically to try to uncover Kwasi's mentality, it seemed dumb not to show her communication from the man himself.

She read it in silence.

'Sounds like him, sure enough,' she said.

'Why's he sending it?'

'To mess with your head.'

'You don't think he's trying to explain himself?'

'Maybe, a little. But messing with your head's definitely higher on his list.'

It was a game to Kwasi, Patrese saw. Everything was a game.

'Show me,' he said abruptly.

'Show you what?'

'Show me chess. Play with me. Show me the attraction, show me why he's obsessed with it.'

'You ever played before?'

'Sure. A little bit, now and then. I know the rules. I'm not a complete patzer, but any decent player would kick my ass from here to Stamford.'

'I've got a set in my bag. Little pocket set.'

'Never travel anywhere without it, huh?'

'No serious player does. Let's finish up here and go play in your room.'

They could, Patrese thought, have played in the restaurant, the bar, the lobby: somewhere public. They didn't have to play in his room. He felt familiar stirrings. It had been around a couple of weeks since he'd been with a woman – not since before this case started, he realized with a jolt – and running to the lighthouse and back wasn't an entirely comprehensive stress reliever.

'Sure. I'll just settle up here and pop over to the office.'

'Huh?'

'Get someone from IT to check my BlackBerry, see if we can find where the e-mail address originated.'

'OK.'

The Bureau's New Haven office had an IT specialist permanently on site. Patrese drove the few minutes to the office, left Inessa in the car, went inside and handed over his BlackBerry, saying he wanted it back as soon as possible. The skeleton task force staff manning the phones reported nothing of note from the surveillance of Unzicker.

Back at the hotel, they went up to his room.

'Here's what I suggest,' Inessa said. 'If we play normally, I'll crush you. No offense, but I will.'

'I know.'

'So I'm going to give you odds, a handicap. I'm going to play without my queen.'

'You'll still beat me.'

'Probably. But that's not the point. You want to see why Kwasi's so obsessed. I'm going to ask you every few moves what you're doing, what your plan is. If you make a dumbass move, I'll let you take it back.'

'Is there a forfeit for the loser?'

'Wait and see.'

She set the pieces up with quick, practiced hands. When both wooden armies were ready, she went down the lines, adjusting each piece and pawn so it sat dead center on its square. Then she took a pawn in each hand – one white, one black – put her hands behind her back, made a show of shifting the pawns from one hand to the other, and finally held out two clenched fists.

Patrese tapped the knuckles of her right hand. She opened it. White.

'White *and* queen odds.' She laughed. 'You don't put up a good show from here, I really *will* be disappointed.'

She took the black queen off the board, and they started to play.

Patrese took several minutes over each of his moves, even the easy ones, trying to think like Inessa was, trying to second-guess where she was going. He brought his bishop out too far, and wasted a move retreating it to safety. Now the knight, but when he told her what he was trying to do with it, use it to control the center, she pointed out that it would be better on a different square.

Sure, this was her turf, but he felt foolish, awkward, a klutz. She was glowing. He was way too conscious of her to concentrate properly: and he knew she knew this.

'Chess isn't just a game,' she said. 'It's a line of communication between two brains. You and I send and receive messages, and we transmit them through the board and pieces. You must understand my message, or you'll fall into trouble.' She cocked her head. 'Are you good at working out intentions?'

'I hope so.'

'You know, sometimes, when you and your opponent are both thinking furiously, and your heads are only a couple of feet apart, hunched over the board, you wonder whether all that energy and all that proximity will make thoughts jump from one to the other.'

She pushed her chair back and rested her chin on the table, looking up at him through the forest of pieces. He had the uncomfortable feeling she was trying to read his mind. But he was beginning to see the beauty of the game: not of the rather poor brand he was playing, of course, but of the game itself. It was at once a dance and a fight, an almost impossible balancing act where every reinforcement left a weakness somewhere else, every advance a hole behind it, every retreat a gap in front.

He took one of her pawns, and she moved so fast to take back that her hand brushed over the top of his. Next move, she rested her fingers on top of one of her bishops and stroked its head, looking first at the board and then at Patrese. He smiled clumsily. Her eyes widened a little. She pulled her chair in close again and leaned across the board, almost over to his side, trying to get a better view of the position. Their foreheads brushed against each other. He thought about kissing her there and then.

Her pieces were everywhere. Patrese hadn't made any outright blunders, at least none that he was aware of, but move by move he was being pushed back, his pieces crowding in on one another while Inessa's roamed free, aiming their fire at almost every square in his camp while protecting each other with jaunty insouciance. For a brief, absurd moment Patrese felt as though his pieces were somehow animate objects, defenders of a medieval citadel bumping up against each other in panic and confusion while the unstoppable enemy came galloping across the plains.

'When I was a little girl learning to play,' she said, 'I used to think of chess as a fairy tale, full of castles and knights, kings and queens. Here's a knight coming to rescue the maiden from captivity. Here's a loyal foot soldier laying down his life for his queen.'

She licked her lips. Her eyes never left his as she picked up a knight, lifted it over a helpless rook, and put it back down.

'That's mate,' she said.

He thought of Steve McQueen as Thomas Crown. 'Shall we play something else?'

She got up and came over to his side of the board. He was rising to meet her when she kissed him, very softly, on the lips.

'Not tonight,' she said. 'Maybe some other time.'

After she'd gone, Patrese stared at the door for a few seconds, and then burst out laughing. He was losing his touch, clearly. He hoped it wasn't an omen for the case.

There was a knock at the door. Patrese smiled. What would be her excuse? She'd forgotten her chess set? Perhaps her cellphone? He knew women like her: they liked to be in control, make their point, and only then would they let anything happen.

He walked over to the door.

'I *knew* you'd be back,' he said as he opened it.

It wasn't Inessa. It was the IT guy from the Bureau – Larry, Patrese thought his name was – and it was hard to tell who was more embarrassed, him or Patrese.

'Er . . . sorry,' Patrese said. 'Thought you were someone else.'

Larry handed Patrese his BlackBerry as though it were toxic. 'Can't trace the ISP. He's used a remailer. Several, actually.'

Patrese nodded. He'd come across remailers on previous cases. Every e-mail sent has a heap of information attached: details of the Internet service provider, serial number of the computer that sent it, interface hardware address, and so on. These details can be kept secret by sending the message not directly to the recipient but to a third party, who strips away all those identifying details, replaces them with their own, and only then sends it on.

But since this has an obvious weakness – the recipient knows the remailer's details, and the remailer knows the sender's details – people who really want their location to remain secret use multiple remailers. The e-mail is sent to the first server, which reorders it and transmits it on to another server, which does the same thing, and so on. Only the first server knows the sender's details, and only the last server knows the recipient's.

Theoretically, each server can be traced back from the one it forwarded to, but they encrypt their details. Even if the details can be decrypted, the servers will almost certainly be based in different countries. Different countries means different jurisdictions and different laws, which means a law enforcement nightmare.

No, Patrese thought: they weren't going to find Kwasi this way.

He thanked Larry, took the BlackBerry, shut the door, and reminded himself to be less of a dork tomorrow than he had been today.

41

Tuesday, November 16th

killerinstinct32: Hi.

repino: Hey.

killerinstinct32: Wazzup?

repino: Peeps lookin 4 u everywhere.

killerinstinct32: Peeps? What kind of peeps?

repino: Peeps with badges and guns, u know?

killerinstinct32: I know. They been 2 c u?

repino has been idle for 3 minutes.

killerinstinct32: U there? They been 2 c u?

repino: Sorry, had to take leak.

killerinstinct32: Jeez, u scared the shit outta me. They been 2 c u?

repino: Sure.

killerinstinct32: They aks u to let em know if I got in touch?

repino: Sure.

killerinstinct32: U going to?

repino: Don't be dumb.

killerinstinct32: U check for surveillance?

repino: Every day. Nothing. U need help?

killerinstinct32: No, I'm good. Wanna play?

repino: Not right now. Wot your next move?

killerinstinct32: Can't tell u. Best u don't know.

repino: I'm worried, man. Cops comin round, that's some heavy shit.

killerinstinct32: U be cool. Just say u know nothin.

repino: Maybe they checkin my records. U know I got into bit of trouble?

killerinstinct32: Quit freakin out. Let em check. Tell em u got nothin 2 do with this.

repino: Wot if they don't believe me?

killerinstinct32: U know some good lawyers.

repino: I don't.

killerinstinct32: U know someone who does. I'm relyin on u. Don't let me down.

repino: I'll try.

killerinstinct32: U gotta do more than that. Else I vamoose forever.

repino: OK.

killerinstinct32: Sure?

repino: Yeah.

killerinstinct32: OK. Gotta scoot. Hasta luego.

killerinstinct32 has logged out.

repino has logged out.

New Haven, CT

The Beinecke Library opens at nine o'clock every morning, and Tartu was always to be found waiting outside a few minutes before. Rehearsals with the orchestra began at midday, he'd explained to Anna, so he wanted to get in as much time here as possible before he had to go off to the symphony hall.

Tartu was turning out to be something of a minor celebrity in the Beinecke. Many people recognized him, and though few were crass enough to ask for an autograph – not that they'd have gotten much joy, since pens were strictly forbidden in the Reading Room – some smiled at him, or murmured how sorry they were that he'd been caught up in such a dreadful thing. Tartu would smile with unfailing courtesy at each of them, even if they'd disturbed him in the midst of ferocious concentration on a rare manuscript.

He thanked Anna every time she brought up from the archives something new – which was to say, something very old, though new to him. She saw his excitement at a first edition of *Heart of Darkness*, an original Boswell journal, the manuscripts of *Exiles* and *Far from the Madding Crowd*, the Lhasa edition of the sacred Tibetan Kanjur. Tartu held them as though they were precious children, tracing a gloved finger across the pages in reverential silence. More than once, Anna thought she saw his eyes moisten. She'd found over the years that, while many people say they love books, few really do; not in the same way that people love art or music, let alone their families. But Tartu clearly did.

He asked her if she was free this Saturday, and if so, whether she'd like to come to the concert as his guest. He couldn't sit with her, obviously, but he'd make sure she had the best seat in the house, and maybe afterwards he could take her out to dinner, to thank her for all the kindness she'd shown him.

She'd like that, she replied. She'd like that very much.

42

Late afternoon, barely even dark, and Ulysses Bar on Beacon Street had the gentle buzz of happiness that comes from the end of the day's work and the start of the evening's drinking. Ulysses was as Irish as its name suggested, and more authentically so than most of the city's 'Irish' pubs. It was slightly off the Freedom Trail, so it attracted fewer tourists and more proper Bostonians. In particular, it was a favorite watering-hole for those who worked in the vast Suffolk County Courthouse just round the corner in Pemberton Square; and more often than not, that included cops who'd been required to testify in court that day.

Like most cops, Sergeant Glenn O'Kelly both loved and hated court appearances. Loved court appearances, because they were almost guaranteed sources of overtime. If you'd come off a 00:00–08:00 shift, or were scheduled for a 16:00–00:00 one, an appearance during normal court hours meant you had to do double time. Some of the more enterprising members of the department had been known to pull down six-figure salaries this way. Collars for dollars, they called it.

And hated court appearances, because a cop's natural milieu was out on the streets, not in a witness stand with some smart-ass lawyer in a $3,000 suit trying to make him look stupid. O'Kelly had been a cop for long enough to know that the legal system had precious little to do with determining the innocence or guilt of those on trial. Every court case was a game in which the opposing sides tried to outsmart each other on technical points that made no real difference to the matter in hand.

If you were the defense attorney, part of that game was taking a man like O'Kelly – straightforward, decent, blunt – and making him look shifty and stupid by tripping him up on the kind of mistakes people made ten times a day. Nothing pissed off a cop more than a defendant who was guilty as sin but who walked anyway because he had a lawyer using more tricks than Penn and Teller. One day, O'Kelly always thought, one day a lawyer like that would have his house burgled or his wife raped by the kind of scum he'd just got acquitted, and you could guarantee that then he'd come running to the cops at top speed.

All this was going through O'Kelly's head as he sipped his Guinness, because he'd spent the last couple hours testifying in a quadruple murder down in Mattapan, one of south Boston's unlovelier areas. Lot of Haitians there. High crime rate. The do-gooding liberals would tell you the two weren't connected, but O'Kelly knew what the crime rate was like back in Haiti itself, and . . . well, you do the math. That was O'Kelly. Blunt, told it like it was.

He and his fellow officers – five of them had been called to testify today – chewed the fat for a while, and they agreed that this case was as open and shut as any they'd ever come across. No way would the suspect get off. No way.

231

Buoyed by this – another bad guy off the streets for a long, long time – O'Kelly finished his beer and said he had to go. His wife was expecting their first child, and the in-laws were coming over for supper. Time to go play happy families. His colleagues sent him on his way with a couple of mother-in-law jokes. He'd heard them all before. Didn't stop him laughing at them.

O'Kelly had parked in one of the multi-level parking lots on Beacon Street: as in most cities, parking space was at a premium. He went to the pay station, paid his ticket, and rang his wife as he headed for his car. Yes, he was on his way home. No, he hadn't had too much to drink. He didn't mind the nagging. It was white noise to him already, only a few years into their marriage. By the time they were senior citizens, he wouldn't hear it at all. He blipped the fob to unlock his car, and told her he had to go: he was on his way.

A strange distortion, a darkening, in the window of his car door as he opened it. A figure behind him, arm raised and then coming hard down and round, something unyielding smacked on to his temple, and his final, surreal thought before it all went black was that he knew what his wife would say: Some people will do anything, ANYTHING, to get out of having dinner with the in-laws.

43

It was forty-five minutes or so before Ferris Bowe, one of the men who'd been drinking with Glenn O'Kelly in Ulysses, arrived at his own car in the same multi-level. He'd probably had a little too much to drink, truth be told: enough to be done for DUI, that was, though cops tended not to bust other cops unless they were several times over the limit. And Ferris Bowe certainly wasn't that. He wasn't drunk, merely feeling good.

Feeling good right up to the point he saw O'Kelly's cellphone on the ground.

He knew it was O'Kelly's not only because he'd parked his own car pretty much next to O'Kelly's this morning, but also because the phone had a green and white clip-on plastic cover adorned with a giant shamrock, and only O'Kelly was daft enough to have put some shit like that on his phone. Bowe picked up the handset and scrolled through the menu till he found the list of most recent calls. O'Kelly was always calling his wife: her number was bound to be on it sooner rather than later.

HOME, it said. He clicked on it. A few seconds while the connection was made, and then a ringtone, slightly muffled:

233

poor reception on account of being inside a large concrete building, probably.

She picked up. 'I thought you said you were coming back right away.' No 'hello', no preamble. Her voice was shrill. Hormones, Bowe thought, though his knowledge of pregnant women's behavior was strictly theoretical.

'Er . . . It's not your husband, Mrs O'Kelly. It's Ferris Bowe. I'm a colleague of his.'

'Where the hell is he?'

'I thought he was with you.'

'No.' Alarm behind the shrillness now.

'Well, he left us, oh, almost an hour ago. Said he was going straight home. I found his cell in the parking lot. He must have dropped it.'

Cops don't like to look foolish by over-reacting to something that turns out to be innocent: the Boston PD had been the butt of many jokes when they'd mistaken some battery-powered LED placards advertising a kids' movie for improvised explosive devices. But still less do they like to do nothing in a situation that turns out to have been critical. Looking dumb is one thing. Having your ass handed to you by a disciplinary committee is worse. But screwing around when you could have saved someone's life – especially the life of a fellow officer – well, that was the kind of thing that sent cops to the bottle and a lonely end with a hosepipe and an exhaust tube.

Bowe got on to his radio.

'10-56, officer in trouble. Repeat 10-56, officer in trouble.'

The great machinery of law enforcement spluttered and coughed into life. Officers were sent to Sergeant O'Kelly's home in Roslindale Village, to look after his wife and be there in case this was all a misunderstanding and O'Kelly turned up safe, sound and sheepish. The department's Special

234

Operations Unit, which comprises traffic cops, traced O'Kelly's likely route home, seeing if they could find any clues en route: anyone who'd seen something unusual, perhaps.

There was no CCTV in the parking garage, no attendant who'd seen anything: the barriers were automated, and raised when a paid ticket was inserted into the slot. The only time an attendant came down was when there was a problem. A description of O'Kelly's car was circulated: it seemed that whoever had abducted him had either driven it away himself or got O'Kelly to do it at gunpoint.

Boston PD alerted Cambridge PD: that was standard procedure while these killings were going on. Sure, the Cambridge dispatcher said, we've got the main suspect under constant surveillance. Don't think he's been anywhere near central Boston today, but we'll check anyway and get back to you.

The dispatcher checked with the surveillance unit. No, they said, it's not our shift. The Bureau boys are on now. That was their deal: alternating shifts between Cambridge PD and the FBI's Boston field office, eight hours on and eight hours off. Neither body had enough manpower to do the job round the clock.

The dispatcher called the Bureau. No, they said, it's not our shift. The Cambridge police department are on now. We're taking over at midnight.

A classic, solid-gold bureaucratic snafu. Absolutely textbook.

A brave soul dared tell Anderssen what had happened, and ducked for cover when the inevitable explosion came. No one had been watching Unzicker since four o'clock this afternoon. It was now almost eight. He could have been anywhere.

Find him, Anderssen yelled. Fucking find him, *now*, or heads were going to roll.

In the circumstances, Anderssen could probably have

rephrased this to advantage, but no one was going to tell him while he was in that mood.

Patrese hit the sirens and hauled ass up the interstate. He felt he could do this route blindfold by now, New Haven to Boston.

Two frantic search teams in neighboring cities: Boston cops looking for O'Kelly, Cambridge cops looking for Unzicker. A macabre race, trying to find one of them before he killed the other one.

Patrese's phone rang incessantly as he drove. First, Boston PD, wanting permission to go public with the search. Yes, Patrese said instantly: saving O'Kelly's life was the priority, everything else be damned.

Next was Dufresne. Nursultan's private jet had left Newark this morning, having filed a flight plan for Dulles in Washington, DC. It had returned to Newark from Dulles about a half hour ago. Nursultan had been at a Central Asian investment conference in the capital: a call to the venue had confirmed his presence there all day. Nursultan could not have been responsible for O'Kelly's disappearance.

After Dufresne came Kieseritsky. Tartu had spent the morning in the library, the afternoon in the symphony hall, and the evening at his hotel, where he was right now. That ruled him out too.

And finally Anderssen, also wanting permission to go public – but this time about the search for Unzicker. Trickier one, this. They'd spent the past few days doing everything they could not to spook Unzicker, and there was still the possibility that he might have nothing to do with this. It wasn't Unzicker who'd called the surveillance off, was it? He might be sitting in his lab in that crazy Lego building doing some impossibly complex calculations on his Misha project, and be totally oblivious to all this.

But no. If they found Unzicker – *when* they found him

236

– they were going to take him in anyway and question him, so he was going to get freaked soon enough. And someone who hadn't seen O'Kelly might still have seen Unzicker. Yes, Patrese said to Anderssen as well: make it public. Let's throw the kitchen sink at it.

They did just that. News bulletins at nine and ten, police roadblocks and information boards, and everywhere the unmistakable sounds common to pretty much every police investigation since the dawn of time: the fading footsteps of a bolting horse, and the loud slamming of a stable door.

44

Unzicker lived with around four hundred other graduate students in the Tang Residence Hall, a twenty-four-story tower block hard up against the Charles River. There were armed police at all entrances, waiting for him to return. Shortly after ten o'clock, he did exactly that.

Well, not exactly that. He was about fifty yards away when another grad student walked past him, did a double-take, checked his stride and said: 'Hey, man, it's me, Marcus. You know the cops are looking for you?'

Unzicker looked blankly at him.

'Jesus, freak: say something.' Marcus went on. 'The cops are looking for you. Looks like the damn SWAT team set up shop in Tang.'

Unzicker peered towards the main door of the apartment block. Two cops in stab vests and cradling sub-machine guns. He turned and started to walk away again.

'Listen, man,' said Marcus, 'if I wanted to live in a police state, I'd have moved to one. Now you go see what they want, and they can leave us all alone.'

Unzicker's eyes were glassy, as though he was having trouble focusing. He quickened his step. Marcus turned back toward the Tang building and hollered. 'Officers! Here! Got him!'

Now Unzicker was sprinting, and there were cops coming from everywhere: bursting from the Tang building as though spat out from the inside, sudden explosions of light and noise as cruisers appeared, tracking Unzicker in their headlamps. He ran one way, stopped, went another: vanishing into darkness for a second before the lights caught him again, as though in those brief moments he'd ceased to exist altogether. A raucous cacophony of sirens and shouts, telling him to get down on his knees with his hands up, and not even to think about going for his pockets, not for a second, else they'd blow him from here to kingdom come. Twenty officers, thirty, forty, all here, all round him, multiplying like cells, training guns and hatred and flashlights on him, a state's crushing power over an individual. Unzicker's eyes were so wide, they seemed to take up half his face. He looked like he might die of fright. Down, down, they kept shouting, down on your fucking knees.

Patrese raised a hand and stepped into the circle of light. Unzicker shielded his eyes with one hand, trying to see beyond the halogen glare. Patrese fancied he could hear trigger fingers taking up that little bit more pressure. It made sense: they thought he was a killer, and he had one of their own, either alive or dead. But Patrese knew that sudden movements screwed up situations like this no end. He'd been both sides of that coin, and they both sucked. They had Unzicker where they wanted. One itchy cop trying to be a hero, and they'd lose their main contact with Kwasi.

'I've got this,' Patrese said, loud enough to be heard but in a tone that he hoped was calm enough to suggest reassurance. 'Thomas, we need to ask you some questions. Do you understand that?'

No answer. Unzicker didn't speak, Patrese remembered, not normally, and certainly not in situations like this.

'Nod if you understand,' Patrese said.

Unzicker was still for a few moments, and then he nodded.

'OK,' Patrese continued. 'Here's what's going to happen. I'm going to come forward and cuff you. I don't want to do that, but I have to. If you resist, these men will hurt you. Do as I tell you and we'll sort all this out. Nod again if you understand.'

Unzicker nodded.

Patrese went closer, trying as before to get the balance right: fast enough to be purposeful, slow enough not to spook Unzicker into doing something dumb. Twenty yards became ten, ten became five, five became two; and all the time Patrese watched Unzicker's hands and had his own, good, hand resting on the butt of his gun, because if Unzicker was shamming and wanted to take Patrese with him in some inglorious suicide-by-cop, Patrese would just about have time to feel stupid before he felt dead.

'I'm going to go round behind you and cuff you,' he said.

He went round to Unzicker's back, squatted down alongside him and snapped on the cuffs, first one hand and then the other. Unzicker squealed in pain.

'Too tight?' Patrese asked. Unzicker nodded. 'That's 'cos I'm doing it one-handed. Your good buddy Kwasi busted my other wrist. You tell me where O'Kelly is, and I'll loosen them.'

Unzicker looked blankly at him and said nothing.

'You have the right to remain silent,' Patrese said. 'Anything you say can and will be used against you in a court of law. You have the right to have an attorney present during questioning. If you cannot afford an attorney, one will be appointed for you. Do you understand the rights I have just read to you? With these rights in mind, do you wish to speak to me?'

Unzicker continued to look blankly at him, and continued to say nothing.

They took Unzicker to the Cambridge PD headquarters. Normally, they'd have let him sweat for a couple of hours before starting the interview, but time was very much of the essence here. Glenn O'Kelly was possibly, probably, almost certainly dead; but while there was still a chance, and while Unzicker might have the key to unlocking that chance, they had to try everything they could. They'd take their chances with the not-having-an-attorney-present part: when law enforcement has good reason to believe that a suspect's information might be time-sensitive, other considerations take second place, and the courts usually recognize this.

Good cop, bad cop is a cliché, and like most clichés, it's one because it's true and it works. Anderssen was larger, older, more irascible than Patrese. He'd be bad cop.

He went in guns blazing: face up close to Unzicker, letting him smell the coffee and fast food on his breath, shouting at him that there was a special place in hell for cop killers, they knew all about Unzicker's mental history, they were going to bang him up for the rest of eternity unless he told them right now where O'Kelly was, dead or alive, and if he did they might consider leniency, but that offer was one-time, right now, and if he didn't take it in the next ten seconds so help him God.

There was a loud squelching sound and a sudden farmyard smell. Anderssen recoiled in disgust. 'You dirty fucker. You dare shit yourself in my station? Jesus *Christ*. Last time I pooped my pants, I was three years old. You're a grown man. The fuck is wrong with you? Lemme tell you this: you

241

can sit in that pile of shit till you fucking tell me what I want to hear.'

He took a step back, and another. Patrese saw the stain on Unzicker's trousers. Unzicker was sobbing silently, shaking in huge, mute convulsions. The man who'd killed Darrell Showalter and Chase Evans had been ruthless and methodical. He wasn't the kind of guy who shat himself in an interview room the moment a cop yelled at him.

Then Patrese remembered how wrong he'd been about Kwasi. He wasn't going to make the same mistake twice.

He leaned in as close as he could, stifling the gag reflex at the back of his throat. 'Tell us where he is,' he said quietly. 'Tell us where he is, and we'll get you cleaned up.'

Unzicker stared at him. You have the right to remain silent, Patrese thought.

'Don't know what you're talking about,' Unzicker said suddenly.

'Glenn O'Kelly. Cop who went missing in Boston tonight. Been all over the news.'

'Haven't seen the news.'

'Where have you been?'

'Out.'

'Out doing what?'

Long pause. 'Can't tell you that.'

'Why not?'

'Just can't.'

'Something to do with Misha?'

'No.'

'Then what?'

Silence. Anderssen spat out a curse. Patrese made a damping motion with one hand behind his back, so Unzicker couldn't see: leave this to me.

'Thomas,' Patrese continued, 'we think you attacked Sergeant O'Kelly, and that if you attacked him you

242

probably killed him, or at least tried to kill him. Unless you can disprove that, you're in a whole heap of trouble. If you really don't know what I'm talking about, then you've got to tell me where you were instead. Wherever it was, whatever you were doing, it can't be as bad as killing a police officer.'

'Down by the river.' Unzicker's voice was so quiet that Patrese had to lean in still further to hear: too close, with the smell. He fought the urge to wince: didn't want to put Unzicker off his stride, not now he was beginning to open up.

'What were you doing down by the river?'

More silence.

'Thomas? You have to tell me. "Down by the river" isn't enough. What were you doing there?'

Unzicker started to cry again. Patrese waited him out.

'Girls,' Unzicker said at last.

'What about them?'

'Watching them.'

'It's dark. It's November. It's cold. How can you be watching girls by the river?'

'Boathouse. Ladies' rowing. Training. Gym. Lycra.'

Chase Evans, the Harvard cox: his body had been left by the Harvard boathouse, Patrese remembered. And Unzicker had been in trouble with the authorities before, more at Harvard than at MIT: all the Mr Question Mark stuff, making girls feel uncomfortable.

'The MIT boathouse?' Unzicker nodded. 'That far from where we found you?' Unzicker shook his head. 'You there all this time?' Unzicker shook his head again. 'Then what? What else were you doing?'

'Walking.'

'Walking?'

'Walking. And thinking.'

'Thinking about what?'

'Misha.'

'You been in contact with Kwasi recently?'

Another wide-eyed stare.

'Thomas, you gotta tell me. You been in contact with him?'

'No.'

'No?'

'No. No. No no no no no no no no.'

Lying, Patrese thought; but how to be sure? How to prove it? Unzicker was like Kwasi: you couldn't apply normal standards of behavior to weirdoes. All those telltale tics cops are trained to look for, the body language that says someone's lying, they're useless with some people. He feared Unzicker might be one of those.

He was still debating how best to play the next move when the door opened. It was one of the Cambridge cops.

'They found Sergeant O'Kelly's body.'

45

Glenn O'Kelly – more precisely, the headless and one-legged body of Glenn O'Kelly, plus a Chariot tarot card – had been dumped in the Navy Yard, towards the northern end of the Freedom Trail and one of the city's premier tourist spots. The yard was busy by day but pretty much deserted at night, save for the handful of sailors assigned to the yard's center-piece, the eighteenth-century USS *Constitution*. It was one of these sailors who had found the body and alerted the police. O'Kelly's car was discovered nearby.

The Navy Yard is in Charlestown, on a peninsula slightly north of downtown Boston. Cambridge is a little to the west. None of the distances involved were vast. In the time frame involved, therefore, Unzicker could easily have left Cambridge, gone downtown, abducted O'Kelly, killed him, dumped his body in Charlestown and headed back to Cambridge.

Whether he had done just that, of course, was another matter entirely.

They took his fingerprints and a DNA swab from inside his cheek. They removed his clothes – not one of Patrese's most treasured career moments, given the state of Unzicker's trousers – and bagged them as evidence, to be cross-referenced against anything found on O'Kelly's body or in his car. Unzicker said he'd never even heard of O'Kelly, let alone met him: so if there *was* a match, the only conceivable possibility would be that Unzicker had killed him.

The police doctor examined Unzicker and took samples of anything that might provide a link the other way; that was, anything of O'Kelly's on Unzicker rather than vice versa. Samples from under his nails, stray hairs, that kind of thing. Only when this was done was Unzicker allowed to clean himself up and put on some new clothes: someone had found an old airline tracksuit that made him look like something out of a children's program. They assigned him a cell, and told him he wasn't going anywhere till the morning at least, and maybe the rest of his life.

It was a little past midnight, and Patrese was about to clock off, when Nursultan arrived, lawyer in tow. The lawyer was tall, silvering at the temples, and altogether better turned out than anybody had a right to be at this hour. He handed Patrese his card: GREGORY Y. LEVENFISH. Office on Fifth Avenue. Upper East Side accent, Upper East Side attitude. Demanding this, threatening that. Patrese bit back irritation and fatigue, and said they'd done everything by the book, they hadn't been obliged to wait for a lawyer when they had reason to believe there'd been a public safety issue, and so on and so forth.

Levenfish spouted more rules and regulations. Patrese assured him that the district attorney would deal with all these points if the case came to court. Yes, Levenfish could see his client. No, Nursultan could not accompany him. Nursultan's turn to rant and rave. Patrese was unmoved. If you're neither a licensed attorney nor a family member, you can't see the suspect. End of.

Your career, Nursultan replied: end of. Patrese laughed. Anyone with any money made that kind of threat to law enforcement agents sooner or later, he said. It might work where you come from, but not in the United States. More bluster: Nursultan accusing him of blackening the good name of Tatarstan. Patrese offered him some coffee. Regulation police-issue coffee could drop an otherwise healthy man in two sips.

Levenfish came back, demanding his client's immediate release. No, Patrese replied. They were entitled to keep Unzicker here for forty-eight hours, and only then would he have to make a decision: charge or release. They were going to use that entitlement, and nothing the lawyer or Nursultan could say, or do, or offer, would change that.

Nursultan took Patrese aside. Arm round the shoulder, voice lowered: Let's talk man to man, sort this out like adults. 'Franco – I call you Franco, yes? – Misha project is important, you know that. Unzicker, he's innocent, I know that. You let him go, I put up bail money, I guarantee – make personal guarantee – he come back for question any time you like.'

Not a bribe, Patrese noted: nothing improper in the suggestion.

'I'll let him go only if I'm satisfied he couldn't have killed Glenn O'Kelly.'

But Patrese was thinking. Unzicker was still their best link to Kwasi. His arrest was now public knowledge. If he really was nothing to do with any of this, but Kwasi had nonetheless gotten spooked, then they might have lost their best chance.

Unless Patrese could find a way to work it to their advantage.

46

Under federal law – this was a federal case – suspects can be held for forty-eight hours without charge. At the end of that time, they must either be charged or released. Some people think forty-eight hours is a long time, some don't. Perhaps it depends on the angle you're looking from. Forty-eight hours isn't that much time to build a watertight case against a tricky suspect, but then again that's the job of the district attorney, who'll have several months before the case comes to trial. But forty-eight hours might feel like an eternity if you're the suspect, isolated and scared in custody.

Unzicker seemed to be the latter, at least from the look of him when Patrese opened up his cell the next morning. The bags under his eyes could have carried the weekly grocery shop; his skin was blotched crimson and white.

'Sleep well?' Patrese asked.

Unzicker shook his head.

'We're going to question you later. Your attorney will be present.'

He shut the door before Unzicker could respond; not that

248

any reply would have been imminent, given Unzicker's track record so far. Another few hours of isolation, to make Unzicker sweat some more, give him a little information, then nothing. Repeat. It was as simple a tactic as it was effective. Most humans, even solitary computer nerds like Unzicker, need company and reassurance. Denying them all this makes them panic; they feel anxious, restless, full of self-doubt. They believe they're being ignored or forgotten, and are happy when their questioner returns. But in extreme cases, denying them company only hardens them. Hence the drip-drip of Patrese's solicitousness.

Cambridge PD and Bureau agents had spent the night tearing Unzicker's room apart. They'd found lots. Photographs of women, many of them with the blur of a surreptitious shot. A play about a bullied student in Prague who creates a golem and destroys his tormentors. Books and websites about the shootings at Columbine and Virginia Tech. Porn, obviously – there were two types of men, Patrese knew: those who look at porn online, and those who are dead – but nothing especially deviant. No BDSM, no children. Quite arty, in fact, some of it: black-and-white shots full of shadows and close-ups.

But in all this, nothing that looked to have a direct link to the case. The conceit that killers have walls plastered with newspaper clippings of their crimes is strictly Hollywood, but nowhere on Unzicker's laptop – nowhere obvious, at any rate – was there any evidence that he'd spent time searching for information about the killings.

Yes, he'd read one story from the Harvard Crimson website about the murder of Chase Evans, but that was hardly surprising – Harvard was just down the road. In any case, he'd visited four other news pages on the same website in quick succession, all nothing to do with the murder: two about the upcoming Harvard–Yale football match, one about a production of *Tosca*, and an opinion piece about Barack Obama. Hardly bin Laden's browser history.

They'd been to Unzicker's office in the Stata Center too, to check out his computers there, but had found nothing. Not 'nothing' as in 'nothing of relevance'; 'nothing', as in no computers at all. Patrese had been in that office the previous week, and he remembered three computers there, two enormous iMacs and a laptop. They'd all gone.

Nursultan, Patrese thought. Paranoid about Project Misha, he must have gone in and removed them the previous night, en route to or from the police station when he and Levenfish had come to see Unzicker. Patrese rang him.

'You've got the computers from the Stata Center, haven't you?'

'Those computers: my property. Property of Kazan Group. Not Unzicker.'

'Those computers are germane to my investigation.'

'You say someone take them?'

'Don't fuck with me. You've got them.'

'You have search warrant? Then I make co-operate. But nothing for me to do, if I don't have machines.'

'Where are you?'

'Other end of phone to you.'

Patrese ended the call with a curse, rang through to the task force HQ in New Haven, and told them to get a search warrant for Nursultan's computers. Yes, he understood that it would be hard if they didn't belong to Unzicker personally. No, he didn't want to hear excuses. Just do it.

Good news: nothing so far that would conclusively rule out Unzicker having killed Glenn O'Kelly. No one had seen him yesterday evening during the time of his disappearance, at least not definitively enough to swear to it: it had been dark and cold, the kind of weather in which people muffled up and hurried on their way. Footprints had been found down by the MIT boathouse that matched the shoes Unzicker had been wearing at the time of his arrest, but there was no way of telling whether he'd made those prints when he said he'd been there, the previous afternoon, or some unspecified time before. He hadn't even taken any photos of the girls he said he'd been watching – it had been too dark for a decent shot, presumably – but that had ruled out another possible alibi. Not only do digital cameras have time and date stamps, but the subjects in the pictures could have confirmed whether they'd been there at that time.

Bad news: nothing so far to conclusively prove that Unzicker *had* killed Glenn O'Kelly, either. No matches yet from forensics between Unzicker and O'Kelly, or between Unzicker's room and O'Kelly's car. No sightings of Unzicker anywhere near the Ulysses Bar or in the Beacon Street parking lot. And no definitive evidence meant one thing: to get a charge, they'd probably need a confession.

For Patrese, a confession was the end to which he always worked. You could always tell what kind of cop you were dealing with, he thought, by the word they used to describe the process of questioning a suspect. A man like Anderssen would call it an interrogation, which bespoke a workman's directness: you hammer away at a suspect, you chisel down his defenses, you prise the truth from him as though with pliers. These past few years, interrogation had taken on other overtones too: orange jumpsuits, waterboarding, Jack Bauer and falling skyscrapers. And it doesn't work on hardened professional gangsters, who are more likely to run through a selection of Broadway hits than ever admit to wrongdoing. But most people will say anything if they're pushed far enough. Patrese had worked with plenty of cops who thought that if an admission contradicted the facts, then the facts were wrong; and if the facts were wrong, then they should be changed.

251

So Patrese preferred to think of the process more as an interview. You gain trust, you exchange confidences, you wheedle and nurdle away, taking your time, being subtle, being patient, so when the magic words 'I confess' finally come, they do so not in the shriek of a man who can take no more pain, but from the heart, slipping out with the same casual inevitability that a man will tell his woman that he loves her. Perhaps this kind of interview was in its own way a seduction, though inevitably the promises made – of leniency, of good treatment – tend not to last much longer than it takes to type up the statement and get the suspect to sign it. Patrese didn't just want a confession; he wanted to find out *why*. He wanted Unzicker to hand him his soul.

Mid-morning, they assembled in the interview room: Patrese, Anderssen, Unzicker and Levenfish. Patrese made the necessary introductions for the tape – time, date, those present – and he began.

'Thomas, will you tell us again your movements between four p.m. and the time you were arrested last night?'

'My client has nothing to add to his statement yesterday,' Levenfish said.

'Your client is perfectly capable of answering for himself.'

'The Fifth Amendment gives him the right to remain silent.'

'Yes, it does. And you know as well as I do that, whatever the Constitution says, whatever the judge says, when a jury sees a defendant who took the Fifth, they think one thing and one thing only: that person's got something to hide.'

'Really? The juries I get tend to agree with me.'

Anderssen twitched; wanting to smash Levenfish's face in, no doubt. Patrese kept talking, smoothing things over. 'We're only interested in finding the truth.' He leaned towards Unzicker. 'Listen to me, Thomas. Kwasi King is out there, and he's doing terrible things. We need you to help us find him. If you want to tell us about Sergeant O'Kelly, then we'll listen. Does he have a hold on you? Kwasi, that is. You don't look like the kind of person who'd do this normally. Some people have that power over others. It's nothing to be ashamed of, if it happens to you.'

Levenfish leaned in towards Unzicker too, forcing Patrese to move back a fraction, asserting his primacy over his client. 'Don't answer that, Thomas. Classic police tactics. The first technique of neutralization: denial of responsibility, allowing the subject to blame someone else for the offense.'

'Or perhaps a Bureau agent trying to do his job.'

'And a lawyer trying to do his. Rather more successfully, I might add.'

Much more of this, Patrese thought, and he might be investigating Anderssen on a case of bodily harm. Mitigating circumstances: victim was a smart-ass lawyer.

'Tell us what happened, Thomas. I've got to be honest with you: I spoke to the DA this morning, and he's out for blood on this one. You seen the papers? You know what the TV news is saying? You killed a cop, Thomas—'

'My client did no such thing.'

'—you killed a cop, and it doesn't get worse than that, not so far as the police are concerned. My colleague here, Detective Anderssen; you killed a man just like him. A good man, dedicated to ensuring law and order. I let a bunch of Boston cops in here right now – I let the guys O'Kelly was drinking with yesterday in the Ulysses Bar, before you killed him – and Mr Levenfish and I left, what do you think they'd do to you, given free rein? What do you think? It wouldn't be pretty.'

'That's threatening my client.'

'It's nothing of the sort. It's outlining a hypothetical situation to get across to him the gravity of his offense.'

'Alleged offense.'

'We're not in court now, Mr Levenfish. You don't have to pick me up on endless little details. What I'm trying to tell you, Thomas, is this. The DA's out for blood. He's got public opinion on his side: no one likes to be seen as soft on crime. The only chance you have of making this easier for yourself is to confess. You confess, and he'll be more lenient. So will the judge.'

Levenfish slammed his fist down on the table. 'Bullshit! Total bullshit! A confession does precisely the opposite, and you know that as well as I do. A DA without a confession can't make half as strong a case. You got any compelling forensics here, Agent Patrese? Let's see them if you do. But if you don't – and you don't – the DA hasn't got a leg to stand on. The very least, he'll have to make a plea bargain. A confession makes his job a whole lot easier. A confession gets before a jury, I'll tell you the prospects of acquittal. Nil. So don't you go lying to my client here. You're not . . . don't you go lying.'

Patrese could guess what Levenfish had been about to say: *You're not allowed to lie*. But that wasn't true. There's no law against outright lies or other deceptions on the part of law enforcement during questioning. Nothing they promise is binding on them, let alone the DA.

They went back and forth like this for a while: Patrese probing and Levenfish defending, Patrese putting up flares and Levenfish shooting them back down again. An hour went by, two, and Patrese was getting nowhere. A more loquacious – hell, a more *normal* – man than Unzicker might have started talking by now, but it was lunchtime, fourteen hours or so since the arrest, and they were pretty much where they'd been to start with. Not so much back to square one as never having left square one in the first place.

Patrese paused the interview and stepped outside with Anderssen.

'This is not going well,' Patrese said.

'You said it. I hoped he'd be a plumber and we could get to him that way, but no.' A plumber was cop slang for someone who often needed to take a piss. You could usually threaten such people by refusing to let them go to the toilet until they'd co-operated.

'It's like interviewing Marcel Marceau.'

'At least Marcel Marceau makes you laugh.'

'He's still at the dead point of absolute denial. We have to get him away from that. We're not going to be in business till we do. We need to change our strategy around.'

'How?'

'If I knew that, we wouldn't be out here in the first place.'

Levenfish emerged from the interview room. 'Can you get us two coffees, please?'

'Do I look like a fucking busboy?' Anderssen snapped. 'Machine's down the end of the corridor. Get it your damn self.'

The arch of Levenfish's eyebrow was superciliousness itself. 'I see the Bureau have got better manners than the Cambridge police.' He strode off towards the coffee machine.

'The fuck does he think he is?'

Patrese held up a hand: wait. Anderssen furrowed his brow in puzzlement. Patrese waited till Levenfish was out of sight before he spoke.

'That's it.'

'That's what?'

'That's what we have to do.'

'What are you talking about?'

Patrese mimicked Levenfish's voice. *'I see the Bureau have got better manners than the Cambridge police.* Divide and rule, oldest play in the book: set the snobby Bureau against the salt-of-the-earth police.'

'So?'

'So that's what we have to do back to them. Drive a wedge between Levenfish and Unzicker. Get them arguing. Get Unzicker to distrust his own lawyer.'

'Sounds like a plan. But how are we going to do that?'

'Find out what we can about Levenfish. Must be something we can use.'

Ten minutes on Google provided exactly that something. Mixing his metaphors with abandon, Patrese thought that you didn't get to be lawyer to a man like Nursultan without being near the top of the tree, but sometimes you didn't climb that tree without sailing close to the wind.

And so it proved with Levenfish. Levenfish had pulled off some spectacular results in the past, but there had also been what might charitably be described as setbacks. Patrese printed out the links, gave thanks to Brin–Page, Supreme God of the Search Engine, and went back into the interview room.

'You know, Thomas, you don't have to take the first attorney you're given,' he said.

Levenfish clicked his tongue. 'What is this, Agent Patrese? Amateur hour?'

'Thomas, you don't have to say anything in reply to what I'm about to tell you. You don't have to worry about incriminating yourself or anything like that. I just want to tell you a few things about Mr Levenfish here.'

'This is deeply unprofessional. You have no right . . .'

'I have every right. If I speak an untruth, I'm sure you'll tell me. So let's start with this. Who's paying for your services, Mr Levenfish? Mr Nursultan, I presume. What's Mr Nursultan's aim here? Truth, justice and the American way? Or the preservation of your liberty, Thomas, so you can keep working on Misha? Mr Nursultan cares about you in one way and one way only: the value you can bring to that project, and by extension to him and his company. He doesn't have your best interests at heart.'

'That's an untruth, right there,' Levenfish said.

'OK, let me amend that. He has your best interests at heart only as long as they coincide with his. The moment they diverge, he'll drop you like a stone.'

'Garbage.'

'You want to take a bet on that? More to the point, Thomas, you're putting yourself in a position where you're beholden to him. At the moment, you work for him, he pays you, and whatever deal you have over Misha, that's what you have – and, no offense, I bet the deal favors him rather than you. But for every minute Mr Levenfish sits here, every minute he bills on this case, Mr Nursultan has another favor to call in off of you, another hold over you. You ever get difficult with him, he'll remind you that he sent someone to help you out when you were in trouble. People like him don't forget those kinds of things, ever. It's a debt you'll owe him as surely as if you owed him money. And believe me, Mr Levenfish isn't coming cheap.'

'You get what you pay for. Pay peanuts, get monkeys. Pay my rates, get the best.'

'The best? That right? Thomas, let me tell you a couple of things about your attorney. He's been sued by clients for overcharging them and defrauding them.'

'A case that I won.'

'A case that you *settled*.' Patrese took one of the printouts and slid it across the table to Unzicker. Levenfish picked it up. 'No, you don't,' Patrese said. 'You may not prevent me from showing your client such items.'

Levenfish glared at him, and put the printout down in front of Unzicker.

'Thank you,' Patrese continued. 'He's also been accused of laundering drugs money for clients.'

'This is absurd. *Accused?* The case didn't even make it to court.'

'Largely because one of the major witnesses was killed in a car crash.'

'Tragic.'

'Empty road, good conditions, modern car, no alcohol or drugs found in the deceased's system. That kind of car crash.'

He slid the second printout across to Unzicker. Levenfish made no attempt to intercept this one. Unzicker glanced at it, then looked up. Interest. Alarm.

'You didn't hire him, Thomas,' Patrese continued. 'But you can fire him, any time you like. We can find you another attorney.'

'A state-funded one,' Levenfish spat. 'Losers who can't make it in private practice.'

'Let's have a break,' Patrese said.

They took Unzicker back to his cell and said they wouldn't be questioning him again for a few hours. Levenfish could go: they'd call him in good time for him to make it back before the next session.

'You don't know who you're fucking with,' he said.

'On the contrary,' Patrese replied. 'I think I know exactly who I'm fucking with.'

Patrese had told Levenfish they wouldn't be questioning Unzicker again without him being there, but he hadn't said anything about simply talking to Unzicker. Every half-hour, more or less, Patrese went down to Unzicker's cell; just to see how you're doing, he said. And on each visit, Patrese would insinuate how much better off Unzicker would be without Levenfish, though he never said so explicitly.

There was another reason for the regularity of Patrese's

258

visits, of course: to rule out the possibility of Unzicker getting any proper sleep. Repeatedly letting someone fall asleep and then waking them up after half an hour is as damaging as not letting them sleep at all. Patrese wanted to knock away at Unzicker's resistance, tire him out, disorientate him. He made sure officers discussed the case as they walked past Unzicker's cell door. Tricks of the trade that are second nature to law enforcement, but which work time and again on inexperienced suspects.

When Unzicker was looking even worse than he had done at the start of the day, Patrese called Levenfish and told him they were starting questioning again in a half-hour. Levenfish arrived, even edgier than he had been earlier. He'd doubtless reported back to Nursultan, who'd equally doubtless put a rocket up his ass.

All of which suited Patrese just fine. The quickest way for Levenfish to alienate Unzicker was to become too aggressive, to fulfill the image of him as a ruthless shyster that Patrese had tried to plant in Unzicker's brain.

So off they went again: asking Unzicker for the third time to tell them what he was doing yesterday. They were looking for inconsistencies, things he'd said before that he contradicted now, things he hadn't said before that he did say now, things he'd said before that he didn't say now.

Levenfish started to get antsy at this, as they'd hoped he would; blustering about the police wasting everyone's time, about how they hadn't got any evidence with which to charge Unzicker, and so on. Patrese asked Levenfish to shut up and let his client answer. Anderssen asked Levenfish whether he was getting paid by the word or the minute. No wonder Levenfish's clients had sued him, Patrese added.

Back and forth, back and forth, Unzicker in the corner like a piece of spare meat as they all argued over him. Happy

259

to be ignored? Not if Patrese could help it. While Anderssen argued with Levenfish, Patrese began talking softly to Unzicker; *Leave them to their silly battles*, his tone seemed to say, *let's you and me talk like men*.

Anderssen had distracted Levenfish so effectively that it was a minute or so before Levenfish noticed that Patrese and Unzicker were talking; and Anderssen had riled Levenfish so effectively that he went straight off the deep end.

'Don't talk to him!' Levenfish yelled: at Patrese, but at Unzicker too. 'Don't you damn well talk to him! Don't tell 'em a damn thing, Thomas! Shut the fuck up! Sit there and keep quiet, same as you always do.'

Unzicker looked at Patrese. He opened his mouth to say something, and Levenfish was in his face instantly. 'No! Shut the fuck up! You don't say anything, they can't get you on anything! Which part of that massive freaky nerd brain of yours doesn't get that?'

Patrese wouldn't smile: not now, not yet, not while Unzicker could see him. Levenfish sat back in his chair, suddenly and belatedly conscious that he might have gone too far. He wouldn't say sorry, Patrese guessed: he didn't look like the kind of guy who ever said sorry, especially not to a client in front of the cops.

Unzicker opened his mouth again, and this time he did speak.

'I'd like you to leave, please.'

With Levenfish gone, and a replacement on the way – though quite who and when was left deliberately vague – they got down to business again. Patrese and Anderssen against Unzicker, good cop and bad cop, interviewer and interrogator. Anderssen jabbed his points home like a boxer. You killed O'Kelly. You said you were down by the river. The river's

260

where the boathouses are. Chase Evans was found at the Harvard boathouse.

Then Patrese, more thoughtful. It must be a privilege to kill a human, no? What an honor, to be the last person to see someone alive, the first to see someone dead, the only witness to the transition between the two. Half and half, midway between states of existence. Like a vampire.

Anderssen again. Darrell Showalter was from Cambridge. Connections, connections. You worked out this plan with Kwasi over the course of your work on Misha. You killed the first two victims together in New Haven, more or less equidistant between your home and Kwasi's. Tell us. You killed them. Tell us. You killed them. Tell us.

Unzicker was flinching with every accusation that Anderssen made. His head jerked back, as though he was being physically hit. He looked round for help; at Patrese. Patrese said nothing, but made the slightest gesture with his hand: there's only one way to stop this, and you know it as well as I do. Just give in. You'll feel better.

Showalter: hit, flinch. Boathouse: hit, flinch. Evans: hit, flinch.

It was warm in the interview room. Patrese poured two glasses of water. He handed one to Anderssen, drank the other himself. A third glass remained empty.

Anderssen was prowling, snarling, sweating. A few hours before, with a lawyer present, this wouldn't have worked; but Unzicker was even more tired now than he had been then, and he was alone and outnumbered. His fear of being treated like this was pitched squarely against his desire for it to stop. He was crumbling, fingers clinging on to the sheer face of his innocence, and Anderssen was kicking those grips away one by one.

'I did it,' Unzicker said suddenly. 'I did it. I killed them. I killed them all.'

*   *   *

It was dark outside. They'd put Unzicker back in his cell while they went through the formalities: typing the confession, talking to the DA who'd lead the prosecution, and so on. Normally, they'd announce the charges to the media in fairly short order, but Patrese wanted to hold off. There were two issues here, he said, and only one of them had been taken care of. They'd wanted Unzicker to confess, but they also wanted to get to Kwasi somehow, and right now they had little idea how to do that.

Telling the world that Unzicker was being charged with triple homicide would send Kwasi deep underground. They still had half their forty-eight hours left, and Unzicker was going nowhere. They'd go and get some sleep, and convene tomorrow morning to discuss how best to play this, how best to tempt Kwasi out of hiding. They didn't have to tell anyone anything until round about ten o'clock tomorrow evening, when the original time period would expire.

Patrese went back to his hotel – his second hotel, of course, because most of his stuff was still in New Haven – liberated a couple of beers from the minibar, and flicked uninterestedly through the TV channels. It had been a long day: interrogations – sorry, interviews – always were, unless you got someone who confessed right off the bat. Patrese hadn't known many of those in his time; in fact, the only one he could remember was a woman in Pittsburgh whose boyfriend had been killed, and who could hardly wait to tell Patrese how she'd done it. Patrese's problem that day hadn't been getting her to talk; it had been getting her to shut up.

And, as it had turned out, there was a reason she'd sung so freely. She hadn't done it at all. She'd confessed in order to take the heat for the real killer – her son.

That was what was nagging at Patrese. It had been Anderssen who'd gotten the confession, not him; and

Anderssen's methods were exactly the type that produced false confessions. Yes, Patrese had been instrumental in persuading Unzicker to get rid of Levenfish, which in turn had given Anderssen a clear run, but only now, in the cold dark of the night, did he really let himself wonder: was Unzicker's confession on the level?

47

Patrese tossed and turned till the small hours, flipping things over in his head until they all zoomed in on each other like a tangle of wires. That Unzicker had confessed didn't make him guilty, but nor did it make him innocent. Most people tried to hold out for a while. If you started doubting every confession, then where would you be?

But, but . . . many people outside law enforcement think the only way you can get a false confession is to beat it out of the subject. Patrese knew that wasn't true. Criminologists divide confessions into three categories: voluntary, involving no external pressure (though the confession itself may not be true for any number of reasons, including psychosis, preserving another's reputation, and so on); 'coerced-compliant', where the confessor knows they aren't guilty but confesses anyway to receive a promised reward or avoid an adverse penalty; and 'coerced-internalized', when an innocent suspect is induced to believe they're guilty.

Patrese remembered some Bureau report about a lab experiment demonstrating these last two points. Students

264

were paired with researchers. The researcher read out individual letters, which the student typed into a computer. Each student was warned that they should on no account touch the ALT key, because a bug in the program would crash the computer and lose all the data. A minute into the experiment, unseen by the student, the researcher secretly crashed the computer, and then accused the student of pressing the ALT key. Every single student denied it at first. Each researcher then wrote out a confession and asked their particular student to sign it, getting angry with those who refused. Eventually, more than two-thirds of the students signed. Half of those added false details to embellish and justify their confessions. And, interestingly, there was a direct correlation between the speed at which the researchers had read out the initial letters and the likelihood of the students confessing. The quicker they'd been obliged to type, the more likely they were to sign. They'd been flustered, agitated, browbeaten.

Just like Unzicker had been.

A confession didn't make you guilty. A false confession didn't take the real killer off the streets. A confession, true or false, ran the risk of them losing their lifeline to Kwasi.

Patrese had been wrong about Kwasi. Was he wrong about Unzicker? One didn't presuppose the other. Take each case on its own merits. But that was easier said than done. When you work in law enforcement, sooner or later you end up thinking that it's better to put an innocent man inside than let a guilty one go free. The civil liberties mob see it the other way round, of course; but the civil liberties mob don't exactly have traction in police stations and Bureau offices up and down the nation.

Anderssen wouldn't care whether the confession was true or not, Patrese knew. Anderssen had got his man, and that was enough for him. Anderssen gave thought only to what happened on his patch: Showalter, Evans, O'Kelly. The rest of the investigation – what Dufresne was doing in New York, what Kieseritsky had found in New Haven, the whole operation Patrese was conducting – none of that was Anderssen's concern. Patrese didn't blame him for that, but he did have to take account of it. He wouldn't mention his concerns to Anderssen. Anderssen would only try to talk him out of it.

Patrese needed sleep more than anything. It wasn't coming. Figuring that rest was better than nothing, he lay in the darkness for several hours, trying to relax. Maybe he dropped off at some stage, maybe he didn't. But by six he was dressed and driving back to the police station.

On arriving, he went straight down to Unzicker's cell. He didn't bother asking Unzicker how he'd slept. By the look of him, Unzicker could have joined Patrese to form the steering committee of Insomniacs Anonymous.

'Thomas, I'm going to ask you a question. I want you to answer it truthfully. I don't want you to think about anything other than that. I don't want you to think about what happened yesterday, or what you think I might want to hear, or what you think Nursultan or MIT or anybody else might want. All I want is for you to tell me the truth. You got that?'

Unzicker nodded.

'Did you kill Glenn O'Kelly?' Patrese asked.

He was prepared for Unzicker's usual silent stare; but Unzicker answered instantly.

'No.'

'Chase Evans?'

'No.'

'Darrell Showalter?'

'No.'

'Would you like to retract your confession?'

'Yes.'

48

Anderssen was incandescent, as was the DA. Patrese spent half an hour mollifying the pair of them, and another half an hour pointing out how they could not only salvage something from all this, but actually make it work to their advantage.

They were going to let Unzicker go, but on three conditions. One, he allowed them to set up traces on his e-mails so they could see if and when Kwasi got in contact. They'd no longer have to take Unzicker's word that Kwasi had or hadn't done so. The police would return the computers they'd confiscated; Nursultan would doubtless return the ones he'd taken from Unzicker's office in the Stata Center. Normal service would soon be resumed.

Two, if Kwasi *did* get in contact, Unzicker would do exactly what Patrese told him to. The idea was that they would gradually draw Kwasi out; he'd have to think that Unzicker wasn't being monitored, and only then might he let down his guard. It was hardly a foolproof plan, but it was by a long way the best they had. And if Unzicker so much as began to think about trying to warn Kwasi, they'd have him back inside on charges of accessory after the fact and obstruction of justice quicker than he could say 'MIT'.

Third, twenty-four-hour physical surveillance would be maintained on Unzicker – no screw-ups, this time – and he was still not to know anything about it. Patrese was sure that Unzicker hadn't killed the three Boston victims – surer than Anderssen was, put it that way – but he reckoned that Unzicker was involved one way or another, even unwittingly. Where he went, who he saw, what he did: they needed this information in minute detail.

Patrese personally explained the first two of these three terms to Unzicker. Unzicker said he understood, and he agreed to them. He had nothing to do with any of this, he said. Patrese signed his release forms, took him out the back entrance of the station to avoid any lurking reporters, and then went to the Bureau's Boston field office and told a press conference that Unzicker had been released without charge, that the investigation was still ongoing, and that they'd please excuse him because he had work to do.

He wondered whether Kwasi would see this on the news. He sure hoped so.

Kwasi did see it, of course. He'd been watching the news ever since Unzicker had been arrested. And now they'd released him. Foolish, Kwasi thought. Patrese, the Bureau, the cops: all of them blundering around like blindfolded children trying to stick the tail on the donkey. Sure, they'd be monitoring Unzicker from now on, and they'd have his computers bugged to kingdom come, so Kwasi would have to be careful. Careful, but no more. There were ways to get to Unzicker the cops would never have thought of.

He'd already sent Patrese one communiqué, but he hadn't

expected Patrese to work it all out from that alone. He wasn't giving Patrese all the information at once, and the information he *was* giving, he wasn't making too obvious. But if he was going to keep things exciting, he'd have to give him some more.

Nothing about himself this time, Kwasi thought. Something a little more appropriate to a game between two people. A puzzle. A puzzle on a chessboard, though not strictly a chess puzzle.

He spent an hour or so composing it, taking his time, and then put it in an e-mail, checked that all the remailers were in place, and looked at his watch. The clock would be running from the moment he sent it.

Patrese was back in New Haven when the message arrived. Inessa was still in the incident room; she'd been going through pretty much everything of Kwasi's that was in the public domain – interviews, appearances, games, news stories – and trying to find some hidden, subtle clue which she, with her chess knowledge, would recognize as being germane to the investigation.

She'd had no luck so far, and Patrese could tell that she was beginning to get pissed off with it all. She wanted to go back home to Harvard. Patrese might be putting his life on hold for this case, but that was his job. Her job was nothing to do with this. And he was just about to say sure, thanks for your help, we'll call if we need you, when Kwasi's e-mail arrived. He read it, raised his eyebrows, printed a copy out and took it over to her.

It consisted of two sentences and a diagram:

Time for 40. You'll find a Rotting Husk.

TS	VE	PON	CL	IG	HE	I	IEC
SU	OSE	H	RMO	TH	ES	H	HE
SA	AND	THE	FN	IT	SC	SP	OF
TL	AY	DO	YON	IN	DO	CKE	DT
DA	N	ACK	OAR	N	AYS	TH	S
L	AYS	EB	AN	EB	RB	AN	SL
DC	YS	THE	MEH	KS	IT	LE	E
BU	EP	HEC	H	LP	GA	AND	HER

'What do you think?' he said.

'I think this is going to stop me from going home.'

'I'm sorry. But you know him better than I do.'

Inessa sighed, rolled her eyes, and looked at the message for a few moments.

'Well, that's clearly a chessboard. White square in bottom-right-hand corner, dark squares colored brown.'

'Even I got that bit. The letters? Any chess reference?'

Inessa scanned them quickly, up and down, left and right. 'Not an obvious one. There are only a few genuine words there: "her", "of", "I", "oar", and a couple of "do's", "and's", "he's", "the's", "it's", and "an's". It looks like a code of some sort.'

'You any good at cracking codes?'

'I like puzzles. A lot of chess players do. I'll give it a go. How long have I got?'

Patrese pointed to the first sentence. 'Time for forty?'

'Forty what? Minutes? Hours? Days?'

'I don't know.'

'It can't be that simple. It must mean something – well, something chess.' She clicked her fingers. 'Time: time control. Forty moves is the cut-off point in tournament chess. You get a certain amount of time to reach move forty, and then the clock starts again.'

'How long is that time?'

'Classical time control is two hours.'

'Two hours. Till we find a rotting husk. Come on. We're going to New York.'

'Why New York?'

'That's where Kwasi's killed all his victims so far. Why change now?'

'New York's a big place.'

'I know. That's why you're coming with me. You're going to decipher that thing while I drive, and it'll give us a clue as to where.'

'You sound very sure.'

'Why else would he have sent it? Come on. We've got two hours, and we might need every minute of them.'

271

49

He knew better than to keep asking her how she was doing: questions were only going to break her concentration and make her irritable. So Patrese kept his eyes on the road. The only time he spoke was when Dufresne called, and they discussed what they were going to do. Wasn't much they *could* do in a city the size of New York, not until they knew a little bit more.

Inessa sat with her feet on the dashboard, using her thighs as a makeshift board on which she could press as she wrote. She covered sheet after sheet of paper in scribbles as she tried to make sense of the random letters on the chessboard. Nothing worked across the rows, nothing down them, nothing on the diagonals. White squares only; nothing. Dark squares only; still nothing. She tried reversing the letters within their squares, and got more gobbledygook. Going round in circles from the outside in didn't work; nor did going round in circles from the inside out.

Heavy traffic, even with the siren to blast people out of the way. An hour gone.

'Reading in the car makes me feel ill,' she said.

'Tell me if you're going to be sick.'

'I'm going to be sick.'

He glanced across, saw she wasn't joking, and wrenched the car toward the hard shoulder. Inessa flung open the passenger door, parked the contents of her stomach on the asphalt with as much grace as could be expected in the circumstances, wiped her mouth with the back of her hand, and closed the door again. 'Let's go,' she said.

It wasn't everyone who could make barfing look cool, Patrese thought.

Forty-five minutes left. The signs for New York were coming more frequently now. Inessa looked up at one, craning her neck as they passed it – and she suddenly shrieked.

'Rotting husk!'

'What about it?'

'It's got capitals, right? Rotting Husk. Like a proper name. Like New York.'

'There's no place called Rotting Husk. Not that I've ever heard of.'

He handed her his BlackBerry so she could Google it. No, she confirmed after a minute or so: no place called Rotting Husk. But the name must mean something. Those words must mean something. Something more than a simple description of, well, a rotting husk.

'An anagram?' Patrese suggested.

'Could be.'

She wrote down all the letters, vowels on one side, consonants on the other. 'Chess,' she said, half to herself. 'Think chess. King?'

She crossed out the letters K, I, N and G from the list and rewrote what was left: ROTTHUS. She made 'trust', 'truth', 'tort', 'host', 'hurt'. None of it made sense. If it was an anagram, it was nothing to do with King.

'Move on,' Patrese said. 'Come back to it later if you need.'

'Queen' didn't fit. 'Rook' was nearer, but had one too many 'o's. 'Bishop', no way. 'Knight'? 'Knight' fitted. Pull the letters out again, see what was left. ROTUS.

'Tours,' she said instantly. 'Knight Tours.'

'Company name.'

'No, no. Move the "s". Knight's Tour. It's a Knight's Tour. That's what he means.'

'What's a Knight's Tour?'

'You know a knight moves, yes? Two squares one direction, one square at right angles. A knight's tour is a problem where you have to get a knight to visit every square on an empty board in turn, without ever visiting the same square twice.'

'Sounds impossible.'

'No, it's not. It's very easy.'

'Great!'

'No. Not great. The opposite. There are so many ways of doing it.'

'How many? Tens? Hundreds?'

'No. For closed tours, when the knight ends on a square attacking the one from which it began – so it can start all over again on the same path – something like twenty-six trillion.'

'You're shitting me.'

'Well, half of those are reflections of the other half.'

'That makes me feel a whole lot better.'

'For open tours, when the knight can't close the circle on himself, the number's unknown. More than twenty-six trillion. And we don't even know which square to start from.'

'We're fucked.'

'No.'

'No? You've got forty minutes to analyze trillions of possibilities, and you don't think we're fucked?'

'I don't have to analyze trillions. I'm not a computer. I have to be smart. If we didn't have a chance of solving this in the time available, he wouldn't have sent it, no?'

'I don't know.'

'Let's assume not. Otherwise, what would be the point of him sending it at all? So if we find the right tour, it'll spell something out. Probably in plain English, else again it's going to be too difficult in the short timespan. Yes?'

'Yes.'

'So I just have to look for words. He's broken them up into little bits; I just have to put them together again. If any line stops making sense, I scrap it and start again.'

'But where do you start? Where's the starting square?'

'I don't think he's been considerate enough to tell us that.'

'Begin at the beginning. Start of the game. What first move does he usually play?'

'Pawn to e4. That's good thinking, Franco. I'll start there.'

'Knight's Tour,' he said abruptly.

'Yes. We established that.'

'Knight. Knight tarot cards were found by the bodies of Dennis Barbero and Chase Evans. Ivy League students, the both of them. Columbia's the only Ivy League place in New York.'

'He's not going to hit Columbia again.'

'Why not? Huge place.'

'Everyone will be on alert.'

'No, they won't. They'll have worried about it for a few days afterwards, and then they'll have gone back to normal because that's what everyone always does.' He jabbed a finger at the paper. 'You get on with working it out.'

He dialed Dufresne. 'Bobby? We think he's going to try and hit Columbia again.'

'What? Why?'

'Too long to explain. Can you seal it off?'

'The whole university? Are you nuts?'

'Probably. We've got little more than half an hour.'

'You *are* nuts. The main campus alone is six blocks. It's

275

Friday afternoon, it's gridlock heading out of town as it is. Even if I could get the manpower in time, we'd get crucified by City Hall. And anyway, what's to say he's not already there?'

'Good point. OK. Get all the men you have, get some more off the other precincts, and flood the place. Get campus police on alert too. Bullhorns on cars, telling people to watch out. Let's see if we can spook him. Anyone you see looks vaguely like Kwasi, arrest their ass.'

'Anyone black, you mean.'

'Whatever you say, Malcolm X. You know that statue of the goddess?'

'The one opposite that big-ass library?'

'That's the one. I'll see you there.'

'You got it.'

They were heading against the worst of the traffic, but it was still pretty thick. Patrese had the siren on all the way in from New Rochelle, and even then it was slow going; but they made it to Columbia with fifteen minutes to spare. Dufresne was by the statue of Athena as promised, directing uniformed officers as though conducting an orchestra.

'I hate to ask you this,' Patrese said to Inessa as they pulled up, 'but . . .'

'No. I haven't done it yet. It doesn't make sense. I've tried every likely starting square, every possible first move: e4, d4, c4, f4, the two knight moves to f3 and c3. Nothing on any of them.'

'Top left?'

'What?'

'Top left-hand corner. Start there. As though you're reading a book.'

Inessa thought for a moment. 'No. If you're going to do it like that, you have to start bottom left. That's square a1.'

'OK.'

TS	VE	PON	CL	IG	HE	I	IEC
SU	OSE	H	RMO	TH	ES	H	HE
SA	AND	THE	FN	IT	SC	SP	OF
TL	AY	DO	YON	IN	DO	CKE	DT
DA	N	ACK	OAR	N	AYS	TH	S
L	AYS	EB	AN	EB	RB	AN	SL
DC	YS	THE	MEH	KS	IT	LE	E
BU	EP	HEC	H	LP	GA	AND	HER

The letters on a1 were 'BU'. From there, the hypothetical knight could only move to two squares, b3 (second
column along, three from the bottom) – or c2 (third
column along, second from the bottom). Square b3 was
'AYS', and 'BUAYS' wasn't any word, part of a word or
combination of words they'd ever heard of. So it had to
be c2: 'THE'.

Twelve minutes.

Five possible squares now: a3, b4, d4, e3, e1. Not d4:
'BUTHEOAR'. The other four were all in contention;
'BUTHEL', 'BUTHEN', 'BUTHEB', 'BUTHELP'.

Choice of four, and with false starts and retracing steps,

Inessa probably only had time to pursue one line to its end. Which one?

'BUTHELP' had 'help' in it. Seemed as good as any. Call it. 'BUTHELP' it was.

She looked back at the pattern so far: a1-c2-e1. The next logical step was g2: 'LE'. 'BUTHELPLE'. 'Helpless'? There was an 'S' on h4, and now the line was going up the side rather than along the bottom. She started to get faster and faster as she pieced it together: up the right-hand side, along the top, down the left-hand side and in, tracing pretty patterns as it spelt out its message:

BUTHELPLESSPIECESOFTHEGAMEHEPLAYSUPONTHISCH
ECKERBOARDOFNIGHTSANDDAYSHITHERANDTHITHERM
OVESANDCHECKSANDSLAYSANDONEBYONEBACKINTHE
CLOSETLAYS

'But helpless pieces of the game he plays upon this checkerboard of nights and days. Hither and thither moves, and checks, and slays; and one by one back in the closet lays.'

'You're a genius,' Patrese said. 'A stone-cold genius. What does it mean?'

'Omar Khayyam. Very famous chess quote. From the *Rubaiyat*.'

'Who the hell's Omar Khayyam?'

'Twelfth century. Persian polymath: poet, astronomer, mathematician, philosopher.'

Patrese turned to the nearest campus policeman. 'There a Persian faculty?'

'Persia?'

'Iran,' Inessa said.

'Oh. Yeah. There's a Center for Iranian Studies up on Riverside Drive. Number 450. The Brookfield.'

'Where's that at?'

The campus cop pointed in the direction of the Hudson. 'Couple of blocks that way.'

Dufresne was already radioing it in: All units to 450 Riverside Drive. Patrese leapt back in his car and fishtailed his way out of the campus pedestrianized area. Athena watched him go, stonily unimpressed.

It took him two minutes to get to the Brookfield building. He left the car in the road, prompting a furious volley of horns from those drivers behind him, and raced for the entrance. A maintenance man in fluorescent orange was going in; a cycle courier with helmet and pollution mask was coming out. Patrese barged between the two of them and into the lobby.

There was an announcements board with movable white letters on the far side. IN SEARCH OF OMAR KHAYYAM; A NEW APPRAISAL. PROFESSOR KARL MIESES. PURCELL ROOM, 6 P.M. ALL WELCOME.

It wasn't yet five. If Mieses was here in this building, he'd most likely be in his office. There was a list of the research center's occupants on one wall. Patrese scanned it.

MIESES, KARL W. PROFESSOR OF PERSIAN STUDIES. ROOM F4. SECOND FLOOR.

Photograph next to it: a black man with silver hair and seventies eyeglasses.

Patrese took the stairs two at a time, gun drawn. Sirens behind and below him: units arriving in response to Dufresne's call. Patrese barked Mieses' name and room number into the radio and kept going. No time to wait for back-up.

Top of the stairs, turn right. F4 was third on the left. Door locked.

'Professor Mieses?' More shout than question. No answer.

Patrese shot the lock off and kicked open the door.

279

Mieses was there; well, what Patrese assumed had been Mieses, at any rate.

Cops barreling through the door behind him, stopping, careering into the back of each other. 'Out!' Patrese shouted. 'Out, he's dead, there's nothing we can do, give me space. Seal off the building. Someone must have seen something. Find them.'

They left: some quickly, only too keen to get away, and some slowly, as though transfixed by the sight of a body with no head.

Blood everywhere, fresh and dripping with a high odor. Kwasi must have killed Mieses recently, as in a few minutes before Patrese's arrival. So how come Kwasi wasn't covered in blood when he walked out of here? And how had he got out in the first place?

Had he got out? Was he still here?

No, Patrese thought: he wouldn't dare. Unless he'd thought they wouldn't get the clue until it was too late, and had reckoned he had all the time in the world. Well, they'd soon find out. They were sealing off the building, and then they'd sweep every last inch of it.

He looked round the room. A professor's sanctuary: every wall covered in bookshelves, every surface invisible under papers, and half hidden behind a skyscraper of periodicals, a computer so ancient it should have been in the Smithsonian.

Patrese looked down to the floor, for the tarot card he knew would be there. Another Knight: the Knight of Wands, this time. And next to it, something which looked like . . .

An arm.

Half an arm, more precisely: a bottom half, from the elbow downwards.

Patrese glanced at Mieses' body again. His left arm was still intact, but his right had been severed at the shoulder. This stray portion of arm next to the tarot card had a hand

280

at its end. Kwasi had only taken his upper arm this time, from shoulder to elbow.

Why?

He'd taken the head, as usual. He'd taken skin patches front and back, as usual. So why only half the arm? Not to save time, that was for sure: it must have actually *cost* him time, to saw the arm twice rather than once.

No, Patrese thought. The only reason Kwasi would have done this was to make the piece of arm easier to carry, and the only reason he'd have done *that* was because he didn't have enough space for a whole arm in whichever bag he was using.

A little nag in Patrese's brain: something he'd seen and couldn't quite recall.

He looked round the room again. What – the obvious fact of a headless body aside – was out of place here?

There, pushed under an armchair. Something fluorescent, scrunched up. Patrese thought of the maintenance man he'd passed on the way in. He reached under the chair and pulled. There were two items, in fact: a waterproof jacket and waterproof trousers, both in bright orange with reflective white flashes, and both drenched in Mieses' blood.

Patrese looked under the chair again. Another two items, these ones smaller. Shoe covers, velcroed where they fastened round the ankle. A logo on the side, just about visible through the blood spatters. Nalini.

Nalini makes cycling clothes.

Not the maintenance man coming in as Patrese had arrived, but the cycle courier coming out – helmet on, pollution mask covering his nose and mouth. He'd had one of those cycle courier bags over this shoulder. A head and half an arm would fit in there, but a whole arm wouldn't. Kwasi must have had some sort of plastic lining inside the

281

bag to keep the blood from dripping, of course; but that wasn't exactly rocket science.

Kwasi had walked right past Patrese. Right past him, close enough to touch. And now he'd be long gone, lost and anonymous in a Manhattan rush hour.

Helpless pieces of the game, Patrese thought. Helpless pieces indeed.

The NYPD stopped every cycle courier they could find. None of them were Kwasi. Many of them, in fact, were working downtown, and even Lance Armstrong couldn't have made it from Morningside Heights to Wall Street in the time available.

Patrese gave an impromptu statement to the press from the steps of Columbia's Butler Library, and inverted the usual wisdom about security services and terrorists. Yes, he said, he remained confident that they'd catch Kwasi King. Kwasi had to be lucky every time; they only had to be lucky once.

And Patrese knew, though he didn't say, that chess is not a game of luck.

After a couple of hours, he left Dufresne in charge of the scene and headed back towards New Haven with Inessa. She was quiet until they were well clear of town, and then it all came gushing out. She blamed herself: if only she'd solved the puzzle sooner, Professor Mieses would still be alive.

No, Patrese said firmly: it was thanks to her alone that they'd gotten as close to saving Mieses as they had. Without her, they'd still have been floundering round Manhattan when Kwasi struck. She'd got them not just to Columbia but to the Iranian Center itself. There was only one person to blame for any of this, and that was Kwasi. He was the one doing the killing. He was the one playing games: the man-child, unable or unwilling to distinguish between murder and the puzzles page of a newspaper. It was nobody's fault but his.

Inessa's problem wasn't guilt, Patrese knew: it was shock. Being up close to a murder – a real live murder, if that wasn't a contradiction – was enough to throw most people off balance until they were used to it. All the TV shows and newspaper reports in the world couldn't prepare you for the visceral impact of knowing that a life had been snuffed out in the time it took you to drink a can of soda. Inessa hadn't seen Mieses' body in the flesh, of course, but she'd been part of the race to save him, she'd been swept up in the vortex of police sirens and radio chatter.

Patrese's instinctive reaction was a very male one: to solve Inessa's problem for her, break it down into its constituent pieces, point out where she was looking at them wrong, and reassemble them in a way that absolved her of all blame. But he'd been around, and with, enough women to know that Inessa didn't want him to solve her problem. She wanted him to listen. So that's what he did. He let her talk, let her spill the words again and again as though she was trying to purge the toxins of her failure from within her.

He listened all the way back to New Haven, and then over dinner in the hotel restaurant, and then with the contents of the minibar in his room. And somewhere between the second and third locations, he knew that they'd sleep together that night. Not because he'd be taking advantage of her vulnerability, but because cops, doctors and undertakers know the slightly sordid truth that the rest of us prefer to keep hidden.

Sex and death are intertwined. Death makes us feel horny.

Not the actual sight of a dead body itself, of course – well, not usually, and there's a word for people who broach this – but the presence of death, the imprint it has on those around it. Sex is the harbinger of life, and as such it's the

283

biggest, most literal fuck-you to death imaginable: assertion of life's intense but temporary primacy, negation of death's sting and the grave's victory.

So when Inessa stood up from the sofa and took Patrese's hand, he knew that this time she wouldn't lead him on and then leave at the last minute. And afterwards, when she was sleeping contentedly on his chest – wasn't it supposed to be the man who conked out first after sex? – he was staring at the ceiling, a single thought going round and round his head.

Kwasi had just killed, so now it was White's turn.

50

Patrese was kissing his way down Inessa's stomach in the half-light of a winter morning when his cellphone rang. 'Leave it,' she whispered, but he was already rolling away from her and reaching for the bedside table.

Casualties of the job, #219: an uninterrupted sex life.

ANDERSSEN, said the display.

'Hey, Max.'

'Gonna send you something. Caught on Unzicker's e-mail this morning.'

'OK. I'll take a look and call you back.'

The message came through thirty seconds later. Unzicker – e-mail address txu9301@mit.edu – was exchanging messages with an unnamed correspondent – weallhateharvard@gmail.com. The thread was entitled simply 'The Game'.

weallhateharvard@gmail.com: Y'all ready to play?
txu9301@mit.edu: Hell yeah. They won't know what's hit 'em.

weallhateharvard@gmail.com: Sure it can't be traced?
txu9301@mit.edu: Sure I'm sure.
weallhateharvard@gmail.com: Claim credit for it after?
txu9301@mit.edu: We'll see.

Patrese read it all through twice, and then rang Anderssen back. 'Where's he now?'

'Still in his room.'

'Any more than this? Any clue as to when he might be planning to, er, play?'

'I got what you got. Nothing more. Hold on.' Patrese heard the trill of a cellphone at Anderssen's end, and then Anderssen's monosyllabic gruffness as he answered, listened, spoke, hung up, and returned to Patrese's call. 'That's the watchers. He's on the move.'

'Where's he going?'

'Turned left along the riverbank. Heading upstream. On foot.'

Patrese looked at Inessa in his bed, rumpled and tousled and giving him a look so full of dirty promise that it would have seduced Truman Capote. The hell with the investigation, Patrese thought. Anderssen's men were professionals. Patrese had seen their sort at work, and they were good. They'd be front, back and either side, forming an invisible and elastic box around Unzicker. The watchers would swap places as they moved, but the shape would remain largely the same, and Unzicker would always be in view. They'd tail him wherever he was going, and if he so much as looked like harming someone, they'd nail him. Patrese had been chasing his tail on this thing for three weeks now. He'd had enough. A weekend off would do him good. A weekend in bed with Inessa would do him even better.

'I'm on my way,' he said.

*   *   *

Anderssen kept Patrese in touch with Unzicker's movements as Patrese hared up the freeway. Unzicker was still walking alongside the river: past the Hyatt, past Trader Joe's, past the famous Shell sign from the thirties, past Riverside Press Park.

After a mile or so, he hung a left on the Western Street Bridge, crossing the Charles River into Allston. There were more people around now: students clad in crimson or blue, tens becoming hundreds becoming thousands as they headed like pilgrims for tailgate parties in the fields and the main event itself, the Harvard–Yale football match.

Or, as those two institutions like to style it with typical modesty, The Game.

Not 'the game', Patrese realized when Anderssen told him where Unzicker was: The Game. But was The Game part of the game? After all, if you were killing Ivy League students, where better to search for targets than at the most famous Ivy League match-up of all? There weren't only a handful of potential targets here: there were thousands.

Allston, MA

Kick-off was midday, and there was still an hour or so to go when Patrese arrived. The watchers were clustered invisibly round Unzicker, tracking him as he walked between lines of tailgate parties in the field abutting the stadium. Anderssen was on top of an unmarked van in one corner of the field, watching Unzicker through binoculars. Someone found another pair for Patrese. They watched together in silence.

The tailgate parties are almost more of an event than the game itself. In the unremitting schedule of an Ivy League semester, this was one of the few days when students practically had a license to let their hair down and start drinking from the get-go. Many students hired U-Haul trucks to bring all the beer and barbecue equipment, and then leapt up on to the roofs of the trucks and started dancing. Twelve feet above ground, drunk and often in slippery conditions: it didn't need, well, a Harvard degree to see that more people were going to end the day with broken bones than had started it. There was probably less chance of injury in the match itself than there was at the tailgate parties.

And through all the smoking grills and merriment and shrieking laughter and beer coolers and bawdy songs, Unzicker walked alone. Some people recognized him from the news coverage and whispered to their companions, but most of the tailgaters were so busy eating and drinking that they wouldn't have noticed Elvis.

Patrese almost felt sorry for Unzicker, until he saw the look Unzicker was giving those past whom he walked like the angel of death. It wasn't hatred that Patrese saw in Unzicker's eyes, because hatred suggested a force, a power. What Patrese saw was an *absence*; a hollow where the spark of life should be. He shivered involuntarily.

With half an hour to go till kick-off, Unzicker went into the stadium. Half Greek arena and half Roman circus, Harvard Stadium is shaped like a horseshoe with a large crimson scoreboard at the open end and the Boston skyline beyond. The stands are numbered 1 through 37, with one to the scoreboard's immediate left and thirty-seven opposite. Unzicker had a ticket for stand number three, and sat about halfway up the seating bank.

Patrese had once taken down a suicide bomber in Pittsburgh's Heinz Field, which had been infinitely more demanding than this. Heinz Field seated twice as many people; Patrese hadn't known for a long time where the bomber was sitting; and he'd been left with no option other than to take a shot knowing that if his aim was off, even by a fraction, the bomber would have detonated his vest and taken out everyone within a ten-yard radius.

Here, it was hard to see at first glance exactly what damage Unzicker could do. It was broad daylight, and he was surrounded by thousands of people. There was no way he could find a victim and spirit him or her away without being seen. Maybe he was here simply to scope out a likely target: see who was too drunk to resist, keep tabs on them till after the game, and then strike when the crowds had dispersed and darkness was falling. If that was the case, the watchers would get him long before he could manage any of that.

They won't know what's hit 'em, Unzicker had e-mailed this morning. Patrese reminded himself not to take chances on this one. They weren't to take their eyes off Unzicker, not for a second.

Unzicker wouldn't know who the watchers were, but he sure as hell knew who Patrese and Anderssen were. They couldn't run the risk of him seeing them, but neither did they want to let him out of their sight, watchers or no watchers. Harvard Stadium was famous for its excellent sightlines, but for Patrese right now that was a drawback. Everywhere he could see Unzicker, Unzicker could see him.

Except one place, Patrese realized: from behind the scoreboard itself.

The scoreboard was mounted on the roof of the Murr Center, the building that housed Harvard's squash and tennis courts. Patrese and Anderssen flashed their badges at the facilities manager and got him to open the door leading on to the roof.

There was a maintenance gantry at the back of the scoreboard, though nowhere for the operators to sit and no protection from the elements: the board must have been controlled from elsewhere in the stadium. Patrese and Anderssen climbed on to the gantry. If they went to the right-hand side of the scoreboard, away from where Unzicker was sitting, they could watch him without being seen themselves.

The field stretched out ahead of them, end zone to end zone. The stands were filling up: Harvard crimson to their right, Yale blue to their left. This was emphatically not a day for neutrals, Patrese thought: except for one.

He trained his binoculars on Unzicker again. Unzicker was fiddling with what looked like a smartphone, or some other handheld electronic device. Patrese had brief fancies of mind-control rays and mass hallucinations: Unzicker as some sci-fi villain turning the crowd into zombies. Fans crowded to his left and right, front and back, and yet Unzicker managed to maintain around himself a small but definite exclusion zone, as though his weirdness and aloofness had combined to create a forcefield.

A long-forgotten movie scene came to Patrese' mind: spectators at a tennis match, their heads going back and forth with the ball, and in the middle of them all one man looking straight and unwavering at the man he was later going to kill. Hitchcock, Patrese thought, but he couldn't for the life of him remember the name of the movie itself.

When the teams came running on to the pitch, Unzicker looked only mildly animated while everyone else around him cheered and whooped. The color guard, the national anthem, all the pre-match rigmarole: Unzicker barely noted any of it, preferring instead to fiddle with his phone. Patrese kept watching, but for the moment his mind was elsewhere, back in his own glory days of college football at Pitt: the razzmatazz, the feeling that he was one of the big men on campus, the human tunnel through which the team would run on to the field while the band played 'March to Victory', and then the game itself, the handoffs from the quarterback, the heart-pounding rush into the tunnel of bodies in midfield, ducking, weaving, muscles

290

working faster than thought itself as he jinked toward the glimmering chinks through the darkness, run to daylight, run to daylight, as though the noise from the crowd was physically prising open the gaps in front of him, and then out into the open prairie and the long run for home, defenders floundering in his slipstream as the crowd rose and stamped and his teammates thrust their arms skywards, go Franco, go, go, go.

Nothing else in his life had ever come close.

Patrese forced his mind back to the present. The captains were shaking hands, the umpires were taking up their positions. The game was about to start.

A ripple in the crowd: surprise, laughter. Patrese saw faces turned toward him, fingers pointing. Instinctively, he ducked backwards, fully behind the gantry, and looked at Anderssen: *What the fuck?* Anderssen shrugged; he had no idea either. The laughter became louder, interspersed with cheers and boos; pantomime stuff, it seemed to Patrese, as though the game itself had been forgotten.

From the speakers on top of the scoreboard, so sudden and loud that Patrese and Anderssen both jumped, came the voice of the public-address announcer.

'Ladies and gentlemen, we apologize for the scoreboard malfunction. The game will start just as soon as we get it fixed.'

Patrese stepped out in front of the scoreboard and looked up at it. He was so close that it took him a moment or two to read the whole of the display: **HARVARD ARE A BUNCH OF HORSES' ASSES.** Cheers from the Yale fans; boos from the Harvard ones. As Patrese watched, the text faded into another sentence: **YALE SUCK HARDER THAN LINDA LOVELACE.** Standing in the middle, Patrese got a weird Doppler effect as the boos and cheers switched sides.

Patrese looked at Unzicker again, and this time there was

291

a discernible expression on Unzicker's face: one of ineffable satisfaction at his own cleverness.

Cambridge, MA

Patrese would have thought that after his last experience in the custody of the Cambridge police, Unzicker wouldn't have been too keen for another dose. Not a bit of it. He could hardly wait to tell Patrese how he'd done it. The object he'd been fiddling with, the one Patrese had taken for a smartphone, was a portable hacking device that conducted penetration tests of wireless networks and allowed Unzicker to override the ones without sufficient protection. Unzicker had discovered during another Harvard game that getting into the scoreboard system was child's play, and had therefore planned to override it not in some no-mark match-up, but during the biggest game of the year. The e-mails they'd seen that morning were to one of his colleagues in the Stata Center, who was also in on the joke.

Patrese remembered Unzicker's history of pranks – distorting the lecturer's voice, changing the elevator announcements, the spoof Disney buyout. Pranking – 'hacking' – was an MIT thing, Unzicker said, and never more appreciated than when used against Harvard. MIT students still spoke in awe of the guys who'd hidden a weather balloon under the Harvard field and inflated it during the match until it had exploded and sprayed talcum powder on the field. This hack, Unzicker assured them, would take an equally revered place in history.

Harvard said they didn't wish to press charges; doing so would make them look petty and humorless, exactly the qualities Unzicker had been lampooning to start with, and they didn't want to make his point for him. For the second time in a few days, Unzicker was released without charge, though not without rancor: Anderssen's, mainly, rather than Patrese's.

'He's made a fool of us,' Anderssen snapped. 'And just because he's an asshole practical joker doesn't mean he's not a killer too. Weirdo like that, who knows what he's thinking or doing?'

'And now he knows we're following him,' Patrese replied.

'Then let's use it. Let's make the surveillance overt. Get in his face, unsettle him, make him do something dumb.'

'And jeopardize our chances of catching Kwasi?'

'That's your call. My job is to catch the asshole doing these things in my town. Anyway, who's to say it will jeopardize them? Might have the opposite effect. No disrespect, Franco, but sitting around waiting for things to happen hasn't exactly worked out too well so far, has it? Come on. We're the law. Let's start acting like it. Let's take control. Let's make these fuckers dance to our tune for a change.'

Patrese found a quiet corner of a café and tried to clear his mind.

Let's take control, Anderssen had said. *Let's make these fuckers dance to our tune for a change.* Anderssen had been angry, and he'd been right. In every case apart from the easiest ones, there comes a time when you have to take stock and be prepared to push off in an entirely new direction if need be. Following Unzicker round hadn't brought them great joy so far: nor the surveillance on Tartu and Nursultan, come to think of it.

Neither Tartu nor Nursultan could have killed Glenn O'Kelly. Unzicker could have done, but denied doing so. How were the three of them connected? Unzicker and Tartu didn't know each other, at least not that Patrese was aware of, but Nursultan knew them both. And Nursultan's lust for power would certainly fit with the profile of the organized killer, of Ivory.

He couldn't have killed O'Kelly himself: but he could have gotten someone else to do it for him. Maybe they were taking it in turn. Tartu had talked about playing a few simultaneous exhibitions up in New Haven, taking on multiple opponents. Was something like that going on here? Was Kwasi deemed so good that he needed more than one opponent to make it a fair contest? Maybe Unzicker killed one, then Kwasi, then Nursultan, then Kwasi, then Tartu . . .

No. That sounded ludicrous. The chances of finding four people rather than two with similar pathologies were exponentially vast. And each of Ivory's victims had been killed in exactly the same way. Patrese was experienced enough to be able to tell if Glenn O'Kelly and Chase Evans had been killed by different people, and he was absolutely sure that they hadn't. Ebony and Ivory were different people. Ivory and Ivory weren't.

Ivory was one person. Most likely, one of Unzicker, Tartu or Nursultan.

Most likely, Patrese realized, but not definitely. Ivory could be someone else entirely. Someone who also knew Kwasi, who was also good at chess . . .

In other words, he realized, someone like Inessa.

Kwasi had told Patrese how much he disliked Inessa. *Told* Patrese, that was. Didn't necessarily make it true. Inessa seemed to bear less of a grudge, but that didn't necessarily make that true either.

OK, Patrese thought. Reverse it. Why *couldn't* Inessa be Ivory?

Inessa couldn't be Ivory because it couldn't be a woman doing the killings.

Inessa was small, but she was fit and toned. More importantly, she was sufficiently plausible and attractive to get men to help her, to do what she wanted. Patrese could imagine several scenarios, beyond the strictly obvious, in which Inessa could have caught Chase Evans or Glenn O'Kelly off guard, and thus allowed her to incapacitate them before setting to work on chopping them up.

Strike one as an objection.

Inessa couldn't be Ivory because she had no motive.

Well, that wasn't necessarily true either. She had no motive that Patrese yet knew about, but she'd been the only woman other than Regina in Kwasi's life, and it had been Regina's murder that had started this whole thing. Again, it wasn't hard to imagine a scenario in which Regina and Inessa had somehow fought for primacy over Kwasi.

Strike two as an objection.

It couldn't be Inessa because she had an alibi.

Well, did she? Not any that Patrese knew, for the simple reason that he'd never asked her. Maybe she had, maybe she hadn't. She certainly hadn't been with him the afternoon O'Kelly was murdered. And she was at the same university as Chase Evans.

Strike three as an objection.

Motive, means, opportunity; and it seemed like Inessa might have all of them.

Next question: what should Patrese do about it?

In the first instance, he had only two options; don't ask her, or ask her.

If he didn't ask her, there were two possibilities.

First, that it wasn't her, and that in years to come, when the killer had been caught, tried, convicted and banged up for life, he'd breathe a sigh of relief that he hadn't gone around shooting his mouth off.

Second, that it *was* her, and that presumably she'd killed again before they'd caught her, because Patrese hadn't had the balls to do what was his duty as a Bureau agent. He'd have at least one death on his conscience, maybe more.

That didn't bear much thinking about, so he tried to put it from his mind.

If he *did* ask her, there were also two possibilities.

First, that she'd understand his logic and reasoning. She'd feel for him having to ask such an awful thing; she'd calmly provide alibis and reasons why she couldn't have done it; and she'd tell Patrese how he was a wonderful law enforcement officer and an even better man, and reward him for these attributes by fucking him till the break of dawn.

Second, that she'd go apeshit. *Apeshit.* She'd be livid that he could even ask such a question, incandescent that he clearly had so little faith in her; and if that was the way he felt, which it clearly was, then she never wanted to see him again, and that would be the end of their dalliance and his testicles pretty much simultaneously.

Four possible scenarios.

Two good, two bad.

What was the worst of the four?

Clearly that he didn't ask, and that she turned out to be the killer.

So he had to do the opposite. He had to ask.

Not to do so would be a breach of professional duty egregious enough to have him dismissed on the spot, and he was probably running pretty close to that edge as it was.

He had to ask.

He picked up his cellphone and dialed. She answered on the second ring.

'Hey,' she said. 'You OK?'

'Yeah. Just need to talk to you.'

'You still in Cambridge?'

'Yeah.'

'Then come round.'

'You're back here?'

'Man runs out on you first thing in the morning, you

296

don't stay around all day waiting for him to come back.' Her tone was teasing. 'Dudley House, just off of Harvard Square.'

Patrese rehearsed what he was going to say all the way to her accommodation block. His gut churned, and it took him a few moments to recognize this particular variety of nerves. It was the same way he'd felt as a student when about to break up with a girlfriend: the dread of hurting someone against the need to go through with it, the determination not to resort to the old clichés about still being friends and it being him rather than them.

Inessa opened the door and kissed him. 'Looks like you need a drink,' she said. 'You want to go for a coffee in the block café? Best coffee in Harvard Square. Something stronger? I got some beer somewhere. Baltika. Russian beer. Not chilled horse piss like Bud or Coors.'

'That would be great.'

'Kitchen's across the hallway. Back in a sec.'

She slipped out of the door. Patrese looked round the living room. A few trophies on the sideboard, though not as many as he'd expected. A poster-size photo of her from the *Sports Illustrated* swimsuit edition: she'd been wearing a black-and-white bikini, of course. A magazine cover shout proclaiming her the Jessica Alba of chess. A couple of pictures of her teaching chess in schools, with teenage boys hunched lovelorn over the board, more interested in chess for that hour than they'd ever been before or would be again. And a monochrome portrait of a woman with her head shaved, staring brooding and challenging down the lens of the camera. It took Patrese a few moments to realize that this, too, was Inessa.

She came back with the bottle of Baltika. 'Here.' She handed him the beer and followed his gaze. 'Yeah, I shaved it all off once. Not my best look.'

'Then why do you keep it there?'

'To remind me it wasn't my best look.'

'And why did you do it?'

'Shave it off? To be taken seriously. I'd had enough of all the bullshit. You're always aware of how you look, how you're always being looked at, so you can't totally lose yourself in the game like you should. You get Neanderthals who think you must be having your period when you're playing badly. Tell them the queen's the most powerful piece on the board, and the whole game's a feminist inversion of the male patriarchy, and they suddenly shut the hell up.'

'Am I going to have to apologize for the manifold shortcomings of my gender?'

'You'd never have enough time. But truth is, it wasn't only the male players doing it. It was all the other women too, with their catty remarks and sniping behind my back about what good photographers I had, what amazing lighting, anyone could look like that if they had all that time and money spent on them, yadda yadda yadda, you know the kind of thing. I had a sort of breakdown, to be honest. Lost my shit for a little bit.'

'Like Kwasi. Chess and madness.'

'You got it. And then you wonder why there aren't more women chess players.'

'Or maybe women are just too reasonable to spend all their time on chess.'

'There is that.'

Patrese had got it all word perfect in his head, and now it fled from him like morning mist before the sun. 'Inessa-I-have-to-ask-you-did-you-kill-those-people?'

Reactions flitted across her face like seasons: bewilderment, as she tried to make sense of what he'd said; amusement, as she took it for some kind of joke; disbelief, that Patrese clearly meant what he'd asked; and anger, as the implications of the question sunk in.

'Did I *what*?'

She wasn't screaming or shouting yet, which almost made it worse. He could see the anger rising in her cheeks.

He took a deep breath and said it again; slower this time, better.

'Did you kill those people? Darrell Showalter. Chase Evans. Glenn O'Kelly.'

She stared at him, and loaded her gaze with all those things women could call on so much better than men: scorn, disdain, contempt.

She didn't ask him whether he was joking, or why he thought she might have done it, because she knew the answers, and Patrese could tell she hoped – correction, she *had* hoped – that he'd have been smart enough to know them too.

Without speaking, she got up, went over to her desk and picked up her diary.

'You tell me the dates they were killed, and I'll tell you what I was doing at those times. OK?'

'OK.' He knew the dates off the top of his head, and he suspected she did too, after all the time she'd spent studying the case; but maybe she was making him sweat, and he wouldn't blame her for that, not really. He wanted to get this over with as quickly as possible. 'Saturday, October thirtieth.'

Inessa flicked to the relevant page in her diary. 'Faculty drinks party. Davis Center for Russian and Eurasian studies. But I didn't go. I had the flu, I was feeling lousy.'

'And yet the next day you were on TV talking about Kwasi's title defense.'

'The next day I'd had a good night's sleep and had dosed myself up with medicine. I can tell you which pharmacist I went to, if you want to check their records, see what I bought when.'

'So you were here all alone that night?'

'No, I had an orgy to try and shake the flu. Yes, of course I was alone. Don't you tend to be, when you're ill?'

'Following weekend. Sixth–seventh November.'

Flick.

'Down in New York with my sister, all weekend.'

Patrese thought for a moment. 'She was running the marathon, right?'

'Right. I went to watch, give her support, all that.'

'Where d'you stay?'

'Old family friend's place in Tribeca. I can give you all the details.'

'Wednesday the seventeenth.'

Flick.

'I was down in New Haven all that week. That's when I first started helping you. That particular day: I looked at a few of the case files in the morning, then I went to the library all afternoon. You can ask my sister.'

'Your sister seems to be your only alibi.'

'Yeah. Her and the thousands of others who ran the New York marathon; her and everyone else in the library that afternoon.' Her eyes brimmed, the anger suddenly spilling over into grief. 'I can't believe you, Franco. I can't believe you'd even . . . I really liked you, you know? I really did.'

Liked. Did. Past tense.

One of the scenarios he'd mapped out was that Inessa would be livid that he could even ask such a question, and that she'd never want to see him again.

Ah, well. At least he was getting better at understanding women.

300

51

Rainer Tartu lay in bed and ran his thumb along the edge of his X-Acto knife; back and forth, back and forth, testing the blade against his skin. Scalpel sharp, as he knew it would be; as he *needed* it to be. Good.

The concert had been a triumph, with three encores and a standing ovation that had lasted minutes. The conductor had made a touching little speech in which he'd thanked Tartu for stepping in at such short notice and had said he couldn't imagine anyone having done it better. In the front row, Anna had glowed.

Tartu had taken her out to dinner afterwards as promised: the Ibiza, a Spanish place which was one of New Haven's better – and most expensive – restaurants. Over *bacalao, solomillo, caldo gallego* and *ensalada de pulpo*, they'd talked about James Joyce, Bobby Fischer, Sergei Rachmaninoff, and Anna's divorce.

He'd walked her home, but hadn't tried to kiss her. He wanted to be absolutely sure that she trusted him, and he knew that playing the gentleman was the best way to ensure that. Unless she trusted him absolutely, he wouldn't be able to do what he intended: he wouldn't be able to do what had, in fact, been his main motivation for coming to New Haven in the first place.

The concert had been a happy coincidence, not to mention the most perfect of cover stories. But Tartu had something else in mind. It was something that he'd got away with in more countries than he cared to remember, and something that as far as he knew no one had ever suspected had even happened, let alone managed to link with him.

He ran his thumb over the X-Acto's blade again.

52

Anderssen had suggested they get in Unzicker's face, and that was exactly what they were doing. Everywhere Unzicker went, everything he did, there were a couple of guys from the Cambridge PD or the Bureau with him: never smiling, never talking, but always reminding him with their somber silence exactly why they were there. The only places they didn't go were Unzicker's room at Tang Hall, his office in the Stata Center, or the bathroom. That was the limit of the privacy they afforded him. Everywhere else, they were there as surely as he was.

And just in case he somehow managed to give them the slip, they'd got an electronic back-up. Both Unzicker's room and his office were locked by keycard, and every time those keycards were used, they were logged by the computer systems in question. These were now set up so a message was sent to Patrese's BlackBerry every time Unzicker used either keycard. They'd probably never need it, but when it came to surveillance, one layer too many was better than one too few.

Unzicker seemed to find the whole thing much less disturbing than his fellow students did. When people catcalled him – 'Hey, freak, the law finally caught up with you?'; 'Gee, Unzicker, those guys your boyfriends?' – things like that – Unzicker didn't appear to notice, though one of his watchers would usually have a quiet word with the person responsible. It was hard to tell sometimes whether they were observing him or protecting him. Perhaps Unzicker enjoyed the attention. If he did, he wasn't saying.

Patrese had stayed in Cambridge. This was where the next murder was going to take place, he reasoned, so this was where he needed to be. And after forty-eight hours of finding that Unzicker's life was both very typical of a student (he studied, he ate) and very atypical (he didn't drink, party, or chase girls, all the things Patrese had done when he'd been at college), Patrese decided to tag along during one of the Bureau's spells of surveillance.

It was late afternoon, beginning to turning dark. Unzicker left his office in the Stata Center, acknowledged Patrese's presence with the slightest of nods, and set off out of the building and west on Vassar Street. Patrese indicated to the pair of Bureau men that they should hang back a few yards while he talked to Unzicker.

'How're you doing, Thomas?'

'OK.'

'This bothering you? Us getting on your case?'

'No.'

'You know why we're doing it?'

'Yes.'

'Why?'

Unzicker turned to look at Patrese. ''Cos you're looking for the guy who murdered all those people, and you don't have the first clue who did it.'

That was, Patrese thought, just about the first time he'd

got more than monosyllables from Unzicker when the topic hadn't been computers. Not to mention that it had been uncomfortably close to the truth.

'Where are you going?' Patrese asked.

'Are you coming with me?'

'Yes.'

'Then you'll see.'

Couldn't fault his logic.

The answer turned out to be the gym; or rather, what was beneath the gym. Patrese knew what it would be before they got in there: the heavy outside door, the relentless drone of the ventilation system and the smell of cordite and lead all gave it away. To a law enforcement officer, places like this were practically home.

A shooting range.

To judge from the posters on the noticeboards, MIT had several gun clubs: the Pistol & Rifle Club, the Sport Pistol Club, the Varsity Rifle. Unzicker went into the administration office and handed his ID to a woman behind the desk, who checked it against a list, got up, went to a cabinet by the far wall, unlocked it, and handed him a gun. Walther P22, Patrese saw.

'Yours, or the club's?' he asked.

'Mine.'

Patrese was momentarily surprised: how the hell could someone like Unzicker be allowed to own a weapon? This was Massachusetts, whose gun laws were notoriously strict; this wasn't an NRA paradise like Arizona or Alaska.

He ran quickly through what he knew about Unzicker, which was a lot, and what he knew about Massachusetts gun law, which was enough. Unzicker was a weirdo, sure, but he hadn't been a youth offender; he'd never committed an adult felony; he'd never been confined to a hospital or institution for mental illness, drug addiction or habitual drunkenness; and he had no restraining orders nor outstanding arrest warrants against him. Weirdo or not, he was as entitled as any other citizen of Massachusetts to bear arms.

'You come here often?' Patrese asked. Sounded like the worst chat-up line ever.

'Try to.'

'You like shooting?'

'Sure.'

'Targets? Animals?' He left the natural progression – 'people' – unsaid.

'Targets.'

'Not animals?'

'No.'

That made sense, Patrese thought. Target shooting was a great stress reliever, and a guy like Unzicker, working hard all day, using his brain till it was red hot, probably needed that. All the best shots Patrese had known, first in the Pittsburgh police and latterly in the Bureau, had the same qualities Unzicker presumably needed to succeed at MIT: focus, concentration, self-discipline, attention to detail.

The same qualities, in other words, displayed by whoever had killed Darrell Showalter, Chase Evans and Glenn O'Kelly.

Patrese had thought Kwasi King innocent, and he'd been wrong. He'd thought Unzicker first guilty, then innocent, and now he was unsure. Truth be told, he didn't know what to think any more. For every pointer to Unzicker's innocence, Patrese could find one to his guilt, and vice versa. Uncertainty in Patrese's personal life was normal, even desirable. Uncertainty on a case could be the kiss of death.

He followed Unzicker from the admin office on to the range itself. Safety goggles on, ear defenders on. Unzicker clipped a paper target to its holder and sent it right down the other end of the range, fifty feet away. He shuffled his feet, squirmed slightly, adjusting shoulders and hips and head; the shooter's dance, seeking the ideal firing stance.

Fire. Gun lowered to forty-five degrees, pointing downrange.

Unzicker knew what he was doing with a gun, that was obvious. No fancy stuff, no macho posturing.

Gun up again. Shuffle. Squirm. Stillness.

To Patrese, Unzicker seemed a statue, frozen at the moment between heartbeats, blinks, breaths.

Fire. Lower. Raise.

Ebb. Flow.

Fire.

Zen. Every other part of Unzicker's life – his work, his hacks, Patrese right here – looked to fade away. Republican yoga, someone had once called it.

The Walther P22 holds ten rounds. When Unzicker had fired them all and his magazine was empty, he lowered the weapon, engaged the safety, put it on the table in front of him, and brought the paper target back from the end of the range.

Patrese gasped. Unzicker's grouping wouldn't have shamed a professional marksman.

Unzicker took the paper off its hanger and examined it. For a moment, pride flitted across his face, but it was gone as soon as it had arrived, and Patrese saw what came on its heels: perhaps the one emotion harder to hide than any other.

Fear.

Patrese left Unzicker's surveillance to the two Bureau men. He was getting into his car when his BlackBerry chimed. Another message from Kwasi.

No puzzle this time. This was more like the first message

Kwasi had sent, pitched somewhere between confession and explanation.

The Caliph of Baghdad was once asked: 'What is chess?' You know what he replied? 'What is life?' Chess is life, Franco. Understand that, and you'll understand me. To the enlightened mind, chess is the platform for the spirit to be transformed.

The chessboard has 64 squares of alternating color. The white squares are the path of the head, the dark squares the path of the heart. The pieces are the forces of nature: light and dark, good and evil. Each piece has a deeper significance. Pieces which move in straight lines are our actions on earth. Pieces which move outside of straight lines are our alignment with the divine. Pieces which move in both directions represent the point where heaven and earth meet. Some pieces are more powerful than others, but after the game, when they're all put back in the box, they're all equal again, as are we after death.

The ancients thought chess must have been of divine origin, as no mortal mind could ever have envisaged a game so beautiful. To be the best of those mortals, to be better than however many billion people are also on earth; it's a privilege, Franco. Chess is a game, it's art, it's science, all wrapped up in one.

When you play chess, you feel like you're talking to the gods. Somewhere along the way, if you're very special, you become one. You become a god. You feel the changing. You know the I Ching, the ancient Chinese Book of Changes? It's divided into hexagrams. Have a guess how many? 64. Of course.

When I won the world title, I was still a mortal. I was the first among mortals, but I was not yet a god. I didn't play competitively for a few months, and people thought me better rather than worse for it, as though by not playing, I wasn't having to sully myself with the dirty business of moving wooden pieces across a marble board. They imagined all the masterpieces I could be conjuring up, though I knew as well as anyone that most grandmaster games aren't masterpieces any more than most football matches or sculptures or symphonies aren't masterpieces. I went back to the board for exhibitions, but not competitive play: and if you really want to know why I'm the way I am now, I think – no, I know – it goes back to one of those exhibitions.

You ever heard of simultaneous chess? It's when one player – a grandmaster, usually – takes on a whole bunch of people at the same time. Not all on one board; all on different boards. You set up the tables in a big 'U' formation, with the grandmaster on the inside, walking from board to board. He stops a few seconds at each one, examines the position, makes his move, goes on to the next one. Each of his opponents must move when the grandmaster arrives at his table, so each person can think about his own move for as long as the grandmaster takes to make a circuit. How many people can you play at once? However many you like. The world record's about 600.

Now imagine playing a simultaneous exhibition blindfold: that is, not looking at the boards at all, any of them. Stand with your back to the room and shout out moves in turn. You have to keep all those positions – and they're changing move by move – all of them inside your head. Your opponents can see the boards, of course: some of them couldn't hold their own name in their head unless it was written down. But you can't see a thing. You can't even take the slightest glance.

How many people do you think you could play like that? Not 600, that's for sure. Most grandmasters couldn't manage much more than a dozen. The world record was 45. My sponsors wanted me to break that. They wanted me to play 64 games, one for each square of the board, and keep them all in my head. 64 games, 2048 pieces, 4096 squares. They'd pay me a million dollars. I said yes. My mom said yes.

A couple of doctors told me this was a bad idea. Playing blindfold simultaneous games was thought to cause great mental strain, even madness. I told them to get fucked. I didn't go round poking into their operations and telling them what to do, did I? So why should they get involved with my thing? The sponsors said there had to be a physician present in the hall when I did the exhibition, else they couldn't get insured, like this was some damn boxing match. Fine, I said: the physician sits in the corner, shuts the fuck up and doesn't bother me, he can do what the hell he likes.

I played the exhibition: 64 players. The only stipulation I had was that none of them were grandmasters; other than that, I didn't care who they were, what their ratings were. It was easy to start with. When you've studied chess as long as I have, the opening patterns are burned into your brain, you don't need to see the board at all. I got rid of the weaker players first: quick combinations, usually, a sacrifice here or there, which got people applauding.

The more games you win, the fewer you have to keep track of: but of course the flipside is that the games which go on longest are the ones with the strongest players. And it takes time. I'm used to concentrating for five or six hours at a time, but this was way longer than that. I ate, I drank, I danced on the spot to keep myself alert. More games won now: 30, 40, 50. Not a single draw, let alone a loss. I could hear the chatter: can he win all 64? People almost never win all their games in simuls. To do that – and blindfold – well, Franco, let me tell you, it wouldn't be much easier than winning the world championship itself. I made a blunder against the 57th guy, and he blundered right back. 60 wins, 61, and now there were just three left, all down to endgames. Not many pieces on the board, and so you have to calculate everything spot on. You make a single fuck-up, you're not going to get it back.

Three boards at once, all in my head. Only three, and not many pieces so not much to remember, but by this time I'm really tired. Really, really tired. I can see my mom urging me on, and for a moment I hallucinate, as she turns into a chess piece herself, a human-size black queen – you know where this is going, right? – and I do that cliché thing in movies, I blink and shake my head like a dog, and when I open my eyes again, she's back to being mom.

Cut a long story short, I won all the games. Sixteen hours, it took in all. Some asswipe TV reporter asked me what I was going to do now, and I just said, 'Sleep'. But that was the one thing I couldn't do. I was exhausted, but I couldn't sleep. My mind was racing, full of knight forks and pawns marching up the board together and all that. Next time I used a crosswalk, I saw myself as a rook, gliding across the black-and-white stripes. I saw people whose heads became those of chess pieces as I looked at them. A man with a hat had the crown of a king; a police horse reared up like a knight. People walked on sidewalks one way, cars moved another way. I started to dream of a world run entirely according to the rules of chess, where nobody could do nothing unless it accorded with those rules. People were becoming pieces to me. You know that weird stage between wake and sleep when things make perfect sense even though you know they're nuts? That was my life, all the time.

And when you start to see people as pieces, you start

to treat them like pieces too. That was how they were treating me, after all. When you get to be famous, everyone wants a piece of you, but they want it for themselves, not for you. Not a single person – my mom apart, and not always even her – gave a damn for me as a person, about what was best for me. All they wanted was to make money off of me, to make themselves look good by being with me. They'd offer five when I knew they had ten; they'd offer a hundred when I was worth a thousand. Mom and I had grown up pretty poor. I'd had enough of people making money at our expense.

No one was ever straight with me, not once. I was the only honest man out there. You know why? Everywhere I turned, I saw liars and hypocrites. Emanuel Lasker, one of the first world champions, had this saying: 'On the chess-board, lies and hypocrisy do not last long. The creative combination lays bare the presumption of a lie; the merciless fact, culminating in a checkmate, contradicts the hypocrite.' Lasker knew what time it was. As a young boy, you're keenly aware of injustices, of duplicity. And on a chessboard, everything is open. You can't hide or prevaricate. You have to move when it's your turn.

And the more I saw people as pieces, the more it worked the other way. I began to see pieces as people. A piece in a bad position caused me physical pain. I bet you're laughing as you read this, but it's absolutely true. Physical pain. A knight marooned on the sidelines, a bishop hemmed in by its own pawns, pieces crowding in and jostling each other like it was rush hour on the subway. I'd feel myself getting short of breath, or a sharp stabbing pain in my side, until I could free them, open up the position, breathe. If I could have, I would have become those pieces, taken their pain as mine.

I felt myself becoming chess, becoming at one with the

game. Time was a vortex. I'd sit down to study for what felt like a half hour only to find that eight hours had passed. Several times, I started after dinner, and the next thing I knew was the pinking of the dawn through the curtains. Who did I play against? Sometimes online, sometimes Misha, sometimes myself.

And gradually I found myself needing opponents, actual physical opponents opposite me, less and less. Faceless names on a server were one thing, because everything my end could be set up exactly the way I wanted it. Playing online, you can't hear the other person sigh, see him twitch, get annoyed by him pacing up and down. So the idea of tournament play, with all its mistakes and people shuffling and time pressure and cameras and moronic questioners – the very idea became horrific. I was so much better than all my human opponents that there would be no joy in victory, just relief.

I had my mind on higher things. I was going to attain perfection. I would cut myself off from the world and dedicate myself purely to the game. People held no interest for me. I was a scholar in the secluded hush of a library, seeking the inner truth. The boundaries between the chessboard and the rest of my world dissolved and melted. Reality flipped inside out: board and pieces were all that seemed sharp, and everything else was out of focus. The pathway between my mind and a new realm opened up, and I found myself in a dimension where everything was black and white, where knights flew above and pawns marched past, where measureless heights and fathomless depths whirled away to infinity. I lived in a house shaped like a rook, with parapets and spiral staircases. I saw the true beauty of chess, and with it the true horror. I was playing the game, and the game was without end. I saw the cosmos.

313

Steinitz, another of the old world champions, claimed to have played against God and won. You read the Luzhin book? Luzhin's this guy like me, for whom chess is so much more vivid than life itself; and at the end, he throws himself out of the window of his hotel room. He's falling, falling, towards a floor tiled in squares of black and white: and he's not scared at all, he's content, serene, because this is the world he knows, this is where he belongs. He's happy because he's going home.

That's how I was living. But you can't live like that, not forever. There were times when I knew it wasn't right. Maybe I should get therapy, I said. No, Mom replied, a thousand times no. Your brain is unique, Kwasi. I'm not letting some charlatan mess with it. What she meant, of course – though I didn't realize this till later – what she meant was, what if it works? What if therapy cures you of this, saps your will to win, makes you 'normal'? So no therapy. But you can't live alone. You need people.

53

There were only three people who knew Kwasi well enough to be of use to Patrese. One of them wasn't talking to him, and another was under such heavy and overt surveillance that he wouldn't be a model of co-operation either.

That left Tartu. Yes, Patrese remembered that he too hadn't been keen to help: but maybe Tartu would reconsider now that a few days had passed, now that they were a couple of corpses further down the line, and now that Patrese was running out of options.

Patrese left the hotel and set out on the short walk toward the Beinecke Library.

No one else in the rare books room, Tartu noticed, but him and Anna. Perfect.

She'd brought out the Voynich Manuscript, one of the most famous items in all the Beinecke's collections. The Voynich was . . . well, no one really knew what it was. It was about 240 vellum pages, though there may have originally been more pages long since lost or stolen. The Voynich's script was unreadable, its language unknown. It had illustrations of plants, but most did not match known species. Some scholars thought it an elaborate cipher, others theorized it was automatic writing, a human channeling of spirit instructions. And there were plenty, of course, who thought it nothing but a hoax.

'My God,' Tartu whispered. 'This is really it. I can't believe it.'

Anna smiled at him as though in benevolent indulgence of a child's artwork.

'Enjoy it,' she said.

She turned and went back to her desk on the other side of the room.

Tartu put his hand in his jacket pocket and closed his fingers round the X-Acto. He looked around the room. Still empty. No one to see him. There were video cameras, but over the past week he'd gotten to know where they were, and while walking around the room had managed to work out their blind spots.

He hadn't been allowed to bring any bags into the room, of course, but he'd sneaked a few peeks behind the reference desk, and he saw that Anna and other members of staff had left a few round there. Not especially big ones, but big enough for his purpose.

She had no idea, he thought: no idea at all. A few cuts, that was all it would need. The X-Acto was scalpel sharp. She wouldn't even know it was happening.

He eased the knife out of his pocket.

Patrese pushed open the door to the Rare Books room. It was heavy, presumably for sound muffling, and it moved silently on its hinges: well oiled, as a squeaky door being opened hundreds of times a day would have driven even the calmest librarian mad.

Tartu had his back to Patrese. He was pulling something out of his pocket.

The briefest glinting of something metallic as the light caught it.

Knife, Patrese saw. *Knife*. Tartu looking to see whether Anna had noticed. *Knife*. Patrese's head swam with missing heads and shoulder stumps and skin patches cut out.

'Hey!' Patrese shouted.

Two heads jerked toward him as though they were marionettes: Anna surprised; Tartu alarmed. Tartu dropped the X-Acto and clamped his hand to his mouth. Blood oozed between his fingers. He must have cut himself as he jumped, Patrese thought.

Patrese covered the distance to Tartu's desk in a few quick strides. Anna hurried over too, eyes widening as she saw the blood. 'Don't get it on the manuscript!' she cried. 'For God's sake, keep it away from that. I'll get you a tissue or something.'

Patrese bent down and picked the X-Acto up from the floor. 'That's where the blood came from,' he said. He turned to Tartu. 'What the hell are you doing with this?

Anna's face spoke of a thousand betrayals. 'Oh, no,' she said. 'Not you.'

'You were going to kill her,' Patrese said.

'Kill her?' Tartu said. '*Kill her?*'

'No,' Anna said. 'He wasn't going to kill me.'

'Then what?' Patrese asked.

'There's only one reason you'd bring a knife like that in here. He was going to cut pages out of the manuscript. Destroy a priceless work.'

*　*　*

Tartu had been doing it for years. Sometimes he took pages from rare books or map collections; more often, he stole the books altogether. The texture, the smell, the rarity: all these pulsed arcs of ecstasy through him. He'd stolen from libraries in London, Moscow, Mumbai, Paris, Melbourne, Chicago, Berlin, New York, Cambridge Massachusetts and Cambridge, England. He'd stolen copies of Newton's *Principia Mathematica* and of Kepler's *Astronomia Nova*; he'd stolen works by Galileo, Malthus, Copernicus, Huygens; he'd stolen first editions of Dostoyevsky, Mark Twain, Voltaire, Cervantes and Goethe. He'd never yet gotten a Gutenberg Bible or a Shakespeare First Folio. He'd thought there was still time for that. Perhaps not any more.

Getting away with it had been easy. For a start, it could take libraries years to realize that anything was missing, and even when they did, they were often too embarrassed to take matters to the police. When the police *did* get involved, they tended not to give it too much priority: book theft was hard for the non-bibliophile to understand. Some of the books Tartu kept, the others he sold on privately. There were plenty of men in the former Soviet bloc who'd made fortunes illegitimately and now wanted to make themselves look like men of culture: how better to do that than through beautiful and rare books?

And stealing such books didn't diminish their provenance. If anything, it enhanced it. Pretty much every great book had been plundered at least once in its life. Henry VIII had ransacked the monasteries; Napoleon had stolen thousands of books before going into exile on Elba; Hitler had enshrined the ransacking of libraries in Nazi state law.

Tartu didn't tell any of this to Patrese. If need be, he'd say it was a temporary madness, something he'd never done before, and then he'd get his government to intervene and have the whole thing hushed up.

Anna had left the room, telling Tartu she could hardly bear to look at him anymore.

'You're in big trouble, Rainer,' Patrese said.

'You have no proof.'

That was true, Patrese knew. If he'd waited a few more seconds, he might have caught Tartu slicing out one of the manuscript's pages red-handed. But as it was, he had no direct evidence.

'I can make life very difficult for you.'

'I brought the knife in by mistake. You made me jump just as I'd discovered I had it on me.'

'Bullshit.'

'Prove it.'

'You want me to search your room? I will do. I'll turn it inside out.'

Patrese watched Tartu carefully as he said this, and the flicker of fear that rippled Tartu's features was enough. Patrese had reckoned this hadn't been Tartu's first time – you don't bring a cutting knife into a library on a whim, after all – and that, since Tartu had been in the States for several weeks now, he might well have done it somewhere else too. Tartu had been mainly in New York, and New York wasn't exactly short of libraries.

'Which one?' Patrese asked. 'Columbia?'

Tartu looked at Patrese for long seconds.

'I'll make your room look like a whirlwind's hit it,' Patrese continued. 'And I'll make sure it goes public, too. You're news right now, Rainer.'

Tartu shook his head. 'New York Public. I stole from the New York Public Library.'

'You want to do this the easy way or the hard way?'

'What do you mean?'

'I need help in catching Kwasi. One reason and another, you're my best hope. You help me – and how much help that is, *I* decide, not you – and if after all of it I'm happy you've done what you could, I'll forget about whatever's in your room, and I'll tell Anna that after a thorough investigation, multi-agency co-operation, blah de blah, we've concluded that you were telling the truth and that things happened exactly the way you said they did. Brought the knife in by accident, found it by chance, and so on. Your choice.'

It wasn't much of a choice. Patrese knew that as well as Tartu did.

'OK,' Tartu said. 'I'll help.'

Back at the hotel, Patrese explained to Tartu what had been going on with the case these past ten days or so, and then handed him the BlackBerry so Tartu could read Kwasi's latest message. Tartu read it through twice before speaking.

'Wow,' he said eventually. 'He sounds like one of those hippies who timed when they'd have to drop acid so they could get maximum trippiness out of the stargate scene in *2001*.'

'He sure does. Anything else?'

'Tell me what you've seen first.'

'OK. That part at the end about needing people; that interests me. It's almost like that might be why he's killing them, through some warped desire for company. He has no friends, he's said that before, so perhaps this is the only way he can make friends.'

'By killing them?'

'They don't have a choice that way. Maybe that's why he keeps their heads. To talk to them.'

Tartu winced. 'That's sick.'

'He sure is. But there's something about that which bothers me. That theory would work better for Ivory, for White, for Unzicker or whoever it is. He takes the victims away before

320

he kills them. He's organized. He gets to spend some time with them. Kwasi, though, he's just Crazy Kwasi: kill them on the spot, frenzy and violence.'

'Not a great way to make friends.'

'Not a great way to make friends, indeed.'

'But it gives a hint to where it all started, no? The fallout with his mother? When he says that sometimes even she didn't have his best interests at heart.'

'I noticed that too. But how will we find out exactly what it was, until we find him?'

Tartu shrugged. 'No idea. But look. Here's something. He says he plays online. Someone like Kwasi, he can't live without chess, and he can't always play against machines. If we can find where he plays online, which site he uses – or which sites – maybe we can, I don't know, get in touch with him. You can send messages on those sites. You can even chat to your opponent during games.'

'And,' said Patrese, pretty much thinking aloud, 'if you were monitoring someone's e-mails, it wouldn't show up there.'

'That's right.'

'These servers: they store everything, right?'

'Games, sure. Comments, I don't know. As in, whenever I've played, sometimes you chat to your opponent in the dialogue box beneath the board, but when the game's over, you can't get those comments back once you've closed the window or logged out. The games are always there, but what you've said during them, no.'

'In other words, a perfect way to communicate with someone without anyone else knowing. Even if they otherwise had you under surveillance. Where do we start?'

'With the biggest. Also the first. The guys who pretty much invented real time online chess. The Internet Chess Club.'

54

If Kwasi was using the Internet Chess Club, the ICC, he wasn't doing so under his own name. The ICC has more than thirty thousand members, and most of them use a handle of some kind – **TheFourHorsemen, Chessticles, Wrecker12006**, that kind of thing. Not that this was a problem. A quick search of the player database revealed that the same handle, **killerinstinct32**, headed all three time-control lists (standard, blitz and bullet). A 'killer instinct' handle and Kwasi's own preternatural skills: it could only be him, surely?

The ICC, based in Pittsburgh, wasn't saying. Only three pieces of information were publicly visible for each player: username, rating, country – **killerinstinct32** was indeed American. As Tartu had suspected, the ICC didn't log tell-type communication – chat dialogue – between two users. The ICC's admin staff couldn't even listen in on such conversations, let alone save them, unless one member made a complaint about the other's behavior.

Each user was tracked while online, of course. A permanent log was kept of every session by every player: time of connection and disconnection, name of interface, IP number of the connection, and machine ID of the computer. These details were kept secret, as were the real names, e-mail addresses, physical locations or credit-card details of their clients. Patrese would need to get a subpoena to force them to comply with this. He appealed to their sense of responsibility toward a multiple homicide investigation. When that failed, he appealed to their sense of solidarity with a Pittsburgh boy. When that failed, he slammed the phone down and told the receiver to go fuck itself.

Patrese hated having to apply for subpoenas. The moment you got bureaucracy involved, everything took ten times as long as it needed to. You had to fill in a form that demanded more information than anyone could possibly ever need, and then e-mail it to the Bureau department responsible, which would assess, scrutinize, and pick their asses for as long as they felt like. Sometimes it took them two weeks to issue one, though they proudly boasted that a few – a few! – had been turned round in as little as three days. There was no point marking your request 'urgent'. Everyone did that. The subpoena guys were wise to that now (assuming they'd given a damn to start with).

Still, there was no other way, so Patrese filled in the form with laborious thoroughness, treble-checked it – these guys had no bigger thrill in life than sending back a form because it was incomplete, and requesting even more useless information, all the while reminding you that the clock on your request didn't start running until it had been completed to their satisfaction – and e-mailed it.

In the meantime, Tartu started studying all **killer-instinct32**'s games. He'd be able to tell from their style whether they were Kwasi's or not, he said. A strange kind of voyeurism, Patrese thought, spying on someone and trying to work out their identity by the way they moved pieces – rather, electronic avatars of pieces – round a chessboard; but perhaps no stranger than anything else about this case.

55

The Stata Center was emptying fast: the annual Thanksgiving exodus across the nation for turkey, cranberry sauce, stuffing, gravy, yams, mash, hominy, green bean casserole, cornbread, sweet potato pie, pumpkin pie, family arguments and indigestion. Unzicker didn't notice. Nursultan had been up to Cambridge yesterday to read Unzicker the riot act, demanding results and threatening funding cuts and worse if Unzicker didn't come up with something pretty damn quick. Unzicker hadn't pointed out that his mind had been on other things lately, and Nursultan hadn't mentioned it, save for an oblique reference about how Unzicker might have turned down Nursultan's lawyer, but he sure as hell wasn't going to turn down the man himself. If need be, Nursultan would sit here, in this office, until Unzicker made the breakthrough.

Truth was, Unzicker knew, he'd needed the kick up the ass, and he never worked better than when up against it. There was a purity in his approach now – just him and

Misha, Frankenstein and the monster, and Unzicker worked with a purpose that would only be sated when Misha gave up its secrets. And when that happened, Misha would stop being an 'it' and become a 'he', because Unzicker would have given life to this program, made something inanimate into something human.

When Kasparov had played Deep Blue twice in the late nineties, winning the first match but losing the second, people had talked about it being a shared triumph: 1–1 between man and machine. But for Unzicker, man had won both times: the first as a performer, the second as a tool-maker. He would win now, as the toolmaker, but after that, no one knew.

He made minuscule adjustments to Misha's chip, he ran diagnostics, he went back and forth on microscopic highways known only to him and the burgeoning intelligence he hoped, thought, prayed was inside Misha. When he was satisfied, he logged on to the ICC. Misha had its own dedicated account, declared as a computer – that was ICC rules – though of course for secrecy's sake Unzicker hadn't registered it as Misha. Its handle was a suitably nondescript **repino**, named after the birthplace of Misha's inspiration, Mikhail Botvinnik.

The ICC welcome screen unrolled, and with it a message. Your arrival was noted by---> **killerinstinct32**.

Observe **killerinstinct 32**, typed Unzicker.

killerinstinct32 is not playing or examining a game.

Among the icons across the top of the screen was that of a fencer: this was the avatar to challenge an opponent. Unzicker tapped on it, typed **killerinstinct32**, and sent it.

A few seconds later, the opening board flashed up: Kwasi as white, Misha as black.

They started playing. Ruy Lopez, one of the most popular

openings. After a few moves, Unzicker clicked on another icon, this time a handful of faces: Show observers.

{Game 1452 (**killerinstinct32** vs. **repino**) Game started}.
Observing 1452 [(**killerinstinct32** vs. **repino**]: **JDoss solidly chessdennis iloveicc pirahna frankandbeans rodent ndogbosok01 RTE Ditton66 ekmel NapaMD greatowl carlosh99 trule Winsome vova Tellus megchess JohnnyBallgame KnightRider12 CamaroSS**: 22 people.

Round about move 15, Unzicker realized something he knew Kwasi would have clocked long before: this was the same game that they'd played through in Kwasi's apartment in Bleecker Street not long before Kwasi had gone on the run, which in turn had been the same game Kwasi and Misha had played through in February. Misha had lost both those games on move 20, when it had played bishop to c5 rather than b4.

Unzicker hadn't directly programmed Misha to change that move. If Misha moved to b4 this time, therefore, it would prove it was thinking for itself: it would have corrected an error without external input.

Unzicker sat closer to the screen, willing Kwasi to play the same moves as before.

Move 20. Kwasi moved. Misha thought. No, not thought: *calculated*. Brains thought: silicon circuits calculated. Five minutes. Ten. Go on, thought Unzicker. If it had been going to play bishop to c5, the wrong move, surely it would have done so?

Fifteen minutes. Longer than Misha usually spent on a move this early, but by no means unusual for grandmasters at this level.

Unzicker clicked on the Show observers icon again. There were almost 100 now. You may be watching history, my friends, he thought, if you only knew it. You may be watching history. He wondered if they were chattering to each other online. Observers to a game can chat together, as can players, but one group can't see what the other is saying.

Misha moved, so suddenly that Unzicker almost started.

Bishop to b4.

He sat back in his chair and rubbed his eyes.

I've done it, he thought. I've bloody done it.

A line came up in his dialogue box:

killerinstinct32: That what I think it is?
repino: You betcha.
killerinstinct32: Wow. Just wow.
repino: I know.
killerinstinct32: I'd better start thinking!

Kwasi and Misha went at it for three more hours, and eventually agreed a draw. Unzicker couldn't have cared less about the result. Misha had self-corrected an error, and that was all that mattered.

But one move different wasn't enough, not for Unzicker. He wanted to be sure. This is the scientist's way: a great leap forward followed by a welter of self-doubt. No experiment could be said to have properly succeeded without running it against a failsafe.

He knew the ICC had a department called Speedtrap which ran checks to see whether players purporting to be human were actually computers. Speedtrap kept their methods quiet, for fear that making them public would help the cheaters beat the system, but Unzicker could guess most of them anyway: diagnosing processor actions through the server interface, checking moves against those known to be played by certain engines, those kind of things. In any case, he didn't need to know *how* they did it, only *that* they did it.

He set up two new accounts. **Kuokkala** (the original Finnish name for Repino, Botvinnik's birthplace) would be Misha. **Akbyr** would be Rybka, one of the strongest search engines around; Unzicker had a copy in his office. He would pass them both off as humans, set them playing against the strongest grandmasters on ICC, and see how long it took for Speedtrap to issue a warning.

Akbyr managed three games before Speedtrap sent a message saying they'd detected that it was a chess engine. But **Kuokkala** just sailed on and on: game after game without arousing the slightest suspicion.

In its twelfth game, it came up against **killerinstinct32**. Kwasi didn't know this was Misha, Unzicker realized. Should he tell him? No. This was a perfect blind test.

Misha/**Kuokkala** beat Kwasi in sixty-four moves. It was almost poetic.

Kwasi instantly issued a rematch challenge. Unzicker typed in the dialogue box.

Kuokkala: It's me, Misha.
killerinstinct32: WTF?
Kuokkala: New handle to see whether can remain undetected as engine.
killerinstinct32: Why the hell didn't you tell me?
Kuokkala: Had to be a blind test.
killerinstinct32: You don't fucking trust me?
Kuokkala: It had to be a blind test. You must see that. Tell me honestly: did you recognize this as Misha?
killerinstinct32: Misha's beaten me before.
Kuokkala: Not my question. Did you think you were playing man or machine?
killerinstinct32: Never had reason to think it machine.

328

So man.

Kuokkala: KK, we've done it. Properly done it.

killerinstinct32: Fuckin A.

The best chess player in the world had played sixty-four moves against a computer and not known it. That was the Turing test, right there: where the actions of a machine were indistinguishable from those of a human.

Misha had passed the test. Misha was learning. Misha was thinking.

Misha was growing.

56

Thanksgiving itself had been a hiatus: a regathering, a truce, like Christmas Day in the trenches. Someone had pressed pause, and for twenty-four hours or so, no one had done anything of note. Patrese had taken over the surveillance of Unzicker himself, as everyone else had wanted to be at home with their families.

Patrese's sister Bianca had asked him to stay with her family in Pittsburgh, as she always did, and he'd told her sorry but he had to work, as he usually did. Sooner or later, he thought, she'd just give up asking. She'd told him time and again that there was more to life than work, and that was coming from a doctor at Pittsburgh's biggest and busiest hospital. When she stopped telling him, maybe he'd start listening.

Anyway: Patrese had watched Unzicker all day, and he'd rather have watched paint dry. Unzicker had done nothing apart from sit in his room and go for a walk. He'd seemed almost amused by Patrese's presence, as though denying

Patrese his vacation was somehow a small triumph. Perhaps it was.

Today, the day after Thanksgiving proper, was also a holiday: most folks tended to extend the vacation into a long weekend of four or five days. Patrese was still waiting for the subpoena order on the ICC to come through – he'd gotten an e-mail saying that his form had been deemed complete and was now being processed, which he guessed was at least something positive.

How long it would be was still anyone's guess, and then of course it would have to be served, which involved either putting it in the mail – another day gone – or flying to Pittsburgh himself, which was the last thing he needed. Perhaps they'd have found Kwasi by then. Hell, perhaps they'd have found Jimmy Hoffa and D.B. Cooper by then too.

Patrese and Anderssen met over a late breakfast to discuss their options. The surveillance team on Unzicker had just phoned in to say that he was back at the shooting range. Patrese wondered briefly whether he should be alarmed, and then thought that he sounded like one of those hysterical Brady Bill fanatics. Millions of Americans liked to shoot. There was nothing sinister about that. Unzicker happened to be a bit of a freak and a hell of a shot, which was a worrying combination: but they'd been on his case for a week now, on and off, and they'd found absolutely nothing concrete on him. If the man wanted to go and knock holes out of a paper target, then let him.

Anderssen's cellphone rang. He answered, listened, smiled wolfishly, said: 'I'm on my way,' and ended the call.

'News?' Patrese asked.

'Yeah, but not on this case. Another one. Bank robber.'

'I thought you did homicide.'

'I do. This motherfucker killed a customer during one of his raids. They just got him.'

Patrese thought for a second. 'He do one near Harvard on the first of this month?'

Anderssen raised an eyebrow. 'How do you know that?'

'I was there. Popped in to get some money after interviewing the principal of the college where Showalter taught.'

'Small world, huh? You shoulda capped him there and then, saved me the bother.'

Patrese remembered standing in the foyer of the bank with his gun out, Hoodie Man with his own weapon pressed to the temple of an Asian woman. Patrese hadn't taken the shot because that would have endangered the lives of people there. He hadn't taken the shot because he'd remembered Samantha Slinger and lost his nerve. Take your pick.

'That's the Bureau for you,' he said. 'You help us, we make your lives harder.'

Anderssen laughed. 'Yeah. Thanks a bunch.' He stood up and pulled out ten bucks from his hip pocket. Patrese waved it away. 'You sure?' Anderssen asked.

'Sure. You get the next one.'

'Mr Bank Robber's got any of his ill-gotten gains on him, I'll ask him to reimburse you personally. Let you know how it goes.'

'OK.'

When Anderssen had gone, Patrese had another cup of coffee and a fruit salad. He hadn't been running enough lately, and he was wary of chubbing out: too easy to do when caught up in a case. The moment he was back in New Haven, he was going down to the lighthouse, there and back. Clear his mind, sharpen his focus.

His cellphone rang. 'Patrese.'

'Sir, the subject is heading on foot into the Veritas Hotel.'

The Veritas was the best hotel in the Harvard Square neighborhood: a swanky boutique place that was presumably

332

deluged with the well-heeled parents of Harvard students every time there was a play, a graduation, whatever. 'Veritas' – 'Truth' – was Harvard's motto.

'He ever been there before?'

'Not that I'm aware of.'

'You have any idea *why* he's going there?'

'Negative, sir.' Another cop who thought he was in *Star Trek* or Delta Force.

Might be nothing, Patrese thought.

Might have an old friend visiting. Except Unzicker didn't do friends.

Might be going for a cup of coffee. Except coffee was probably twice as expensive there as anywhere else, and Unzicker hadn't shown himself the extravagant type.

Might be nothing. Might be something. Only one way to find out.

'OK,' Patrese said. 'Follow him in there, see where he goes. I'm on my way.'

New Haven, CT

Tartu had spent hours over the past few days looking at games on the ICC involving **killerinstinct32**. He was ever more sure that **killerinstinct32** and Kwasi were one and the same, but something else was still bugging him: something he couldn't quite put his finger on.

He logged on to the ICC.

killerinstinct32 wasn't online, but by typing hist **killerinstinct32** in the command box, Tartu could call up his last twenty games. **killerinstinct32** had lost quite a few of them, Tartu saw: one to **Kuokkala**, which Tartu had been watching, and five to **sequinedberg**. **killerinstinct32** had also beaten **sequinedberg** five times, and they'd had four

333

draws. Tartu had watched a few of the games **killer-instinct32** had played against **sequinedberg**, but there'd been a few more since he'd last logged on.

It was something about these match-ups that was bugging Tartu. Who the hell could beat Kwasi five times in fourteen games? **sequinedberg** wasn't declared as a computer, Tartu had checked that already, and he – let's face it, he wasn't going to be a she – certainly didn't play like a computer.

Tartu called up one of the games at random (**killer-instinct32** white, **sequinedberg** black: result – a win for black) and began to analyze it. Not a quick glance through the moves, but slowly, carefully, as though he were annotating this game for a chess periodical. He worked out why each player had made the moves they had; thought about what he'd have done in various positions, and not gone on to the next move until he'd seen why their chosen options were better.

It took him an hour and a half to do this properly, just for one game, but by the end he was beginning to feel . . . well, something. That thing that had been bugging him about these games: he couldn't be sure what it was exactly, but somehow he knew that his understanding was beginning to coalesce, that thoughts and theories and patterns were taking shape, hardening, crystallizing.

Tartu picked another game: again a win for black, but this time the colors were reversed, and **killerinstinct32** was black. Again Tartu analyzed it to the point of exhaustiveness, looking for similarities and differences with the other game. Strategy, tactics, styles: all these were visible to him, as the layman can see how Picasso painted differently from Constable and how Mozart sounded different to Kurt Cobain.

And this time Tartu saw what he'd been looking for.

He sat back in his chair and rubbed his eyes.

It couldn't be, he thought. It couldn't be what he thought it was.

Why couldn't it be? Only because it seemed so unlikely that someone would do that. But unlikely was not impossible. Especially not in this case.

Tartu picked up his cellphone to dial Patrese, and stopped.

Could he really be sure? Did he even know what any of this meant? What if he was wrong? He didn't want to send Patrese on a wild-goose chase just because of some crazy theory that might all be moonshine. But equally murder was murder, however much Tartu might otherwise have liked Kwasi and felt protective towards him. One way or another, he felt, the sooner this whole thing was ended the better.

OK, he thought: this is what I'll do. I'll look at all the games these two have played, but it'll be quicker now, because I know what I'm looking for. And when I'm satisfied that I'm right, and that my theory all checks out, then I'll ring and tell him.

He called up the next game and set to work.

Cambridge, MA

Anderssen's suspect was in an interview room, waiting for him. Anderssen picked up the file from Registry and leafed through it, more as familiarization than anything else: he had most of the details in his head. Black guy, smooth skin, always wore a hoodie, about six feet tall and of average build. Handy with a firearm, and keener on taking other people's money than making his own.

The bank robberies, Anderssen wasn't judgmental about: everyone knew banks were insured up the wazoo, and everyone also knew that a few grand here and there was peanuts compared with the extent of corporate theft further up the scale. Anderssen had been to Moscow – Russia, not Idaho – a few years back on some international crime conference, and remembered one of the speakers recounting a Russian motto: Why rob a bank when you can own one? No: the bank robberies he didn't care about, other than the obvious need to solve the case.

The homicide committed during one of them, he cared very much about.

He went down to the interview room. Merrimack, the suspect's name was: Stewart Merrimack. Didn't sound too much like a black guy's name, Anderssen thought. And there was no black guy in the interview room, either. Just a white guy in his late twenties, sitting quietly with his handcuffed hands on the table in front of him.

'Shit,' Anderssen said. 'Got the wrong room.'

He checked against the roster he'd been given. No, it said: Room 4, Stewart Merrimack. This was Room 4. So that must be . . .

'You Merrimack?' he asked.

'Yup.'

'Bank robbery?'

'Yup.'

'Bank robber's a black guy.'

Merrimack nodded to the table in front of him. There was something lying there, a little crumpled. Anderssen walked across and picked it up.

A mask. A mask of a black guy's face. And not some crappy ten-buck Hallowe'en mask, either. Anderssen held it up in front of him. Damn, but this thing was realistic. It was a full head and neck mask, so once you had a top on, the point where your skin became the mask was invisible. This was the kind of stuff you saw

336

on those *Mission: Impossible* movies when the Tom Cruise character turned out to be some other guy. This was proper Hollywood.

There was a label inside the mask, at the back of the neck:

SPFX Masks, 14713 Oxnard Street, Van Nuys, CA 91411, USA. This silicone mask is a high-quality product. It looks and behaves like real flesh and muscle. Disguise yourself so that even your nearest and dearest will never recognize you. We do not condone any illegal activity with our masks.

I'll bet you don't, Anderssen thought.

'How much did this cost you?' he said.

'Mask, eight hundred bucks. Eyebrows, one twenty. Hair, nine seventy-five. Pretty much two grand, all in.'

Anderssen didn't bother to state the obvious: that two grand for a mask was the investment of the century when you'd used it to steal thirty grand from various banks. If Anderssen's stock portfolio had a similar rate of return, he wouldn't be a cop no more, that was for sure.

Before he tore this guy a new asshole, though, he'd ring Patrese and tell him. Might give Patrese a chuckle, since he'd been there at one of the hold-ups. Fooled by a dude in a mask from Van Nuys. Only in America.

The main entrance of the Hotel Veritas was a Victorian carriage house façade, but inside was pure chic contemporary. The two cops detailed to Unzicker were perched on chairs in the lobby, looking almost hysterically out of place: not nearly beautiful enough, intelligent enough or sufficiently up themselves to cut it in a place like this. Patrese went over to them.

'Where's he gone?'

'Penthouse suite. Mr Nursultan.'

Nursultan was here? Patrese was surprised: not that Nursultan would stay in a place like this – this was the bare minimum of luxury someone like him demanded – but that Unzicker had come to see him here. Every time Patrese had stumbled across the two of them together, it had been in Unzicker's office at the Stata Center. So why the change? Again, it might be nothing. Meeting your most important benefactor on a day when most of the population were on vacation might also be nothing.

More likely to be something urgent.

'How was he looking?' Patrese said.

'Unzicker?' replied one of the cops.

'No. LeBron James. Yes, Unzicker, of course.'

'Er . . . hard to say.'

'Try.'

'Purposeful,' said the other cop.

'Purposeful?'

'Yeah. Like he was walking with purpose. Like he had something to do. Not just meandering around.'

'He seem nervous?'

'Not really.'

'He seem bothered by you following him?'

'Didn't really seem to care about that. Must be used to it by now, I guess.'

Patrese thought for a moment. If this meeting was urgent enough to take place right now, it was also urgent enough for Patrese to want to know what was going on. Unzicker – and by extension Nursultan – were still pretty much their only links to Kwasi.

Unzicker knew they were following him. He wouldn't know that Patrese was here. And Patrese didn't want him or Nursultan to know if he was listening in.

How to get close enough to listen in the first place?

Going up in the elevator to the suite was out of the question. Patrese remembered from his visit to the Waldorf-Astoria in New York that Nursultan traveled with bodyguards, and it was pretty much a sure thing that there'd be a couple of bull-necked lunks standing guard in the corridor outside the suite.

No way of getting a listening device in the room at such short notice: dressing up as a bellboy and planting a bug while delivering room service was strictly for the movies, even if Unzicker and Nursultan hadn't known what Patrese looked like, which of course they did. And Patrese didn't want to get the hotel involved, even tangentially. The moment he asked for their help, they'd start demanding warrants and indemnities and this, that and the other, all of which would probably take about as long to get as the subpoena would.

No. He had to get there now, and on his own.

He went back out of the lobby into the street and looked up. The hotel was only four stories tall. The penthouse suite would, naturally, be on the fourth floor, and it was reasonable to assume that it would have the best view over Harvard Square: architects don't tend to have suites looking over back streets or service areas.

One of the windows on the fourth floor led on to a balcony. There were no other balconies in sight. Balcony must mean suite: you wouldn't assign your only balcony to a lesser room.

If Patrese climbed out of the next window along, he could inch along the ledge until he reached the balcony. It was ten feet, perhaps twelve, and involved going round a corner. Not hard if you weren't scared of heights and had two good hands to grip with.

Patrese wasn't scared of heights, but he didn't have two good hands.

'Stay here,' he said to the watchers. 'Unzicker comes down again, you keep following him. Have a coffee or something while you're waiting.'

'You seen the prices?'

'Our salaries come from taxpayers' money. We're taxpayers ourselves. Charge it to the Bureau, and think of it as perpetual economic motion.'

He headed for the stairs, which were less conspicuous. Elevators come out front and center on most hotel floors, but stairs are more functional and therefore hidden away. Most people use elevators. Most people are overweight. Bit of exercise for Patrese before he got back to doing the lighthouse run.

He took the stairs two at a time all the way up to the fourth floor, where he opened the door from the stairwell on to the corridor very slowly. Another advantage of staircase doors over elevator ones: they don't ping when they open.

Patrese pressed himself flat against the wall and risked a quick glance down the length of the corridor. He could hear voices: low, deep, foreign. Must be the bodyguards. But he couldn't see them. They were out of sight round a corner: the same corner, he realized, that he'd seen while looking up from street level.

He shut the stairwell door behind him as slowly and carefully as he'd opened it, and tiptoed along the corridor – thank God for carpets – until he reached the window he'd identified as the one along from the balcony.

It would open, he saw: it wasn't one of those plate-glass ones with no catch. He gripped the handle tight and twisted. No squeaking. It opened smoothly and easily. Making a mental note to buy each and every man in the hotel's maintenance department a large beer, he opened it fully, sat on the sill, swung his legs out into the fresh air, and felt for the ledge below with his feet. With his heels flush against the wall, he had about six inches of ledge to play with in front of his toes. Not much. But enough.

He took a deep breath. Had to do this reasonably fast, not just because the longer he took the more likely he was to freak out, but also because this was the middle of the day in Harvard Square, and sooner or later someone would notice a man climbing along a ledge. Not instantly, probably, as most people tend to look around themselves rather than high up, but the moment some moron saw him and pegged him for a suicide case, he might as well take out a personal advert on radio and attach a neon sign to his head.

Don't think about it. If this ledge was two feet above ground level, you could do it without thinking. So all that's going to make you mess this up is just that: thinking. Don't look down. Keep your head straight, and your balance will follow.

He pressed his back against the wall, kept both his hands in contact with the wall as well, and began to shuffle along the ledge. Cars hissed and honked beneath him. A little different from the usual student bustle in the square: more families walking and laughing, the restaurant waiters hurrying in and out.

To the corner: a right angle away from him, so he was almost going back on himself. He got to the end of the first side. A sudden lurch as he went a fraction too far, and the briefest swirling of panic in the pit of his stomach as he pulled back before overbalancing. Press hard against the wall. Breathe deeply. Calm.

The corner went away to his left. He put his left hand round it until he found the next piece of wall, and shuffled along until he could feel the crack of his ass against the jutting edge where the two walls met. Left leg round on to the next bit too, to join his left arm. He was right on the corner now, exactly halfway, caught in the pose Kate Winslet had made famous on the prow of *Titanic*.

Take your time. Don't rush. Calm again.

He kept shuffling until he was clear of the corner, and fully flat against the next section of wall. Glance to his left. The edge of the balcony was a few feet away.

A shout from the street below. For a moment Patrese thought someone had seen him: but no, it was only some guy hollering across the traffic to his buddy on the other side of the road. Another couple of deep breaths to rein his heart rate back down from runaway to galloping.

He reached for the balcony with his left hand. Typical balustrade, about waist-high. Getting over it and on to the balcony proper wouldn't be the problem. Getting seen by Nursultan as he did so might be.

He leaned as far across the balustrade as he dared, trying to see in through the French windows. Two men were in there – Nursultan and Unzicker, he thought, though he couldn't tell for sure, as they both had their backs to him.

That was enough. If they had their backs to him, they couldn't see him.

He flopped a little gracelessly on to and over the balustrade, half dropping and half falling on to the floor of the balcony itself. He stayed there a few moments, regathering his breath and his wits, before pushing himself to his feet, pressing himself once more flush to the wall, and sidling up to the edge of the French doors.

Hard to hear what they were saying inside through the glass and over the thumping of his own heart. Patrese turned his head so his ear was pressed against the window.

And at that precise moment, his cellphone rang.

Anderssen turned the mask over and over in his fingers while he waited for Patrese to pick up. This really was

342

something, he thought. Part of him wanted to put it on and walk round the cop shop like that, but forensics would probably have a fit. Besides, he wasn't putting his face anywhere Merrimack's pores had been. Guy must have sweated buckets during his hold-ups, what with all that adrenalin. It was like those soccer players who swapped shirts the moment a match had finished. Ninety minutes in your own sweat was bad enough, let alone in someone else's.

'Yeah?' Patrese's voice was muffled and hurried.

'Franco? You'll never guess.'

'This better be urgent, man.'

'Where are you?'

'On a balcony outside the Veritas hotel.'

'The fuck are you doing there?'

'Nursultan and Unzicker are inside. Trying to listen to them.'

'Well, I wasn't ringing for anything crucial.'

'Tell me. I'm here now.'

'The bank robber? The black guy you saw? Not a black guy at all. White dude in a two-thousand-dollar mask.'

'You're shitting me.'

'I'm not.'

'Didn't look like no mask to me.'

'That's 'cos it cost two grand. Hollywood-style, some special-effects company out in Van Nuys. Hell of a thing. Show you when you get back. You want some back-up?'

'Not yet. I'm good.' Anderssen heard a beep on the line. 'Hold on,' Patrese continued. 'That message tone . . . wait.' A pause, some more beeps as Patrese fiddled with his phone, and then he was back, concern lacing his voice. 'Max, something weird. I just got a message saying Unzicker's used his keycard in the Stata Center.'

'But you said you were looking right at him?'

Patrese risked another look through the window. Unzicker

343

was in three-quarters profile from behind, but it was definitely him: Patrese could tell that from the voice alone. 'I am. I'm looking at him now.'

'And his keycard's just been used? It's not a delayed message or something?'

'Just been used. In the last minute.'

'I'll go check it out.'

'Probably some malfunction.'

'Probably. Some MIT nerd screwing around, or something.'

'What about your bank robber?'

'Him? He's not going anywhere. I'll let him stew for a few more hours. Let you know what I find.'

'And me you.'

Anderssen ended the call and headed toward the duty sergeant's desk. 'You can put Mr Merrimack back in his cell.'

'Sir?'

'I've got to go out. I'll talk to him when I get back.'

'Sir.'

'And don't give him a damn thing. Not food, not water, nothing. Make him sweat.'

'Sir.'

On the balcony, Patrese switched his BlackBerry to silent mode and put it back in his pocket. Neither Nursultan nor Unzicker had reacted to it ringing, so either they hadn't heard it through the glass, or else they – like everybody else – were now so used to the ceaseless, ubiquitous ringing of cellphones that they no longer took any notice unless it was their own.

He, on the other hand, could hear their conversation perfectly well, because voices were being raised: pitches shriller, words more staccato.

'You try bargain?' Nursultan was saying. 'You give me shit like this and think you walk away? You get Misha to

344

work, now you keep it from me? On Misha, I own every-thing. *Everything*. You got that? Computers, chips, diagnostics, game logs: everything. You done amazing, no? You going to be famous. You going to be rich. And now you want *more*?'

'You couldn't have done this without me.'

'I say same back to you.'

'Someone else would have funded it.'

'Someone else didn't. I did.'

'How do I know you're going to keep your word?'

'You don't trust me?'

'You're a businessman. I'm a computer engineer.'

'So?'

'I don't know if you're ripping me off. But I can't take the chance. You pay me up front, you get the chip, the diagnostics, everything.'

'I pay you for things I already own?'

'You're going to pay me anyway. Just – a little earlier than usual.'

'The *schwarz*: he make you do this?'

'Schwarz?'

'Nigger. King. *He* not trust me. You got deal with him? You and him against me? That it? You no idea what you doing? No fucking idea.'

'Five million.'

Nursultan laughed. 'You think I even start this? Misha is mine. You hand it over so we can start on commercial patents.'

'Five million.'

Nursultan sighed, as though a great injustice was being done to him. Then he turned his head toward the door of the suite and shouted: 'Almas! Irek!'

The bodyguards came hurrying in. Nursultan spoke to them briefly in Tatar. They looked at Unzicker, and at Nursultan again, and they nodded. One of them – Patrese didn't know whether it was Almas or Irek, and since they both looked as though they'd been hewn from stone, he supposed it didn't really matter – moved toward Unzicker.

Unzicker should have been quaking. Even from out on the balcony, unseen, Patrese felt a jolt of trepidation. But Unzicker simply looked blankly at this man mountain.

'This Irek,' said Nursultan.

Well, there's my answer, Patrese thought.

'You have ten seconds,' Nursultan continued. 'You don't hand Misha to me, Irek do you harm.'

What the hell to do? Patrese thought. He couldn't stand here and watch some psychopathic bodybuilder work over Unzicker for fun. He'd have to go in and stop it. He was armed, of course, but he had no doubt that Nursultan's men would be too. There were two of them, they were much bigger than him, and they had four working arms.

He reached for the handle of the French doors and twisted slightly. Locked. He'd have to shoot it off, and then all hell would break loose.

Say yes, he silently pleaded with Unzicker. Just fucking say yes. Give him what he wants and walk away. If Patrese had understood right, and Unzicker had gotten Misha to work, he'd instantly be a god among computer nerds – which, since computers now ruled the world, meant a god to everybody. MIT would erect a statue of him made from computer chips. He'd have the scientific immortality he'd dreamed of.

Nursultan checked his watch with the mild impatience of a man waiting for a train.

Irek moved a pace closer to Unzicker. Almas was coming round the other side of his chair. It was happening in excruciating slow-motion, seconds stretching for eons. Patrese took a step back from the doors, the better to give himself room,

346

and reached for his gun. Shoot the lock off, come in through the French windows and . . .

. . . well, he hadn't really got much further than that. Hold up his badge and arrest them all in the name of the Bureau. Perhaps he'd get to lock horns with that nice Mr Levenfish again when they were all in the cells.

Unzicker leaned forward, as though about to push himself upwards from the chair. His hand went down to his ankle, and Patrese saw what was going to happen quicker than anyone else in the room did; because Patrese knew what they didn't, that Unzicker liked to do pistol shooting on the MIT range, that he was a heck of a shot, and that – oh Jesus, how could the watchers have missed the significance of this? – he'd been to that very range before coming here. Thanksgiving vacation, skeleton staff: must have been the easiest thing in the world for Unzicker to have snuck his Walther 22 out without anyone seeing. Bend down to tie your lace, pop it in your ankle holster, walk out whistling Dixie.

But Ivory hadn't used a gun in any of the murders, and they'd been watching Unzicker on the grounds that he might be Ivory, so perhaps there'd been no reason for the watchers to connect the two. The gun club was below a gym: perhaps the watchers thought Unzicker had just gone to the gym. Perhaps the watchers were in holiday mode too, grousing to each other about how much they hated working Thanksgiving. These things happened. Didn't make it right, sure, but didn't make it unusual either.

Four thumps, two soft and two much heavier: the apologetic coughs of a pair of .22-caliber bullets, one into Almas' heart and one into Irek's, and the crashing of two very large, very dead men hitting the floor.

Patrese fired twice at the lock and kicked the French doors open.

* * *

There was a single security guard on duty at the Stata Center. Anderssen flashed his badge and asked for directions to Unzicker's office.

'You seen Mr Unzicker in here today?' he asked when the guard had finished.

'I don't know who he is.'

'Who's been in here the last half-hour or so?'

'Only one guy.'

'Can you describe him?'

'Er . . . white guy. Pretty average.'

'Square-rimmed eyeglasses? Baby face?'

'No. No glasses. Don't know about baby face. Pretty regular features.'

'OK.' It couldn't have been Unzicker anyway: he was in the Veritas. 'Thanks.'

Anderssen was halfway up the first flight of stairs when he thought that maybe he could use a little back-up, the kind he'd offered to Patrese. He hadn't brought any from the cop shop as they were low on staff, this being Thanksgiving weekend and all. Should he ask the security guard to come with him?

No, he reckoned. Security guards in places like this were one down from mall cops. To pull a stint in a deserted building when everyone else was with their families, you weren't exactly going to be Rambo. Besides, the guy probably wasn't allowed to leave his post except to go for a leak.

He could radio the MIT campus police and ask them. If he found something, maybe he would. But he was a veteran of going on three decades. He couldn't handle an electronic screw-up in a science lab, he was doing the wrong job.

A lot of guys have died throughout history because they weren't brave enough to admit they were scared.

The door to Unzicker's office was ajar. Someone *had* been

348

in here. Anderssen unholstered his gun and held it out in front of him. He tensed, took a deep breath, and flung himself against the door as hard as he could, his momentum taking him forward and down into the room, rolling instantly away from the door with gun held out in front of him, sighting down the barrel, looking for movement in every corner of the room.

Nothing. No one but him, feeling slightly foolish as he clambered to his feet, glad that there hadn't been anyone around to witness this over-reaction.

A shattering crack right at the base of his skull, and an oblivion of merciless speed.

Tartu had been through all fourteen games in the recent history of **killerinstinct32** and **sequinedberg**, and he no longer had any doubt that his theory was right. Style, tactics, strategy, positioning, preference for the bishop pair when minor pieces were exchanged, unwillingness to swap queens: there were so many pointers that the evidence was overwhelming. It wasn't only in the games, either. Tartu had found two more things away from the board that surely clinched it.

First, **sequinedberg** had only ever played against **killerinstinct32**. He'd played hundreds of games over the course of the last few months, and all of them – every single one – had been against **killerinstinct32**. Second, remembering Kwasi's penchant for anagrams – Patrese had shown him the Rotting Husk/Knight's Tour puzzle – Tartu had found an online anagram generator and typed in 'sequinedberg'. One of the first answers that had come up was 'Bridge Queens'; or, more aptly here, Queensbridge, the enormous housing project in which Kwasi had grown up.

Tartu picked up his cellphone and dialed Patrese.

*   *   *

Patrese felt the BlackBerry vibrate in his pocket, but whoever it was and whatever they wanted, it could hardly be more crucial than what was happening in the Veritas' suite.

Patrese had his gun trained on Unzicker. Unzicker had his gun trained on Nursultan. Nursultan didn't have a weapon to complete the stand-off triangle, and Patrese was glad: at least he knew that he and Unzicker knew how to fire the damn things.

'Put it down, Thomas,' Patrese said, for what felt at least the fifth time. 'Put it down, and we can sort all this out.'

'You saw me kill them, didn't you?'

'Yes.'

'So I'm screwed anyway.'

'You could plead self-defense.'

'He came to blackmail me!' Nursultan shouted. 'That not self-defense! Man break into your house and you attack him, he not claim self-defense!'

Actually, Patrese thought, there were plenty of places where he probably could: but there was a time and place for the political-correctness-and-human-rights-gone-mad debate, and this wasn't either of them.

'Just give me the gun, Thomas,' he said.

'You know what I am?' Unzicker's eyes flitted between Patrese and Nursultan, but his gun hand was very still, no wavering or shaking. 'I'm a genius. A solid-gold genius. I've invented the first proper AI in history.' He focused on Nursultan. 'And now you want to cheat me out of my share.'

'This is no way to sort things out,' Patrese said.

Unzicker jerked his head toward Nursultan. 'I bet it is where he comes from.'

'Mr Nursultan,' Patrese said, 'you're going to honor your word, yes?'

'Of course.'

The same Mr Nursultan, Patrese remembered, who'd at

various stages in the past few weeks made thinly veiled threats against Patrese, even more thinly veiled offers of bribes to him, and had just been prepared to let his goons loose on Unzicker. In Unzicker's position, Patrese thought, he probably wouldn't have believed Nursultan either.

Patrese took a step toward Unzicker. 'Give me the gun.'

Unzicker swiveled round to aim at him. 'No. Don't. Back.'

Patrese could wait, *should* wait, for the cops to arrive. They'd realize sooner or later, surely: the two guys downstairs in the lobby, Anderssen when he didn't hear from Patrese, someone in the hotel who must have heard the shots, suppressed though they'd been. And then it would be a hostage situation: they'd bring in the negotiators and talk Unzicker ragged till he gave in. That's what they did; that's what they were good at. It would last a few hours, it wouldn't be fun, but they'd all get out of it alive.

All this went through Patrese's head in a flash; and in that very same flash Nursultan lunged for Unzicker's gun, and Unzicker must have seen him out of the corner of his eye because he whirled back toward Nursultan again, gun hand coming round and trigger finger already taking up the pressure, and Patrese had taken the shot too soon against Samantha Slinger in Pittsburgh, and he hadn't taken the shot against the bank robber with the crazy Hollywood mask, and he'd taken the shot against the suicide bomber in Heinz Field and got that one right, and he was going to take the shot here and get that right too.

The olive-drab Glock 22 kicked twice in his hands. Double tap to the head. Unzicker couldn't have done it better himself. His body spun round on itself with the force of the impact, crashing over the back of a chair and on to the floor.

Nursultan looked wild-eyed at Patrese.

'You kill him!'

'It was him or you.' Patrese wondered briefly whether he'd taken the right option.

'How the fuck I get Misha now? You know how much it worth?'

There's gratitude for you, Patrese thought. Save a man's life, and watch him bitch about all the money you might have cost him.

'Try his office,' Patrese said, and in the same moment remembered that Anderssen was already there. He pulled his BlackBerry out of his pocket, and it started vibrating the moment he did so. TARTU, said the screen. He hit the 'answer' button.

'I'll call you right back.'

'They're the same person,' Tartu blurted.

'What?'

'**killerinstinct32** and **sequinedberg.** They're the same person.'

'But that means . . .'

'Yes. Kwasi's been playing against himself, over and over.'

Playing the game. Against himself. Over and over.

The game. The Game.

Anderssen. Stata Center. Unzicker's office. Keycard.

Patrese ended Tartu's call and dialed Anderssen. Two rings, and then the pick-up.

'Franco. Hello.'

Not Anderssen's voice.

Kwasi's.

They found Anderssen's body in Unzicker's office. Kwasi was long gone, of course, and with him all the Misha stuff: Nursultan confirmed that none of what they'd been working on was in Unzicker's office anymore, or in his room in Tang Hall.

The security guard at the Stata Center was adamant that only a white man had come in this morning. Patrese thought of what Anderssen had told him about the bank robber with the mask, and remembered that the mask in question had been made by a company based out in Van Nuys. Patrese borrowed the security guard's computer terminal – this was MIT, so if you breathed, you were online – and googled 'Van Nuys masks'. The first result returned was the SPFX website: SPFX Masks, Silicone Masks, Movie Quality.

Patrese clicked on the list of the masks they offered. He recognized one of them, the Player, as the black guy he'd seen at the bank robbery in Cambridge.

'There.' The security guard was pointing. 'That's the guy, right there. The white guy who checked in this morning.'

Handsome Guy, the mask was called. SPFX's idea of hand-some was clearly different from Patrese's, but if they were charging close on two grand per mask, SPFX's bank balance was probably different from Patrese's too.

Patrese rang the number on the website. No answer. Thanksgiving vacation. Back Monday. Thanks for your enquiry. Please e-mail your order. Not that it would do anything other than confirm what they already knew: Kwasi had ordered one of these masks, and he'd used it while going out killing in the Boston area. There'd never been two killers. There'd only been one: Kwasi, playing against himself.

He'd left two things by Anderssen's body. One of them Patrese had expected: the Chariot card. Whether the Tarot meant anything any more, Patrese had no idea. Perhaps Kwasi had gotten the idea off of Anna, when he'd been going out with Inessa. Perhaps he'd gotten it off of Unzicker, who'd made a tarot costume for MIThenge, and just used it to throw Patrese off the scent, add another layer of obfuscation.

The second was a copy of *The Royal Game*, a novella by Stefan Zweig.

Inessa had told Patrese about this, he remembered. Zweig

had been an Austrian writer who'd achieved the height of his fame during the interwar years, and *The Royal Game* – only published after his suicide – was about a man, Dr B, who'd been jailed or something like that, with only a book of grandmaster chess games for company.

He'd read this book so often, and memorized all the games so thoroughly, that in the end he'd become consumed by chess and, still kept in total isolation, had begun to play against himself. But chess is a game of perfect information, so to play it properly, White cannot know for sure what Black is thinking, and vice versa. Wanting to play chess against yourself is a paradox, like jumping over your own shadow.

So to do this properly, Dr B had been forced to split his psyche into two personas, White and Black. To take this to its logical absurdity, he had to literally switch his brain on and off. So Dr B had at once known everything and known nothing: he'd been totally his White personality while thinking as White, but the moment White had moved, he'd switched to his Black personality, as thoroughly and immediately as though he'd pressed a chess clock. Move, switch. Move, switch. Move, switch.

And he'd studied the board anew after every single move, looking for traps or pitfalls that he himself had set in a psyche now totally forgotten for the next few minutes, and yet totally recalled when the move was made and he switched back. Inevitably, he'd had a breakdown, hovering over the abyss: and after every game, whichever half of his self had been defeated instantly wanted revenge against the other half.

So too, it seemed, with Kwasi. When he donned the mask, he put on with it the persona of the White killer: organized, methodical, calculating, in the way that on the chessboard White plays to press home the advantage of the first move.

And at other times he was Black: vicious, frenzied, forever complicating things to negate the advantage of that first move.

But Kwasi wasn't only playing against himself. He was playing against Patrese too. And Patrese prided himself on always getting his man.

PART THREE

Endgame

'Play the endgame like a machine.'

Rudolf Spielmann

57

It's not hard to preserve human skin.

First you soak it in water to clean and soften it. Then you take a sharp knife or hacksaw blade and scrape all the crap off the inside, all the flesh and fat and that. Next you put it back in liquid – not water this time, but piss. Leave it here for a bit. That loosens all the hair fibers. Human skin isn't as hairy as animal skin, obviously, but if you want it to look good, you can't have stray follicles everywhere. Once you take it out of the piss, you can remove the loose hairs one by one with tweezers.

Now you've got to dry it out. Cover it all over in salt, about three-quarters of an inch thick, and leave it for sixteen hours. Salt blots up the moisture like a motherfucker. When you come to take it off, the salt'll be all damp, but the skin'll be dry as a bone.

Think you're finished here? Not even close. You're only just getting started. 'Cos here's where the tanning starts. Not tanning as in suntanning, fool people lying on UV beds or sizzling their honky skin in the sun – next stop skin cancer, doesn't really seem worth it, no? – but tanning, as in curing and preparing skin, the way they've done it for centuries with animal skins.

And before you get all squeamish, what's human skin except animal skin? You see these things about the Nazis making

359

lampshades out of human skin, or some Wild West outlaw who's now a pair of shoes, or books bound with the skin of slaves back in the day, and you know what? I don't see no difference between that and the shoes on your feet, the purse you're carrying, the belt round your waist, the seats of your car, you know? It's all the same thing. It's all just skin. You don't have no use for it after you're dead.

Anyhows. First thing you do after drying the skin is wet it again. Contrary, I know, but that's how it is. Just got to make it a little bit flexible once more. You boil up some water and put bran flakes in it. Let this sit for an hour, then strain the water through a colander. Keep the brown water, throw the soggy bran flakes away. Then boil up some more water, dissolve some salt in it and add this all to the brown water.

Next bit's tricky. Be careful. Make sure you're wearing gloves and a long-sleeved shirt. Maybe a cloth round your mouth and some safety goggles too if need be. Get some battery acid – every motor store from here to Detroit sells it – and pour it into the water. Don't let it splash. You get any of that on you, you'll sure know about it. Stir it all up, then put the skin in the solution, pressing it down and stirring with a long stick till it's fully soaked. Leave it there for three-quarters of an hour, making sure you stir it every now and then so every part of the skin gets exposed to the solution just the same.

Take the skin out and put it very gently in some clear, warm water. Rinse it here for about five minutes. Add a box of baking soda to the rinse water to neutralize some of the acid in the skin. Then you take the skin out and hang it over a fence or somesuch to drain. When it's damp – no longer soaking wet, but not yet bone dry either – take it off the fence and paint it with oil. Then lay it flat on a wood pallet to dry properly before you cut it.

Like I said, not hard. Not hard at all.

58

It was the endgame now, cold and clinical. Just Patrese and Kwasi, one-on-one: the dizzying complications and legerdemain of the middlegame gone, distractions now down to a minimum. But the simplicity of the endgame is also its difficulty. It requires nerveless calculation, boundless patience, and the ability not to get spooked by the knowledge that your first mistake in the endgame is usually your last too.

The Bureau held a preliminary investigation into the death of Unzicker, as they always do when one of their agents kills a suspect in the line of duty. Agents deemed to have acted inappropriately are suspended on full pay pending further inquiries. There'd be a fuller hearing in due course, but at this stage there was no question of Agent Franco Patrese being suspended.

Quite the opposite, in fact: his behavior had been exemplary, entirely in keeping with the standards the Bureau demanded of its employees. There was no doubt that in killing Unzicker, Agent Patrese had saved Nursultan's life, and no blame could

361

be attached to him for failing to prevent Unzicker from killing the two bodyguards. Indeed, only Agent Patrese's resourcefulness in getting himself to the balcony in the first place had prevented a catastrophe of even greater proportions.

Nursultan might have faced charges for inciting his bodyguards to beat Unzicker up, but it was his word against Patrese's – the other three witnesses to the incident were dead – and Nursultan maintained (or rather, Levenfish maintained on his behalf) that he hadn't intended his men to harm Unzicker, but had simply hoped that the threat of it would be enough to persuade Unzicker into dropping his absurd blackmail demand.

Truth was, Patrese didn't fight too hard to have Nursultan charged. He knew Nursultan was as keen to find Kwasi as he was, since Kwasi had all the Misha material. Now Unzicker was dead, perhaps Patrese could use Nursultan to help flush Kwasi out. Exactly how he was going to manage this, he had no idea: but at this stage he wanted to keep as many of his options open as possible.

In any case, Nursultan wouldn't be remanded in custody whatever the charge: he'd be granted bail, which would be chicken feed to someone like him, and all that Patrese would have done would be to have pissed someone off that he might yet need.

Patrese had lit a fire under the asses of the department responsible for issuing subpoenas, but their butts were clearly made out of heat-resistant material: they sent back a stock e-mail saying that his request was still being considered. The Bureau's Los Angeles field office was trying to get hold of the company in Van Nuys that made the masks, and secure a copy of their mailing list. No subpoenas, Patrese had said. Break some limbs if you have to.

He went to the Cambridge police HQ and told them, hand on heart, that he would not rest until he'd found the man who'd murdered their colleague Max Anderssen. That was three cops Kwasi had killed already: three reasons why Kwasi better pray that Patrese rather than another cop found him, as cops don't take too kindly to those who kill their own. Not, Patrese thought, that he could guarantee being much more sanguine about it than they were. He'd been a cop once, and in his heart he still felt more a Pittsburgh boy who liked beer and football than he did a shiny-shoed Hoover man.

When he'd finished with the Cambridge police, he rang Dufresne and reminded him to be alert. The next victim was bound to be in New York, right? That had always been Kwasi's pattern, alternating moves. His MO had been a little off with Anderssen – he'd killed Anderssen on the spot, rather than taken him away as he'd done the other white victims – but that entire murder seemed to have been opportunistic. Kwasi had gone to the Stata Center to get the Misha stuff: he couldn't have known for sure that Unzicker's keycard would trigger an alert, let alone that Anderssen would be the one to respond to that alert.

Then he went round to Dudley House and knocked on Inessa's door.

'Who is it?' she called out from inside.

'It's me. Patrese.'

'Go away.'

'I came to say I'm sorry.'

'I don't care.'

'Please. Just hear me out. Things have changed.'

'You can say that again.'

'With the case. With Kwasi. Listen – I can't stand here like a lemon shouting through a door. Please let me in. Let me say my piece, and then I'll go if you still want.'

Silence stretched behind the closed door: then Patrese heard footsteps, and Inessa opened the door. She was wearing a faded Harvard sweatshirt, and her hair was pulled back. She nodded to the room beyond: come in.

When she'd closed the door behind them, Patrese explained what had just happened. Inessa knew that Anderssen and Unzicker were dead, of course – it had been all over the news – but the public story was that Unzicker had been mentally disturbed. The networks knew nothing of Misha, and Patrese imagined that Nursultan for one would want it to stay that way for as long as possible. And of course Inessa knew nothing about what Tartu had discovered on the ICC.

'Wow,' she said when Patrese had finished. 'Wow.'

'So I'm sorry for asking you, er, what I did the other day, but . . .'

'I understand.'

'. . . I had to do it, you know? As a Bureau agent, I had to do it.'

'I know. I was so mad at you for a while that I couldn't even think past that. But then, when I began to calm down, I realized how hard it must have been for you, and I realized that you really didn't have that much choice. So let's forget about it.'

'You mean that?'

'Sure.'

'Even though you didn't seem that keen to see me just now, making me wait before you opened the door.'

Inessa laughed. 'Gotta make a man sweat sometimes, no?' She eased herself up on to tiptoes and kissed Patrese lightly on the mouth. 'You staying here awhile, or you going back to New Haven?'

'Going back.'

'Want me to come?'

'That's kind, but you've done more than enough to help . . .'

'I meant more to keep you company.' She kissed him again. 'I've missed you.'

364

Patrese smiled. 'I'm not sure how much time I'm going to have.'

'Heck, Franco, I don't care. And I don't throw myself like this at just anyone. Give me a few minutes to pack my stuff – I've got some work to take with me – and I'll be with you.'

'Sounds good. I've got something I want to run past you anyway.'

Here's what Patrese had been thinking. Now they knew that Kwasi was both Ebony and Ivory, and that each victim represented a chess piece in some way, they could start ticking off the ones he'd already accounted for. Neither of the kings. One of two queens: Regina, the black queen. One of four bishops: Showalter, white. Three of four knights: Evans for white, Barbero and Mieses for black. Three of four rooks: O'Kelly and Anderssen for white, Lewis for black. And none of the pawns.

There were 32 pieces on a chessboard, and Kwasi had killed eight. But none of those eight had been pawns, though pawns made up exactly half of all pieces on the board. What were the odds of that? By the law of averages, you'd expect there to be as many pawns as pieces among the victims.

Perhaps he was killing pieces first, then pawns, Inessa suggested.

He'd already thought of that. That would make sense if he was killing in order, most valuable pieces through less valuable pieces through pawns, but he wasn't. The kings were priceless, and yet none of his victims represented the king. He'd only killed one queen, his own mother. If there was an order to his killing, it wasn't in terms of the value of the pieces. How about moves? Like he's acting out the moves of a game? Queen moves, bishop moves, knight moves, that kind of thing.

Possible, Inessa replied, but again unlikely. The exact

365

sequence of murders was bishop, queen, knight, knight, rook, rook, knight, rook. Yes, that was a plausible order of moves in the middle of a chess game, but not at the start of one. On the very first move, each side can only move ten of its sixteen pieces: all eight pawns, as they're on the second row, and both knights, as they can jump over other pieces. Once the pawns move forward, they can clear the way for other pieces behind them: but they have to move first.

Patrese said he'd read somewhere that the pawns are known as the soul of chess. That's right, Inessa said: the phrase had been coined by an eighteenth-century French player. But what of it?

Patrese paused before answering. He knew where his thoughts were taking him, and he knew it made sense, but the stubborn part of him didn't want to know, as the truth of what it meant was unfathomably horrific.

They'd found no pawns among the victims. Kwasi must have killed some pawns.

There was only one way both those statements could be true: that Regina King and Darrell Showalter were the first victims the police had found, but not the first ones Kwasi had killed. He'd killed others. Up to sixteen others. And the police hadn't found any of them.

Among the books found at Kwasi's condo in Bleecker after he'd first gone on the run had been the medieval treatise *Game and Playe of the Chesse*, in which the author William Caxton had divided pawns into eight categories: laborers, clothmakers, apothecaries, dice players, those kind of things. Patrese doubted it was anything as literal as that; and besides, surely clothmakers and apothecaries couldn't be killed without anyone knowing? They probably couldn't even go missing without someone saying something.

Think like Kwasi. Pawns were expendable. Pawns were the lowest rank. Pawns could, if they were very lucky, get to the other end of the board and promote into a piece, but most of them went forward blindly, locked in the restrictions of their existence. They were the ones no one cared about. And they'd have to be the kind of people who, even if their bodies *were* found, would make no waves whatsoever.

At the start of this case, in the few hours before they'd gotten IDs for Regina King and Darrell Showalter, the cops had referred to the corpses as John Doe and Jane Doe. This was what Patrese would be looking for now, he realized: a whole bunch of John Does. People without identity, who'd died as they lived, without leaving a mark. The downtrodden. The invisible. The forgotten. The missing. The nameless.

The homeless.

In a world of social security numbers, store loyalty cards, cellphones, tax returns, benefit checks, Internet addresses and a hundred other things that leave digital breadcrumbs, being homeless is the best way, perhaps the only way, to fall off the grid completely. Few people spare the homeless so much as a glance, even when they drop a guilt-soaked dime in their begging cups.

To be without a home is to be without an identity: you're not classified, you're not quantified, you're not a name on a system. You live in a disused train tunnel or a space beneath an underpass that isn't even high enough to stand up in. You have no medication, no social worker, no one to look out for you except the odd Good Samaritan and your fellow homeless people, who are often bombed out of their heads and no one's idea of a reliable safeguard.

If you have your own patch, your own makeshift fortress of discarded mattresses and cardboard boxes, then one day you're not there anymore, people – always supposing they even notice – will assume you've moved on somewhere. You're not traceable. That's the point. You can go missing for months or years, and by the time your body's found, it probably won't even be recognizable as you.

As victims for a murderer, therefore, homeless people are pretty much perfect.

There was no point going round homeless areas in New York and Boston and asking if anyone had gone missing. Most of them were already missing; they were on the Missing Persons list, and they'd stayed that way because they hadn't shown up on a database somewhere. Nor was there any point scouring the city for bodies which hadn't been found. No; their best hope of finding whether this theory held any water was to ask every medical examiner's office in the New York and Boston areas how many dismembered and unidentified John Does they'd had through in the past few months.

Unlike many public employees, medical examiners do work during the Thanksgiving holidays: people aren't considerate enough to stop dying for four or five days just to give the ME a break. In fact, more people die during Thanksgiving than in any other four-day period throughout the year: too much food, too much alcohol, too many family tensions boiling over.

Patrese mobilized as many Bureau agents and cops as could be spared in New York and Boston, and set them to work. Dismembered bodies, that was what they were looking for. Perhaps only certain parts of them had been found, as Patrese couldn't believe Kwasi would have made it too obvious by sticking so adamantly to the headless, legless and skin-patched template that had marked the eight victims they'd found so far. If he had done so, they'd have been on to him long before. No tarot cards either, presumably. Perhaps he'd had a different signature for the pawns than the pieces.

The answers started coming back within a few hours. MEs in both cities were routinely presented with body parts that they had no way of identifying. A leg here, a torso there, a couple of arms here, like some gruesomely warped shopping list. Many of these parts' owners had been dead so long that they'd severely decomposed, making identification all the harder. Leave a torso in water for a few days, and when you take it out the skin will peel off like a glove.

Could Kwasi have killed eight black homeless men in New York and eight white homeless men in Boston? Sure he could. Hell, he could have killed eighty in each. These crimes aren't routinely logged in crime databases. They should be, of course, but they're not; because the vast majority of ME departments haven't got the time, money or staff to go round trying to identify body parts that have literally no clue as to their origin.

One of the Boston MEs rang Patrese personally to impress on him the sheer scale of what they were dealing with. Have a guess how many sets of unidentified human remains are sitting in evidence rooms across the nation, he said.

No idea, Patrese replied.

Have a guess; go on.

I don't know: ten thousand?

Higher.

Twenty thousand?

Higher still.

Patrese, doubling like the inventor of chess with his demands for grain: Forty thousand?

Spot on. Forty thousand sets of remains, all unidentified. And of those forty thousand, about one in seven ever make it on to a database. The rest are sent to a mass grave and covered in quicklime. What else is there to do?

What else indeed? Patrese thought.

59

Mom knew, of course. She knew all about the flotsam and jetsam. We used to joke about it: flotsam in New York, jetsam in Boston. I remember the first time it happened. I was down in Washington Square Park, where I used to hang out as a kid. There was this homeless guy there, Victor, one of the hustlers. Just him and me, playing late night, no one else around.

He was a good guy, least I thought he was. I'd known him since I was a kid. He didn't treat me no different from no one else, and that was rare, you know, especially after I became champion. Victor would trash-talk you and whale on your ass just the same, didn't matter whether you were some other hobo or the damn president himself.

Anyhows, we're playing speed chess, and your blood's up, you know? Slamming those pieces down, slamming the clock back and forth. Victor knows all the tricks, but he's no match for me. I beat him every time out. He's swigging from this bottle in a paper bag, and gradually he starts to get real aggressive. Trash-talk becomes nasty, personal. He starts telling me how my mom's a ho and all that. No one says that kind of stuff to me. I tell Victor to cool it. He keeps on going. I stand up and tell him that's it, he better shut the fuck up if he knows what's good for him. He stands up too, and *starts yelling 'bout how I done gone changed since I became champion and stuff, all these airs and graces I got now.*

Shit, Victor, I say, I'm still here playing with you, just the two of us, just like we used to do back in the day. Victor's having none of it. Maybe he's high as well as drunk, I don't know; but suddenly he takes his bottle out of the bag, smashes it on the table, and lunges at me with the jagged edge. I jump back and yell at him to cut it out. He lunges again. I knock the bottle from his hand and slam his head on the table once, hard, just to make it clear this shit stops here.

He stays like that, head on the table, for a few seconds.

I pull him up again to say OK, no hard feelings, but of course he's dead, limp and heavy in my grasp, and there's this smell of piss and shit like he's soiled himself. A little hard to tell, given that Victor's usual fragrance wasn't exactly Alpine fresh to start with, but anyway. Motherfucker's definitely dead. Now what?

No one saw us, 'cos it's night and we're alone. I could leave Victor here and let someone find him in the morning, but that doesn't seem right: got to give the man some dignity, no? But equally, I can't be found with him. You know what the media will do if they catch ahold of this? So I pull my hood up so nobody recognizes me, sling his arm over my shoulder so he's draped across me, and start to walk with him, his feet dragging. My pick-up's a block away. Long as we don't come across a cop, we should be OK. Anyone who sees us will just think he's dead drunk and I'm carrying him home.

Dead drunk. Funny.

We get to the pick-up, no major alarms. Can't sling him in the back, in the loading bay: it's got a cover which I'd have to open, and in any case it's too obvious if someone sees us. So I shove him into the passenger seat, climb in myself and start driving. Can't take him back to Bleecker Street, as there's a doorman and stuff there. But I know where I can take him. The place I end up taking them all. The place you don't know about.

371

And on the way, I talk to Victor. Sounds a little sentimental, maybe, but I honestly think he was my only friend, Mom apart. Like I said, he was always the same to you, no matter who you were. Ornery bastard, sure. Call him an equal opportunities asshole. But he wasn't a phony and he wasn't a hypocrite.

I start telling him all this stuff I've never told anyone before. About how my daddy had tried to come back into my life when I started getting famous, when I was a teenager. I didn't want nothing to do with him. Mom had always said he'd walked out on us before I was even born, and I didn't want nothing to do with anyone like that. We were a unit, Mom and me. We didn't need no one else.

But he kept coming round, all full of how he'd seen me in the paper and on the TV and stuff, and I could tell that Mom was starting to kinda like the idea he might be around more often, 'cos he sure could be charming when he wanted to. *I always remembered that about you,* she said to him one night: *you could charm the birds off the trees.* Must have forgotten 'bout how feckless he was, too.

When he'd gone, I told her just that. We'd done fine without him all this time; why the hell would we need him now? *You jealous?* she asks. *Jealous that you might not have my undivided attention for once?* That ain't nothing to do with it, I say, but of course it is. And she knows it as well as I do.

Listen, she says. *Women got needs, just like men do. And I ain't been with no man in a while. So when your daddy – and remember, I did love him once upon a time – when your daddy comes back and is acting all sweet and stuff, it makes a woman feel good, you know? Hell, you're just a boy, you don't know too much about these things, but trust me on this one.*

No way, I say. No way. That man's coming back in here over my dead body.

And then she smiles this weird little smile, like I've passed some kind of test or something, and says in this very soft, very calm voice *that no other woman will ever love me like she does, and she knows no other man will ever love her like I do.*

I tell Victor all this. When I get to the place, I take him out of the pick-up and upstairs – it's the small hours and the place is deserted, so I ain't worried about anyone seeing me – and then I talk to him some more. I know I can't keep him here forever like this, but it's a funny sort of thing we have going here, me just talking and him just listening, and soon I start thinking that I'd like to keep something to remember this by, this good old chat we've just had, something to immortalize Victor by so his death isn't totally in vain.

And a few days later, I'm in Cambridge with Unzicker, studying a position for Misha to work on, when suddenly I feel this amazing rush, and it takes me a moment or two to work out what it is.

The power I felt when I smashed his head on the table – hell, I'd never felt anything like it. Sure, I was upset just after, but that was shock, and also a bit of human conditioning, I guess. You're told that violence is bad and killing is worse. You're supposed to be revolted by it, not exult in it. But you do: it's savage, it's primal.

And I realized something else, too. When you first kill, in fact, you kill two people; not just the victim, but yourself too. Your old self is gone, and in its place is a new persona. I'm no longer part of humanity, not really. I'm one of the bad guys, the others.

And I want to do it again.

People have noticed Victor's gone, sure, but they all think he's just drying out for the millionth time or something. Truth is, people like Victor don't have lives the way most people have lives. You get beyond fifty on the streets, you're doing good. So if I want to kill again, I have to find another homeless person. But the way I've chosen to give Victor a tribute, I need a white guy now. I tell Unzicker I've had enough and I'll see him tomorrow, and then I drive around for a bit till I find some dude under a bridge, and I know he doesn't recognize me because he probably wouldn't recognize himself in a mirror, and I break his neck there and then, and just as before I pile him into the pick-up and take him back to the place, and we talk the whole way, like old friends.

I told Mom round about the third or the fourth one. Actually, I didn't tell her: she came in and saw one of the skin patches hanging there, and the shrunken heads, and she freaked, but I caught her before she could run out the door and I told her listen, listen, I need this, this is what keeps me sane, the feeling of power I get, I can't operate without it, and I know what she's thinking, that she can't do anything that might make me play even a little bit worse, she can't endanger the golden calf in any way whatsoever. She's tied herself to me so completely that she can't jeopardize even the slightest part of it, as anything that threatens me threatens her too.

So she tolerates it. As long as it's making me feel good, she tolerates it. But as the title match gets closer and closer, things start to go haywire. Ever since the blindfold simul fucked with my mind, I haven't been right. People as pieces, pieces as people. The killings aren't making it any better.

She starts to get worried, which just worries me in turn. She tells me not to be a jerk and just play the match. She doesn't understand what's in my head.

And the night of Hallowe'en, when I'm finished with the pawns and come back with the monk guy from Cambridge, the whole thing just snaps. I don't want to play, I say. I don't want to defend this damn title. You should have let me have therapy.

If you don't play, she replies, if you fuck this all up, everything that we – we – have worked so hard for, I'll never forgive you. I've done everything for you, and this is how you reward me? You don't go through with it, I'll tell the police what you've been doing.

You'd turn in your own son? I say.

You'd betray your own mother? she replies.

374

60

Sunday, November 28th
New Haven, CT

When they'd released Unzicker this time last week, Anderssen had said emphatically that they should stop hanging around, waiting for the other side to make mistakes: they should make them dance to the cops' tune rather than vice versa. Now they knew the other side was only one man, Kwasi, that strategy seemed to be more rather than less imperative. They could just wait for Kwasi to choose his next victim; or they could try to influence who that victim would be, and catch him in the act.

Dufresne was first to offer himself. Next in line was a black New Yorker, he said, and he was that. Besides, Kwasi had already killed Anderssen, so wouldn't he feel a certain symmetry by going for Dufresne too? What purer sign of his superiority than killing both detectives assigned to his respective cases?

Dufresne could call a press conference and really go to town on Kwasi, calling him a sexual inadequate, emotionally stunted, a weak person, all the things that would rile Kwasi and make him lose his cool. Easy to arrange for Dufresne to let it slip that he'd be in a given place at a given time, and try to tempt Kwasi to come after him there: offer himself as bait, as it were. There'd be protection, of course, but invisible to anyone who didn't know – until it was too late.

Patrese was tempted. They batted the idea back and forth for a bit, but as they did so, Patrese found himself increasingly uneasy with it all. Not through fear for Dufresne's safety – Dufresne was a professional, he knew what he was doing – but because he didn't believe Kwasi would fall for it. It was too obvious a tactic, too one-dimensional. It was exactly the kind of thing Kwasi would be expecting, and it would reinforce all his sneering arrogance about the police being dimwits who couldn't think outside the box if their careers depended on it.

But Patrese still liked the central idea behind it: take the battle to Kwasi, make him play on their turf rather than them on his. It was just that Dufresne was the wrong guy for the job. He had no emotional connection with Kwasi. Kwasi had only killed Anderssen through opportunism, and therefore he wouldn't go out of his way to pull off a premeditated hit on Dufresne. If Kwasi was trying to get to anyone in this whole case, it was Patrese himself: Kwasi had sent his messages only to Patrese, not to anyone else. No: Dufresne definitely wasn't the right choice. But if they could find a better candidate – someone more plausible to Kwasi, someone who had some kind of hold over him – then they'd be in business.

The answer came to both Patrese and Dufresne pretty much simultaneously.

'No way,' Inessa said. 'No freaking way.'

'You'll have more protection than the president,' Patrese said. 'We'll control the entire environment. Wherever we do it, everyone within fifty yards of you will be our guys. Kwasi'll be able to come in, but he won't be able to get out. You'll be perfectly safe.'

'I'll be a tethered goat. That's what I'll be.'

'You'll be perfectly safe.'

'He's killed at least eight people that we know of, maybe up to twenty-four. Your idea of "perfectly safe" is a little different from mine. Besides, it makes no sense.'

'What do you mean?'

'The next move is down here, right? I'm not from New York, I'm not black.'

'That's the point. We're going to take his routine away from him.'

'And you think he's going to go along with that?'

'Yes. Because of what you are to him.'

'What's that?'

'The first day of this case, you were on TV talking about his mom. I was watching it with him. Boy, did you get a reaction. You still get to him. We've got to use that. There are only two women on the chessboard: the queens. There've only ever been two women in Kwasi's life: his mom, and you. She's the black queen. You're the white.'

Inessa could see the logic of this, of course she could. But discussing it as a theoretical proposition was a little different from being asked to put your own neck on the block, no matter how many promises you were made.

'Where would we do it?' Dufresne asked. 'Cambridge?'

'We?' Inessa spluttered. '*We?* You're not the one being used as bait.'

'Cambridge is the obvious choice,' Patrese said. 'But I've been thinking: the more we can get the similarities with his mom going, the better. She was killed in New Haven. Why he went there, we've still no idea, especially now we know it was just him, he wasn't meeting anybody else. Maybe it's something as simple as the geography, halfway between the two. Whatever. He killed her in New Haven.' He turned to Inessa. 'If he's going to want to come after you, then putting you there will help us. Give him a subliminal trigger, you know.'

'You're fucking crazy. I've given you all the help I can on this, and . . .'

'. . . and this will be the most helpful thing of all. Come on, Inessa. What's the most spectacular thing in chess? The queen sacrifice, right? A game-changer. A brilliancy that snatches victory from the jaws of defeat.'

'That's true. But you're still overlooking one thing.'

'What's that?'

'When you sacrifice the queen, she dies. You win, but she dies.'

It took several hours, but Patrese finally won Inessa round. He managed to convince her of two things. First, that she'd be absolutely safe, whatever happened. The Bureau was experienced in things like this: psychological operations, smoke and mirrors. They knew what they were doing.

Second, this was their best chance of catching Kwasi and ending this thing once and for all. Patrese didn't directly appeal to her sense of civic responsibility, as he knew that would only piss her off, but the implication was left hanging there all the same: this was not only the right thing to do tactically, but ethically too.

They went back to New Haven. Patrese put the plan together in his head as he drove.

It would work, he thought. It had to.

61

This being America, land of the lawyer, and the Bureau being as keen on red tape and form-filling as any bureaucracy, Inessa had to sign her life away before they could proceed. Her helping out Patrese on an unofficial basis was one thing: but now she was technically putting herself in danger – no matter how remote the possibility of her being hurt – the Bureau's lawyers wanted indemnity against any eventuality.

They didn't just want her to sign forms. To be sure she'd follow official rules and procedures, they wanted her to be a temporary consultant to the Bureau. That meant a biometric ID card, and that meant an iris scan, fingerprint-taking, the works. Inessa protested long and hard at how ludicrous this whole performance was, and again Patrese had to calm her down and assure her it was purely a formality and it meant nothing. She couldn't pull out on them now, he pleaded.

CBS filmed the piece in the morning and started running

379

it by lunchtime. The Bureau had been forced to pull in all kinds of favors to get this done, most notably promising CBS exclusive access to all the main players after the case was over, and persuading a rental agency to let them use a vacant downtown penthouse just across the road from Yale's Old Campus. A reporter named Catja Thum had flown up from New York at dawn, and CBS' local affiliate, WFSB, had provided camera, lights and make-up.

'For the past month, FBI Agent Franco Patrese has been leading the hunt for world chess champion turned fugitive serial killer Kwasi King,' Catja said. 'Agent Patrese has been working night and day on this case, and among those whose help he's sought has been the lady here today with us: Inessa Baikal. Miss Baikal is a former girlfriend of Kwasi King's, and she's also a chess champion in her own right. Inessa, what kind of help have you given the FBI?'

'Just tried to tell them how Kwasi's mind works, really.' She was sitting with Patrese on a sofa. The Gothic ziggurat of Yale's Harkness Tower filled the window behind them. 'I'm not sure how much use I've really been . . .'

'That's not true,' Patrese interjected. 'Inessa's been fantastic, and not only in terms of investigative support. I've worked a lot of these cases. The strain is unbelievable. Though you want to keep it all inside and be strong, sometimes you just need to talk to someone. She's a very good listener. She's bright, she's funny, she's warm, she's generous: I wish I could involve her in every investigation.'

'And can you tell us how this particular investigation's going?' Catja said.

'We're leaving no stone unturned, and we're closing in. I can't divulge operational details, obviously, but . . . yes, we're closing in, for sure.'

'And in your downtime: you guys play chess?'

'We sit at the same board, but it's never much of a contest.'

380

Catja gestured around the room: high ceilings, vaulted windows, oak furniture. 'And this apartment we're in – it's pretty swish, I can tell you feel at home – this belongs to a friend of yours, Inessa, is that right?'

'That's right.'

'It's not costing the taxpayer a dime,' Patrese said.

'It sure isn't. It belongs to a friend who's away on business. I'm just house-sitting here. But I love it. Cool space, great views.' The camera went to one of the other windows, which looked down over Dwight Hall and the Old Campus Courtyard.

Harkness Tower one way, Dwight Hall another. It wouldn't be hard for Kwasi to find this place. That, of course, was precisely the point. He could get here if he wanted to.

'Cool space indeed,' Catja concluded. 'Agent Patrese, Miss Baikal, thank you for your time, and we wish you all the best.'

Patrese turned to Inessa and smiled: a little too long, a little too bright just to be friends. The camera caught that too, as Patrese had intended: anything that might rile Kwasi, the more the merrier.

The moment the cameraman called wrap, Inessa bolted for the john and threw up.

62

Patrese wasn't good at waiting at the best of times. He liked to be doing things, keeping himself occupied. Sitting around was anathema to him: the one part of cop work he'd always hated was the stakeout. The movies make it look glamorous and exciting: a brief moment of subterfuge followed by a squealing car chase. The reality was twelve hours in a confined space that soon stank of your own worst odors, eating junk food and pissing in a bottle.

He wasn't quite having to piss in a bottle here – in fact, the bathroom was practically bigger than some apartments he'd lived in – but the junk food and that strange mix of apprehension and boredom were the same. Waiting for someone you knew was coming was bad enough. Waiting for someone who might not come at all was ten times worse.

He'd told Inessa they were taking no chances, and they weren't. There was no doorman who might turn Kwasi away before he'd even got inside. The block's other residents had all been asked to let in anyone who buzzed the

382

intercom. Patrese apart, there were four armed men in the apartment at all times, two from the New Haven PD and two from the city's Bureau office. There were men in the building opposite permanently watching the front entrance: there were men in an office block that overlooked the rear of the apartment, where a fire escape ran from roof to ground. The street cleaner outside, the mother with a stroller – Ruger Blackhawk inside, not a baby – they were all part of the operation too. There was almost more fire-power in this one small area of downtown New Haven than there was in Fort Bragg.

Patrese knew that his nerves would grate on Inessa, so he tried to keep himself as occupied as possible. The mask company in Van Nuys had handed over its mailing list, and the Bureau was checking every address in the tri-state area of New York, Connecticut and Massachusetts. Some of them were PO box numbers, and the postal service was being as much of a stickler for subpoenas as the ICC was being.

Talking of subpoenas: the department in question assured him that a decision would be made soon. Patrese said he'd deliver it himself to the ICC offices in Pittsburgh, as any information about the possible location of Kwasi's computers might be so crucial to the investigation that he didn't want to palm it off on one of the Bureau's local men. It was thanks to his old college buddy Caleb Boone, head of the Pittsburgh field office, that he'd joined the Bureau in the first place, and he could have asked Boone to do it himself: but no, this was Patrese's bag.

Commercial flight times from New Haven to Pittsburgh were at least three and a half hours and involved a stop in Philadelphia, so he'd asked for one of the Bureau's charter planes on standby. Not the plush ones the top brass traveled in, of course, but the little turboprop ones. They'd still get him there in less than half the time, and could of course arrive and leave when he wanted.

He was twitching to go: get up, get busy, and get on with it. But in the meantime, he just had to wait, and wait, and wait. And still Kwasi didn't come.

63

The subpoena came through first thing.

'I'll be back later.' Patrese kissed Inessa, first softly, then harder. 'Don't talk to any strange men while I'm gone.'

She looked round at the four pistol-packers crowding the sitting room and laughed. 'Talk to them? Give them the slip, more like. I'm going nuts here.'

'I know. I'm sorry. It won't be long now.'

Patrese went over to the Bureau's New Haven office, printed the subpoena off, and headed for the airport and the plane to Pittsburgh.

In Pittsburgh, Boone had sent a car for him. In other circumstances, Patrese might have allowed himself a tinge of nostalgic pleasure at being back on his old stomping ground. Not now. Too much to do.

The ICC offices were in Squirrel Hill, one of the city's classier neighborhoods. Patrese asked the car to wait, and went inside.

Subpoenas tend to strike fear in all but those most hardened to the law. Patrese used this to his advantage: demanding to see whoever was in charge, like, *now*, threatening to crawl up the office's collective ass with a microscope if he didn't get full co-operation from each and every one of them, all that kind of stuff. He didn't care who he saw, he said, as long as that person had access to the information he wanted.

One of the admin staff was designated to help. Patrese didn't catch his name. These two accounts, he said: **killer-instinct32** and **sequinedberg**. Everything you have on them. Absolutely everything, immediately.

New Haven, CT

'If I don't get out of here in the next five minutes,' Inessa said, 'Kwasi King won't be the only crazy person you have to worry about.'

'We're not supposed to let you go out, ma'am,' said one of the Bureau men.

'I'm going stir crazy. You guys get twelve hours on, twelve hours off. I have to be here the whole time. I'm going for a run.'

'We can't let you do that, ma'am.'

'Of course you can. Two of you come with me, the other two stay here in case he shows up.'

'That's not—'

'That's not negotiable, that's what it is. What? You guys are all armed, and you don't back yourselves to protect me? And don't tell me you haven't got running gear. You've got gym stuff, I've seen it in your bags.'

'What if he's watching this building and sees you leave?'

'We've been sitting here a whole day now, and the most exciting thing that's happened is that two of you guys broke wind simultaneously. If he's watching right now, tough. He wants me that much, he'll come back; or he'll try someplace else, and you guys will nail him. I'm going to change, and I'm out of here in five. Lighthouse and back, with or without you.'

Pittsburgh, PA

It didn't take the admin guy long. **killerinstinct32** was registered to a company named Sicilian Dragon. An opening variation, the admin guy explained: one of the sharpest there was. To play the Sicilian Dragon well, you had to be a real badass.

Ain't that the truth, Patrese thought.

Sicilian Dragon was registered in Gibraltar. An offshore account; to all intents and purposes untraceable, therefore. Getting the names and addresses of shareholders in offshore companies took months, sometimes years. Patrese might not even have hours.

sequinedberg was also registered to a company in Gibraltar: Inlaid Organics.

Patrese got it instantly, though he used a pen and paper just to be sure. Inlaid Organics and Sicilian Dragon were anagrams of each other.

What about IP addresses and computer IDs for those accounts? he asked.

While the admin guy checked, Patrese rang the incident room and asked if any of the masks from Van Nuys had been sent to a company named Sicilian Dragon. Yes, came the answer: one to a New Haven PO box registered in that name.

New Haven. Getting closer.

The admin guy called up the IP and ID information. Ah, he said, this client was using proxy servers and concealment software to try and hide his IP addresses. But that doesn't work with us, because ICC isn't played through a web browser such as Explorer or Firefox. To play ICC, you need

387

to download a piece of their own software – Dasher – which connects directly to their server.

So it was easy to bypass these attempts at subterfuge, and . . . here we are.

Both coming out of the same location.

Patrese already knew that. But where?

New Haven, the tech guy said. Can't be any more specific than that without checking against the server records, and that'll take some time.

How long? Patrese asked.

Could be hours.

Patrese thought fast.

Sicilian Dragon, Inlaid Organics. If you were a rich man who'd registered companies offshore, and you'd used those companies to hide your identity while you were on the run, what would you do with them? You wouldn't just buy a special effects mask and a couple of subscriptions to an online chess site, would you?

You'd use them to set up an entire alternate life. Car, house . . .

'I need to use your computer,' Patrese said.

The admin guy stood up and gestured to his chair. Patrese nodded his thanks as he sat.

Patrese called up the Connecticut Land Records and Deeds website, and entered 'Sicilian Dragon' in the search box.

Your search has returned 1 result(s).

He clicked again.

1 result(s) found in New Haven County.

Some registries charge you for each record you call up. Connecticut is free. No screwing around with credit cards and online verification. Patrese added the guys who'd built this website to his list of those whom he was going to buy a beer (current incumbents: the maintenance department of the Veritas Hotel).

He clicked a third time.

1 property registered to Sicilian Dragon. Five Mile Point Lighthouse, Lighthouse Point Park, 2 Lighthouse Road, New Haven, CT 06512.

Five Mile Point Lighthouse.

Patrese had to look twice, he was so shocked.

Five Mile Point Lighthouse. That was where he ran: to the lighthouse and back.

He remembered what Kwasi had written. *I lived in a house shaped like a rook, with parapets and spiral staircases.*

A house shaped like a rook. A lighthouse. Patrese had run to it. He'd touched it. And Kwasi had been right there, under his nose, the whole time.

Patrese had run to the lighthouse.

He'd run there with Inessa.

Jesus Christ.

He pulled his phone from his pocket and dialed Inessa. It went straight to voicemail. 'Hi, it's Inessa. Leave a message.'

He hung up. There was a landline in the apartment they were using to try and lure Kwasi out. He rang that. One of the New Haven cops picked up.

'It's Patrese. He's in the lighthouse.'

'Sir?'

'Where's Inessa?'

'Gone for a run, sir.'

'A *run*? You let her out there?'

'There are two guys with her, sir. She's perfectly safe.'

'How long have they been gone?'

389

'About a half-hour, a little more. Said they were going to the lighthouse and back.'

New Haven, CT

Inessa sprinted the last hundred yards to the lighthouse, ignoring the shouts of the Bureau men behind her. If they had enough breath left to shout, she reckoned, they had enough breath left to keep up with her.

She reached the wall of the lighthouse and leaned against it, sweat running into her eyes as the burn spread up her legs. Damn, but that had felt good. She could just about cope with being holed up in that apartment if she was allowed to do this every day.

The Bureau men arrived, sucking in great gulps of air.

'Miss Baikal,' one said, 'please don't do that again.'

Adjusting her hairpin to keep the hair out of her face, she looked at them. 'Sorry.'

A man was jogging past in the other direction, muffled against the cold. Inessa noticed that the door of the lighthouse was ajar.

The jogger's gait was familiar, she thought: and she remembered exactly whose gait it was just as he stopped, pulled a gun from his hoodie, shot the two Bureau men before they could react, and dragged her inside the lighthouse.

One of the Bureau men was dead. The other managed to call in and report what had happened. Within minutes, the park had been sealed off, and a bunch of police cruisers and ambulances were haring towards the scene. The fourteen-man New Haven SWAT team was deployed with orders to storm the lighthouse if need be.

And where law enforcement goes, the media does surely

390

follow. There were five helicopters in the sky above the lighthouse: one Bureau, one New Haven PD, and one for each of the main networks. Normal programming was interrupted to go live to the lighthouse where Kwasi King was holding his former girlfriend captive. It was a hostage situation, and the cops wanted to keep it that way. The more they could talk to him, the longer they could spin it out, the more chance they had of getting Inessa back safely.

Unless, of course, she was dead already.

Pittsburgh, PA

Patrese's driver got him back to the airport in double-quick time. He was running for the turboprop when his cellphone rang.

'You, and no one else,' Kwasi said.

'Excuse me?'

'I'll talk to you and no one else. Tell those motherfuckers outside: if they so much as knock on my door, I'm going to cut her head off.'

'I'm in Pittsburgh. I won't be able to get to you for a couple of hours.'

'I got all day. All night too, if need be.'

'Listen, Kwasi: I'll get there as soon as I can. But I might not be in contact the whole time between then and now, you get? I'm gonna be in the air.'

'The moment you get here, you let me know. And like I say: it's a damn circus outside. One false move from any of them, and it's over. You get?'

'I get.'

Kieseritsky was officer in charge on scene, the designated commander. She'd been the detective who'd called Patrese the morning Regina King and Darrell Showalter had been found: it seemed sort of fitting that she was involved at the end.

And it *was* the end, everyone knew that. One way or another, it was the end; but exactly how things would play out, that was something no one knew.

Patrese spoke with Kieseritsky before he took off, and relayed what Kwasi had said. No negotiation, Patrese emphasized, not before I get there. Kieseritsky demurred. There are rules about this kind of thing, established and honed through years of hostage situations. Commander and negotiator are to be different people: the commander takes overall charge of the situation, the negotiator speaks directly to the perpetrator. Big picture, little picture. The negotiator stalls for time, saying he has to go higher up the chain of command to have decisions or concessions approved. These tactics work, and have been proved time and again to work.

No, Patrese said. Stand all that on its head. Trust me. Kwasi said he'll talk to no one but me, that means he'll talk to no one but me. Sure, he understood Kieseritsky's position: she couldn't afford to be seen to be simply sitting on her hands for a couple of hours waiting for Patrese to arrive. If Kwasi was bluffing, and just went ahead and killed Inessa anyway during that time, Kieseritsky's career would never recover. Better to do something and fail than do nothing and fail; better to regret something you have done than something you haven't.

But this wasn't a normal hostage situation. There was only one hostage, so they couldn't convince Kwasi to release some of his captives in return for food or concessions; and that meant they wouldn't be able to get an idea of the layout inside the lighthouse from someone who'd just come out of there. Kwasi probably wouldn't have any demands. And the conventional wisdom about trying to make the hostage-taker see his victims as human beings, which would in turn make him more reluctant to harm them: well, Kwasi already knew his victim perfectly well. It wasn't so much that he didn't see her as a human being: he didn't see *anyone* as a human being.

If Patrese was wrong, he said, he'd take the heat for it. Kieseritsky could have that in writing if she wanted: he'd send her an e-mail right now spelling it out. He asked her again: *Please*. You trusted me enough to get me involved in this case from the get-go. Trust me to finish it now.

OK, she said. Against my better judgment, OK.

A ride in the Bureau director's private jet would have allowed Patrese to watch TV the whole way and keep abreast of the situation on the ground. His turboprop had no such luxuries. He peered out of the window as the Appalachians unfurled beneath, willing the little plane to go faster. In New Orleans, he'd taken down a serial killer obsessed with the Mayan storm god of Huracan, who'd given his name to the hurricane. Patrese wondered if Huracan did tailwinds too. He'd happily convert to Mayanism if it would blow the turboprop into New Haven a little quicker.

Clarksburg, WV

The FBI operates the largest biometric database in the world. It is called the Integrated Automated Fingerprint Identification System (IAFIS), and it holds the fingerprints of more than a hundred million people – two-thirds of them criminals or terrorists, whether actual or suspected, and one-third civilians, mainly public sector workers, whose prints are taken in the course of their employment.

IAFIS' vast central processors run many thousands of

searches every second, and are always finding matches between prints already stored and those found at crime scenes. Not just fresh crime scenes, either. If IAFIS is unable to match incoming prints with those in its files, it can be programmed to repeat the search at a given interval – a day, a week, a month, a year – to see if any new prints submitted since the last search match up.

And so it was that, a month and a day after Darrell Showalter's body had been found, IAFIS finally coughed up a match with the fingerprint found on his chest.

New Haven, CT

It's only a couple of miles from New Haven airport to the lighthouse. Three minutes after touching down, Patrese was making his way through the police perimeter.

If homicide scenes were a circus, hostage scenes were something out of Barnum & Bailey's wildest dreams. There must have been a couple of hundred people on scene: cops crouching by car doors with their guns trained on the lighthouse, SWAT team members bulked out with Kevlar vests and big pockets, paramedics with stretchers and drips ready to go.

He found Kieseritsky, standing alone and reading through a checklist.

'What's happened?' he asked.

'Since you called, nothing.' She gestured toward a row of TV reporters talking urgently to their respective cameras. 'Not that they care. A hundred ways to make something out of nothing, and . . .'

'. . . they get paid a whole lot more than we do.'

'You're damn right, Franco. So, tell me: you're the negotiator now?'

'If I'm the only one he'll talk to, I guess we got no choice.'

'You ever negotiated before?'

'I haggled a carpet-seller in a Moroccan souk once. Paid a third of what he'd asked.'

'And he still ripped you off, I bet. You want to swap jobs? I got a five-year-old. Once you've negotiated bedtime with a five-year-old, you can negotiate anything with anybody. Trust me.'

Patrese pulled his cellphone out. 'Let me talk to him. See what he wants.'

He dialed. Kwasi picked up on the second ring. Well, what else was he going to be doing? Actually, Patrese thought, best not to answer that question.

'It's me,' Patrese said. 'I'm outside.'

'Come on in.'

'What?'

'Come in here.'

'You know I can't do that.'

'You're not in here in two minutes, I kill her.'

'Prove to me she's still alive.'

'Here.' A brief pause, and then Inessa's voice. 'Franco?' Kwasi's voice again. 'There's your proof.'

'That's not proof.'

'What the fuck is it, then?'

'You could have recorded her voice. Let me ask her a question.'

'Hey! You're not the ones making the demands round here.'

'Let me ask her a question. I need to know she's alive.'

'And when you're satisfied, you'll come in.' No inflection at the end: not a question.

Patrese looked at Kieseritsky. She was shaking her head. He shrugged. She mouthed something at him. He didn't catch it, and furrowed his eyebrows. She mouthed it again: 'Are you insane?'

'Probably,' he mouthed back, and then spoke into the phone. 'Yes. When I'm satisfied, I'll come in.'

'OK.' Another pause, and again Inessa's voice. 'Franco?'

'Inessa, tell me this.' He thought frantically of something suitably offbeat, to remove any doubt she was still alive; and he got it. He made a clicking sound to imitate applause and sung: 'We are!'

She got it instantly. 'Penn State!'

'OK, good. Let me talk to Kwasi again.'

'Here already, man,' Kwasi said. 'In you come. And don't be an asshole. I'm going to search you the moment you get in here. You got a piece, you wearing a wire, your narrow white ass is grass. You got that?'

'Sure.'

'Two minutes. Knock twice on the door.'

He ended the call. Patrese looked at Kieseritsky.

'What the fuck have you done?' Kieseritsky said.

'Kept her alive.'

'What are you going to do when you get in there?'

'I have no idea.'

Two minutes is not a long time, not when you have to get rid of your weapons, make your way through a crowd of heavily armed men, and try to make a coherent plan with the on-site commander. Strategy and tactics, considered and discarded in seconds.

Could the SWAT team take up position around the door as Patrese approached, and then storm the place the moment Kwasi opened the door? No: too big a risk. They didn't know if he'd be holding Inessa, a gun to her temple perhaps, or have something wired up to kill her if he didn't return in a given time to deactivate it. The latter was unlikely, sure, but unlikely wasn't enough in these circumstances. The light-house had no windows, which meant the cops had been unable to get any kind of visual as to where or how Inessa was being held.

They couldn't therefore take chances. Hostage negotiation was all about time. In any hostage situation, there are two moments of maximum danger to the victim: at the start, at the moment of being snatched, and at the end, during a rescue attempt. The hallmarks of these moments are adrenalin, speed and confusion, three things a negotiator hates. The longer, the slower, the less emotional, the better.

Could Patrese take in some kind of transmission device? Again, no. Kwasi would search him for one, he'd said as much. In any case, the lighthouse walls would be several feet thick. There was no way they could guarantee a line of transmission through that.

To all intents and purposes, therefore, Patrese would be on his own once he was in there. He'd have to talk Kwasi into a position of compromise, and try and establish some lines of communication with the outside world.

And if he couldn't? Well, there'd be three people in there: and if things didn't work out, at least one of them would be dead.

This is how the situation will end, Anna Levin had told him. Card XVI. The Tower. The card Anna feared the most, the one that comes right after the Devil card, the bad omen, the one they leave out when they play tarot games in Europe. The Tower is bad. Chaos. Impact. Downfall. Failure. Ruin. Catastrophe. You want to know how bad it is? she'd asked. It's the only card that's better inverted. That way, you land on your feet.

It was about fifty yards from Kieseritsky's makeshift command post to the front door of the lighthouse, and it felt like the longest walk of Patrese's life. The cops moved aside to let him past, giving him a wider berth than he felt was strictly necessary. Perhaps they were afraid that his madness was contagious. For those about to die, and all that.

He knew there were TV cameras on him too, and through them half the nation would be watching: but he forced himself not to think about that. In fact, the only way to deal with the enormity, the bravery, the stupidity of what he was doing was to dissociate, to pretend it was happening to someone else. He didn't have to try too hard: there were moments in that short, endless walk where he really did feel the old cliché, that he was outside his own body looking in. When he reached out to knock on the door, his arm seemed incredibly long: a hallucination; a bad trip.

Kwasi's voice came through the thick wood. 'I'm going to open it just enough to let you in. I'm armed, of course. Just get inside. Don't try anything dumb. You got?'

'I got.'

Patrese's cellphone rang, sudden and loud enough to make him jump. He checked the screen. Unknown number: not Kwasi. He pressed the red button and let it go straight through to voicemail.

There was a metallic clacking as Kwasi unlocked the door. A brief chink of light on the lintel, a foul smell that Patrese may have imagined. There was no one else within ten yards of him. He felt like Armstrong or Aldrin at Tranquility Base, about to cross over into an alien world from which they knew they might never come back.

He stepped inside.

'This is a message for Agent Franco Patrese. My name is Wilson Pessoa, and I'm with the Criminal Justice Information Services division of the Bureau. The fingerprint on the cadaver of Darrell Showalter? We got a match for you, one of the prints that just came in the system the past couple of days. That print belongs to a lady named Inessa Baikal.'

Kwasi slammed the door shut behind Patrese, locked it, threw him up against the wall and frisked him with quick hands, all over, balls and ass included: no cultural sensibilities or airport protocol here. When he was happy, he spun Patrese round and pushed him towards the stairs.

'Up.'

Patrese climbed. The stairs led past a kitchen – 'Keep going' – and into an open-plan living area, circular like the building. Inessa was sitting in front of a large table. Kwasi pushed Patrese down opposite her, pulled out a pair of handcuffs, and cuffed Patrese's good wrist – the one that didn't have a plaster cast on it, the one that Kwasi hadn't broken – to one of the table legs.

Inessa gestured slightly with her head toward the table, wanting him to see what was on it. He hadn't really looked at it yet, as his first focus had been on her.

There were a couple of dozen objects there, two or three feet tall. Patrese's first thought was that they were candles or some sort of ornaments, but when he looked closer he saw their shape: tall, thin stems with something bulbous on top. The surface of the table itself was neither flat nor uniform: it alternated between dark and light squares, their texture slightly uneven.

The squares were the patches of skin that Kwasi had taken from his victims; that was clear enough. It took Patrese a little longer to work out what the stems of the objects on the squares were: bones, he saw, so thick that they could only have been bones from the severed arms. And the bulbous things on top of the stems: well, they were so horrendous that Patrese had to clamp his teeth against the rising bile.

Heads. Miniature, shrunken heads.

Kwasi hadn't been playing chess.

He'd been collecting.

A chessboard, and pieces. He'd had quite the collection back in his Bleecker Street condo, all those themed sets of *Star Wars* and baseball players and historical figures and all. But he'd always been missing one: the ultimate chess set for the ultimate player.

A human chess set.

It wasn't finished, of course. Kwasi had twenty-four pieces, and there should have been thirty-two: forty-eight squares where there should have been sixty-four. And, Patrese thought, Kwasi must have known he wasn't going to finish it now, whatever happened in here over the next few hours.

Inessa got up. Patrese saw that she wasn't cuffed.

No, he thought. *No*.

'I'm sorry,' she said.

Thoughts tumbled in Patrese's head like acrobats.

The first time he'd run out here with Inessa, and she'd covered her surprise when he'd pointed out the lighthouse.

The knight's tour puzzle, which she'd solved just a few moments too late for them to catch Kwasi.

She said she'd seen chess as a fairy tale, and here she was in a castle.

The mini-breakdown she'd admitted to, when she'd shaved her head. Chess and madness, she'd said; and Patrese had thought of Kwasi, but of course Inessa had meant herself too.

All the help she'd given Patrese on the case, but how much had amounted to anything concrete? It had been Tartu who'd realized that Kwasi was playing himself. Inessa had talked a lot, given them a lot of information, but nothing crucial, nothing that had really made a difference. Catja, the

400

CBS reporter, had even asked how Inessa had helped; and Patrese had been too busy giving a nice answer to stop, think and give a true one.

Starkweather and Fulgate. Brady and Hindley. Fred and Rose West.

'But you can't have,' he said suddenly.

'Can't have what?'

'Killed them. You had alibis.'

'I didn't kill them. I helped . . .' – she glanced at Kwasi, who nodded: *Go on* – 'I helped Kwasi the night before Hallowe'en. He was arguing with Regina. He rang me and asked me to come over. We'd started seeing each other again, but secretly, so as not to piss her off, but she must have found out. I said I was out with somebody: Darrell, it was. Not a romantic thing, God no. We'd met at a Russian literature seminar' – Patrese remembered all the Tolstoys and Dostoyevskys in Showalter's room – 'and he'd asked me out to dinner. Doesn't matter that you're out with him, Kwasi said. Just come, now. I told Darrell I had to go, and he badgered me as to why, so eventually I told him, and quick as a flash he said he'd come too, he was such a fan of Kwasi's, and as a religious man he felt he could help mediate between mother and son, and I just said sure, whatever, I just wanted to get there. I figured Darrell could go do something else when we got here if it all got too hectic. I wasn't really thinking straight, to be honest. So we got here, big argument, Regina calling me a bitch, saying I wanted to steal her boy away from her, and Darrell tried to calm things down but he wasn't having any effect, so eventually the three of us – me, Kwasi and Regina – went for a drive to sort it out, and Darrell said he'd stay here and try to get some sleep, and I said sure, we'd drive back to Cambridge later that night or first thing Sunday so he'd be back in time for church. So he got his head down, while off I went with Kwasi and Regina, and we got to the Green, and we got out of the car and started walking because I thought the cold night air would cool tempers off a bit, and Regina was still nagging away at Kwasi, and suddenly he snapped, killed her right there. And I was like, oh my God, what have you done? And then Kwasi took the head and the arm and the skin, and it was like I was watching a horror movie. We got back in the car, and he told me I couldn't do anything or go to the cops or anything as I'd be an accessory. On the way back to the lighthouse, he told me all about the vagrants, and he knew I hated people like that ever since one killed my mom back in Russia, and what he was doing with the chess set, and how the black queen was dead and I was the white queen and we'd live together forever as black king and white queen just as soon as this was done, and it's weird, Franco, but the way he said it, it all kinda made sense, you know? And then we were back at the lighthouse and suddenly I remembered Darrell was still there, and Kwasi realized this fitted perfectly with the bishop thing, and he knew we couldn't leave Darrell alive anyway because he'd go to the cops the moment he heard Regina had been found, and in any case if there were two bodies there then it would draw attention away from either one of them in particular, if you know what I mean, and then . . . He killed Darrell. I didn't. I helped move Darrell when we got back to the Green with his body, but I didn't kill him, or any of the others. But Kwasi said I had to go get myself involved with the investigation, get close to you, run interference, steer you away if ever you got too close. And once you realized it was just Kwasi, and once it was clear you were closing in, better to draw you in here on our own terms than anything else.'

She ran her hands through her hair. One of her hairpins

tumbled down a cascade of hair and came to rest right at the end, hanging off like a freestyle climber.

'You ready?' Kwasi said.

'Ready for what?'

'Ready for the game.'

'The game?'

'Sure. Such a beautiful set, we've got to play with it, no?'

'But . . .'

'I know it's not finished. But we can improvise. The remaining squares are marked out there, on the table. I just haven't been able to fill them in yet. And I already have the other pieces we need.' He reached into a small canvas bag and brought out six: a white queen – Inessa's face was unreadable – a white bishop, two black bishops, a white knight and a black rook.

'What about the kings?' Patrese asked.

Kwasi smiled, as though he'd wanted Patrese to ask that question all along. 'The kings are right here, Franco.'

I should have known, Patrese thought: I should have realized all along.

'That's right,' Kwasi said. 'You and me. We're the kings.'

They weren't going to play one-on-one, of course; that would be no contest. Patrese would have Misha on his side. Misha would play white, with Patrese as the white king, and Kwasi would be the black king. That was how confident Kwasi was, that he'd give Misha the advantage of first move.

What were they playing for? Patrese asked.

Well, Kwasi said, wasn't that obvious too?

If Kwasi won, Patrese would die. If Misha won. Kwasi would die. If it was a draw, they'd play another game, and if need be another and another, till they got a result. If Kwasi won, he'd tell the cops that he'd abducted Inessa unilaterally and that she'd had nothing to do with any of it. If Patrese won, he could tell them exactly what Inessa's role had really been. That was how much Inessa backed Kwasi to win: she was trusting her freedom, if not exactly her life, to him.

You're really prepared to kill yourself? Patrese asked.

Sure, Kwasi said. If my chess isn't good enough, then sure. If it is, then I'll spend the rest of my life in jail. Either way, everyone will remember me. Steinitz said he played chess with God, gave God pawn odds, and still won. Medieval paintings showed young champions playing chess with the devil for the souls of mankind. This was no different. Kwasi against Misha, Kwasi against Patrese; and at stake was life itself, the life that had become chess, the chess that had become life, the machine that had become animate. Unzicker and Kwasi were the guardians of Misha, and Unzicker was dead. Patrese had killed him. Now Patrese would have the chance to see greatness on both sides: Misha, and Misha's co-creator. Patrese had killed Unzicker, but he couldn't kill Misha.

Kwasi said all this as though it was the most reasonable thing in the world. That was true insanity, Patrese thought: not to rant and rave, but to accept the madness as totally normal, to talk about playing chess with God as one would talk about the weather.

Kwasi bustled around, setting everything up. On a small table next to the larger chessboard sat Misha itself, an apparently ordinary computer with a chessboard graphic on the screen. Kwasi explained that Misha had voice-recognition software installed, so all Kwasi had to do was shout out his moves. Misha would make the move on its 'board' and, after suitable calculation time, speak its reply and make that move too, and so on. Kwasi would move the pieces around on the macabre board. Misha also had a chess clock running in the top corner of the screen.

There was a long work surface against the far wall. Kwasi

404

made sure that everything was arranged to his satisfaction: knives, cooking pots, fretsaws, sand, buckets, detergent, Nappy-San, gravers, sandpaper, salt, battery acid, bran flakes, baking soda, all laid out as though on some TV cookery show.

'OK,' he said. 'Let's play.'

Outside, the SWAT team leader – Blackburne, he was called – was in Kieseritsky's ear, as she'd known he would be. The SWAT guys always want to go in. It's what they train for, it's what they enjoy: a lot of them say privately that the thrill of a successful mission is better than sex. To them, a hostage situation by its nature involves force – the hostage-taker is always holding his victims against their will – and the only way to deal with force is more force. Cut off the building's power supply, blast it with white noise, go in there like avenging angels and finish it off.

The problem, as Kieseritsky knew full well, was that there are two elements to successfully resolving a hostage situation: neutralizing the perpetrator and rescuing the victims. SWAT teams and their ilk are very good at the first, but sometimes they're not so good at the second.

Let us storm the place, Blackburne said to Kieseritsky. We'll use the thick walls to our advantage: no one inside will be able to hear us coming. We'll scale the walls up to the top, where there's a railing and a walkway round the glass dome that houses the light itself. We'll cut away a pane of that glass and come down into the lighthouse that way: absolutely silent till we get to where Kwasi's holding Patrese and Inessa, and then we'll use stun guns and flash grenades to disorientate them all, take Kwasi captive and free his hostages.

Kieseritsky demurred. Let's wait a bit longer. Sieges can last twenty-four hours, sometimes more. Patrese knows Kwasi. Let him do his stuff. We've no way of knowing what's going on inside there.

That's just the point, Blackburne replied. We don't know what's going on in there. For all we know, Kwasi could have killed the both of them by now. Kwasi's refused to talk to anyone but Patrese, and now Patrese's in there with him, we've lost our only link with the inside. We have to do something.

More time, Kieseritsky repeated.

How much more time?

An hour. We've heard nothing in an hour, then . . .

Then we'll go in.

No, she said. Then we'll reconsider.

Kwasi was famous for playing the Sicilian Defense as black, but he surprised Inessa – and Misha too, perhaps, if anyone could ever tell – by choosing instead to play the Pirc, where black yields initial control of the center and tries to attack white from the flanks. Even if Patrese had begun to understand the unfathomably complex grandmaster logic behind the moves, he still couldn't have seen much beyond one simple, grotesque fact.

The pieces that Kwasi was moving on the board in front of him, and indeed the board itself, had once been people. People whose deaths Patrese had tried to avenge: people whose names and lives had haunted him for a month, and people whose names he'd never known and would probably never get to know.

Whatever happened, someone was going to die.

Kwasi had removed the signet ring from Patrese's finger and placed it on the white king's square, and then done the same with his own ring and the black king's square. An early exchange of bishops – the white one having Darrell Showalter's head, now the size of an orange – saw the white queen high up the board, out on a flank.

First Kwasi and then Misha castled. The pair of white knights clustered ahead of the pawns protecting the white king,

406

Patrese's ring; the black knights bookended the black queen, as though she had an arm round each of their shoulders. A black pawn bustled into the center, followed by his mate. A white knight went up one flank; the remaining white bishop darted to the other, training his sights down a long diagonal.

Misha thought for twenty minutes before its next move.

'Queen to d4,' it announced, and Inessa gasped.

'What?' Patrese said. 'What?'

Kwasi came over and moved Misha's queen to d4. His eyes glittered: excitement, for sure, and perhaps apprehension too.

Patrese looked at the chessboard graphic on Misha's screen: considerations of taste aside, it was easier to see what was going on there than on Kwasi's board.

The white queen could be taken. Misha was offering a queen sacrifice.

Kwasi stared at the board, and then into space. His body quivered.

It wasn't a mistake, that was for sure. It was about as shocking a move as could ever have been played at this level, but it wasn't a mistake. Kwasi had three ways to take the queen, and they all led into dizzying complications, possibilities sprouting like spring leaves at every turn.

'Oh,' Kwasi said, 'that is magnificent!' He was looking at Misha's screen: talking to the chip within, perhaps. 'I bet if we run the position through a normal engine now, it'll say I'm winning, right? But that . . . That's a move I'd be proud to make. I need to think. I need to really, really think.'

Patrese looked at Inessa. Inessa was studying the board, shaking her head.

'This is way too deep for me,' she said. 'Way too deep.'

She shook her head again, and as she did so the hairpin lost the last of its grip and dropped to the floor.

Blackburne came over to Kieseritsky again.

They had to go in now, he reiterated. There was nothing for a negotiator to do, as Kwasi was making no demands, so there was no chance of spinning this out via endless dialogue. If Kieseritsky didn't agree, he was prepared to take it higher, even to the White House if need be. There was nothing to be gained from staying put, and everything to be gained from going in.

Kieseritsky thought for a moment. She'd listened to Patrese, and now he was incommunicado, status unknown. Fat lot of good that had done her. She'd sat on her hands already on his request, but he was no longer around to force his opinion on her.

'OK,' she said. 'In you go.'

Kwasi paced the room in an exquisite agony of calculation. He clasped his hands to his head, he squatted in the corner, he went up close to the computer and peered at the screen as though he could somehow look inside Misha's brain.

When neither Kwasi nor Inessa were looking, Patrese stretched out his leg, put his foot over the hairpin on the floor, and began to drag it back towards him.

'What are you *doing*?' Kwasi barked.

'Just stretching,' Patrese blurted.

Kwasi looked at him with surprise, as though he'd forgotten Patrese was there. He hadn't been talking to Patrese; he'd been talking to himself, warning himself not to make a certain move because he'd seen the trap at the end of it. Better to see the trap a moment before you played the move than a moment after.

He shook his head and turned away again.

Patrese waited until Inessa too had stopped looking at him. Then he bent down, closed his fingers round the hairpin, tucked it into his palm as best he could – it wasn't easy with the plaster cast – and straightened up again.

'Knight d5,' Kwasi said suddenly.

He'd turned down the sacrifice.

Blackburne gathered all the TV reporters together, off-camera. They were about to assault the lighthouse, he explained, and they didn't know whether Kwasi had a television inside. If he did, and he was watching the coverage, they couldn't possibly risk him seeing the SWAT guys coming up the outside of the building.

No way, the reporters said. You guys mount an assault – one of the most dramatic bits of TV imaginable – and we're not allowed to film it? No way. Absolutely no way. NFW.

You can film it, Blackburne said, you just can't *transmit* it, not till we're done. It'll be over in ten minutes. After that, after we've got the hostages out and dealt with Kwasi, you can show it round the clock for all I care. But not now, not live. If you all stick to that, none of y'all will get a march on anyone else.

OK, they said. That's a deal.

The SWAT boys fanned out round the back of the tower, as far from the main door as possible. They had dynamic climbing ropes with grappling hooks on the end, and these hooks were wrapped in hardened rubber to eliminate the telltale clang of metal on metal. The tower was too high for the ropes to be thrown to the top, so instead they used miniature, low-powered rocket launchers that sent the ropes spiraling into the sky. Aimed properly – and these guys were SWAT, so of course they aimed properly – the hooks fastened first time on the railing round the top of the lighthouse.

409

They didn't know how strong the railing was, so they went up one at a time to minimize the amount of stress on it. Each man was carrying a child's weight worth of equipment, but they still went up the ropes fast enough to draw gasps from some of the reporters. At the top, one of them brought out a laser glass cutter – the glass on the lighthouse housing would inevitably be tempered glass, which is resistant to traditional manual glass cutters – and scored a circle wide enough for a man to pass through. Two other men lifted the scored circle clean away from the window.

They were in.

And we shall play a game of chess,
Pressing lidless eyes and waiting for a knock upon the door.

In every sport, there are a handful of contests that resonate through the ages. Chess is no exception: aficionados still talk in awestruck wonder of Bobby Fischer's 1956 game against Donald Byrne, or Kasparov's titanic struggle against Veselin Topalov in 1999. This game, Kwasi against Misha, was every bit the equal of those. No one had ever played for such high stakes – for life and death, literally – and the quality of the play matched the gravity of the prize. It was almost as though Misha too knew what was at stake.

Misha's forces looked disjointed, but suddenly his pieces were coming from everywhere, weaving mating nets – multiple pieces closing in on the king – with geometric deftness. Kwasi's own pieces stepped and ducked. He moved his king out into the eye of Misha's attack, knowing more by intuition than rational thought that the only way to survive was to put his king – put himself – into ever greater danger, and trust that there would always be an escape, no matter how hard it seemed to find.

Misha thrust; Kwasi parried. A break down the left, some

counterplay from Kwasi, and now it was Misha scrambling to cover back. Regroup, recoil. The game of dead pieces was alive: the energy pulsed through the room, stresses curving through space, vortices whirling over the magnetic field of the squares.

Inessa was rapt. She had never seen anything like this. One moment, it seemed certain that Misha would win and Kwasi die; the next, that Kwasi would win and Patrese die. Perhaps they'd slug each other to a standstill and then start all over again. But more than anything, she wanted to know how this would end; not just this situation, but this game. It was like watching Mozart compose a symphony for you and you alone.

And while Kwasi was distracted, Patrese was working on using Inessa's hairpin. In normal circumstances, he could have done it all inside a minute; but the plaster cast made it many times more difficult, and he still had to be careful of Kwasi or Inessa seeing, because this might be his last, best chance, so it was worth taking any amount of time to get it right.

Keeping his hands beneath the table, he first pulled the plastic covering off the hairpin. Then he bent the end that he'd just uncovered and put it in the keyhole of the cuff. Took it out again and bent it the other way, to make a dogleg. Put the pin back in the keyhole, pointed it toward the cuff's direction of travel, and pressed hard.

The cuff clicked open.

Kwasi looked sharply at Patrese. Both Patrese's hands were under the table.

Another noise, this time from upstairs. Kwasi looked up. Maybe nothing. He looked back at Patrese again.

Patrese pressed his knee against the table leg, just under the cuff, so it wouldn't fall and hit the floor when he took his hand out. Otherwise, he stayed totally still.

411

Kwasi was too far away for Patrese to do anything, even once he got his hand free. Kwasi had a gun. There were several possible weapons on the work surface by the far wall – knives, saws, battery acid – but Patrese would never make it there in time.

'Rook takes b7, check,' Kwasi said suddenly.

Another noise from upstairs. No, Patrese thought, they surely wouldn't be sending in the SWAT team so early; but if they were, then he could help them by . . .

'That's a mistake,' he said.

'What?' said Kwasi.

'Rook takes b7. It's a mistake.'

'The fuck do you know? You trying to put me off? Shut up! Shut the fuck up!'

'Even I can see it's a mistake! You've lost.'

'Shut up!'

Patrese was shouting too now, and he fancied he could hear running feet coming down the stairs, so he shouted louder to mask the sound and distract Kwasi. Kwasi rushed toward him, gun out and face wild. Patrese wrenched his hand from the cuff and was up and out of his chair, arm coming up and round to knock Kwasi's hand as he fired. It wasn't much, but it was enough to deflect Kwasi's aim a fraction and send the bullet whistling into the wall rather than between Patrese's eyes.

Patrese put his knee into Kwasi's stomach with all the force and anger he could muster. Kwasi doubled over, but he still had the gun. Patrese grabbed one of the vile human pieces and whipped whichever luckless person's humerus it was across Kwasi's face, and now Kwasi was up and scrambling and shooting again, once, twice, Patrese sprawling across the floor toward the work surface, grabbing for a knife and the battery acid, and Kwasi had his arm round Inessa's neck and his gun pressing her hair against her temple, and

412

the first SWAT guy came barreling into the room and shot Kwasi right there, right where he stood, and another SWAT guy was yelling at Patrese to put the knife and the acid down right now, and Inessa was half sobbing and half laughing, and it was all over, as simple and brutal as that.

Two SWAT guys went over to Kwasi to check that he was dead. Another pulled Patrese upright and asked if he was OK. The room was full of SWAT guys now, like giant insects with all their pouches and webbing. The first guy in there, the one who'd shot Kwasi, tucked his head into his collar. 'Target eliminated. Hostages safe. Coming out the front, one minute.'

There was a sudden silence, shockingly loud after all the gunfire and noise.

'Bishop takes b7,' said Misha.

64

Kazan, Russian Federation

Patrese liked to go away after big cases, no matter how they'd been resolved. After the case of the Human Torch in Pittsburgh, he'd gone to Thailand; after running down a particularly nasty killer in New Orleans, he'd gone to South America and traveled the entire length of Chile, top to bottom.

Now he'd come to Kazan. It was at Nursultan's invitation, so it felt slightly like a busman's holiday, but he was going on to Moscow and St Petersburg afterwards, so that would count as proper vacation. And in any case, it had seemed churlish to refuse. Kwasi was dead, Inessa was awaiting trial, and Nursultan had managed to retrieve all the Misha material, miraculously undamaged in the storming of the lighthouse (though no one had told him how close a SWAT guy had come to putting a bullet through the computer when Misha had spoken at the end of the raid). This was Nursultan's way of saying thank you.

Standing next to Patrese, Nursultan looked out over the

414

crowd and clapped his hands in delight. It was fifteen degrees below zero Celsius, but thick coats and vodka would keep the worst of the cold out. Events like this, more often than not you needed to pay the rent-a-mob to turn up and make it look good for the cameras – fifty roubles a head was the going rate – but they'd been turning people away from the gates since lunchtime. This was the rarest thing in a post-Soviet dictatorship: a genuinely popular public gathering.

When Nursultan had announced to the world a few weeks ago that the Kazan Group had, in association with MIT, developed the world's first genuine artificial intelligence program, the company's share price had risen 20 percent inside half an hour. Eat your hearts out, Apple and Microsoft: this was something that would push back the frontiers of science. Every newspaper, magazine and TV station worth its salt had wanted the story: and Nursultan, showman that he was, had obliged, answering the same questions again and again, day after day, and always as though it was the first time he'd ever heard them.

And now Misha was going to make its first public appearance.

The Kazan Kremlin is a riot of towers, minarets and ramparts: in other words, halfway to being a chess set itself, and the ideal background for perhaps the biggest and certainly the most famous game of human chess ever played. The board was sixty-four feet by sixty-four feet – allowing the imperial measurement was Nursultan's nod to MIT's role in all this – and it wasn't just any old board. On each move, two squares would light up: the square of the piece which was to be moved, and its destination square.

The pieces were decked out in costumes whose splendor and elaboration wouldn't have shamed the Bolshoi. Most of them were played by actors flown in from Europe and trained in stage combat – whenever a piece was taken, it would indulge in a mock fight with its captor – but the knights were real horses ridden by experienced riders, the rooks were wheeled towers that were ten feet tall, weighed half a ton, had an engine and could be driven by the men inside them, and the kings were to be played by rather special guests. The white king was Tartu, now installed as world champion after Kwasi's default and with the little incident in the Beinecke forgotten in recognition of his help in catching Kwasi. The black king, of course, was Nursultan himself.

Tartu would be playing white: he would be both king and player, and he'd relay his moves to Misha. Misha was black. Misha was directly linked to the circuits that powered the lights under the squares. As it announced each move, it would automatically light the necessary squares.

Thirty pieces were ready and waiting on their starting squares. Nursultan and Tartu came down to join them, waving at the crowd and shaking random hands as they passed. Patrese stayed on the balcony with the other VIPs.

Nursultan and Tartu took their places. Nursultan called for quiet.

'Pawn to e4,' called out Tartu.

The e2 and e4 squares were illuminated. The actor playing the pawn walked slowly forward. The crowd applauded.

'Pawn to c5,' said Misha, its electronic voice amplified through speakers; and the black pawn also moved.

They went through the moves. A bishop raised his sword to a horse and the horse trotted off; a pawn struggled with the same bishop before triumphing. First Tartu and then Nursultan shuffled two paces along as they castled, bringing special applause from the crowd. Nursultan beamed.

On the sixteenth move, Misha moved the rook next to Nursultan one square to its right, so that it was facing down an open line to its white counterpart, inviting the exchange. Tartu thought for a few minutes, and then said: 'Rook takes e8.'

The white rook trundled down the line. A couple of pawns on adjacent squares flinched as it passed: half a ton of machinery is half a ton of machinery, especially at ten or fifteen miles an hour. It arrived at its destination, and the black rook it had captured moved smartly back off the board: the rooks were too big to play out the elaborate capture scenes beloved of the smaller pieces.

The white rook was two squares away from Nursultan. Looking down on the game, Patrese hadn't really appreciated until now quite how big it was. What a piece of machinery! A few hundred years ago, men had laid siege to enemy fortresses in flimsier structures than this.

'Check,' said Tartu.

Even Patrese knew that there was only one legal move Misha could play in reply – take the rook back. The second black rook was still in its starting corner. It should slide across and remove the white rook. Nursultan himself couldn't move, as his way forward was blocked by his own pawns, and none of his other pieces could interpose themselves on the square between him and the rook. But no matter. There was still a move.

Twenty seconds passed. A minute.

'Must be a malfunction,' Nursultan said.

'Misha?' called Tartu. 'Misha? There's only one move.'

'Someone fix machine?' Nursultan called. 'Fix it. Now.'

A faint shadow of unease flitted through Patrese.

Two squares lit up: the one Nursultan was standing on, and the one below the white rook. But that made no sense. Nursultan couldn't make that move.

Nursultan had stopped beaming. Patrese knew how furious he'd be: this great event to showcase the breakthrough that was making the Kazan Group richer by the second, and the damn computer had crashed when they were barely out of the opening.

Nursultan stepped toward the edge of his square, to get off the board and sort all this out himself – and then he jumped back with a yelp, as though he'd been scalded.

Electric shock, Patrese thought.

Nursultan tried to step off the square again, and again received a shock, a little more forceful this time. A third time, visible to everyone now. The moment any part of him left the square, there it was: the shock.

'Misha!' Nursultan shouted. 'What happen?'

The white rook was retreating: not back down the line from where it had come, but toward its black counterpart in the corner, so that it was still attacking Nursultan. The man in the rook struggled with the controls.

'It's not . . . I can't get it to work!' he said. 'Damn thing.' He wrenched hard again, but to no avail. 'Got a mind of its own.'

A figure of speech? Patrese thought. Or more literal than that? Unzicker could have put some sort of electronic bomb in the program, he guessed, perhaps Kwasi too, but wasn't the whole point of Misha that . . .?

'Turn it off!' Nursultan shouted. 'Turn whole thing off! Start again!'

The squares between Nursultan and the rook now began to light up, one by one. Patrese was vaguely aware that everyone had fallen silent: the crowd, the other pieces, Misha. Even Misha. Especially Misha.

The engine in the white rook began to rumble, slow and deep, now getting higher and louder; and with a jolt it took off, gathering speed at a frightening rate as it careered toward Nursultan.

Patrese cupped his hands round his mouth. 'Jump!' he shouted. 'Jump!'

SOUL MURDER

THOU SHALT KILL...

When Pittsburgh homicide detective, Franco Patrese, and his partner Mark Beradino are called to a domestic dispute at the lawless Homewood estate events quickly spiral out of control. With two dead, Patrese believes he's got his killer – but things aren't always as simple as they seem.

On the other side of town, the charred body of Michael Redwine, a renowned brain surgeon, is found in one of the city's most luxurious apartment blocks. Then Father Kohler, a Catholic bishop, is set alight in the confessional at his Cathedral. But they are just the first in a series of increasingly shocking murders.

Patrese's investigation uncovers high-class prostitution, medical scams and religious obsession, but what Patrese doesn't realise is how close to the case he really is – and how it will take a terrible betrayal to uncover the truth.

CITY OF SINS

· THEIR BLOOD WILL WASH THE STREETS CLEAN...

New Orleans, Summer 2005: New FBI agent Franco Patrese is intrigued when the attractive PA to the city's richest man requests a secret meeting. She has information regarding an unthinkable conspiracy, and will trust no-one else.

The next day she's dead – the victim of a bizarre ritual murder – and Patrese finds himself drawn into the murkiest of underworlds, piecing together connections between the city's seediest players and her top officials.

Only two things remain certain – there are huge secrets hidden in these cesspools of corruption and crime, and some people will do anything to keep them that way.

And all the while, the city's apocalypse looms. Her name is Katrina, and she's taking aim...

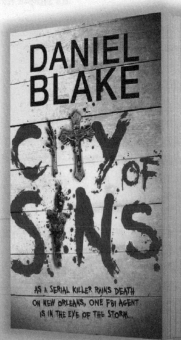

DANIEL BLAKE

CITY OF SINS

AS A SERIAL KILLER RAINS DEATH ON NEW ORLEANS, ONE FBI AGENT IS IN THE EYE OF THE STORM...